THE NEST EGG

THE NEST EGG

S.L. Sparling

Macmillan of Canada
A Division of Canada Publishing Corporation
Toronto, Ontario, Canada

Canadian Cataloguing in Publication Data
Sparling, Sharon L.
 The nest egg

ISBN 0-7715-9127-6

I. Title.

PS8587.P37N48 1991   C813'.54   C90-095832-4
PR9199.3.S62N48 1991

1 2 3 4 5   95 94 93 92 91

Jacket design by Linda Gustafson

Jacket illustration by Donna Gordon

Macmillan of Canada
A Division of Canada Publishing Corporation
Toronto, Ontario, Canada

Printed and bound in Canada by John Deyell Company

For Hazel
my mother

CHAPTER ONE

I never knew my grandmother. She died before I was born by freezing to death when she locked herself out of the house one abnormally cold winter night. This always struck me as bizarre since she was living in the center of Westmount at the time, not isolated on a prairie farm. Why didn't she simply knock on a neighbor's door? It is incomprehensible to me that anyone in that situation would curl up in the potting shed and allow herself to freeze to death, but I am told hypothermia is disorienting. Connie found her by following footprints through the fine powdered snow.

The potting shed is gone now and the garden overgrown with spruce, but the shed must have been in the angle of the stone wall surrounding the property, for it was there I found fragments of clay pots and a rusty trowel. I came upon them when I was five as I was digging with a large kitchen spoon. I know I was five because the memory of that day is the first complete recollection I have.

It was the day of Mother's annual garden party for the employees of Payton Furniture Manufacturing Ltd. Every party Dolores ever threw was a disaster or, worse still, a bore. She believed that if you invited enough guests, provided enough food and enough booze, that a party would be a success. Unfortunately she failed to realize that none of her employees or business associates wanted to attend her garden parties and only came because they were dependent on her for jobs or custom or charitable donations.

Few people enjoyed themselves. I never did. On this particular occasion, Dolores had dressed Leslie and me to the nines in smocked eyelet cotton batiste with matching bloomers, white mary janes, idiot straw hats, and white gloves. All the children of the factory workers were in simple cotton sundresses, some in shorts and sneakers. Leslie reveled in her role as precious little princess, curtsying, offering her pristine white-gloved hand for a shake, her rosy cheek for a kiss. I felt like a perfect fool. Because of my scars I wasn't allowed to wear ankle socks, and my fat little legs were encased in white tights.

It was hot. Some of the other kids had given up the attempt at propriety and were up to their knees in the goldfish pond, whacking one another over the head with water lilies the gardener had carefully transported from some Laurentian lake. Dolores, of course, was too much the good hostess to interrupt their play, although from the way her jaw muscles bulged I could tell she was furious.

I hated the whole scene. I hated the way everyone was making a fuss over Leslie, I hated the way Mother whispered at Daddy so loudly that anyone standing nearby could hear her call him a drunk, and I hated to see him slink off, a quart of vodka in his hand, to drink in the toolshed with the lawn mower and broken garden furniture. I hated the voice Mother used when she talked to the wives in their pretty flowered dresses. It was the same way she talked to her dressmaker—too nice, too sincere. All I wanted to do was go up to my room and watch the Mickey Mouse Club. I wanted to get away from the whispering and pointing.

I knew what they were saying: "Isn't it unbelievable that Greer and Leslie are identical twins?" Did they think that because I was only five I didn't understand, or because I was fat I was also deaf or simpleminded? First I cried, then I fouled my underwear. Dolores exploded with all the pent-up anger and frustration of the afternoon. Not only did she yell, she whacked me across the head with the flat of her hand, knocking me onto the grass. We were quite the spectacle but I got what I wanted. Connie carried me indoors, washed me, and changed me into my favorite pink corduroy overalls with kittens printed on the fabric. I was removed to his house with Dolores's blessing because she didn't know how to deal with a filthy-humored five-year-old and it was the nanny's day off.

Connie gave me a spoon and instructed me to dig in the dirt. I ventured to the far corner of the yard, beyond the spruce trees with their soft feathering of new growth. He remained close to the house in an iron garden chair and puffed on his pipe. I attacked the soil as though it was my sister's face. First I hit the trowel, then the terra-cotta shards, then—oh, the bliss of it all— earth of the most lovely sticky consistency that held the imprint of my chubby hand in perfect mold. I wielded the old trowel and excavated a great clot of the stuff, making impressions of leaves, rocks, my feet. Then it occurred to me that I could manipulate it into shapes. I rolled a snake, then a rudimentary dog. I had always wanted a dog but Dolores said they were loud, smelly, and messy, and she wouldn't allow it. Instead Leslie and I were given an aquarium of tropical fish that we weren't per- mitted to touch.

I shaped a fish but couldn't make it stand up, then I tried a person, but the only way I could get it to remain upright was by making it terribly fat. I remember taking great care carrying them to the porch steps, one by one. Connie smoked his pipe and stared into the middle distance as the sky turned indigo and the mosquitoes came out. I tugged at his sleeve to show off my creations, and to this day am grateful for his reaction. Instead of dismissing them as a childish effort, he examined each one in turn, discussing its strengths and drawing comparisons to primitive art. Then he suggested we bake them in the oven so they'd last forever. The snake and fish cracked, but the dog and man still sit on his mantel.

Connie is my grandfather, Constantine Fletcher. In another of my early memories he is sitting on the long green leather couch reading *Izvestia* and *Pravda* while I, crouched on the Persian carpet, examine sepia photographs in a crumbling album. He read Russian newspapers because he had been raised in Russia and he didn't want to forget his mother tongue. The name Fletcher came from his father, who was British. It was because of his father that he was sent to school in England and wound up in the British army after the outbreak of the Great War. Then the revolution broke out and he couldn't get home.

At my side was a pink kitchen plate, chipped at the edge, covered with honey-drenched squares of baklava. The little black triangles that at some earlier time had anchored the pictures into place had dried and loosened, and attached themselves to my sticky fingers. I peeled them off to line them up along the stem of a flower, part of the rug design. The stem appeared to have thorns.

"Who is this?" I asked, pointing to a picture of a lady in white sitting in a horse-drawn carriage before a tall stone house. She was holding a parasol. The shade obscured her face.

"That is my mother," he answered, lowering the paper so he could see. "And that's the house where I was born."

"In Russia," I said, proud that I remembered. "How come you were born at home and not in a hospital?"

"One only went to hospitals if one had to, and certainly not to have babies. Hospitals were filthy places."

I considered that, and imagined my grandfather being born on a kitchen table.

"Were you and your brothers born at the same time?" I could see the doctor putting one pink baby after another in a blanket-lined basket. "No. Only two of my brothers, Mischa and Peter, were born at the same time. Like you and Leslie."

On the next page was a snapshot of a large white house circled by a wide veranda and surrounded by elms. Connie's paper lowered with a crackle as he squinted down at the book. "That's the summer house."

"Did you ride horses there?" I was mad for the idea that people used to ride horses instead of driving in cars. The only

horses I ever saw were mounted patrols in the park and wheez-
ing old nags pulling tourists in calèches.

"Yes. Sometimes. We were among the first people in St.
Petersburg to have a car." He knelt on the floor beside me with a
grunt and flipped pages forward until he came to a photo of a
high shiny automobile packed with children. All boys. A man
who I assumed was his father sat proudly at the wheel. Beside
him sat the same lady, her face in the black shade of a broad-
brimmed hat, a gauzy scarf.

"The journey to the country took three full days, and we had
to back up hills or the petrol wouldn't run through the fuel line.
That's me." He indicated a gangly youth in a sailor suit perched
on the running board. "Around 1907," he added.

"And them?" The heads of five little boys were just visible
over the car door, and another sat on the folded hood.

"Mischa, Sascha, Peter, Karel, and Nicky. The other one is
my cousin Ivan, son of my mother's sister, Catherine. He used
to come to the country with us. He was an only child and my
mother felt sorry for him. He was always over at our house and
he might just as well have been a brother. We were very compet-
itive. I remember once our Uncle Ferdy, he was Mother's
brother, brought us a defanged cobra from India and all it
would do was sleep. We tried throwing lit matches at it, prod-
ding it with sticks . . . nothing. Finally we killed it and slit the
skin off, then we couldn't decide who would have it. Ivan
wrestled me for it and won so I made my brothers watch me
roast the carcass over the nursery fire and eat it. Of course, they
told everyone and Ivan was jealous I had stolen his thunder.
Eating a cobra was so much more impressive than just having
its skin. He tried to outdo me and ingested spiders, fish, a
mouse, even his mother's canary, for which he paid dearly, but
it was no good. I'd won." He noticed my attention was wandering as I was gluing corners to my nose and cheeks.

"You know Uncle Michael?"

I nodded. I knew Uncle Michael but I didn't like him much.
He worked in Grandfather's shop and stank of perfume. He

wore dark suits, tickled me when I didn't want to be tickled, and put on a sickly sweet voice when he spoke to women customers, then laughed at them as soon as they were out the door.

"My cousin Ivan is Michael's father."

"Oh." I finished eating the baklava and sucked the residual honey and flakes of pastry from my fingers. "Can I go and play with the clay?" One of the attic rooms had been outfitted as my own little studio, and Connie had bought me some real artist's sculpting clay.

"Just a minute." He stood and reached into the blue cloisonné bowl on the fireplace mantel, found a key, and unlocked the glass doors of the curio cabinet. One by one he removed some little stones from a shelf and lined them up on the coffee table. I was excited and thought that he was giving me more rocks, but as I looked closely I saw that they were actually little carved animals. I hadn't noticed them before because I wasn't tall enough to see into the cabinet. He motioned for me to sit next to him on the green couch. He placed a blue rabbit with pink eyes on his wrinkled palm. I thought blue was a peculiar color for a rabbit, but all the animals were odd colors.

"When each of us was born, my father went to Fabergé and ordered an animal for the baby and a piece of jewelry for Mother. His craftsmen were artists and now people pay through the nose for his work."

This meant nothing to me. I was entranced by the blue stone shot with golden streaks and flecks. I had never seen anything quite so lovely. I touched the smooth pink eye with the tip of my sticky index finger.

"Cabochon ruby. This was my brother Karel's. Hold it if you like. Gently."

The bunny, a mere inch and a half in length, burrowed snugly in my hand. The stone was warm, like living flesh. Grandfather was talking Russian, softly, absently. He did that now and again. I had no idea what he was saying but hung on to the sounds, repeating every curling syllable in my head. As he spoke he swung his right foot, shod in a black carpet slipper.

At last he returned from his long digression to lift another animal from the table.

"This is mine. Onyx. You see, the eyes are tiny black pearls. There is no variation in the color of the stone. The craftsman had to carve the feathers. The claws are green gold. That is accomplished by adding fine silver to the gold. See how nicely it stands?" He perched the raven on the table and we admired the cunning twist of its head. The bird considered us as intently as we considered him. I was slightly unnerved and turned him to face the other way. Grandfather chuckled, understanding perfectly.

"The sculptor had to work with the stone. Every animal was trapped from the beginning of time, waiting for release. Look here." He picked up a lizard delicately between his thumb and forefinger, turning it so I could examine the workmanship. "This is a nephrite chameleon. Sascha's. Can you imagine it carved any other way?"

Mossy patches in the dark stone dictated precisely how the artist was compelled to work, and I shook my head, gazing with awe at the sparkling diamond eyes. We proceeded to examine in detail the animals remaining on the table. Nicky's fox, the rusty sardonyx changing abruptly to white at the tip of the bushy tail, peered slyly over his shoulder; Mischa and Peter's pair of agate bear cubs tumbled on their backs; Baby Stefan's ivory ermine with black opal eyes licked his paw. A monkey of translucent rose quartz peeked with one eye through fingers clasped across his face.

"There's no brother for the monkey."

"No. I picked that up later."

"Why do you have your brothers' animals?"

"They died a long time ago."

"How?" The glue on the corners had dried and was itchy. I peeled them off and scratched. Grandfather laid his hand on my shoulder and squeezed.

"The twins and my father were killed fighting the Bolsheviks during the revolution. The other brothers and my mother died of typhoid fever soon afterward. I'll explain more when you're older."

"How are these made?"

"When you work with clay, you add material on to make a figure. Here, a sculptor took rock and chiseled some away."

"Can I do that?"

"When you're a little older. For now, take a big lump of clay and try carving instead of molding."

"Okay. I'll try now."

"Wait a moment." He returned the animals to their shelf and returned with a yellow egg. A network of vines spread across the surface and he opened it, like a box, from a hinged center. There was a golden bird inside on a golden nest and like magic it lifted, flapped its wings and tail, and twirled as an unfamiliar melody chimed from a clockwork interior. I was entranced.

"My father bred and trained carrier pigeons. He used them to send my mother love notes from the city house to the lake."

"Can I have it?" I asked, with the effortless greed of a five-year-old.

"As of this moment, it is yours, but we'll keep it here, shall we?"

"Oh, thank you, Connie. I think keeping it here is a good idea. Mummy would probably take it away from me anyway."

"Probably."

"Have you anything else to show me?"

He stared at me, scratched his chin, then carried the musical egg to the cabinet, returning with a shiny ball. As he sat and displayed it to me in his cupped hand, I could see that it was an eye, hazel-colored and shot with a network of fine veins. I gazed in fascination. When he rotated it, I saw that there was a picture on the back, of the house in the photographs, large, white, rambling, with a veranda and trees. I touched the surface, which had absorbed the heat from Connie's hand. It was hard and smooth.

"It's an artificial eye. I was wounded at the Somme—a big battle in a war, long ago. I was so messy, they mistook me for dead and threw me in a grave."

"Ugh." I shivered.

"When they threw quicklime on me, it burned and I regained consciousness. I was in a hospital for months. I lost an eye. The doctors sewed me up but my mother went to the same jeweler who had made the egg and the animals, and they fabricated this eye. I wore it for a while, until I switched to a ceramic one. Would you like it, too?"

"Maybe you could give it to Leslie," I suggested diplomatically, but he only laughed and put it back on the shelf. As he crossed the carpet he scattered my perfectly ordered line of black triangles, then seeing what he'd done, he stooped to replace them.

It always seemed as though it was raining from inside Connie's house. The ornamental Boston ivy, its growth unchecked, smothered the entire wall surface including the windows, and from May until November the thick leaves filtered all incoming light into a shade of watery green.

I spent most of my free time at Connie's big stone house on top of the mountain because my mother couldn't bear to have me around. That suited us both fine. I preferred being with Grandfather where I didn't have to witness the obvious preference of the world in general for my sister Leslie. I didn't like her. I know I ought to have, us splitting from the same ovum and all, nurtured in the same placenta, swimming in the same sac, probably sucking each other's thumbs, for God's sake, but when I compared my lot to hers even my unformed little mind balked at the capriciousness of fate.

To start with, my mother had lowered me into a sinkful of scalding water when I was barely three weeks old. Most mothers would have checked the water temperature with an elbow, but not Dolores. Begrudging every moment she was not at the factory, she was screaming instructions at her shipping clerk into a telephone receiver tucked between her shoulder and ear when she dumped me in. My tender baby flesh suffered second-degree burns from the waist down, and I had to spend three weeks in the hospital. From all reports, I screamed like a ban-shee every waking hour for a solid year. A bottle with an enlarged nipple oozing diluted pablum and mixed strained fruits laced with analgesics and sedatives was stuffed into my increasingly willing mouth, so that by my first birthday I was a very fat, unpleasant, unattractive baby. The only person who could stand the sight of my latexy scars was Grandfather, who, having scars of his own, great keloid welts from the burning quicklime, was not easily repelled.

On the other hand, my sister Leslie (second in line to bathe that fateful day), was not burned. She was not a tearful, gro-tesque reminder of Dolores's maternal incompetence. Her skin was healthy and pink. She was not overfed. She smiled and cooed, was held and cuddled, and got to sleep in a pink room with a frilly canopied bed on the second floor. I was removed to the attic with peeling wallpaper so my crying wouldn't disturb everyone's sleep. As soon as the lights dimmed, the trellis pattern with blobs of red berries transformed into giant spi-derwebs that stretched over my bed. Dolores promised me a room on the second floor "the next time I redecorate," but it never happened. When I left home, she gutted the third floor, installed huge acrylic bubble skylights, thick carpets, and moved in my father's black leather reclining chair, his huge television, his VCR, and his mini-refrigerator (to chill his vodka and mixers—he disliked ice because it melts and dilutes the liquor). To this day, however, I still see invisible spiders on the walls.

So to everyone's relief, Grandfather took me most weekends and school vacations. I had my own room, not a pink confection like Leslie's, but an exotic masculine cavern with objects culled from his dealings. There was a Turkish carpet with geometric shapes in reds and blues and burgundy leather club chairs flanking the small coal-burning fireplace where we snuggled on cold winter evenings and he read to me from Robert Louis Stevenson, his boyhood favorite. There was a large sleigh bed with floral designs of inlaid fruitwood and a satin eiderdown in faded rose. A drop-front secretary held infinite treasures —I remember ivory pick-up sticks, an old embossed leather back-gammon set, tarot cards, a game of Go with marvelously smooth black and white pebbles and a worn wooden board that lived in the bottom drawer. There was a set of lead soldiers of the Napoleonic era, French, Prussian, Russian, and British all jumbled in a leather hatbox, the paint worn and muskets bent, and best of all, there was an electric train that Connie set up in an empty bedroom.

He also had wallpaper put up, not trellises and cherries but a William Morris reproduction of complex florals that transformed the room into a gift with the wrapping on the inside. He hung paintings with little intrinsic value but fascinating for a child: shaggy highland cattle grazing beside a loch, a copy of a rollicking wedding feast by Brueghel, a primitive American village scene, and four Dürer woodcuts depicting stations of the cross.

My only sorrow with the arrangement was that I occasionally had to go home. Dolores's sense of what was right and proper denied Connie his desire to act as my official and legal guardian. It would have reflected badly on her, no matter how little she wanted the job, so home I went, to my attic, my absent mother, my spoiled sister, and my sweet, indifferent, drunken father.

My classmates called me "Fats." Their ringleader was a child called Abigail whose mission it was to torment me. Each week a different girl was chosen to select ten vocabulary words. These would be written on the blackboard and had to be learned by the others. Abigail would twice yearly approach the blackboard to the mounting expectation of her clique, then with deliberate malice scratch on the board in her deliberate, square handwriting words like obese, corpulent, plump, portly, fleshy, whacking, thundering, mountainous, massive, huge, bloated, gross, elephantine, porky, swollen, mammoth, lumpish, gargantuan, whopping, stout, voluminous, poundage, tonnage, rotund, bulk, volume, amplitude, enormous, Brobdingnagian, behemoth, leviathan, colossus, thumping, bulky, burly, turgid, adiposity, tumid, hypertrophied, dropsical, edematous, distended, bulbous, and inflated, to the hysterical giggles of those little wretches in box-pleated tunics. Year in, year out, the words grew in syllables but remained constant in definition. She was probably the only kid in grade six competent in the use of a thesaurus. I blame the staff equally for turning a blind eye to the cruelty. How many synonyms for "fat" did they consider it necessary for us to know?

When I was twelve we had an Easter fashion show at school, at which we modeled our creations from sewing class for our parents and anyone else who cared to show up. Out of a group of twenty, eighteen were wearing the teeny little miniskirts that they'd stitched in a half hour—two seams, a waistband, and a hem—with tank tops and brilliantly colored tights. Abigail was announcing because she'd broken her arm spring skiing and hadn't been able to sew. I was slated to appear last in a flowered granny gown. I'd spent four weeks of evenings hunched over a sewing machine correcting the gathers, painstakingly applying a round collar, adding lace to the cuffs, and creating what I thought was something simple and dignified. The PA system crackled and Abigail's voice spat out, "A floral fantasy tent capable of sleeping six." I could have died. The audience collapsed in the aisles, clutching at their sides. They probably thought it was planned comic relief but at the time I wanted to melt into the platform. I ran out of the gym and onto the sidewalk, sobbing uncontrollably. Connie (who'd taxied up to represent the family—Dolores never took time off work for school events and Daddy was agoraphobic) bundled me into a cab and took me to his house, where I spent a good hour pounding clay until I had the self-control actually to sculpt something.

When I'd finished, I took a long, leisurely, perfumed bath, changed into clean clothes, and carried my creation down to the living room where Grandfather had lit a fire and covered a card table with a damask cloth. Two candles were lit, and some lilacs from the garden spread their fragrance from a bowl in the center. I placed my statue on the coffee table where it underwent Connie's scrutiny.

"I see you've opted for a caricature. Let me guess. Young female person from the middle of the twentieth century. Um. May I deduce from the pustules on her visage that she has acne?"

I nodded.

"And the eyes are stitched shut. I presume the blindness is metaphoric. I like the tail and the pointy ears. Doberman? So this is a bitch. But the cloven hooves . . . perhaps you're overdoing the symbolism. Oxfords would be sufficient. Have you any fingernail parings—an article of clothing?"

"What?"

"I think a hat pin is traditional."

"What are you talking about?"

"Isn't this a fetish? A voodoo doll?"

"It hadn't occurred to me."

"What had you planned on doing with it?"

"I thought I'd glaze it, maybe black, and fire it, and enter it in the arts competition."

"Nice touch. Is she recognizable?"

"Oh, yes."

"You could get into trouble."

"So what?"

He grinned, took my arm, seated me, and served up ordered-in Chinese food in delicate ceramic bowls. I remember trying to use chopsticks and giggling as he pretended to be a torture device salesman going through an imaginary catalogue, expounding on the superiority of his thumbscrews over the competition's—his racks, his scavenger's daughters (which, unlike the rack, compressed the victim into a ball), his iron maidens, his bilboes, his boots. I settled on an oubliette for dear Abigail, soothed by the image of her forgotten in a dark, dank hole with spiders and rats.

Cousin Michael ran the shop, but the real goods were dealt with privately and many passed through Connie's house. I crept out of my bed at night and watched from the window as the trucks were loaded and unloaded. Things never remained long, for Connie's first dictum was: "Never buy anything you haven't already sold." His second was: "Never buy anything you can't sell at a profit in five minutes." The two may have seemed to contradict each other but they worked for him. I learned about art and *objets de virtu* by his testing me when new shipments arrived. He pried open crates, spilling wood shavings or straw or shredded newspaper on his living room floor, and held up objects for scrutiny.

"Cellini, cast bronze model for a never-completed or subsequently lost sculpture," I said.

He smiled, satisfied, and irreverently dumped the study on the chesterfield to lift a framed sketch from another box.

"Too easy," I complained, glancing at the sepia crosshatching of an anatomical drawing. "Leonardo."

"Well, you're wrong," he gloated. "It's a nineteenth-century forgery."

"You're kidding!" I pored over the detail with a magnifying glass, impressed that the anonymous forger had avoided incorporating the taste of his era on the work.

"Are you selling it as a forgery?" I asked, but he only smiled.

"What's this?" I lifted the wrapping from a lovely van Eyck portrait.

"Hitler's booty."

"Pardon?"

"Step back and look again."

I did. After a few moments it became apparent that this work too was a fake.

"What do you mean, Hitler's booty?"

"Hitler planned to make Linz the cultural center of Europe. Can you imagine?" He snorted contemptuously. "Linz! He plundered private collections and galleries but the war escalated beyond his control and he stashed all the loot in a salt mine. The Americans discovered it and most was returned to the rightful owners. Some wasn't. If I find a good fake and a gullible buyer with more money than brains, I'll palm it off as Hitler's booty and warn him not to insure the work or exhibit it openly or he could lose it."

"Oh." I wasn't sure how I felt about that and my dismay must have shown.

"Don't worry. I only say that to people who deserve to be cheated."

"Who deserves that?"

"People who themselves are cheats. It's a kind of game."

"Oh."

"I only supply what the market demands." He propped the portrait on the mantel and admired it from the middle of the room.

"The gentleman who is purchasing this is an expatriate German living in Argentina. Does that summon up any images?"

I shook my head.

"He was personally responsible for thousands of executions. Call it rationalizing, but I feel no compunction about selling this worthless man worthless art. I'm sorry if I have to tarnish my image in your eyes, but life is complex."

"I guess it's all right. Was the forger a Jew?" I asked.

"No," he said, laughing. "Justice, even poetic justice, isn't quite that symmetrical." He ruffled my hair and pointed out the invisible brushwork, the delicate cracking across the canvas.

"It's almost a pity that it will never be seen again except by an old Nazi."

"I think you're beginning to understand. Better a forgery than the genuine article."

"Yes. I see." And by an act of faith, I did.

When I was fourteen I peered through the latticework of the gazebo in the backyard to watch Leslie having a rollicking old time with the gardener's boy. His hedge clippers lay on the wooden floorboards, and they humped and grunted on Mother's custom-made chintz cushions in the brilliant midsummer dawn to the accompanying chatter of hungry starlings. I was planning to collect irrefutable photographic evidence for Dolores, to use as blackmail, but as I watched I realized that Leslie wouldn't care. And what could Dolores have done anyway? Sent her to a convent? Not bloody likely. So I watched as they pulled on their shorts. The boy collected his shears and wandered whistling to the ragged bushes at the front of the house. Leslie tapped on the wood and said: "You can come out now, Greer. Peep show's over." I stood up in the bushes, blushing purple, and said:

"I'm telling Mother."

"I'll deny it and she'll believe me."

"She can have you examined by a doctor."

"Get real. This isn't the Dark Ages. What's this?" She yanked my arm from behind my back and snatched the Polaroid from my hand. "Give me the pictures."

"I didn't take any."

She pushed the button ten times and yanked out each exposure.

"You creep. You just wasted an entire roll of film. You know how much they cost?"

"So what. I had to be sure you hadn't taken any."

"I hope you get pregnant," I hissed.

"I'm on the pill. Look, Greer. I like balling. If you have a problem with that, well, it's really none of your concern, is it?"

I picked at the leaves of the bush, too embarrassed to face her.

"Well, is it?" she pressed.

"No."

"No, what? No, Leslie, it's none of my damned business."

"No, Leslie. It's none of my damned business if you fuck yourself hollow and expire from the clap," I yelled, tears pouring down my chubby cheeks. She finished buttoning up her blouse and tucked it into the elasticized waistband of her shorts. My own were splitting at the seams.

"Better that than eat myself into a disgusting mountain of flab that no boy would want to touch in a thousand years."

"I have my virtue," I shouted.

"Yeah. That and a dime'll buy you a Coke." She laughed and strode on her slender tanned legs back to the house for breakfast.

But Mother did find out. I don't know the circumstances of the revelation, I only saw the scene through a crack in Leslie's bedroom door. The best part was when the little plastic pill container smashed against the wall. The boy, who had unfortunately celebrated his eighteenth birthday, was prosecuted for statutory rape, but the judge (sizing up Leslie) suspended the sentence. Had Mother foreseen the inevitable consequence of the event, she might have shrugged off the incident, for after charges were laid, she was boycotted by every gardener in the city. The maids were forced to mow the lawn and trim the hedges, and Father and I were dragooned into the job of planting flower beds.

It's a good thing Dolores wasn't of a botanical bent because after our first disastrous season we relied exclusively on marigolds. Dwarf marigolds. Giant marigolds. Orange and yellow marigolds. God's gift to earwigs. Impossible to kill. Miracle flower.

I didn't bother attending my graduation dance, even after Dolores coerced one of her young trainees in upholstery to offer his services as escort. I suffered the indignity of having my hair piled high on my head in a curly mass that might have become Leslie, but not me. Leslie (who had twice failed to advance in the course of her school career) wasn't graduating. She sat on my bed in a pair of hot pants and roared. The dress Mother had selected, long and white with empire bodice, puffed sleeves, and a blue satin sash, hung on my door. I'd only tried it on once and it looked stupid. I swore and stuck my head under the faucet. Downstairs in the living room, the date Mother had bribed was waiting with a corsage of pink roses in his sweaty hands. I'd seen it in the fridge when I was snacking. I looked at the dress, looked at Leslie, looked at the door, fled down the back staircase, and took sanctuary in Connie's cool, tiled

basement kitchen with a bottle of malt whiskey from his storeroom. He found me the following morning passed out in a pool
of my own vomit.

Mother wanted me to go to a Swiss finishing school after spending the summer at a diet clinic. I refused. Connie came up with
an alternate plan. He sent me to London to take a course at the
Victoria and Albert Museum. Mother agreed. I don't think she
cared what I did as long as I left Montreal. Connie said the
distance from my family would do me good. He was right. For
the first time in my life I was serene. Connie found me a basement flat in Chelsea with its own garden, a potting shed, and
azalea bushes. I went to the theater every week, haunted the
British Museum, browsed in the Brick Lane Market, sat in Dr.
Johnson's chair in the Cheshire Cheese, and experienced unre-
quited love.

His name was Simon. I fell in love the first day I saw him
across the lecture room at the Victoria and Albert. I was just
seventeen. He at twenty-one seemed sophisticated and remote.
There was something of the Noël Coward character about him in
the way he languished in his chair and smoked. I despaired that
we'd ever speak, and it stunned me when he plopped into the
next seat and struck up a conversation. He called me "my dear
Greer" as he copied my notes from missed lectures. He could
have copied notes from anyone, so why me? He laughed as he
snatched chocolate bars out of my hand and ate them himself.

Between lectures he often took me to a pastry shop at the
South Ken tube station and treated me to coffee and éclairs.
He'd rattle on about nothing in particular and was an intent
listener when I talked about my family. I knew his feelings
toward me were brotherly, but for the duration of the course I
lived, ate, and breathed Simon. I can't count the number of
times I wrote my first name and his last on scraps of paper.
Greer Beauchamp. Being a Montrealer I was surprised the first
time I saw it spelled out on a page, for he pronounced it Bee-
chum—the same idiot English pronunciation that transforms

Featherstonehaugh into Fenshaw or Cholmondley into Chumly. (No wonder Shaw advocated phonetics.)

It puzzled me that Simon was taking the course at all. I supposed it gave him a queasy sort of accreditation. The third son of an earl, he was raised in a drafty old Elizabethan manor in Derbyshire that was simply bursting at the seams with Gainsboroughs, Romneys, Stubbses, Holbeins, Canalettos, and every conceivable period of furniture, British and continental. I know this because the class chartered a bus and we spent the day there, stroking veneer and crawling around on the floors to examine undersides.

Once he confided that he had been ''sent down'' from Cambridge (lovely euphemism; so much gentler than ''flunked out''), and his father warned him he'd have to get off his duff and earn a living. He figured that with his background and the credentials of the course he could make an easy living dealing in antiquities, and he certainly did have an instinct from being raised around the stuff. He could spot a fake instantly, a skill he demonstrated several times when lecturers tried to trick us.

My favorite memory was of an expert who brought in a small painting on wood, about eight by twelve (an inspired study of the sort artists dash off in situ before executing the work on canvas), attributed to Turner. He invited comment. Not only did Simon expose it for a fake but he identified the forger. Apparently his grandfather had been duped into buying half a dozen of the things in the 1920s by an unscrupulous dealer who claimed that a small cache had been discovered in a hotel in Dunkirk during renovations. The dealer elaborated that since there existed no large canvasses with the same subject matter (insipid beach scenes with clam diggers and so forth), the value was necessarily enhanced. The scam was revealed six months later when another victim had his collection evaluated for insurance purposes, and the dealer and a Mr. Beamish Peck (paint still wet under his fingernails) were both incarcerated for a period of ten years for fraud. Simon's grandfather and a great many others were left holding an estimated two hundred ''Turners.''

I loved Simon. I adored the way his long narrow fingers held a fountain pen, admired his fine bold handwriting, committed to memory the way his thick red hair curled over the rim of his small ears, gloomed the days he was absent, and exulted every time he sat beside me smelling of after-shave and cigarettes. For two years I nightly hugged my pillow for Simon, and for those same two years he dated Lady Portia Stuart, a skinny blonde debutante with sensible shoes and a toothy smile. I hated her. She awaited Simon daily on the museum steps garbed in practical wool skirts and little blouses with Peter Pan collars, cashmere cardigans, her straight blonde hair hanging shoulder length, neatly trimmed, bangs covering her eyebrows.

He'd wave at me as they rode off together in his white Austin-Healey. (I never rode in it myself. The bucket seats would never have accommodated my bulk.) He wore a cap that left exposed only a curly fringe of his auburn hair, and the wind gave his skin a ruddy glow. His eyes crinkled up at the edges, amber-green eyes of a peculiar shade I'd not seen before or since, and his long thin mouth curled at the edges in an expression of perpetual amusement. Perhaps he was perpetually amused, at us and how slow we were. He'd take weeks off, returning tanned, and still be able to knock off brilliant essays on the history of Chinese import ware or techniques and styles of picture-frame manufacture in the seventeenth century.

Shortly after the course concluded he and Portia married in St. Margaret's Chapel, Westminster. I was invited, the only person in the class who was, and though the very thought of his marrying upset my stomach, I found a set of antique fruit knives I could barely afford in the silver vaults for which I received a pro forma thank you from the honorable Portia. I bought a silk dress and a stupid hat and sat in a distant pew on the groom's side of the church as they exchanged their vows.

I can't remember where the reception was held, only that after the receiving line (where Simon pecked my cheek and lied about how stunning I was looking), I stood by a window drinking too much champagne, feeling alien, alienated, and miserable. Simon was understandably preoccupied, and his only further acknowledgment of my presence was a wink and a nod across the room. Needless to say, I didn't catch the bride's bouquet. They honeymooned in Greece, then he started a job in New York. I never heard from him again.

The beginning of my second July in London, Dolores called in a frantic state to tell me that Leslie had been apprehended at the American border in a truck with three roadies and the sound equipment for a rock band. For some misguided reason, Mother believed that an exile in London would remove Leslie from further temptation.

I had a bed-sitting room and a kitchen. I had peace. I didn't need my wretched sister. Mother wanted me to look after her. Whatever was she thinking? Leslie was a smoldering little seventeen-year-old in a transparent blouse and miniskirt up to the crotch. Three days after her plane landed at Heathrow, she arrived at my door on the back of a Harley-Davidson, clinging to a great hairy brute with tattooed biceps. Swastikas were prominent about his person. He introduced himself as Slash and drew the tip of a riding crop down the side of my face. Since dental care was covered by the National Health, I supposed that his cracked, decaying teeth constituted a social statement. Without so much as a by-your-leave, Leslie moved her suitcase and his saddlebags into my bedroom and relocated the cot intended for her into the tiny kitchen. When I protested, Leslie, in the most patronizing tone possible, drawled:

"Greer, darling, somewhere out there is a prick with your name on it."

She played loud music until my landlord threatened to evict me, then deigned to lower the volume, but the following day when I returned from lectures, she'd changed the locks and I was forced to go to a sleazy hotel and eat at Wimpy's. The hotel was so noisy I lay awake nights grinding my teeth and slept in class during slide presentations. Ratting on my sister was out of the question—Dolores would have attributed Leslie's moral degeneracy to my lack of vigilance and used it against me for the remainder of my natural life. I suffered silently until an envelope was delivered care of the school containing the new keys and a note from Leslie explaining that she had met the most "scrumptuous" [sic] man with a Ferrari who had invited her to his villa in Tuscany. Not to worry—she'd make her way back to London in August. No address. No apologies. Typical. She never did make it back. She screwed her way to Nepal where she met the man she would marry.

Dolores placed the blame for Leslie's escapades squarely on my shoulders, so I was in no hurry to go home after I completed the course. I signed up for a few night courses in sculpture at the Royal College of Art and landed a job as a numbering porter at Sotheby's—not the best pay but great experience. The duty of a numbering porter is to handle sale items twice to see that they correspond to the inscription in the catalogue, which is a fine apprenticeship, because looking through glass in a museum isn't an education—you must handle something to learn about it. That was the most important lesson I learned from Connie and his packing crates, which might have contained anything from a Degas bronze to a gilded icon or a Motherwell. I fondled fakes and copies and genuine articles and I learned plenty. My skill as a sculptress was also improving. I bought a two-foot-square block of pale, veined green marble and, working from photographic self-portraits, with a kerosene heater to warm my potting shed studio, I chiseled myself in stone. It resembled something between a Henry Moore and a pre-Columbian fertility goddess, but came in second in a school exhibition.

My only regret in remaining overseas was that after Uncle Michael was murdered, Connie gave up Constantine Antiques and sold the building. (At a huge profit, for at the time Old Montreal was undergoing a process of gentrification.) If I'd been on hand, it might have occurred to me to ask if I could take over and I would never have had to take the job at Ponsonby's. Hindsight. The fact was, I reveled in the distance I'd placed between myself and Dolores. If I hadn't missed Connie I would have stayed longer than four years.

CHAPTER TWO

My second floor office at Ponsonby's overlooked the roof of a fast-food franchise, and from nine in the morning until eleven at night, the whirring aluminum ventilation fans expelled the scent of fried chicken through my window. I leaned back in my large green leather desk chair, vaguely puzzled that my nose never became acclimatized to the smell. I had always understood that people who worked around strong scents eventually experienced a selective olfactory shutdown, be the odor roasting coffee, curing tobacco, or rotting corpses, but four years later I was still susceptible to the fragrance of fried chicken. Several empty boxes were compressed in the industrial green wastepaper basket beside the desk, and a half-full one sat on a stack of recent Christie's catalogues. I stared out the window into a drizzling rain that melted the last of the snow on the flat tarred roof next door into a shallow lake.

I turned my attention to the catalogue that rested on my plump knee and flipped through in an attempt to discover a chair similar to one that had been delivered with an otherwise unremarkable consignment of threadbare Chinese carpets, seventy-year-old walnut bedroom suites, a scratched, stained dining table, and worn, sagging upholstered furniture. What a Louis XV beechwood *fauteuil* with, it appeared, the original petit point was doing in this lot, I could only imagine. The owners, an elderly couple of modest means, had no notion of its value. I was certain I recalled one enough like it to establish a

price, and scratched my head with the pencil stuck in the knot
of hair at my neck. The troublesome chair stood before the
desk, its needlework frayed, and I was anxious to be able to tell
the two old people of my find. They were entering a retirement
home, and I suspected the monthly fee would strain their
resources. On my recommendation, the chair would be sent to
Christie's in New York where someone would bid prettily to tie
a red silk cord around its arms, denying a seat to anyone foolish
enough to consider sitting. I threw the catalogue aside and
shook my head. It was hard to imagine anyone but a museum
paying twenty thousand dollars for a chair you couldn't sit on.
It offended my ingrained utilitarian sense. It was like owning a
Stradivarius when you didn't play the violin.

The office was piled high with overflow from the showroom.
I hated having stock in the office. Every object bore the imprint
of former owners, and their presence crowded in on me with
bristling white noise, making it difficult to concentrate on
work. I stood and threw my large black coat over the Louis XV
chair in case Ponsonby dropped in. Any dealer attending the
auction would immediately recognize the value of the chair. I'd
seen treasures sold in Montreal for a fraction of what they'd net
in New York or London, but Ponsonby didn't give diddly-
squat as long as he got his percentage.

I wiggled another catalogue out from under the red-and-
white cardboard box, and morsels of chicken cried, "Eat me,
eat me." I ignored them and swung my heavy legs over an open
drawer. The swelling in the joint of the big toe of my right foot
was lessening. I wiggled my toes. At the conclusion of my last
physical examination, the doctor had handed me a diet sheet
along with a lecture on hypertension, cardiovascular deteriora-
tion, falling arches, and uric acid buildup in the joints of the
extremities. As he snacked on a jelly doughnut, he insisted a
hundred and seventy pounds had to come off.

"Where are you going with that?" Ponsonby stood in the doorway of his office as I walked through the main showroom, the

chair in my arms. I froze on the spot and cursed the assistant who had assured me that the boss was out for the afternoon. A pair of bifocals rested low on his narrow little nose, and he tilted his head back to scrutinize the chair rather than raise his glasses.

"This?" I widened my eyes, as though the fact I was holding a chair was a revelation.

"That."

"The owners sent it by mistake. They never intended to sell it." At least not there. I had finally established to my satisfaction that the chair was genuine and made arrangements for its shipment to New York. The old couple were ecstatic.

"What is it?"

"A chair," I said. He tapped the arm with exasperation and stamped his little foot.

"You know what I mean. Is it Chippendale, or ... " His furniture vocabulary was exhausted. I was surprised he had come up with the name Chippendale but that was no doubt due to the fact that Walt Disney had never created chipmunks called Duncan and Phyfe. The chair was quite heavy and awkward to hold. When I placed it on the carpet, Ponsonby bent to run a finger along the elegant curve of wood at the base of an arm.

"No. It's just a chair chair. A generic sort of chair."

"Then why aren't they selling it?" He acted as though it was a personal slight.

"The owners have a sentimental attachment. It's been in the corner of their bedroom for forty years." I was beginning to enjoy my fictitious narrative. "He hangs his pants over the back. At night. And his shoes under. She sits on it when she peels off her nylons."

"What would it fetch?" he interrupted, bored with the domestic scenario.

"I don't know," I lied. "It's a fair reproduction, probably done in the 1920s, but as you can plainly see, the wood chosen is of inferior quality. Soft." He poked his index finder into one of the frays in the petit point, and I had to restrain myself from slapping his hand.

Once, when I was new at the job, I made the mistake of informing him of the likely value of an extremely rare but visually nondescript vase, which he then, without my knowledge, withdrew from auction to purchase for himself at ten dollars above the absurdly low reserve price—unethical, illegal, and vile. He resold it in New York at an obscene profit, and the original owners, overseas at the time, were none the wiser. When I caught him out he grew defensive and snapped that what they didn't know wouldn't hurt them and weren't they rich anyway? So I no longer told him anything and snuck things out from under his nose whenever I could.

"It looks old," he argued. He plucked at the fabric with its pattern of roses, faded but still glorious with its muted hues.

"Sixty years is old."

"I've been in this business for twenty years, Ms. Payton." He stretched out the Ms. unnecessarily. "To me, this chair seems very old. Older than sixty years."

"The Keynes keep cats, sir." The "sir" inadvertently came out sounding ironic. I hoped he hadn't noticed.

"Pardon?"

"Cats. They're hell on furniture. See the scratches?" I pointed to the fraying petit point, which could, if imagination were stretched, be the work of claws. He cleared his throat.

"Yes, well."

"Mr. and Mrs. Keynes are waiting, sir."

He dismissed me with a resigned wave of his hand.

Later that afternoon I hurried along Sherbrooke Street in the driving rain, trying to avoid puddles and other pedestrians who like myself were shielded by large dripping umbrellas. The sidewalks, only in the past day or two denuded of ice, had so far been ignored by city maintenance workers, and the decorative interlocking brick was coated with flattened newspapers, beer cans, candy wrappers, animal excrement, and sand. A taxi, speeding through an amber light, threw up a spray of water that drenched me from the waist down, and I cursed not having been able to find a parking space closer than three blocks from the tearoom. I hated April in Montreal.

I turned along a side street, and again into a narrow alley behind one of the few remaining Victorian mansions that wasn't merely a facade fronting some mirrored high-rise. I pumped my umbrella open and shut before entering a tiny hallway with the narrow stairway leading up to the restaurant.

Sitting on the hard wooden bench, I removed my rubber boots and slipped on a pair of new shoes I'd brought in a plastic bag. Orthopedic, although they didn't look it in the least. In my youth, orthopedic footwear had been thick-heeled and laced, only worn by old ladies and polio victims. I turned my foot this way and that to admire the flaming red, open-toed pump that matched my new crepe wool dress. I liked to look my best for Connie at our Tuesday teas.

Connie hadn't arrived yet. I glanced around the room after settling in my usual seat at our usual table, recognizing most of the people, regulars like myself. An old lady with mauve hair sat reading a thick hardcover whose title I couldn't make out, her frail liver-spotted hand absently selecting sandwiches from a plate on the pale yellow tablecloth, absently drinking tea from a flowered bone china cup. Two men in their seventies played chess beside the bay window, the translucent yellow panes casting a warm diffuse light even on this gloomy day. They rarely spoke, playing in silence, as the waitress who had been in attendance since I was a child automatically refilled their cups.

A huge steaming coffee urn of glowing copper dominated a marble console that sat against a wall covered with a rather odd collection of Victorian oils, obviously amateur, depicting children and animals. One, in particular, fascinated me. It was the portrait of a homely little girl with beady black eyes, wearing a fur coat and hat, holding a monkey. The monkey was smiling; the girl was not. When Connie first brought me to the tearoom, the child in the painting had been old enough to be my big sister. Now, I realized with a pang of mortality, she was young enough to be my daughter.

I turned my attention to the handwritten menu. The daily

special was chocolate cheesecake. The door swung open and a young couple laden with shopping bags entered, laughing, shaking water from their coats. They took a table near me and ordered Lapsang souchong and cinnamon rolls. They knotted fingers over the sugar bowl. The woman was noticeably pregnant. I bit the inside of my cheek and rummaged through my purse for nothing in particular, imagining for a moment that a young man sat opposite me, hair damp from the storm, hands cool against my warm skin. "Greer."

I jumped. Connie brushed my cheek with his cold, dry lips and sat down. Water dripped from the ends of his shaggy gray hair onto the collar and shoulders of his heavy tweed suit, and the smell of wet wool wafted across the table. He needed a haircut and reminded me of a mad conductor with his piercing hazel eyes (the glass one a touch cockeyed) and his hawklike nose. As he gestured impatiently for the waitress I wondered how a man of ninety-four retained so much energy. I was only thirty-five but getting out of bed in the morning was a chore.

"What will you have?" Connie asked. The waitress didn't bother with a pad. I ordered the chocolate cheesecake and café au lait in the secure knowledge that not only would Grandfather not make a snide comment, he wouldn't even think one. Of my entire family, he was the only one who never plagued me about my weight.

"Can you accept a consignment? Alex is driving a truckload up from Boston tonight and the house is ... " He threw his arms up in a gesture of despair. I'd been to the house over the weekend to deliver groceries and knew what he meant. There were packing crates stacked to the rafters, and he wasn't expecting a pickup until the first of the month.

"When for? Is it a large consignment? I'm up to my eyeballs in crap."

"Is next Monday too soon?" I thought of the already overcrowded showroom and figured we'd have to start putting things into the employees' lunchroom. Wonderful. I wondered what Ponsonby would say if I insisted that we store furniture in his office.

"Sure. Okay. But no sooner, please. As it is I don't know if I can find room. Have Alex deliver them at about ten."

"Thank you." He smeared raspberry jam over a scone and ate half in one bite. A small blob of sticky red dangled from the end of his otherwise immaculate mustache. I dipped the corner of a napkin into my water glass and reached across the table to wipe it off, feeling fond and maternal. It would be nice to have a daughter, I thought. We'd shop downtown, then come here for tea. She'd have silky blonde hair like a Fletcher, parted in the middle, falling to her shoulders with bangs that needed trimming every two weeks. They'd just fringe her green eyes. She'd wear a dark green smocked dress and a fitted coat with a velvet collar. And a hat with a brim. Emily. People would turn on the street to admire her, she'd be so lovely.

"Greer!" Connie tapped his spoon against his cup and got not only my attention, but the attention of the couple at the next table, the woman with the book, and the two men. I blushed when I realized how near I had come to ordering an éclair for my imaginary child.

"Were you on the moon?"

"Sorry. I was just thinking how nice it would be if I had a baby."

Connie stroked his chin thoughtfully. "A baby." He said the word slowly, as though he was considering an art object of dubious value. "Why would you want a baby?"

"If I don't have one soon, I might never have one."

"That's a reason? Don't be banal. Some people weren't meant to have children."

"Well, thanks a lot. That's nice."

"No offense intended. Think rationally. What on earth would you do with a baby?"

"Love it."

"Oh, please."

"I can't explain. It's not a rational urge."

"Irrational urges should be identified as such and ignored."

"You don't understand. I don't feel complete."

"Well, don't be so naive as to believe that the encumbrance

and responsibility of another body will fill the void in your life. That's why I married your grandmother after my family was wiped out. I felt empty and I thought she might fill the space."

"She did, didn't she?" There was an uncharacteristic bitterness in his voice, and I felt a sinking in my chest. I had always assumed they had had a great romance.

"For a time, perhaps, but that was lust. We had nothing in common and neither of us could provide what the other needed." He shrugged. "There was no animosity, but unless the subject was our children, we didn't talk."

"But you had children."

"Everybody did. They needed boys to crash Spitfires." His face assumed the inscrutable expression it always did when he recalled his sons. We sipped our tea in silence for a few minutes until he focused on the present again. "That's what you did. You married, and you had children. Anything else was considered aberrant behavior. There are no such societal pressures today. Besides, your child could turn out like your nephews."

I thought of Pascal, Honoré, Anatole, and Émile. The fact was that they were monsters. Bright, attractive, five-year-old monsters. What else could Leslie produce?

"One has no control over these things. I imagined a daughter would be like Maudie, but Dolores is exactly like her grandfather. He drank and whipped the horses. I expect if Dolores drank, she would have beaten you. She oughtn't to have had children, but that's what one did thirty years ago. Selfish people shouldn't reproduce."

"I'm not selfish."

"Yes, but your child might be, and then where are you?"

"But what about me? You practically raised me. Was I a burden?"

"Frankly, yes. Children aren't my favorite people, but I recognized your potential and had to save you from Dolores."

"So according to you, no one should have babies."

"It would be a gentle end to the human race. I rather like the idea of mountain lions roaming the streets of New York, don't

you? Eagles and falcons nesting on the World Trade Center. I
wonder how long it would take for a skyscraper to fall down?''

"I don't know," I muttered gloomily. I stared at the painting,
and the ugly little girl with the pet monkey suddenly replaced
the image of little Emily. I imagined her sitting in Connie's
place, demanding another round of French pastries, growing
fatter and fatter until her black eyes peered like raisins from her
greasy, sallow face. I, meanwhile, would be chasing the monkey
because the child had neglected to tie it to the table leg. The
filthy simian would swing by the tail from the light fixture
curling back its lip and pelting us with cream puffs. As I, tippy-
toed on the table, strained to reach the beast, the flimsy pedestal
would snap under my weight and I would topple . . .

"Greer!"

"Pardon?" I shook the horrible vision from my head and
looked up.

"Are you here?"

"Yes. Sorry." I watched him open his pocket datebook and
smooth it flat in the middle of the next month. The tight Cyrillic
script in India ink covered the pages. Funny that he still wrote
notes to himself in Russian. A discipline, he'd once admitted.
Since he thought, dreamed, and functioned in English, writing
was the only way he could remember his mother tongue.

"The seventeenth to the twenty-third." He began scribbling
the unintelligible characters on the vacant space next to the
seventeen. "Have you anything on your agenda?"

I didn't have to think. I never had anything scheduled.
"No."

"Can you move into my house and take care of Alex?"

"I suppose so. Where to this time?"

"Manaus."

"Manaus?" How odd. Back in elementary school we'd been
shown a scratchy black-and-white film about rubber production in the jungles of Brazil. V cuts in rubber trees and half-
naked Indians collecting the milky sap to be boiled and dripped
into dense balls. The film had been made in 1935, well before
the advent of synthetics, and a full ten minutes of the reel dwelt

on the glory of Manaus, upstream on the Amazon, built, metaphorically speaking, from rubber, and specifically on the opera
house, inaugurated by a performance of the great Caruso.

"There's a lady there who wants to divest herself of a rather
fine ceramics collection."

I rarely questioned his travels. In his years as a dealer the
combination of reliable contacts and an unerring instinct
landed him in profitable troves six months ahead of the competition. I had once heard another dealer refer to him maliciously
as "the skimmer," an apt title, I thought, for he did tend to
make off with the cream.

"Is that all? Ceramics?"

"Certainly, that's all," he said curtly. "What else would
there be?"

"I don't know. It just seems like a lot of trouble for you to fly
all the way down there when one of your agents could just as
easily acquire it for you."

"I haven't been to Manaus in a long while."

"Oh."

"Yes. Don't I deserve a vacation?"

"I thought this was business?"

"Business, pleasure. What's the difference?" He finished
writing and placed the agenda in his pocket.

"If you don't want to tell me why you're going, just don't. It
doesn't make any difference to me."

"I told you, I was buying ceramics."

"Fine. I'll feed Alex. Any deliveries?"

"No. But there will be a pickup on the seventeenth. Can you
be there?"

"No problem." I could always take time off when I needed
to. Ponsonby didn't dare fire me, for if I went elsewhere, so
would Connie's consignments. Granted, the stuff he foisted on
Ponsonby's wasn't first rate—only things he was left with when
forced to purchase a houseful of goods in order to acquire a
single Ming vase or an Elizabethan saltcellar, but the general
quality was certainly superior to the production-line dross that
constituted the bulk of Ponsonby items.

"And I'll be making a side trip to Mexico to supervise the transport of a stela from a newly discovered archeological site."

"How newly discovered?"

"Well . . . " Connie grinned and pulled at his earlobe. "Two weeks. My source had some young friends who have been investigating suitable sites for, ah, their, ah, crops." He winked. "And they stumbled on an undisturbed temple."

"How the hell are you going to get a stela out?" It isn't legal to remove archeological treasures, and stelae are big, like obelisks.

"Mexico is a very poor country. To have the complicity of the authorities is as good as having their permission. And we'll get there before the *esteleros*." *Esteleros* are looters who pillage archeological sites with power saws, hacking monuments into fragments that can easily be transported on the backs of donkeys. Museum curators turn blind eyes to questionable provenances, and certain collectors will buy anything they can get their hands on. Connie, bless him, preferred his art intact.

"The plan is elegant." He rubbed his hands gleefully. "We've arranged for the use of a military helicopter capable of lifting a tank. All we have to do is loosen the stela, which I am informed is over twenty feet high, and lower it gently into a canvas sling—the type used for lifting whales in and out of aquariums—and fly it to the coast."

"You have a buyer?"

He tsked as though I ought to know better. "Of course I have a buyer. My customer is an importer of a certain commodity who feels a special affinity with the Maya. I've supplied him with much pre-Columbian art over the years, and when I told him he could have a whole stela, I could hear him swoon over the phone. Fortunately, he owns an isolated island off the northern coast of Maine and can display it openly in the middle of his garden."

"Well, good luck."

"With good planning, you don't need luck."

"Right."

Connie massaged his left eye with the heel of his palm.

"Ache?" I asked. He nodded.

"Perhaps you should have it checked? Maybe there's an infection?"

"No. Just the ordinary pain. It comes and goes."

"Go home and lie down."

"No. I promised Jules we'd finish the chess game. I think he believes that he won't die until the game is over, and he very badly wants to die. It's the least I can do. Want to come?"

Jules was my brother-in-law. Eighteen years ago, at the tender age of seventeen, my sister had shocked almost everyone by marrying the notorious, wealthy, sixty-year-old Senator Jules Dansereau.

"No. I have things to do at home." A lie.

"I don't blame you. I'm beginning to think the man's going to live forever. He keeps falling asleep between moves. We've been playing the same game for three weeks. I think the next time he dozes off I'll do him a favor and plop a pillow over his face."

"Just be sure you remove it when he stops twitching."

"Unless you can think of a better way."

"No. Suffocation sounds good to me." I peered into the teapot.

"More tea?" He glanced in the direction of the waitress. I guessed he was reluctant to quit the cozy tearoom for the dubious comforts of the Dansereau mansion. While we'd been talking, late-afternoon shoppers had drifted in from nearby department stores and the room reeked of wet clothing. Colorful umbrellas that hung on hooks beside the door dripped steadily. I again considered the small flowered teapot, the pattern of tea leaves in the dregs of my cup, and the fact that my only alternative for the remainder of the afternoon was to return home and read or watch television—perhaps do a little carving on the chess set, but I wasn't in the mood.

"Sure," I said. "Why not? And more cheesecake, too."

By the time we finally dragged ourselves from the tearoom it was black and miserable. I maneuvered the car through the rush-hour traffic. Connie had turned up the heat to its maximum level and was absentmindedly drawing pictures on the fogged windshield with his index finger. I was stinking hot but didn't dare open the window as we were trapped behind an exhaust-spewing bus. Connie added details to what looked like a Ukrainian Easter egg.

"How many Easter eggs were made by Fabergé?" I asked. He obliterated the oval with a swipe of his glove.

"Why do you ask?"

"I don't know. Your little drawing. I saw in the paper yesterday that Forbes paid $1.7 million U.S. for a Kelch egg, and they also mentioned that there were six of those." Kelch, an industrialist, had kept the Fabergé folk almost as busy as Nicholas II.

"Oh. I think about fifty-nine Imperial eggs were created, but whether they all still exist ... There are ten in Russia. Forbes owns about twelve, and the Queen has a few. Then there were ones like my mother's. It would be difficult to give an exact count. In many cases the documentation is fragmentary. You must remember that during the depression one could pick up an egg at an auction for about a hundred pounds. They got around and there are probably more than a few gathering dust in curio cabinets."

If I had suspected it was going to be so dark when I arrived home after dropping Connie off in Westmount, I would have left a light burning. I hate coming home to darkness. I flicked on the light and was greeted by the familiar austerity. My highrise with its southern exposure overlooked the city but if I sat on the floor all that was visible was the sky. It was the chief reason I'd rented the apartment—its undistracting blandness. I sat on the floor a lot, staring at the sky or the white ceiling. The place suited me more for what it wasn't than for what it was. It wasn't big, it wasn't ornate—the walls and ceiling met at uncompromising right angles—and it wasn't dark. I had tolerated enough clutter for one lifetime, what with the auction house, Connie's crates, and Dolores's need to cover every wall with gloomy oil paintings, every table surface with decorative knickknacks. My bedroom contained only a bed, a worktable, and a set of shelving to hold rocks, drills, knives, hammers, mallets, and chisels.

A box packed with rough blocks of carnelian and heliotrope waited beneath the flat table upon which lay sheaves of loose paper-charcoal studies of birds for the chess set I was carving for Connie and florals for the tomb. The green marble statue of myself sat on a pedestal in the corner.

I dropped my keys in a blue porcelain dish on the hall shelf and tossed my mail on the white marble table for later examination. Mostly important and confidential information addressed to the occupant. I carried my groceries to the kitchen: four tins of smoked oysters, a container of whipped cream cheese, a bottle of inferior locally bottled Chianti, a loaf of egg bread, a wedge of ripe brie, a barbecued chicken, some microwave popcorn, a pound of butter, a bag of peaches, a pint of strawberry ice cream, and a large Toblerone. I had also bought flowers.

I pressed my palm against the kitchen light switch and felt a glow of contentment as the warm light flooded the pale counters. One by one, I unloaded my provisions from the bag, then I found a tall vase under the sink and filled it with water. The narcissus, daffodils, and pussy willows had just appeared on the stands in the past few days and made a refreshing change from limp roses and wilted carnations. I put the arrangement on my round white table then set it with a yellow place mat, a napkin, and a wineglass of engraved amber Bohemian crystal. That was cheery. The bread and brie went on a board, the chicken on a plate, and I uncorked the wine. Then I opened the door to the cabinet, turned on the television, and slipped the film Daddy had lent me into the video recorder. *Dark Victory* with Bette Davis, George Brent, Geraldine Fitzgerald, Humphrey Bogart, and Ronald Reagan. Hokey, but a good wallow. I settled in my chair to watch and eat. The same as last night. The same as most nights.

CHAPTER THREE

I dreaded Saturday nights. That was "dinner with the parents" night. Leslie lied her way out of it nine times out of ten, which was a source of relief to us all because she would bring the boys who invariably escalated the proceedings into chaos and disorder. I, dolt that I was, came Saturday after Saturday, for there was Daddy to consider, poor dotty man, and I wouldn't have hurt his feelings for the world.

The temperature had taken another unseasonable dip to extreme cold and a light snow fell on the newly flowering crocus. Erratic swings in the weather usually give me a cold. I was fumbling in my handbag for a kleenex as the cook let me in. I threw my coat over a hall chair and settled in the dark living room, waiting for my parents to make an appearance. The portrait of Sean Payton, founder of Payton Furniture Manufacturing Ltd., hung over the mantel. A carpenter and joiner by trade, he fled Ireland in the middle of the last century to set up shop in Montreal. I didn't like the look of him, even in a reputedly mellow old age when the work had been commissioned. His eyes had the guarded look of a wary predator, and the manner in which he held the adze was downright menacing. It may have been my imagination, but I always sensed that the dark reflections on the razor-sharp tool were actually smears of blood.

The room was suddenly flooded with light, and I turned to see Dolores in a tailored dress of turquoise wool crepe that, apart from the belted waist, fell in a straight line from the

shoulders to the hem. She smoothed the side of her French roll
(she'd worn her faded red hair this way since 1958 when she had
decided she was too mature for a page boy; thirty years later the
unyielding tug at her facial skin accomplished the same result as
a face-lift) and sipped a highball. A new maid stood behind her
with a tray of hors d'oeuvres.

"Why don't you get rid of it?"

"Get rid of what?" asked Mother, who seated herself on a
delicate little rosewood chair that I avoided because it would
collapse into a pile of splinters under me. I wondered if Dolores
only sat on it when I came over so I'd feel fatter than I already
felt. I eyed her skinny legs, encased in the sheerest of stockings,
and took a handful of raw vegetables from the platter the maid
had unceremoniously dumped on the coffee table before escap-
ing to the kitchen. I harbored grave doubts that they ate crudités
on weekdays. Probably bouchée shells stuffed with crabmeat
salad, triangles of puff pastry filled with creamed spinach, and
smoked oysters wrapped in crisp bacon. I popped a broccoli
flower in my mouth and tried to banish the thought of smoked
oysters. Mother was malicious enough not to serve dip.

"Greer, dear. Get rid of what?" she repeated.

"Why don't you stash the portrait of Grandpa Payton in the
basement or somewhere?" I pointed at the evil face with a baby
carrot. "It's awful."

"I like it." She shrugged indifferently. At Christmas she
would hang a festive sprig of holly jauntily over the edge of the
gilt frame, a touch so incongruous it was funny.

"How is your grandfather?" Dolores politely inquired as she
stabbed at the bottom of her highball glass with a swizzle stick
in an attempt to spear the maraschino cherry. By the time I was
four I recognized that Connie and Dolores despised each other.
Although I sympathized with Connie's dislike of Dolores, it
baffled me why Dolores hated Connie.

"He's fine. Off to Brazil in a few weeks."

"Brazil." She said the word as though it was as inappropriate
for a man of his years as chicken pox. "The man should be in a
home."

"Now why do you say that?"

"He's senile."

"Oh, for goodness' sake—he's no more senile than you."

"Look at the way he lives."

"So he's a bit eccentric."

"Eccentric? The inside of the house hasn't seen a vacuum cleaner since the *Andrea Doria* sank."

"Rubbish. I clean up." Perfunctorily. Occasionally. And exclusively the rooms he lived in, which only numbered three. Since she hadn't set foot in his house for several decades there was no way she could know how casual his living arrangements actually were.

"A representative of the Westmount city council called me again this week. He received a petition from thirty-seven households in Father's neighborhood complaining that the condition of his property lowers the value of theirs. He had to tell them that since the front lawn was kept more or less trimmed there was nothing he could do. Then he pleaded with me to get Father to do something. There's a first-growth forest in the tennis court, for God's sake."

"It's no one's business but his." I stoutly defended Connie although the entire overgrown property was a paradise for birds, squirrels, raccoons, skunks, bats, and insects. Neighborhood youngsters believed that the place was haunted and Grandfather a lunatic.

"The neighbors should be grateful. He's keeping down their municipal valuations," I added.

"And why won't he install a telephone?" Dolores dumped the melted ice in a Boston fern, catching the elusive cherry with her fingers as it tumbled out.

"What difference does that make? You'd never call him anyway." The conversation never changed. Year in, year out, it was either: 1. Connie was crazy, 2. I was fat, or 3. Leslie was perfect. I wished that Daddy, ensconced in his den, would turn off the blasted TV and come down.

"If he can't manage to keep his house and grounds in repair, how can he manage his finances?"

"He's perfectly sane," I protested. "He pays his taxes, buys his clothes, feeds himself . . . "

"And prances off to Brazil on a whim."

"Not a whim. It's business. There's a valuable collection of ceramics for sale."

"Ceramics. Is that what he told you? He'll rot in prison yet. He probably smuggles drugs and guns like that cousin of his."

"Oh for Pete's sake! He does nothing of the kind." I decided to shift the topic. "Is Leslie coming tonight?"

Dolores looked uncomfortable.

"No."

"Oh? Why not? Has Jules taken a turn for the worse?" I asked hopefully.

Dolores stood and began plucking brown fronds off the fern. It was obvious she didn't want to answer the question. Why not?

"What's she up to?" I persisted.

"She's been under a great deal of strain lately."

"Yes. I can appreciate that." Jules wasn't an easy person when he was healthy, but since his illness he'd been impossible.

"She needed a break."

I turned to hide a smile. "So how is Leslie relieving her tension?"

"She has gone to Mustique."

"All by herself?"

"Well, she couldn't very well take the boys with her."

No, she couldn't, and only a sadist would make her. In the third month of Leslie's pregnancy and in view of her family history (my great uncles had been twins, my dead uncles were twins, and Leslie was a twin), her obstetrician suspected that she might be carrying twins. An ultrasound detected three babies but during the premature delivery at thirty-two weeks a fourth baby made a surprise appearance. Four identical boys. Leslie was horrified, but fortunately Jules was wealthy. The top floor of their house was converted to a nursery, nannies were hired, and all proceeded smoothly until the children were old enough to strip off their OshKoshes.

They were so uncannily alike that without the distinction of clothing, no one was able to tell them apart. Noticing the bewilderment that ensued, they quickly determined that it would be fun to keep their individual identities a secret. If Leslie took them to a barber for varied hairstyles, the boys, on returning home, would repair to the bathroom to shear each other's locks to the scalp. If one scraped an arm, all four wore Band-Aids. Tattoos were suggested, a tempting idea rejected more by class prejudice than any rooted aesthetic objection. At five years of age, the boys had all the individuality of a herd, and the consensus was that Pascal, Honoré, Anatole, and Émile should be treated like one. This suited them down to the ground. All attempts at differentiation were abandoned, and when Leslie shopped, she simply purchased four of any given item. Since it was a decided advantage to be able to locate them easily, she tended to choose day-glo colors. A sharpshooter could pick them off at five hundred yards.

"Who's taking care of the boys?"

"She still has the Italian."

"That's been three weeks. I'm surprised."

"Leslie offered her a bonus if she stayed out the month."

"Oh."

"And Yves has moved in while she's gone. The boys always behave better when he's around."

That was true. Yves, fortyish and ascetic, the sole offspring of Jules's first marriage, was an unlikely behavioral restraint, but the boys liked him and didn't pull stunts when he was around. They liked me, too, to my relief, and Connie, but we knew enough to bring presents. For some reason, they didn't expect any from Yves, and it didn't matter.

"How's work?"

"The mill delivered a totally unacceptable batch of wood. Warped. Improper drying. I sent it back."

"What are you going to do?"

"After the current contract expires, I'm changing to Landry."

"For one bad shipment?"

"This makes three in a row. Beaubien's either stupid or incompetent. Dealing with them is a waste of time and money." My, but she was in a snappy mood. Payton Furniture, which she'd been running since before I was born, had dealt with Beaubien's since Sean Payton married a Beaubien daughter. I got up and fixed myself a martini, since gin and vermouth were sitting there, then settled in a more comfortable chair, part of a Payton living room suite from the early 1950s, recently recovered. Well-made ugly furniture. I wondered what that would be in Latin. It would make a fine motto for the company. My parents' entire house was like a historical retrospective of Payton furniture, from Sean's original hand-tooled tables right up to the latest atrocities to roll off the production line represented by a kitchen dinette set, bedroom furniture in the maids' rooms, and some extremely modern lacquered tables and bookcases in Daddy's attic aerie. Just then, Daddy appeared at the door looking sleepy and rumpled. I joined him, we embraced, and the maid announced that dinner was served.

The large dining room, furnished like the rest of the house by Payton Furniture Manufacturing Ltd., seemed vast with just Dolores, Daddy, and me clustered at the far end of the long mahogany table. The maid was forced to walk an additional twelve feet to serve the food—a disappointing salad plate with cottage cheese. I poked at the clotted white mound with a fork then reached for the decanter, which turned out to be filled with iced water. Damn!

"Your father and I had a heavy meal at noon," Dolores explained, clearly lying.

"I didn't," I snapped, instantly regretting it. I quickly turned toward Daddy, and willed him to say something. Anything. Luck was with me. He wiped a curd of cottage cheese off his chin and, sipping from the tall glass of vodka he'd brought to the table, he began to talk.

"I was watching *Random Harvest* this afternoon and was wondering if it was medically accurate."

"Is that the one where Ronald Colman is the artist who gradually loses his sight? He paints his last great work, his masterpiece, a picture of a prostitute, and she is so offended by the representation of her misery that she destroys it, but he never knows because by then he's totally blind?"

"No, no, no," he sighed, irritated that he would have to waste time and energy explaining. "Right actor, wrong movie." He popped a radish rose in his mouth and crunched. "That was *The Light that Failed*. *Random Harvest* is the one where he gets shell-blasted in the trenches and loses his memory. He escapes from an asylum and hooks up with Greer Garson at her dishiest, makes a life, then is hit by a taxi and forgets everything after his initial memory loss."

"I.e., the dishy Greer." Daddy had a thing for Greer Garson. I was named for her. Mother was similarly keen for Leslie Howard.

"Right. So he returns to his old home, Random Hall, and in his unique melancholic Ronald Colmanish way, goes on to become a prince of industry."

"What happens to the dishy Greer, meanwhile?"

"Oh, very sad. Their baby dies. Then she sees Ronald's picture in the paper, immediately realizes what's happened, and contrives to be hired as his executive secretary. They ultimately contract an in-name-only marriage of convenience."

"And he *still* doesn't recognize her?"

"No. Then he goes to settle a labor dispute at the town of Melford, where they met, and he starts to recall things."

"Did I tell you," Dolores interrupted, "that my carpenters are threatening to strike for an extra two dollars an hour, retroactive to last June?"

"Yes, you did," he said tartly, irritated by the very idea of furniture production and real-life labor disputes. "Ronald winds up at the cottage where they once lived, and who should be there but . . . "

"The dishy Greer."

"Exactly. And they fall into each other's arms and live happily ever after."

"Is it still on tape?" I asked. I knew he never watched anything at the time of broadcast. A middle-aged woman called Alice (who looked for all the world like a bag lady) did all his time-shift videotaping, zapping out commercials. Alice, apparently engaged through a domestic agency, had a small windowless room in the basement outfitted with three televisions and three tape machines (for the rare simultaneous airing of several worthy shows). She worked every night from seven until the national anthem, deposited the edited tapes in Father's television room, slept until ten or eleven the next morning, then vanished until six-thirty, when she returned with a bottle of Beefeater gin in a Liquor Board bag. She made no pretense of the fact that she drank, a weakness that Daddy empathized with so long as it didn't interfere with her job. Even as we ate cottage cheese, she recorded, alone, in the flickering light of her little room.

"Yes. Do you want to see it?"

"I'd like to." I didn't have to feign enthusiasm. Once, my father had asked me to watch (for comparative purposes) the three movie versions of a Damon Runyon short story: *Little Miss Marker*, 1934, featuring Adolphe Menjou and Shirley Temple; *Sorrowful Jones*, 1949, with Bob Hope and Lucille Ball; and *Forty Pounds of Trouble*, 1963, starring Tony Curtis and Suzanne Pleshette. This, all on one Saturday evening. Then, as I prepared to leave, my coat half on, he insisted on playing the game. His favorite game—reproducing, rewriting, and recasting the film. "Who would you get to play Sorrowful Jones? The girlfriend? Where would you set it?" I was terribly tired. My back ached. I was unpleasantly full of popcorn and I really didn't think it was a movie worthy of yet another remake, but we spent so little time together that I stayed another hour. "Sylvester Stallone. Sally Fields. Belmont."

But that night he had a film that I actually didn't mind seeing. He grinned with pleasure and grabbed my hand.

"Who would you get to play Ronald Colman?"

"Oh. That's tough. Do you see it in period, or updated?"

"How about a Vietnam vet?"

"Lord spare me." Dolores rolled her eyes, shoved her chair back, and grabbed her glass. "I need another drink."

"Hm." A replacement for Ronald Colman. An American replacement. Gosh. That was harder than trying to find a contemporary Claude Rains, and we'd spent years on that. He'd had a rare balance of menace and sweetness, and we'd reached a compromise with James Mason, who promptly died, leaving us back at square one. Ronald Colman. Ronald Colman. A Vietnam vet. Someone young. That was a mistake they constantly made in the thirties; they cast actors far too old for the parts. Only the very young went to war. Maybe a rock star. But I didn't know many rock stars.

"Do you watch rock videos?"

"No. Should I?"

Dolores, returning with more gin but no bottle, had caught the last exchange and offered her two cents' worth. "I had a man come in last month to make a video of my hand carvers at work, then do a time-and-motion study to see if he could develop a method to improve productivity."

"Mother!"

"He calculated that by recoordinating their movements, and constant monitoring, production could be up a third. He advised me to forbid the playing of radios."

"Radios?"

"They're an unnecessary distraction."

"That's a little fascist, isn't it?" I said.

She ignored me. "The carvers sent a representative who told me they refused to be monitored and he threw the video camera on my desk. They'd pulled it off the wall. He said that they wouldn't be forced to work faster, that carving required concentration—"

"But the radios—"

"—and that music was conducive to the activity. He said they'd strike if I insisted on carrying out the recommendations." She frowned. Daddy looked at the chandelier, shook his head, and continued as though she had never spoken.

"About rock videos."

"You're a pay-TV subscriber. Tune in Much Music."

"Can rock stars act?" He seemed skeptical.

"You've seen David Bowie and Sting. Get an American rock star. Guaranteed box office. But a young rock star."

"You could be right." He stared off into space with a curious grimace. "I wonder who holds the film rights?"

Dolores was silent, preoccupied with mutinous hand carvers. It was remarkable that their marriage had lasted nearly forty years. They led parallel existences that only bisected at suppertime, and even then they had nothing to say to each other. I couldn't conceive of how they ever got together but it probably had something to do with Daddy's simplicity, money, and Dolores's desire to control and to be wealthy. She could never control Connie, or Leslie, or me, for that matter, but Daddy could be bossed like a spaniel. As long as he had his television and his vodka, he was perfectly content. Although he was the sole heir to Payton Furniture Manufacturing Ltd., the management of the business had passed directly upon the death of his father to Dolores. Daddy appeared in the boardroom once every January for the annual shareholders' meeting and reappointed Dolores as president. She had absolute control, which meant Daddy either trusted her absolutely or absolutely didn't give a damn. I couldn't decide which but I was inclined to think the latter. The only opinions he ever expressed related to television or movies that could be watched on television. At the annual meeting, he also appointed me vice-president and Leslie secretary-treasurer, although our only function as directors was to sign documents Dolores gave us no opportunity to examine (not that we would have bothered anyway) and to collect a ten-thousand-dollar honorarium, which paid my rent and created a tax nuisance for Leslie's husband.

My attention had wandered and I realized Daddy was still spinning ideas for the *Random Harvest* remake.

"But what about the validity of the medical premise? Is it

possible for a person to suffer from a traumatic amnesia for three or so years, then get knocked on the head and completely forget everything that occurred during the period of amnesia?''

"You'd have to consult a neurologist."

"It doesn't sound likely. He might remember his life before the initial trauma, but I don't think he'd forget everything after." He shook his head sadly. "And if that's the case, I couldn't make the movie. I just couldn't. No. Couldn't."

"I see your point. Nowadays people are too well-informed about medical matters. You couldn't remake *Dark Victory* because everyone knows inoperable brain tumors just don't permit that graceful a death." I paused, thinking of Bette Davis, brave and beautiful as her maid drew the shades and covered her with a quilt. "At least I don't think so."

Daddy nodded glum agreement.

"But *The Light that Failed* would work. There are certain forms of blindness that creep up gradually, where science is useless. Degeneration of the optic nerve or something."

He raised his head from the melon he rocked with a spoon, hope filling his eyes.

"And we could still cast a rock star," I added.

"Should it be a musical?" he asked.

"Of course. Why not?"

Dolores groaned and excused herself from the table.

My stomach churned. The locks snapped behind me as I leaned against the door and stared into my dark apartment. It had stopped snowing and the sky hung low and starless, a lurid mauve cast of city lights. On the drive home I had demolished two Oh Henrys and, although still famished, resisted an impulse to stop at McDonald's. I failed to see Dolores's logic in feeding me only salad and then not tying me up. She knew full well that there was a world of food out there waiting to be consumed. What was the point? If the exercise served merely to emphasize Dolores's disapproval, well, that was pointless, too. She had been emphasizing her disapproval by word and deed since realizing my baby fat wasn't going to melt away.

Amphetamines had been prescribed when I was six, before anyone knew better, and they worked for a time. Dolores was ecstatic that Leslie and I finally looked alike so she could dress us in matching smocks and bonnets for church. That I hadn't had a proper night's sleep in six months, bounced off walls, and was failing grade one didn't seem to matter as long as strangers gushed over us. Then one night at Connie's I had a psychotic fit and tried to kill him with a model train. He put two and two together and threatened to sue Dolores for custody on the grounds that she was incompetent and abusive. The pills stopped and the fat returned. There followed endless summers of fat camps, years of Metrecal, then Weight Watchers, with measured portions of bland white fish and personal food scales I was too embarrassed to use in public. When I was twelve, Dolores tried to bribe me with a trip to Disneyland if I submitted to having my teeth wired shut. I declined. Who wanted puréed hot dogs? When she read an article about stomach stapling, I left home.

From the kitchen door, I caught sight of my silhouette in the darkened window and stared, transfixed. I never looked in a mirror unless I was driving, and then only to avoid being rear-ended by a bus. There were no mirrors in my apartment. I replaced the sliding panels over the medicine cabinet with a laminated poster of Monet's *Water Lilies*. My toaster wasn't chrome. The glass over the two pictures in my bedroom (one of Connie as a youth in a boater and the other of my twin uncles in RAF uniforms) was nonreflecting. I usually drew the curtains after dark so I wouldn't be confronted by my rotundity. Was that really me? I thought. I lifted my arm to touch the sagging roll of flesh beneath my chin, and the doppelgänger copied my movement.

I quickly crossed the floor and yanked the cord that drew the long gray curtains shut. Maybe, I thought, just maybe I was too fat. Maybe I should lose a few pounds. The notion of diet crossed my mind every other week, and each time the possibility of slenderness seemed a revelation (like the capability of committing murder, of being pregnant: possible, but not probable). Maybe I'd fast. I clutched my pounding chest and tried to imagine a life without smoked oysters and chocolate. No. Wrong approach. Imagine a life without fat. Imagine wearing one of Leslie's silk teddies with lace inserts. Of course, she ate like a rabbit and worked her Nautilus machine into a state of metal fatigue, but if that's what it took to have men invite you out for dinners you didn't eat, I'd do it.

I decided I wouldn't eat. I opened a cupboard and stared at a stack of tinned oysters, marinated mussels, and sardines. I'd starve. Take laxatives. Jog. Induce vomiting. Embrace anorexia as a lifestyle. What time was it? The digital clock on the microwave read twelve-fifteen. I'd wash my hair instead of snacking. I'd drop so much so fast their heads would spin. In six months Dolores would mistake me for Leslie. I stomped to the bathroom, stripped, turned on the shower full force, and stood under it for an hour imagining the fat melting under the steaming jets. I shuddered and scrubbed every inch of my body with a stiff brush as I had done in similar moments of resolve over the years.

After drying and crawling into a flannel nightie, I lowered myself to the living room floor and switched on the blow drier. My pale, baby-fine hair flew upward at right angles to my ears as I flipped through the pages of *Gourmet* magazine with my free hand. It fell open at a recipe for pressed duck. Sigh. If I hadn't vowed never to eat again, I'd dine out every night on pressed duck and lobster thermidor and beef Wellington. If I was pretty like Leslie, men would invite me out. If I'd always been thin, like Leslie, Simon would have dumped the Honorable Portia. If, if, if. The fact was, to look like Leslie I'd have to survive on carrot sticks for the rest of my natural life, which brought me full circle, right back to my great pendulous breasts resting on my vast thighs and dying for a snack. I pulled the plug to the hair drier, stood, and buttoned the thick flannel up to my neck. Loathsome, loathsome body. I could hardly imagine how it would feel to have my knees touch, or see my hipbones, but sometimes, just as people dream that they can speak fluent Chinese, or have the solution to world peace or the cure for the common cold, I would dream that I was thin. I would dream that I could bend over and tie my shoelaces, that I could run my fingers over ribs that jutted like the convolutions of corrugated cardboard, that I could curl up into a ball, wrap my arms around my legs, and still touch my sides. Then I would wake and hunger for croissants.

I sank into my big soft white chair and flicked on the television with the remote. The late show was just beginning. *Desirée*. I'd only seen it thirty-seven times. Marlon Brando as Napoleon was shielding an already drenched Jean Simmons from the rain while Richard Deacon, almost unrecognizable with hair, yelled from an upstairs window. Good, I thought. If this romantic swill couldn't distract me from food, nothing could.

There was a pizza in the freezer that would nuke in five minutes.

Jean Simmons crashed Merle Oberon's salon on the arm of Michael Rennie, her dress plebeian and utterly inappropriate, but Michael Rennie was plainly smitten. Everyone in the scene was holding a glass of champagne.

There was a bottle of Mumm's in the vegetable drawer of the fridge, nestled between a rotting cucumber and three dried-out lemons. I clutched the chair arm.

Maybe a single tin of oysters could quell a raging hunger. Maybe a Toblerone. There were eight chilled Toblerones in the butter compartment. Only twenty feet away. I could taste the honey nougat and almonds on my teeth and tongue and the roof of my mouth. I was delirious with want, but if I ate a Toblerone, I would hate myself. I already hated myself. I was going to walk to the kitchen. I was going to open the fridge. I was going to slide open the butter compartment and eight Toblerones were going to fall at my feet. I was going to tear open one of the triangular boxes and pry out the foil-wrapped chocolate bar. I was going to unfold the silver paper and break off a segment with my teeth, then another, then another. It was pre-ordained. Why did I even bother pretending that I wasn't going to eat it? Them. All eight. Then the oysters. *And* the champagne. What a waste of effort. An absolute waste. And while I was at it, why

not the pizza? Why not the leftover fried chicken I'd brought
home from work three days ago?

Why not?

Jean Simmons flung a glass of champagne at Merle Oberon
and ran from the room. I knew just how she felt.

CHAPTER FOUR

Grandfather's shipment of furniture arrived Tuesday, not Monday morning as expected. Alex and Bartleby (his dog, a predominantly Irish wolfhound who neither sat, came, lay down, nor heeled on command because he preferred not to), arrived in the drizzling rain with a truck loaded the previous Saturday on Mount Desert Island. Why on earth had a twelve-hour run taken two days? Fortunately, Ponsonby was at the hospital having an impacted wisdom tooth chipped out, and I could supervise unloading without his intrusion. Since the next auction was in ten days, I needed to work late revising the listing for our printer who had wanted the copy yesterday.

Bugger it all anyway. I didn't need this. Why didn't I start my own business? Better still, why hadn't Connie kept the antique store for me? He had never actually run the business; cousin Ivan's son Michael had done that in his blue pin-striped suits, dark shirts, and light ties. I remember he used scented oil to slick back his wavy hair and looked uncannily like photographs of Al Capone. And he smoked cigars—butts had littered every bowl and dish in the place. He lived in an apartment above the store but hung around Connie's house enough to make me nervous. He had been a toucher and he used to squeeze my shoulder as I passed, stroke my thigh, pat my bottom. I had had Connie put a lock on the door of my room. Years later, when I learned that his body had been discovered sprawled on a settee in the window of the shop, a bejeweled Turkish dagger stuck in his chest and a wad of hundred-dollar bills jammed in his mouth, I was neither surprised nor displeased. Connie sold the shop shortly thereafter, so when I decided to return to Montreal I wound up with Ponsonby.

Stockboys unloaded the truck as Alex sat in the cab with Bartleby shivering on his lap. So to speak. The dog was so large it would have taken three laps to accommodate him properly. Where had Alex been? My schedule was totally screwed up. I waited inside the door, slapped a numbered sticker on each piece as it passed, and jotted a telegraphic description next to the corresponding number in a loose-leaf binder: 973. walnut ped. tble., 974. Pr. cherry lamp tbles., 975. mahog. hd. brd. (dbl.), 976. cpt. (Col. typ. meas.??), 977. dng.-rm. tble. Chip. tpe. 8 chrs. mahog . . . I should have learned shorthand.

Alex had begun to assist in the unloading while Bartleby rested his large shaggy head on his paws in the open window of the truck, tracing his master's every move with sad, moist eyes. That he was getting drenched didn't seem to register in his dense doggy brain.

The shipment was ordinary enough. Perhaps the furniture was of slightly better quality than usual. More real antiques, and not the factory junk, mass-produced in the 1920s, that people, aching for the feel of real wood, were so eager to buy. I estimated the lot would probably net him over fifty thousand. Not bad, considering he only bought it to get his hands on some old English silver and a pile of rare books. The thing I couldn't figure (and Lord knows I'd been trying for years) was, what did he do with the money? There were, on average, two truckloads a month, which enriched Connie by many thousands of dollars— and this was merely the jetsam of his dealings. The ''good stuff'' was stored at his house until it vanished in the night. He never actually explained his affairs, but I deduced that strangers pacing Connie's dusty living room were middlemen for private collectors. His standard of living hadn't improved in my lifetime, yet to consider the gain from the deals that transpired under his roof—I shook my head, baffled. Did he have a Swiss bank account? Where did the profits go?

I checked my train of thought and continued: 978. chst. drws. mahog., 979. sec. dsk. yew, 980. dsk. Lou. XVI? bk. lq. eb ... I was automatically applying the numbered sticker before what I had seen registered in my consciousness.

"Wait! Stop. Put that down," I commanded, perhaps a bit too stridently, for Alex nearly dropped his end of the long desk.

"What?" he yelped.

I ran my hand over the lacquered ebony and the ormolu mounts with reverence. The neoclassical desk was more than two hundred years old, in superior condition, and could be modestly valued at two hundred thousand U.S. dollars. Someone had certainly goofed. It didn't belong in this lot. Christie's. Sotheby's. Not Ponsonby's.

"When you've finished unloading, put this back in the truck and take it to Connie's."

"Oh, no, Greer. Connie'll be real mad. No daytime trucks. He'll hit me." He cringed apprehensively.

"Don't be silly. He won't hit you."

"Yes, he will."

"Has he ever hit you before?"

He pursed his lips and squinted, thinking hard. "Well, no."

"And he never will."

Alex brushed a fringe of dark hair from his tired brown eyes then scratched his bum. Poor sweet stupid boy, his chief joy in life was grooming the neurotic Bartleby.

Alex was the sole progeny of cousin Ivan's sixth marriage. Ivan, a shadowy figure in the family mythology, had voluntarily exiled himself from Canada in 1937 until the statute of limitations on a real-estate swindle perpetrated on the government of Manitoba expired. He had appeared at Michael's funeral with an adolescent Alex in tow and vanished before the baked meats were consumed, relinquishing the boy to Connie's care. If it was a substitution it was a strange one, for as Michael was a slick operator, so Alex was sweet, trusting, and none too bright.

Alex's hand shook as he pulled a rumpled hankie from his pocket and blew his nose. "I can't take it to the house. It wasn't on the list."

"Alex. It was an oversight. Take the desk. Trust me. It's not supposed to be here. It's a mistake." I intercepted Bartleby, who had left the truck and was crawling underneath the desk. He whimpered and burrowed his head into Alex's crotch. I wiped his dripping dogginess off the fine ebony finish. Maybe it was a reproduction, but I decided to go with my instincts.

"If it'll make you happy, park the truck somewhere and take a nap. I'll meet you there after dark and help you in with it. Now stop worrying. Trust me, he'll be very happy to see this. And if he isn't, you can blame me."

"Can we call him to check?"

"No, we can't." I was ready to scream.

"Please, let's call," he begged, eyes glistening. "If he's there he'll be mad."

"He has no telephone. Remember?"

Another of Connie's socially questionable peculiarities, he refused to have a telephone in his home, claiming they were an intrusion into one's privacy since you were at the beck and call of any idiot who wanted to sell a magazine subscription or poll your brand of underarm deodorant. Parcel services and express mails were kept busy on his account. He passed hours sitting on benches beside the pay phones near the Ritz cloakroom quenching his thirst with malt whiskey from his flask while he conducted his business. The fact that a telephone could be plugged in at a table in the bar didn't interest him. Whenever he needed to relieve himself, he'd hook an "hors service" sign over his telephone to keep the line free and paid the coat-check girls a dollar each time they took an incoming call.

"Oh, yeah." Alex shook his head and scratched Bartleby's ears. "I guess Bartleby 'n' me can sleep till dark. You sure he won't hit me?"

I gave up. "I'm sure. Finish unloading, Alex." How did he manage to navigate roads? Maybe that's why it had taken him two days to drive what ought to have taken twelve hours.

"Alex," I asked. "Why weren't you here Monday?"

"I had to stop a few times."

"Why?"

"Bartleby got carsick."

That was all the explanation he was going to give, so I let it drop. We shifted the desk to one side of the entrance, then I watched him walk to the truck. He was too thin. As thin as his dog. He resembled one of those photographs of released British POWs—all angles.

"Alex," I called as he staggered under the weight of a wing chair. "Would you like to come for dinner tonight?"

He screwed up his eyes as though he had to decipher my words. Lord knows, he'd eaten at my place often enough that there should have been no mystery in the invitation.

"This is the eighth?"

"Yes. Why?"

"Can't. Got to do a delivery for Connie after we take the desk." He huffed as he lumbered past, the heavy chair slipping noticeably lower down his spine. Why didn't he use a dolly? Perspiration glistened on his brow and his pale cheeks flushed with exertion.

"Since I'm helping you with the desk, why don't I help you with the delivery?"

"No. You can't. Connie'd get mad."

"He wouldn't."

"Yes, he would. He said it's a secret and I can't tell anyone or he'd sell me to the lowest bidder."

Christ. Why did Connie have to be so melodramatic? He scared the kid half to death. What was another bloody delivery to me? Who cared where it went? I handed the stickers and book to one of the trainees and examined the desk. The surface was flawless. There were no signs of repair or refinishing. Generations of care had been lavished on the piece. It was almost certainly authentic. What dumb luck for Connie to come by it unintentionally. He'd only purchased the contents of the house to obtain its library and some silver. The drawer interiors were predictably stained with circles of ink. I checked my watch. How long did an extraction take? Maybe Ponsonby would be feeling so miserable he'd go home and bury his jaw in an ice pack. I certainly didn't want him to catch the desk heading out again.

"You really want me to take it to Connie's?" Alex returned, carrying a Victorian folding screen, each panel hand-painted by someone's Aunt Prudence or Cousin Charity to represent a scene from *Romeo and Juliet*, done in the style of Burne-Jones. I shuddered.

"Yes, Alex. Really. Is everything unloaded?"

"Yes."

"Can you come for dinner tomorrow?"

He nodded. Bartleby sniffed the desk leg. I tapped his flank with my foot and he jumped behind Alex, quivering.

"Then take this out, but wrap it first."

He draped a packing quilt over the desk, yanked tight a complicated tangle of knot, and indicated to Bartleby that he should proceed to the truck. Instead, Bartleby collapsed on the carpet, a strand of drool trailing from his jowl. Alex and one of the stockroom assistants heaved the desk up to their chins and carried it to the truck. I scratched my head. Bartleby, realizing Alex had gone, scrambled to his feet and out the door, leaving a noxious pool of milky bile in the corner.

The erratic spring weather had warmed up to a balmy sixty-five degrees, and the mountain's remaining snow was melting at a prodigious rate. Shallow torrents of water streamed down the cemetery roads sweeping along winter debris of sticks and pebbles and sand. Having decided to walk, I was glad I'd worn rubbers. I slung my heavy bag over my shoulder and stepped onto the spongy grass as a hearse, two flower cars, four limousines, and nine vehicles, headlights lit, snailed past. They took a downward curving fork in the road and disappeared into a small ravine. A murder of crows, disturbed by their passage, mustered into the brilliant sky with deafening caws. Then all was silent except for the rushing water.

Every few years, rumors sprang up that there were wolves on the mountain who preyed on raccoons, skunks, and stray pets. Mount Royal, or Mont-Royal (so dubbed by God knows which French explorer), is a regal chunk of real estate that sits in the heart of the city. Perhaps one quarter of its area is covered by a municipal park, which includes Beaver Lake (actually a cesspool of murky water harboring beer cans and catfish). Another quarter holds the elegant pale brick art deco campus of the Université de Montréal. The remaining land houses the dead of our city. There are two huge cemeteries, the Protestant and the Catholic, and a smallish Jewish one. At certain points in the topography the surrounding town is invisible and one is in a valley of the dead as isolated as the tombs of Saqqâra, but I doubt that there are wolves. In the usual incarnation of the rumor, a wolf somehow finds its way from up north, mates with a German shepherd, and their rogue pups take to ground in the brush around the shale precipice to terrorize mourners.

I never believed the story, but it was not without caution that I trekked up the winding road for the first time since the thaw to see how my work on the family tomb had endured the winter. I had once encountered an antisocial dog, more golden Lab than wolf, who bared his gums and backed me against a monument for fifteen minutes until I remembered the tin of smoked oysters in my bag. As calmly and unthreateningly as I could, I withdrew the tin, peeled back the cover, and tossed the oysters, one by one, onto the grass. In a few minutes he was licking the cottonseed oil off my fingers, and after that I never entered the graveyard without a Baggieful of dog biscuits.

The glare of the low-hanging sun stabbed my eyes. I shaded my brow with my hand and stared across at the opposite summit where the tall stone chimneys of Connie's house were just visible above a dense mist of leafless trees. A thin white plume of smoke lazed from one. Connie, happily burning papers. It vaguely concerned me that he had suddenly insisted on incinerating everything: trash, newspapers, old paperbacks, dead leaves, packing crates, stuffing from packing crates, last night's dinner, and the occasional stick of furniture. Someday the place was going to go up in flames, and him with it, I thought.

The tomb was set in the side of a hill with ten others, constructed at the end of the last century by an enterprising firm of stonemasons but for some reason never completed. The archi-tecturally unified facades were set in a semicircular niche beneath the cliff, and over the decades had been forgotten, partially buried under the crumbling shale. When Connie had bought one in 1948, the entire structure had required excava-tion, cleaning, and the addition of a door. I thought it was lovely and was glad I'd discovered its location in the cemetery records. The white marble, quarry marks still visible on the weathered, unfinished stone, was bright against the dull rust-colored shale.

I fitted the heavy iron key in the lock and pulled open the perforated metal door. The hinges shrieked. I lit a small kero-sene lamp that still contained a bit of fuel and the light flickered on three tarnished oval-shaped brass plaques behind which rested my grandmother and two uncles killed in the war. Peter and David. My only impressions had been formed from a single cracked photograph of two young RAF pilots standing on an airfield next to a Lancaster bomber, caps pulled low over their foreheads to shade their faces against the sun. How had they got along with Dolores? Had she been an adored baby sister? Was she devastated when they died? Why had Connie gone to the trouble and expense of shipping their remains from England, and then never bothered to finish the tomb? Because his wife died? The one time I'd asked about them it was as though a cold fog shrouded in around him, and I had to leave the room. I hadn't yet told him I'd found the tomb. Would he mind what I was doing?

My eyes fell on the burlap sack resting beside the door. Hadn't I left it in the far corner? Marble chips spilled over the top, and treads from running shoes left their clear impression in the dusting of white powder around its perimeter. But the door had been locked when I came. I occasionally worked in running shoes and had probably moved the bag when I stopped work last fall. As though to reassure myself that the tomb hadn't been violated, I measured my foot against the print. They were close enough. I shivered and held my hands up to the warmth of the flame.

I pulled on thin white cotton gloves, gray with dirt, and

selected a grinding disk from among the tools lying on the stone bench. Outside, the sun warmed my neck as I tightened the bit on my portable hand drill. Three gray squirrels, slightly mad after the long winter, chattered in a nearby tree. I ran a black-ened finger along my yellow crayon line, marking the raw stone lintel, undecided whether to continue the design or to hire a mason to carve FLETCHER in the space. My grandmother had loved flowers, and I had intertwined delphinium, roses, Canter-bury bells, narcissus, and anemones in the frieze. I stepped back over the squirrels' litter of chestnut casings, leaned against the tree, and studied the effect of my work.

It was my first attempt at relief—so different from the minia-ture animals and birds for the chess set that I could hold in my hand and examine from every angle. I was also accustomed to harder stone. The marble, quarried a century ago, was brittle and hell to work, leaving little margin for error, but shadows lent definition to the stylized blossoms, and I felt I'd achieved a spatial balance. I was especially pleased with the shallow ivy pattern that framed the door, contrasting with the deeper relief of the flowers. Connie was sure to be pleased.

The sudden high-pitched whine of the drill sent the squirrels scattering, and it was several hours before I remembered the barbecued chicken I'd packed in my bag.

CHAPTER FIVE

It had snowed again, a disheartening April blizzard dete-
riorating the following day into a dismal cold rain. I would
rather have been home curled up in my comfortable chair eating
hot cross buns, reading a murder mystery, and listening to
Bach, but a promise is a promise. The only available parking
space was three blocks from Jules's house, and I was drenched
to the skin by the time I reached the door. The colorful paper
bag into which the woman at the toy store had packed presents
for the boys had disintegrated into a pulpy mess that dripped
streaks of orange onto my beige raincoat.

Jules had telephoned earlier in the day to "request" that I
come over after work to play chess. I cursed myself for not
having invented an excuse. It would have been so easy. A late
shipment. Writing text for the catalogue. A migraine. He
always invited me after work, and he never fed me.

Family members had been pandering to his every whim since
he was diagnosed as having lymphatic cancer. Under the circumstances it seemed reasonable to humor the man, but since
virtually no one on earth liked Jules, there was an unspoken
consensus that he was taking an awfully long time to die. I had
no doubt that obituaries were already composed and committed
to computer at all the Montreal dailies in anticipation of his
demise. I wasn't curious about what they'd put in as much as
what they'd leave out.

The public knew Jules as a self-made man who'd made a

fortune in real estate before opting for a career in federal poli-
tics. Minister without portfolio in the Liberal government of
Louis St. Laurent, he was appointed to the Senate a day before
the Conservatives were sworn into power in 1957. His first wife,
the former Louise LaRivière, had died a quarter of a century
ago leaving one son, Yves. (Yves, an erstwhile Jesuit, had discovered his true calling in litigation.)

The facts guarded from general circulation were that
Louise's father, the legendary Paul LaRivière, had done very
nicely spiriting booze to New England in the 1920s, then shy-
locked the profits in the 1930s, acquiring a tremendous number
of businesses from the poor slobs who failed to repay his
"loans." During the depression, Jules had worked his way
through law school as one of LaRivière's "collectors." It was in
those far-off days that he picked up the handle "Doigts Dansereau" for the punishment he'd mete out to delinquent debtors.
His later associates wrongly assumed it was a talent for financial
manipulation that earned him the nickname. He was not a nice
man, but then, my sister was not a nice woman.

After Leslie fled my London flat with the scrumptious man
in a Ferrari, she eventually wound up much farther east and
returned a year later with the notorious senator in tow. They'd
met at a Tibetan monastery catering to credulous North Americans in search of enlightenment. Jules was over sixty. Dolores
accused him of being a despoiler of young girls and a frog
besides. She, a ferocious snob, was endlessly galled that the
names he dropped had a much higher recognition factor than
the names she dropped. Who was he anyway? A self-made man
who proclaimed his humble origins whenever he could. The
eleventh child of a Beauce farmer, Jules recalled ad nauseum the
shack where he was raised, with its packed mud floors, manual
water pump, and outhouse.

The door was half open and I let myself in. Neither Pascal,
Émile, Honoré, nor Anatole ever shut doors, although they occasionally slammed them for effect. The repeatedly shattered bev-
eled glass panels in the entrance had been replaced with thick,
tempered stuff that successfully defied their collective effort to

inflict damage, so they resorted to defacement with crayons. Eschewing the charm of stick men and smiling suns, they opted for maximum coverage, and the door, up to a level they could reach while standing on a bench, was a Crayola horror.

I always brought presents for the children. Insurance premiums. It was wise to remain in their good graces, considering the alternative. If one entered the house without an acceptable offering, a disproportionate punishment was assured. Once they had shaved paths down the backs of sixteen fur coats with electric razors while their owners, the executive committee of the Junior League, nibbled finger sandwiches in the salon. Another time a quart of molasses found its way into Jules's lawyer's attaché case. The one time I neglected to bring gifts, they had dropped my key chain into the sewer, which I interpreted as a warning, for they didn't touch the duplicate set. Connie once narrowly escaped their retribution by telling them some stones he'd picked up in the garden were moon rocks, and they passed the remainder of the afternoon riding the creaky old elevator up and down pretending they were astronauts, which nobody minded because at least we knew where they were.

I shook the water off my raincoat and draped it over a copy of a statue of Artemis, one of twelve worthless plaster reproductions of Greek masterpieces that punctuated the perimeter of the tennis-court-sized atrium. I didn't know what the architect had intended, but the general effect of the house was cold, gloomy, and institutional. Marble columns around the sunken marble floor reached to a skylight ceiling. It would have made a great room for a swimming pool. Put in a few palms, deck chairs, sunlamps. The sole positive quality of the hall was acoustical. You could whisper at one end and be heard clearly and distinctly by any party at the other—a handy thing to know if your purpose was secrecy and discretion. Jules once told me that when he moved into the house, he had discovered a hardwood dance floor stored in the cellar. I couldn't imagine anyone dancing there. The statues were uniformly ugly and the Cats (the boys' collective nickname since birth when the attending

obstetrician had yelped, "Quatre!" at the unexpected appearance of a fourth baby), who had long ago snapped the wings off
the feet of Mercury, the penises off Dionysus, Apollo,
Posiedon, Prometheus, and Achilles, and the fingers off everyone, had made them even uglier.

Out of the corner of my eye, I glimpsed a flash of red as two of
the Cats slithered down either side of the wide marble banister
at the end of the atrium. Their shrill yelps must have alerted the
others, for seconds later the cellar door crashed open and all
four of them were leaping on me like a litter of puppies, screaming:

"Garsbongs! Garsbongs! Garsbongs!"

I patted their dark heads, randomly addressing them by
individual names, at the same time doubting whether after
functioning as a unit for so many years, even they had any
notion who was who. (I had a vision of them at twenty-one,
plucking straws to establish who would be Émile, who Pascal,
who Anatole, and who Honoré.)

"Honoré, tiens. Pascal. Oui. C'est pour toi. Émile. Prends
garde. Anatole." I doled out the inexpensive water pistols and
they dashed off in the direction of the kitchen yelling: "Gringe
bidou," their private language for thank you, or merci
beaucoup. The vocabulary tended to shift, another tactic to
throw adults off guard, and they might have been uttering
private blasphemies. One never really knew.

I trudged up the branched staircase to the sickroom. Jules lay
flat on a hospital bed staring at the ceiling. I waited at the
doorway, wondering whether he was asleep. The open, slightly
glazed eyes indicated wakefulness. Or death. He looked dead.
My heartbeat accelerated as a rush of adrenaline surged into my
system. The yellowish cast to his skin gave him the appearance
of being carved out of old ivory. I withdrew into the hall where
an ostentatiously fragrant purple hyacinth sat on the floor outside the room. Why had the nurse put it out here? Where *was*
the nurse? I thought Jules wasn't to be left alone. Perhaps he
was dead and she'd gone to call a doctor.

I leaned over the balustrade but the atrium below gave no

hint of movement. Even the Cats had vanished into some dark recess of the house. It was eerily silent. At least when Leslie was around, there was music. She always blasted the stereo, indifferently choosing between Wagner, Twisted Sister, or Barbra Streisand.

I glanced at the door but was repelled by the idea of entering. The room's atmosphere combined all the joyless odors of urine, medicine, and antiseptic. No one had bothered turning on any lights (or else the boys had turned them all off), and the house was awash in gloom. Freezing rain pelted the glass roof. I decided to leave and give someone else the pleasure of discovering the body. In the momentary pause before I turned to go, Jules lifted his head off the pillow. "Greer," he called, pronouncing it "Grair." My heart sank. He was alive.

I forced a smile, entered, cranked up the bed so he was in a comfortable position, and rolled over the table upon which sat the ongoing chess game. It took a few minutes to analyze the board (for each match was played by several opponents) to figure out who had preceded me by the configuration of the pieces. Since the balance of the game was recklessly pinned on the position of the white queen (Jules always played black), I deduced it was Connie. Yves, perhaps because of his priestly training, was a thoughtful, overly cautious player whose strategies were primarily defensive, but then, so were Jules's. Their games must be monotonous in the extreme.

The only thing that I enjoyed about the games was the men. Carved by an Inuit over a hundred and fifty years ago, the pawns were seals; the castles, little igloos; the bishops, walruses; the knights, polar bears; the king, a hunter holding aloft a spear; and the queen, a woman with a baby slung on her back. The pieces were ivory and green soapstone with a sheen only generations of handling could achieve. They were gorgeous. The carving suggested a sinuous, flowing movement I wished I could achieve in my work. Jules said it had been a gift in lieu of debt repayment, and I was surprised that he had valued it more than cash.

"Whose move is it?" I asked, hoping it was mine so I could

move the queen to safer territory. Jules looked me dead in the eye.

"Mine." He swung a bishop to capture the piece, exposing his own queen to one of my knights. I was tempted to retaliate, even though it insured the loss of my man by his king. Is that what Connie had in mind? Jules usually resorted to castling, and if he fell for this ruse that option was closed. I slid my knight across the board but instead of capturing it, he (surprise) castled, and I had to content myself by knocking off a pawn. Hardly worth the bother. I considered throwing the game and treating myself to take-out Chinese. Sweet and sour spareribs, lobster cantonese, stir-fried vegetables, and fried rice. And fried wontons. A couple of egg rolls. I kamikazed my king into hostile territory, where Jules could check me three different ways.

"Greer." His voice was so weak that I leaned forward to hear and had to force myself not to turn away from his sour breath. His insides were decaying.

"What is the worst thing you've ever done?" he rasped.

Oh Lord, I thought. Not another game of "I confess."

"I don't know." I fingered my rook in anticipation of the next move while he toyed with the queen's bishop. If he moved it then he hadn't noticed his opportunity to put me in check and I'd have to move a knight. Whatever logic the game might ever have had would be lost. He moved the queen's bishop. I sighed. What difference did it make anyway? It was obvious Jules wasn't interested in playing. Although he was fully conscious, his mouth hung slack, exposing long yellow teeth. Didn't anyone brush them? I felt a sudden stab of pity for his utter helplessness and tried to humor him by dredging up a rotten act from my past.

I crossed my swollen ankles, inadvertently kicking the urine bag that dangled from the rungs of the guardrail. It sloshed as it swung back and forth. He wanted something lousy, but had I ever done anything lousy? All that came to mind was snitching a magnifying glass from Dolores's desk and zapping unsuspecting ants under the burning pin speck of light while I watched them contort and fry with the indifferent cruelty of a seven-year-old. A cruelty I outgrew.

"Greer?" He whined pathetically, tears welling in the corners of his eyes. This seemed important to him, and I was almost sorry I had never robbed a bank, rolled a drunk, or had an abortion. What a blameless, boring, innocent life.

"Just a second, Jules. I'm thinking." My stomach growled. I remembered stashing a bag of Oreos in my purse before I left for work, and reached down to find them. Relief. I removed the package and held it open for Jules. He shook his head. He really needed to confess but the pattern was that he wouldn't until you did. Strange man. I wolfed down four cookies before speaking.

"I haven't really done anything awful, but I confess that I've been tempted to kill Leslie."

"So have we all," he said, and I wasn't surprised. "But there are better ways to punish Leslie than murder." There was a cold finality implicit in his statement that gave me pause. What could he do to Leslie?

He stared glassy-eyed at the ceiling. His bed, in keeping with some weird whim, faced neither the door nor the window, but a wall. The faded green paint was covered with what at first glance appeared to be an abstract expressionist mural, but which on closer scrutiny was revealed to be more Cat artwork. They'd contorted themselves into grotesque shapes and traced each other's bodies onto the wall surface with thick-nibbed felt pens. The resulting silhouettes were then decorated in oddly individual clothing, the one exception a nude with prominent genitalia. The first in line was dressed in a top hat and tails, the second sported scuba gear, the third was the nude, and the fourth wore a ball gown. I hoped Jules's thoughts were more diverting than the view. He turned his face away from me and whispered in a voice so low I almost didn't catch what he said.

"I murdered a baby." A single tear trailed down a crease in his yellow skin, and I dropped a cookie on the carpet before realizing he probably meant that he had got a girl in trouble and arranged an expedient solution.

"Have you spoken to a priest?" I asked. Each succeeding

confession was more lurid than the last, and my initial response had been to regard them as pure fiction. He once claimed to have set fire to a livery stable. Eight horses perished in the blaze and a milkman struggling to open the stalls was so severely burned he lost all his fingers. I asked what year, and he said 1927. To satisfy myself that he was a congenital liar, I went down to the *Gazette* morgue determined to check through all the papers for that year. I only got as far as February. The milkman's name was Lamarsh.

"No priest. Not yet." Jules poised his bishop over my rook, then reconsidered and retreated to a position of defense. I couldn't concentrate on the game, wondering if he was going to elaborate on his confession. Part of me wanted to be privy to every explicit, gory detail and part of me wanted to shut him up. Perhaps I should have confessed to the urge to put rat poison in his saline drip. Would he have been amused? Probably not. His vicious black humor had dissipated with his health. I threw my remaining knight in the path of his bishop and picked the cookie off the rug.

"How," I asked, in as uninterested a tone as I could manage, "did you murder this baby?"

Jules laboriously lifted a glass from the night table and sipped some water through a straw before talking. "It was 1925. There was this small-time gambler. His weakness was horses. He borrowed money from LaRivière to cover his track bets, but he lost and he lost, and he could never repay a cent. I'd already broken eight of his fingers, but every time he got his mitts on a buck, there he was, back at the track. Then I got this idea. He and his wife had this new baby—about six weeks old. I decided to nab the kid and dump it on the nuns. I figured they'd take it to the orphanage, and I'd tell Rourke—that was his name, Rourke—that his baby was safe, but that he wouldn't see it again until he paid up. So I climbed up the fire escape of their building one night, jimmied a window, bundled up the kid, and headed for the Soeurs Grises. I left it in a fruit crate by the main entrance, rang the bell, and ran like hell. A few days later, when I figured Rourke was crazy with worry, I cornered him on the street and said my piece: that his kid was safe, but if he didn't come across, he'd never see it again, and not to bother calling the cops, because there was no evidence linking me with the kidnapping.''

He sobbed as he spoke. It was disconcerting. I'd never seen Jules upset. He hadn't shown any remorse over the eight horses. I handed him a Kleenex.

''Well, it worked. He found the money, somehow or another. Probably knocked over a store, and he paid back every penny. I went down to the convent, playing the repentant father, and begged the Mother Superior to tell me where they had taken my baby. The baby left on their step last week. I can still see her face. All the color drained out of it. She sat me down and held my hands as she told me that their bell hadn't been working. They'd recently converted to electricity, and that one circuit had shorted. The goddamned bell didn't work.''

Jules was bawling. I felt close to tears myself.

''And because the bell didn't work, the baby froze to death on their doorstep. They'd heard it cry in the night, but simply assumed the sound came from a nearby house. It was out there all night, freezing.''

I fidgeted with the Oreo bag.

''What did you do?''

''Drank for three days. Then I figured I was going to get in real trouble, so I sneaked into the orphanage and made off with another baby. Rourke and his wife were so ecstatic, they never noticed the baby wasn't theirs. I guess God didn't want Rourke to suffer. Only me. And I have.'' He sniffed and closed his eyes. ''You are the first person I've ever told.''

''Wouldn't you feel better if you confessed to a priest?'' I reasoned.

''But I can't confess. Confession means repentance.''

''But you're sorry, aren't you?'' I was baffled. Didn't Catholics go around confessing all the time?

''You don't understand the problem.'' Jules sighed, shrugged, and stared hopelessly at the ceiling.

''Well then, explain it to me.''

"I do not repent of my sins. I'd do them all again in the same situation. I am sorry the baby froze, but I'm not sorry I stole the baby. I'm not sorry I burned the stable. I'm not sorry I broke a thousand fingers. I'm not sorry I screwed a hundred women. I'm not sorry I married Louise, even though she bored me to tears, and I'm not sorry I made her life misery by never touching her after she produced Yves, the grandson her father wanted so badly. I knew she'd never complain to the old man. Everything was appearances with her. And if he discovered I kept mistresses? Didn't he also? God. I think we shared a few. I've enjoyed my life. If a few people suffered, well, tough. So you see, I am damned." Another tear left a wet track along the side of his nose. "I am going straight to hell."

Lord. No wonder he was hanging on. He may have been a beast, but he wasn't a hypocrite. I studied the list of ingredients on the half-eaten bag of cookies, not knowing what to say. Why had he unburdened himself to me? Because I was a nonentity? He reached for the large linen serviette that covered the enamel bedpan and blew his nose. Just then, the nurse appeared at the door and to my relief indicated that I should depart. I hurriedly shoved the Oreos in my bag and headed upstairs to see if I could find the boys.

"Papa is preparing for a trip."

"Oh?" I said. We were in the nursery. It was a large room comprising half of the third floor and looked almost like the set for the nursery in *Peter Pan*. Wainscoting painted an Oxford blue lined the wall to a height of four feet, and above that scenes from fairy tales had been rendered by an artist. One wall had Jack climbing the beanstalk to the giant's castle in the clouds, another was Puss in Boots bowing to the carriage of the nobleman, introducing his master, who was naked and shivering in the water, a third depicted the approach of Hansel and Gretel to the gingerbread house, and the fourth I recognized as being from *The Tinder Box*, where the soldier was opening the box filled with gold while on the tablecloth sat the ferocious dog with eyes as big as mill wheels. The style was quaint and old-fashioned; they had probably been commissioned when Yves was a baby, or even Louise.

The water pistols lay discarded on the floor, but enormous splatterings of blue-black ink dripped down the walls. That, I thought regretfully, hadn't occurred to me. I didn't bother chastising them. One of the Cats sat on the stained carpet at my feet while the other three methodically tore leaves from an atlas, which they folded into paper airplanes and sailed out the window.

"Oui. Madame says he's going to heaven." (When the boys deigned to speak a comprehensible language it was clear they had a firm grasp on both English and French.) I admonished one of them about leaning too far over the sill but he gave me the finger and slid out even farther. One of his brothers clutched an ankle and yanked him in. They wrestled on the floor. I ignored them.

"Is he?"

"*Certes*. Madame say so. He will be an angel."

"Really?" What an image—Jules with wings and a harp.

"He will fly like a bird."

"Fly, fly, fly." Overhearing our conversation, the fourth Cat leaped on his bed, began bouncing, and was soon joined by the other three. I watched in awed fascination as the wooden legs slammed against the floor and the mattress gradually slid from the box spring, depositing my nephews into a wriggling, giggling heap.

"He's lucky," sighed one, as their mirth subsided. The others concurred by nodding their shaggy heads.

"Greer, how will Papa get to heaven?"

"I don't know."

"Does God send a limousine? I saw a long white limousine the other day with white streamers."

"No, a boat," said another. "I saw a movie where all these people were going to heaven on a boat in the fog."

"Stupid. An airplane. Heaven is in the sky."

"He won't need an airplane. He'll rise into the clouds like Jesus."

"No. That doesn't happen with ordinary people. They have to grow wings. He'll fly with his wings."

"Ah, yes. I forgot. Wings."

"Greer, can we watch Papa fly to heaven?"

"I don't know." Goodness me. I had a vision of them standing vigil by his bed waiting for him to sprout wings and take off. "I don't think so. It'll probably happen at night when you're asleep, like when Papa Nöel comes." At least I hoped so. The last thing they needed after their elaborate scenario was to see their father hauled off in a black plastic, zippered body bag. One of them looked extremely skeptical.

"We don't believe in Santa Claus. Last Christmas we saw Yves and Maman wrapping all the presents."

"He has to die before he grows wings, right?" another asked.

"That's right." This explanation satisfied them, and I was grateful, as the entire topic befuddled my brain.

"I wonder if his hair will grow back, too. I've never seen a bald angel." They engaged in a heated discussion on the rejuvenation of the newly dead, whether it was instantaneous or whether the transformation was gradual. They couldn't agree and decided to hit on the cook for doughnuts. They said goodbye and in pairs crawled into the dumbwaiter for descent to the kitchen.

The image of Jules, dead, haunted me. For weeks following his death that last week of April, I woke in the middle of the night with his specter floating in that murky level of semiconsciousness so like reality. He was decked in a pair of huge feathered wings and flapped like Icarus up into the clouds. Only when I switched on the bedside lamp did the hallucination dissipate or take on the form of my dressing gown tossed over the edge of the door.

I had arrived for our weekly chess game and found his bed unoccupied and disarrayed. Pills from open bottles were scattered confetti-like across the floor as his disconnected IV dripped steadily onto the sheets. The catheter tube snaked over the bed rail and swung almost imperceptibly in the breeze from an open window. The sheer net curtains were drenched by rain, and I crossed the floor to lower the sash. I stood looking out for a moment.

The configuration of the servants' wing and garage was such that they and the main house formed a three-sided court that provided considerable shelter from the wind. Consequently, it was climatically a week or two in advance of the front yard. The pink crab-apple tree beneath Jules's window was already in full flower. In the deepening twilight it stood out as a great pale sphere from which the strident chattering of starlings could be heard. I turned to face the room. The curtains dripped and pooled milky white on the waxed floor. The bathroom door gaped open, revealing a storeroom of boxes containing saline and glucose solutions, stacks of clean linens, sterile tubing, plastic hypodermic syringes, enema kits, kidney bowls, bedpans, bottles of rubbing alcohol, baby lotion, medicated liquid soap, and disposable rubber gloves, but no Jules. I didn't think he could leave his bed. From the door I glanced up and down the hall. Nothing. I phoned the kitchen to alert the nurse and household staff to the senator's disappearance, and within moments two maids, the cook, the chauffeur, and the gardener were combing the house. The nurse just gaped at the empty bed, shaking her head and muttering, "But he was asleep. I only left for ten minutes to get a cup of coffee."

After half an hour it appeared as though Jules had accomplished the impossible and vanished into thin air. Either that or God, in a quirky mood, had whisked the evil old man off to paradise intact. We all converged in the atrium quite at a loss as to what our next move should be. Rain pattered on the skylight. The cook wrung her flour-dusted apron between her hands. The maids whispered to each other beneath the statue of Demeter, whose furled skirt the boys had recently painted orange. The gardener eyed the statues suspiciously, as though he expected one of them to transform into his boss. It was dawning on me that the boys were absent when the basement door opened and they ambled into the hall. I asked them if they'd seen their father.

"Oui," they responded in unison, shrugging their shoulders as though it couldn't be of less consequence.

"He's in the tree," one stated nonsensically. What on earth would Jules be doing in a tree? Then I shuddered as I recalled the open window.

The Cats led us into the sheltered garden and stood under the crab-apple tree on a carpet of fallen petals. They pointed to the center branches above the gnarled trunk where Jules, horribly twisted, his spine snapped, hung suspended. A canopy of flowers had closed over him as he fell, which was why I hadn't noticed him from above. Fortunately, he appeared to be dead. The maids screamed but the children displayed an abnormal calm. A debate ensued as to whether we should wait for the police before removing Jules from the tree, but the indignity of his position finally decided us, and the gardener climbed into the thicker branches to disengage the corpse and lower it to the chauffeur. After Jules was laid on the ground and covered with a blanket, one of the boys tugged at my sweater and in a confiding tone, whispered:

"He didn't fly."

The circumstances surrounding the death provoked a coroner's inquest, and the one question no one could satisfactorily answer was: how could a man, bedridden for over a year, leap out a window? Lacking a sensible explanation for such an extraordinary occurrence, it was decided that Jules had, in all probability, made a heroic effort to end his life.

Only later did I recall my nephew's words, and it gave me a frisson to realize that the boys were capable of dragging him from the bed, tearing out the tubes, and heaving him over the windowsill. They entirely lacked moral sense, and were certainly undisturbed at the sight of their father's mangled corpse in the tree. Their motive, obviously, had been to watch their father fly to heaven, which, all things considered, was more comprehensible than their motive for microwaving the canary or phoning Ville Marie Social Services to report that they were victims of child abuse and had spent the last four years of their lives locked in the cellar. (Fortunately the testimony of eight employees and seven family members convincingly contradicted their story.) If this is the truth, the Cats will never tell.

Since Jules was a nominal suicide, arrangements had to be made for interment in consecrated ground. I understand it cost Yves something in the order of a ten-thousand-dollar donation toward replacement of the copper roofing on a downtown church.

CHAPTER SIX

"*Papa est dans une boîte*," bellowed one of the boys who hung upside down on the monkey bars beside the house. I paused on the front steps and waved. He wasn't wearing the usual jumpsuit but was oddly dressed in a small tweed jacket with belted back, knickerbockers, argyle socks, and leather shoes that laced high over the ankle—the sort of clothes little boys wore around the time of the First World War. I could smell the mothballs. He blew a large pink bubble that burst and collapsed over his face, then peeled the mess off and stuffed the gum back in his mouth as he swung.

A black mourning wreath of glossy silk roses hung from the wrought-iron grillwork over the glass on the door. How archaic. How ostentatious. Jules's forebears had gone to their rewards in nothing more elaborate than pine boxes but he had stipulated (in a letter, copies of which had been entrusted to Yves, Connie, and myself) that he wanted the works: engraved invitations to be sent out for the funeral service in Notre Dame Cathedral, with Mozart's *Requiem* to be performed by the Montreal Symphony Orchestra and Tudor Singers (or whoever was available). And he wanted spectacle. None of this "in lieu of flowers, donations to cancer research would be greatly appreciated" could satisfy his posthumous megalomania. They'd all send wreaths and bouquets and sprays of roses and glads and mums: everyone who had ever known and hated him. Twenty flower cars would wend through the downtown streets and shoppers would pause and stare and wonder, briefly, who had died.

My nephew (who knows which?) swung his legs through his arms and dropped gracefully to the mud.

"*C'est beau, ça, eh?*" He stood beside me, fingering a silken leaf with the pinched, deprived expression of a street urchin. The smell of mothballs was almost overwhelming.

"Is your mother in?" I asked. He shrugged indifferently and wandered back to the monkey bars. An anemic sun struggled to break through a thin layer of clouds, but failed to dispel the lingering chill. Swollen buds on the trees refused to burst; the crocus had withered. I breathed pale silent puffs. The door swung open and I was greeted by another of my nephews who also seemed to have emerged from a time capsule, only of a later period. He wore a gray flannel blazer and shorts, white shirt, striped tie, gray knitted vest, and matching knee socks with black oxfords and a peaked cap with the crest of Yves's old school. Without bothering to demand a present (I'd brought lollipops) he abandoned me in the vast marble atrium.

No lights were on, and the skylight cast a murky pall. I wasn't sure what to do, or where to go. Dolores had simply demanded my support so, dutiful child that I was, I came. A door slammed, but so peculiar were the acoustics of the hall, it could have been anywhere in the house. Then I heard crying, and Leslie's voice.

"What does it matter if it's next year or next week for Christ's sake? Since when have you been concerned about what people thought?"

"Observances must be made. And must you swear? It's hardly becoming."

"Jesus. You're such a fucking Jesuit hypocrite!" Leslie's shouting filled the huge empty space and Yves appeared at the entrance to the dining room, marched across the atrium and out the front door without the slightest awareness of my presence, although he passed within two yards of me. Then he did something uncharacteristically demonstrative. He walked over to the monkey bars, lifted his little brother off, and clutched the struggling, uncooperative boy against his chest for a good minute.

"Greer! What the hell are you doing here?"

I turned from the window to see Leslie standing beside the statue of Demeter. She was clad in a fuchsia spandex exercise leotard. (My sister—not the statue. Demeter was sporting a firefighter's helmet.) Her entire body was clenched with anger. She didn't budge so I walked toward her, my heels clacking on the stone as loudly as exploding squibs.

"Dolores wanted some help. I'm sorry about Jules," I uttered lamely, but what could I say? Congratulations? I knew the tears she was shedding had nothing to do with her bereavement. She breathed deeply, shrugged, and regained some composure.

"Where is she?" I asked.

"Oh, shit, how should I know? She said she'd be here to organize the frigging caterers. Then I get a call from her secretary informing me that the carvers are on strike and that she's locked up with a mediator. You'd think the old bitch would delegate authority once in a while. What's more important, anyway, Jules's fucking funeral or a few fucking scalloped headboards?"

"I'll call the caterers. Just tell me how many people you expect."

"Don't fucking bother. I'll order in pizza."

"Okay . . . " I stepped back. I'd been witness to more than a few of Leslie's bad moods, and this went way beyond that. She whipped a Kleenex from her sleeve and patted her forehead and upper lip free of perspiration. I tried to change the topic.

"So how was Mustique?"

"Shit! Not you, too. Everyone's trying to make me feel guilty because I was away when he died. What did you all expect me to do? Hover beside his bed for two years? God. First Dolores, then Yves, now you."

"Take it easy. I was only making conversation."

"Bullshit. You're being judgmental, as usual. Well, I don't feel obliged to rationalize my behavior to anyone."

"Fine. Just tell me how many people you estimate will come and I'll get on to the caterers."

"I don't know, and I don't give a sweet goddamn. If I had my way I'd haul him over to the crematorium in the station wagon and fly back to the Caribbean."

"Who *does* know, Leslie? Someone must have the invitation list?" I was losing patience.

"Yves," she sighed, resigning herself to the fact that she was stuck in the role of grieving widow. "Yves knows everything, but he's off to discuss the service with the priest and won't be back until two or three. Since you're here, you might as well come upstairs and give me a hand."

"With what?" I asked, as I followed her up the curved staircase.

"Sorting junk." She entered a large mirrored dressing room. Doors and drawers gaped open and every variety of masculine apparel erupted onto the chairs and floor. Leslie shook open a green garbage bag into which she began stuffing shirts. I took my cue and began folding pants and jackets, destined, one supposed, for the Brewery Mission. Everything reeked of mothballs. That explained where the boys' costumes had come from.

"The man never threw anything out. Do you know there are trunks of old clothes in the attic? I was up there this morning with the boys. There are tons, literally *tons* of clothes. Some of it belonged to old man LaRivière and his wife. Louise's clothes from when she was a baby until the day they carted her away. All Yves's things. Old servants' uniforms. Jules was a pack rat, with an emphasis on the rat. I don't know how he ever imagined they'd be useful. Look at this." She held an opera cape with white silk lining up to her shoulders.

"There are suits upstairs that date from the thirties, all packed away in cedar. Pristine. Once he actually had the nerve to suggest I look up there to see if there was anything of Louise's I could make use of. I mean, can you imagine? She was five foot nothing and dressed like a retired nun. If he had had his way, the boys would have worn Yves's old clothes. All wools and cottons. Everything needed hand washing, and ironing. I convinced him that we'd have had to hire a laundress and it would cost us more than new clothes. God. He was a cheapskate. But he sure didn't scrimp on his own wardrobe budget. Guess how many dress suits he has squirreled away?"

"I don't know." I shrugged and made a guess. "Ten?"

"Thirty-three!" she exclaimed. "Twenty-five with dinner jackets and eight pairs of tails. There are going to be a hell of a lot of strange-looking rummies wandering the streets in a day or two."

I pulled a pair of fawn-colored jodhpurs from the pile and we both burst out laughing. I couldn't picture Jules in them, much less some St. Catherine Street derelict.

"And he didn't even ride." She collapsed on the mess of Harris tweeds, cashmere pullovers, linen shirts, and silk pajamas, helplessly giddy, when two of the Cats shot through the door and landed on Leslie, beating her with their grubby little fists, tearing at her hair. One was wearing a Little Lord Fauntleroy suit and the other a smocked dress and patent leather mary janes.

They began grabbing socks and handkerchiefs, frantically stuffing them back in the drawers. Leslie watched, momentarily stunned by the outburst, then lunged at them, throwing them onto the pile of clothes. She tried to pull a vest away from one of them and lifted the little boy right off the ground. I feared for the child. He dangled a foot in the air, kicking furiously at Leslie until the fabric gave way with a violent rip and he tumbled onto the heap of garments, weeping bitterly. The other child then grabbed her by the ankle and was about to take a bite out of her calf when she yanked him to his feet by his thin little arm. I was afraid she'd dislocate his shoulder.

"To your room. Both of you."

They froze and glowered defiantly.

The one in the dress stamped through the door, defiantly dragging the opera cape. The posture of the other slumped and he started to sob. He reached for a red silk dressing gown and held it against his cheek. His tears left a dark smear on the lapel.

Was he crying for a lost father, or an unloving mother? I couldn't tell, but it was interesting to see the children act as individuals.

"When are they going to let Papa out of the box?" he asked with a pitiful little wail.

Leslie threw up her hands in frustration. "What can I do with this child? He's impossible. They're all impossible. I explained and explained but they refuse to comprehend."

"They're only babies."

"Right. Babies. The morning I was to catch my plane, I came downstairs at five o'clock and discovered that they had flooded the sunken atrium to a depth of eight inches so they could recreate the battle of Acton with paper boats. Among the papers they used were my airline tickets and passport. They had to get up at midnight to plan and execute that one. They aren't children. These are monsters placed exclusively on this earth to persecute me." She lunged at the sniveling child and hauled him to his feet by his shoulders. "Papa is dead." She shouted. "Dead like your cat after it was run over by the garbage truck."

He screamed back. "Papa isn't dead. Get him out of the box. Put him back in bed."

"Don't you understand dead?"

"The cat was bloody. Dead things are bloody. When people are shot and stabbed they're bloody. Papa isn't bloody."

"Bloody people can be bloody dead without being bloody bloody." Her hand was outstretched and I caught her arm as she was about to take a swipe at the child.

"Leslie, calm down."

"Butt out. This is none of your concern." She shook the child then practically threw him onto the floor where he glared at her with an expression of undiluted hatred.

"Out," she commanded and the boy exited, sniffing, trailing the red dressing gown, pausing once on the threshold to regard his mother with narrowed eyes as though he were incanting a curse on her head.

"The little horrors." She kicked a garbage bag and checked her reflection in the mirror. After flicking a few stray hairs into

place she attacked the pile of clothing with renewed determination. I threw the shirt I was holding on the floor.

"Why don't you have the maids do this?" I asked.

"Because I want to do it myself," she hissed as she tore an
armful of cardigans from the pile and compressed them into a
bag with her foot. "It's cathartic. A purge. I want to eradicate
Jules from the house. I want to be able to walk through any
room and not have one fleeting microsecond of recollection
infect my mind. I want to see those hideous statues crushed by a
garbage truck. I can't count the number of times I asked if we
could get rid of the things and have a decorator come in and do
the place up." She yanked at a drawer so hard that it fell onto the
floor, spilling its contents of gloves—soft yellow leather gloves,
lined and unlined, about forty pairs. The man was compulsive.

"I want to paint. The place hasn't been painted since Louise
died. And carpets. All the carpets are beige. I hate beige. I want
bright carpets and comfortable furniture. Everything you see is
production line circa 1935."

She didn't have to tell me this. Similar stuff passed through
Ponsonby's daily, its sole worth being that it was manufactured
from solid wood and not particleboard.

"Some of it is actually Payton stuff. Can you believe it? The
labels are still glued to the undersides. Phony French provin-
cial, phony Queen Anne, phony Louis Quinze. He bought
cheap to fill the place up and never bothered upgrading. He
never even bought a painting because he figured mirrors were
cheaper per square foot. You look surprised. I know. You think
I'm so vain I bought the mirrors so I could gaze at my reflection
all day. Well, they were here when I moved in. I read somewhere
that in 1935 you could have bought a Gauguin for a few hundred
pounds. Christ! *Any* bloody oil would have appreciated in
value, but everything in this house is worth zip. I'll have to pay
someone to cart it away. Perhaps you could sell it at that place
you work." She kicked aside the bag of sweaters and started
jamming ties and cravats in another.

"If you hate the house so much, why don't you just sell
it?"

"Wouldn't I just love to, but I can't sell what I don't own."

"I don't understand."

"Jules didn't own the house. He rented it from Yves."

"Yves?"

"His mother willed it to him."

"Oh."

"Oh is right."

"Then just move."

"I don't want to move. I've lived here for seventeen years. This is *my* house. It has potential. Have you any idea how much I'd have to pay to buy a house of this size in as good a location?"

"Does Yves agree with your plans?"

"He doesn't care."

"Maybe he has a sentimental attachment to the cheap ugly furniture."

"Oh, no. Some of his Jesuitical indoctrination stuck. He is utterly indifferent to worldly goods."

"You sound pretty sure of yourself."

"You're being judgmental again."

"Look, I don't care what you do. As you pointed out, it's none of my business."

"Of course, *you* don't think I deserve anything."

"I never said that."

"No. But you thought it. Well, I deserve plenty. I earned it. Have you any idea what it's like to sleep with an old man?" She poked an accusatory finger at my chest as her lips formed a grimace. I didn't know what it was like to sleep with any man, much less horrible old Jules, nor did I care to linger on the image.

"Look. I don't know. I don't want to know. You married him." I opened a door and escaped into a huge white-tiled bathroom. A breeze blew through an open window making the plastic shower curtain rustle against the tub. A Spartan room, out of keeping with the opulent wardrobe. All for the sake of appearance. Who was to see the worn white towels or the cork bath mat? Even his brushes were wood. An ordinary Gillette razor lay on the edge of the sink. The room must have sat untouched since Jules was moved down the hall a year ago. The soap in the dish was dry and cracked. Leslie, who had followed me, was sitting on the toilet seat folding an argyle sweater.

"I was stupid to have married Jules. I suppose that I was flattered someone like him would even notice me. He was rich and famous. You can chalk one up to the arrogance of youth that I didn't realize he was only after me because I had a tight young cunt. All I could think about was what a blast it would be to watch people's reactions when I came home on his arm. Remember the party Jules gave to introduce me to his important friends?"

"I was still in England."

"I suppose I should count my blessings. If I'd been you I'd have slit my wrists. I mean, God, aren't you just so bored?"

"Boy, you're arrogant. Can't you for one moment imagine life without a man? Look at the price you paid for your limited thinking. You could have left Jules the moment the novelty paled, but you didn't. You could have educated yourself, or even if you'd wanted to languish your life away being someone's decorative other, you could have done better than Jules. The man was an evil old pig. You could have had anyone. Anyone. Why did you stay?"

She shrugged and ran her hand along the length of her spandex-encased leg, from her impossibly slender thigh, which didn't noticibly flatten when she sat, to her shapely calf and narrow ankle. I don't even think she was aware of doing it, but she unconsciously reveled in the feel of her own body. I touched my tentlike tweed jumper that hid serviceable undergarments: an enormous cotton brassiere, size 47 DD, a shapeless pair of drawers (one couldn't call them panties, there was simply too much fabric), and knee-highs. (Even queen size panty hose were so tight that they ran the moment I stretched them over my hips.)

"I don't know. Inertia. One grows accustomed to a certain position in society. It's easy to move sideways or up, but down, no. I don't think I could ever move down, and I had other reasons for maintaining the marriage."

Explicit in the tone of her statement was completion. The topic was closed. "I think I'll go up and check on the boys," I said, anxious to be gone.

"Don't bother. They'll be having lunch about now. Besides, I feel like talking. For the next few days people are going to be coming up to me and telling me what a fine human being my husband was and I'm going to have to keep a straight face. Did anyone really believe he was a fine human being?"

"No."

"A few years back one of his brothers asked him for a loan, a loan, mind you, so that he could make up overdue mortgage payments on the farm Jules was raised on, and Jules refused. The man was eighty years old. Fortunately, Yves took care of it."

"He wasn't a nice man."

"It would not be possible to make an exaggeration of the man's un-niceness. Did you know that before he married me, he hired prostitutes? Young prostitutes."

"Look, I don't care what he did. The man's dead." I wondered if Jules had ever taken Leslie into his confidence about his lurid past. Anyway, I'd had it with Jules stories.

"But I want you to understand. You always thought I was so mean to Jules. Poor Jules."

"I didn't like Jules. Nobody liked Jules. He was evil."

"But he was my husband. My duty. Right?"

"Look, every relationship has its private contracts and negotiations. Forgive me if I'm not curious about yours."

"But you felt sorry for him. You visited and played chess. For some unknown reason, you felt you had an obligation, right?"

"Okay. If you insist. Jules had a compelling personality."

"Compelling. Yeah. Compelling." She considered the notion for a minute while chewing the inside of her cheek. "You can thank your good fortune you didn't have to screw him."

"Really, Leslie. This conversation's inane." I made a move for the door but she blocked the way with her feet.

"If you'd looked as good as me, Jules would have jumped

you. Not that it would have done him any good or you any harm. You would have emerged with your precious hymen intact. You *are* still a virgin, aren't you? The great mystery grows ever greater.''

"Shut up, Leslie." I lunged for the doorknob but Leslie grabbed my hand.

"There's no mystery. It's just fuck and suck.'' She laid the sweater on the edge of the sink and smoothed her eyebrows with the tips of her fingers. I stood, pinioned to the cool white tiles by her hypnotic drawl.

"In and out. Grope and poke. Rub and squeeze. Lick and nuzzle. Really quite nice, but not with Jules. Jules was usually impotent, but that didn't stop him from trying. Or making me try. He'd dangle his pathetic little pecker over my face and expect me to work my mouth raw until something happened. It rarely did. Then he'd have his little go, mushing his flaccid piece between my legs until he collapsed from exertion.''

"You're disgusting. I don't want to listen. Please move your legs.''

"Then I became pregnant. A miracle. He begged me not to have an abortion—Lord knows I wanted one—and in exchange for keeping the brats I made him swear he'd never touch me again, or question my comings and goings or my VISA bill.'' She stood and raised my chin with her finger until I was forced to look her in the eyes. Sweat dripped between my breasts. Her pupils contracted in the light until they were mere pin specks in the center of her green irises. "You see.''

"Yes, I see. Typically mercenary. You know what they call women who trade sex for favors.''

"Your *Reader's Digest* values bore me.''

"How many years were you married before the boys came? Twelve? Are they even his?''

She snorted. "Oh, they're blood of his blood and flesh of his flesh all right. That I'd swear before you and God.''

I'd never questioned their paternity before, they looked so exactly like Jules. The only way she could have managed that feat was to have slept with his double, or Yves, and Yves was, well, if not homosexual, asexual. She swung her legs around, opened the door, and waved me out.

I checked in at work and returned to the house after lunch. One of the Cats sat on the kitchen floor eating a banana. The one in the dress. He was shoeless and the soles of his white ankle socks were black. The spotted peel fell over his small fist like the petals of an exotic flower. He turned the fruit sideways and sucked off the brown bruises first. I tried not to screw up my face in distaste.

It was certainly curious that at a time when one would have expected them to draw even closer together, they'd chosen to be individuals. He looked at me with his great brown eyes and smiled. What sort of a person was I to suspect the boys of having dragged their father from his deathbed and thrown him out a window? The more I thought about it the more preposterous the notion seemed. Jules somehow made his way out of bed and fell or jumped out the window.

Upstairs, the atmosphere was charged. Dolores had arrived late in the morning after suspending strike negotiations, and learned that two of her most reliable caterers were booked Monday. Then her florist informed her that due to an unexpected frost in Florida, there were no orange blossoms to be had in Montreal at any price. (What did she want them for anyway? This was a wake, not a wedding.) A lackey from the office of Jules's lawyer had, at Leslie's request, dropped off a copy of the will. It sat for approximately two minutes on the hall table before being purloined by the Cats, who hid it somewhere. It was a big house and no threats had thus far induced the children to reveal its whereabouts. The chauffeur and two maids were reduced to poking about on their knees in every dusty corner in an effort to find the document, and when Leslie called the lawyer to demand that another copy be sent, she was informed by an answering machine that the office was closed for the weekend.

The kitchen was relatively quiet. A bright morning sun had finally broken the gloom and flooded through the high basement windows, reflecting off the shining black-and-white tiles.

The nurse, her employment extended to help watch the children (the Italian nanny had quit after Jules was found in the tree), swung her white-shod foot back and forth to the rhythm of a Paul Simon song on the radio while Madame, her large bosom heaving under the bib of a flowered apron, slapped across the ceramic floor in her husband's carpet slippers to pour me another cup of coffee. (I had just eaten two slices of tourtière and a bowl of chocolate pudding and was, if nothing else, physically content.) She groaned, arched her back, and sat heavily down. The chair creaked. Her bulk made me self-conscious and I glanced at my ankles to assure myself that they weren't as fat as hers, but they were. The Cat peered out from beneath the table and beckoned me to join him. With difficulty, I lowered myself to the floor and slid under, ducking my head. The space was cramped with me in there and I was cramped in the space. Above, in a different world, an adult world, the two women were talking in a gentle Gallic murmur, but their speech was so rapid and idiomatic, I couldn't understand more than one word in ten. The little boy, surprisingly affectionate and familiar, laid his head on my leg and sighed.

"Are you Honoré?" I asked, stroking his dark glossy hair, not expecting affirmation or denial, certainly not his soft reply.

"Non." He touched the tip of the banana to the cracked skin of Madame's heel. No response. Down a little farther, toward the arch, brought better results. The old cook lowered her cheerful ruddy face below the table and wagged her finger. Then she handed him a cheese Danish on a big white linen serviette.

"Pour toi, Pascal."

That was interesting. She could tell them apart. Perhaps she bribed them into identity with their favorite foods. Pascal smoothed the napkin flat on the floor and placed the gnawed banana on one side, the pastry on the other, then picked his nose, rolling the mucousy blob into a tiny black ball. My back ached from hunching forward but I didn't want to disturb the child, who reached up to press his creation onto the rough underside of the table. The wood was dotted with old dried wads of gum.

"We aren't allowed to chew gum," Pascal announced, as he touched one of the blobs.

"Why not?" I asked.

"Maman says it's a plebeian habit. I wonder who stuck this gum here. Maybe Yves. Was Yves allowed to chew gum when he was little?"

"Perhaps. I don't know. Why don't you ask him?"

"I will." He fingered a purple ball, hard, shiny, and petrified where the top and side of the table made a right angle. Thirty-five-year-old gum?

"I wonder if it still tastes?" He raised himself to his knees, bent his head and before I realized what he was doing, stuck his tongue out and gave the gum a lick. Just then the nurse's foot tapped him on the hip and he fell back, his hand flattening the banana.

"Merde," he muttered, wiping his palm against his dark blue smock, leaving a smear of white.

"Why aren't you guys together today?"

"We have to know what's going on."

"Where did you hide the will?"

"I don't know."

"Did you read it?" I couldn't resist asking.

"We can't read." He was lying. They'd been reading for years. In one of the rounds of testing they were forced to endure, their intelligence quotients were estimated to be in the high 160s.

"Then why did you steal it?"

He shook his head and slid the cheese Danish across the floor until it touched my knee—a bribe to end the conversation.

I accepted it.

The will was found amid the ashes in the breakfast room fireplace. All that was identifiable was a thin triangle of charred paper held together with a staple. Punishment was meted out equally to all four children, who were exiled to their room with sore bottoms and no supper. Since the nursery had been

soundproofed shortly after it was discovered how much noise
four cranky babies were capable of generating, they were forgotten for a few hours until a trickle of water was discovered
running down the stairs from the third floor where all the taps
were running full force, overflowing the bathtub and sinks,
flooding the entire upper landing.

The nurse was fired for neglect of duty.

Jules had died on a Wednesday. Leslie had flown home Thursday. Funeral arrangements were made on Friday. The funeral
was held the following Monday. It could have been held on
Saturday, but Jules didn't want his funeral to be held on a day
when everyone was in the country. He figured people would
rather miss work than weekends. The church was packed, but
only family bothered to show up at the graveyard, and not even
all the family. Jules's surviving siblings (I think there were five)
were conspicuously absent. I doubt that they were invited.

The poor Cats. They stood before Leslie as the priest drawled
on in Latin. (He was a very old priest, and Vatican II had
probably slipped his mind.) The day was dull and damp,
entirely fitting for a burial, and a fine misty rain that gave the
impression of hovering in the heavy air beaded lightly on everyone's somber garb.

The boys were dressed in little gray flannel suits with short
pants and their knobby knees were chapped and red. Their tiny
hands were as white as the roses they held and their liquid
brown eyes were expressionless. I could only imagine their
thoughts as they watched Jules being lowered into the ground.
It was still my understanding that they didn't believe he was
actually dead. Leslie should have left them at home. It was pure
sadism to let them watch their father (as it must follow) being
buried alive.

Leslie was wedged between our parents, giving a fair imitation of Jackie Kennedy that was wasted on the family, who were
wise to her. Stacked haphazardly around the area of the grave
were baskets and wreaths and sprays of flowers (mostly glads in

the gaudy artificial shades peculiar to hybridized species), the only bright spot on the landscape. The trees still hadn't budded in that late spring. Yves stood at Dolores's left, hat in hand, his bowed head revealing a perfectly spiral crown, and Father stood to her right, swaying slightly, gazing skyward, probably oblivious of what was going on. Beside me, on the opposite side of the grave, was Connie, looking vaguely sinister in a heavily padded black overcoat with an astrakhan collar. He unabashedly swigged whiskey from a monogrammed silver flask (the monogram not his: he had picked it up at an estate sale years ago and never bothered to change the initials). Alex waited near his truck, still in jeans but, as a concession to the event, wearing a dark blue raincoat of the variety that folds into a small vinyl snap-close package for easy transport. Bartleby shivered at his side, sodden and rheumy.

No one from the church had come and I thought of the boxes and boxes of catered food that sat in Leslie's kitchen—all the flowers Dolores had ordered. I stared across at her grim face, knowing she was seething that all her preparations were for nothing. Who did she think would want to come anyway? The church, yes. That was a duty. There was press at the church. (A stringer from the *Journal de Montréal*. What an anticlimax.)

The prayer was complete. Yves replaced his hat and held the shoulders of the child before him. I hadn't noticed until then how like Jules he was—the high, narrow cheekbones, the limpid brown eyes and full lips. The boys resembled him, too. Neither the Slavic earthiness of the Fletchers was inherited, nor the Celtic fairness of the Paytons. All five of Jules's children were pure Dansereau.

Leslie lifted her veil to dab the corner of her eye with a handkerchief. She played her part well: calm and dignified. Smeared mascara made her eyes great, dark, and sad like some silent screen heroine. For whose benefit did she act? The priest's?

The stone, already engraved with Jules's name and date of birth, had been waiting since the death of his first wife a quarter of a century before. It was surmounted by a stone angel holding a sword that had been snapped at the hilt. (Had the boys been there before?) He hadn't even had the mason carve 19--, in anticipation of his demise. What an optimist. If he'd made it into the next century he'd have been almost as old as Connie.

I looked at Grandfather and caught him tapping numbers into a pocket calculator. He waited for the answer then clicked the machine off and scribbled the number in his little black notebook. Then he took another gulp of whiskey.

Leslie, her widow's weeds dripping, bent to whisper in one of the boys' ears. The child mustn't have liked what she said because he reacted by tearing off her heavy veil and grinding it into the mud with his little black oxfords. She clenched her fists and looked as though she was about to box his ears when Dolores intervened, pulling her back. Then Dolores, smiling sweetly, tried to make him do whatever it was he was clearly not willing to do. He kicked her shin. She shrieked and his brothers grouped around to protect him against retaliation.

The priest hurridly chanted, "In nomine Patris et Filii et Spiritus Sancti, Amen," and crossed himself. This momentarily brought order to the proceedings and even the children (who had been dragged to church by Yves every Sunday of their young lives) automatically crossed themselves and murmured amen. Then the priest tossed a handful of dirt on the coffin. Unfortunately the wet soil had the consistency of clay and instead of pattering gently on the wooden lid it landed with a moist thunk and sat like an insult, a great dirtball beside the blanket of roses. Everyone stared.

Connie snorted and Leslie glowered as she threw her rose overhand into the open grave. When she took hold of the stem of one of the boys' roses, encouraging him to do the same, he resisted and yelled, "Laisse-moi," tugging at the flower. His brothers then started batting at Leslie with their blooms and white petals drifted like huge snowflakes over the muddy ground. Dolores and Yves pulled the children away just as they were about to force their mother over the lip of the excavation, and they were dragged, thrashing and flailing, to one of the limos. Bartleby, already cowering and shaking, crawled under the truck and howled. Father just stood there, gazing off into the middle distance, unaware that anything out of the ordinary was occurring. What was he thinking? Which funeral in which movie? Finally, he meandered in the direction of their car. The priest stepped over, took Leslie by the arm, and led her away.

The two subtle gray limousines (Grandfather and I had come in my Ford) pulled away, leaving Connie, Alex, and myself alone in the grave-pitted mountain hollow. Grandfather sat on the headstone and continued to drink his whiskey while I ate two chocolate bars. Alex bent down to haul Bartleby out from under the truck and lift the wailing beast into the cab. Then he walked over to where the others had been standing, stooped, and extracted a long slimy object from the mud. At first I thought it was a snake, but he crumpled it into a small ball, kissed it (smearing mud all over his face), and reverently placed it in his pocket. It took me a moment to figure out what the hell it was, then I remembered. Leslie's veil.

CHAPTER SEVEN

Ten people don't take up much space at Leslie's house. The living room, designed for lavish entertaining by Paul La-Rivière, was sixty feet long and thirty wide, which on this occasion worked out to a stunning one hundred and eighty square feet per person. When she realized that only family would come, Dolores ought to have moved the wake into the small study. The three maids supplied by the caterer seemed a little baffled, and two vanished shortly after our arrival, never to reappear.

Daddy collected a quart of vodka from the portable bar and retired to the library to watch some videos he'd brought in a leather attaché case. Five cassettes representing eight hours of prime-time television and two late movies circled by Daddy in *TV Guide* had been dutifully taped by Alice. The children had been removed to the kitchen for a light supper without any complaint or rebellion. Utterly exhausted, they had fallen asleep in the car on the return from the cemetery. They had such presence it was easy to forget that they were just babies. So our number was reduced to five.

Yves kindled the logs in the fireplace and we all gravitated to the warmth: Dolores and Leslie on an ersatz Louis XVI petit-point love seat, Connie and I on matching chairs, and Yves leaning against the mantel. It was deadly. No one said a thing until the cook huffed in, sweaty and frazzled from supervising the children's dinner.

"Oh, what's the problem now?" Leslie moaned. "Have the children had a flour fight, or locked themselves in the freezer, or tried to dissect the cat, or what?"

"*Non, madame. Anatole a disparu.*" She flinched as she spoke, as though she expected Leslie to hit her.

"Oh, never mind. He'll turn up. Unfortunately, they always do. Just put the others to bed." She smiled sardonically and dismissed the cook with a bored wave of her hand. "They always reappear, usually covered in cobwebs or coal dust," she added. Then the room fell into silence once more. Evidently no one cared to reminisce about Jules. I suppppose it wasn't curious that none of his surviving political cronies had bothered making an appearance at the house. Jules dead had no power of intimidation.

"Did you notice that the PM only sent the minister for Health and Welfare to represent him?" Dolores polished off her gin and tonic and unbuttoned her blazer. "I had to put my labor negotiations on hold and only a third-rate minister. Who was that floozy with him? It shows no respect, bringing one's mistress to a funeral."

"That was his wife," said Leslie.

"Oh. Well, she should have worn a more suitable dress. And why didn't anyone come here?"

"Because they didn't want to."

"That's no excuse."

The maid entered with hot canapés (creamed spinach in puff pastry) and refilled Leslie's glass of wine. I have never been at such an awkward gathering in my life. Connie walked over to the bar (the bartender was nowhere in evidence), poured a quarter of a bottle of cognac into his flask, then returned to his seat and proceeded to scribble in his notebook. Yves poked the logs, exciting a crackle of sparks. Leslie drank. Dolores picked at her red nail polish. I cleared my throat to address Connie.

"So. How was Brazil?" I asked in a casual, conversational tone such as one might use to a stranger in the dentist's waiting room.

"Fine," he replied. "Hot, though."

"Really?" I responded. Everyone was staring, hungry for diversion. "It's been bitter here."

"Has it?"

"Rain. Bone-chilling damp. Like today." As if for emphasis, I stretched out my hands to the fire and rubbed them briskly.

"It was ninety in Manaus. Terribly humid. On the river, you know."

"Yes."

"Lots of mosquitoes."

"Oh?"

"Absolutely impervious to repellents."

"What did you do?"

"Ate copious amounts of garlic."

"Did the business go well?"

"Exceedingly. Although at a distance." A pallid joke, but we all laughed anyway.

"I ran into my cousin Ivan."

"In Manaus?" From all I'd ever heard about Ivan, he hadn't been there for his health, and neither had Connie. What was the attraction?

"Yes. At a sidewalk café."

"What was he doing there?"

"Smuggling drugs," sniped Dolores. "The old reprobate."

"The area isn't renowned for drug production," he said.

"Then he was smuggling them in."

"Actually, he was drinking gin and lime. He was surprised to see me and didn't seem to know about the ceramics, so he must have been there for another reason."

"Were the ceramics as fine as you expected?"

"Better. Among other things, a Meissen swan tea service. The woman there discovered it in one of her father's trunks that she'd never bothered opening."

"That's rare stuff. You must be pleased."

"Yes. I've refused three offers so far, but I think I'll hang on to it for a bit. The ceramic market is doing very nicely at the moment."

"Three offers? You only got back Saturday."

"News travels."

"Apparently. Did you see in the last Christie's auction, a set of twelve hand-painted Worcester service plates fetched over a hundred thousand?"

"I noticed that. A bargain. If the buyer was clever he'd go home and smash six immediately."

We giggled but the others looked aghast. I was about to enlighten them with the story of how a cynical philatelist, having acquired two rare identical postage stamps, upped the value of one tenfold merely by burning the other, but at that moment the doorbell rang and a maid ushered in Jules's lawyer. He looked uncomfortable as he shook hands and offered condolences to Leslie. Without budging from her chair she held out her hand and he reached into his jacket pocket for a copy of the will. She took it, unfolded it, read it, snorted, and tossed it on the couch beside her. Dolores grabbed it, read it, and threw it on a side table as though it was infectious. I picked it up, and the contents pleased me so much that I wanted to dance and sing. It read:

> I, Jules Dansereau, being of sound mind and body do
> hearby declare this to be my last will and testament. To
> my wife, Leslie Elizabeth Payton Dansereau, I leave the
> income from the remaining term of my annuity in the
> fixed sum of one thousand dollars, payable monthly until
> the year two thousand and five.

That was it. Connie gave it a quick glance and emitted a sharp burst of sound, more like a report than a laugh. I dropped the papers on the coffee table where they unfolded with a swish. The lawyer shook hands with Yves and exited without further ado. We stared in silence. One page. It was the shortest legal document I'd ever seen.

"That's all there is? That's it?" asked Dolores, shocked and incredulous.

"Yes," answered Yves.

"But what about the house? The real estate holdings? The stocks? Senator Dansereau was a wealthy man."

"Mother . . . " interrupted Leslie, who sounded defeated, but not surprised.

"The house, Leslie, the house is in your name, isn't it? A downtown property this size must be worth millions."

"No, Mother." An ash dropped from her cigarette onto the threadbare carpet. She ground it in with the tip of her shoe. "Yves owns the house. He always did."

"Yves?" She looked baffled. "But you must have stocks? Bonds?"

"No, and no."

"Jewelry?" Dolores's voice raised a despairing octave and cracked on the final syllable.

"Some." Leslie uncrossed her legs and turned to face Yves, who was standing to her right. "Perhaps Yves would explain." Her lips curled at the edges, but she wasn't smiling.

"I don't know that this is the time or the place, or indeed, that it's anyone's business but Leslie's," he responded stuffily.

"Well, Yves, since it is my business, I think this is as good a time and place as any. What did Jules do with his money?" Leslie's face was unnaturally pale. Her longed-for liberation from Jules hadn't quite conformed to her fantasy. Yves replaced the poker in its stand with a clatter, then picked up the whisk and swept stray cinders from the marble surround as he spoke.

"Well, there is a percentage of Father's senatorial pension that as his widow you receive automatically. All the LaRivière money he had was only in trust until he died, at which time it passed to me. He transferred his remaining assets to the boys when they were infants, only retaining the income that now reverts to their trust."

"Administered by?" Leslie's green eyes were fixed on Yves, but I couldn't read what she was thinking. What I was thinking was that Jules's gift to the children had been subject to a thirty percent tax. He really must have loathed her.

"Father entrusted me with the management of the estate," said Yves.

"Were you aware of his intentions?"

"Yes. I tried to convince him to leave you a fair portion of the estate, but he was determined to have things his way."

"You could sue." Dolores slammed her drink on the table and stood up to pace. "He had no right to cut you out. You were married for seventeen years. Seventeen years. When did he write it? He was sick for two years. I'll testify that he was non compos mentis. This is an insult. You're entitled to much more."

Just then there was a small rustling, and the misplaced child appeared from behind a painted screen (a rather poor duplication of *The Allegory of Spring* in three panels) and ran over to me.

"*Nous sommes riches?*"

"*Je pense que oui,*" I answered, uncomfortably aware that Leslie was glaring. She looked as though she wanted to drag the usurper upstairs by the hair. He must have picked up on this, for the next thing he said was:

'*Et maintenant je vais regarder la télévision avec Grandpère.*" With that, he pushed open the sliding doors and marched across the hall with the dignity of a little king. Dolores was the first to speak after this demonstration of seigneurial aplomb.

"I don't believe this. So am I to understand that Leslie gets nothing but some puny pension?"

"And the annuity," added Yves.

"Oh yes. Such munificence. She couldn't keep clothes on her back with that, while you and the children share a fortune." She had reached the far end of the room where we could barely hear her muttering. She clutched the window frame until her knuckles turned white.

"Forget it, Mother," Leslie snapped in a tired, impatient tone. "This is typical Jules treachery. I should have anticipated it. I mean, we despised each other, right? Why should he leave me anything?" She shrugged and pulled the combs from her hair, which fell in a fluffy permed cloud over her shoulders. She lit a cigarette, stuck a pillow behind her head, and leaned against the back of the couch.

"How did he expect you to live? Did he want you to buy your

clothes at Sears?'' Dolores almost shrieked. Her jugular vein swelled alarmingly. "You must contest the will."

I wondered if Dolores really believed Leslie had been dealt a rotten hand or if, even as she opened her mouth, she realized the nonsense she spoke. The pension was about fifty thousand, the annuity twelve, her fee from Payton and Company another ten or so, and she could always count on Mother for a shekel or two at regular intervals. Even after taxes it was certainly not a sentence to penury, and if I understood the tax system, all child-related expenses could be paid from their personal incomes, including house maintenance and food. Dolores addressed Yves.

"When was the will written?"

"Five years ago. His holdings were gifted to the children at the same time. Leslie has no legal recourse."

"But a spouse is legally entitled to a third of the estate."

"Only if Jules had died intestate," he explained patiently. Dolores clenched and unclenched her fingers. I wondered if she had suddenly realized that Connie wasn't obliged to leave her a dime. (Not that she needed a dime, but the possibility that her father's presumed fortune might go elsewhere was something she might not have hitherto considered.)

How cunning of Jules. So that was what he meant when he said there were better ways of punishing Leslie than killing her. What elegant vengeance. Leslie is one of those people who get things because they expect things, leaping from conquest to conquest, triumph to triumph, never paying the price, never suffering. I have actually spent days with my sister where the most crucial decision she was forced to make was what to wear for dinner. As for the Cats—well, to give her her due, she tried. It was she who schlepped them off to child psychologists for endless evaluations and analyses, a career as consuming as that of a stage mother. I don't know why they hated her. Perhaps she didn't give them enough presents.

"Who are the executors?" asked Leslie.

"I am," answered Yves.

Leslie relaxed visibly and sighed with relief, which was odd.

I'd never found Yves to be a sympathetic character, nor had I sensed an affinity between him and my sister. On the contrary, I had always thought they disliked each other.

Yves lowered his eyes and rubbed the dark stone in the ring on the small finger of his left hand. It looked like heliotrope. He avoided further eye contact with Leslie. She examined her nail polish. I had hoped for more excitement. Even Dolores had calmed down and poured herself another drink. Connie closed his notebook and began calculating on his pocket machine. I don't know where the maid had gone. Apart from three spinach puffs, I hadn't eaten for hours and was feeling my mortality. Through the doorway I could see a buffet had been laid out in the dining room. I glimpsed a platter of huge succulent pink shrimp and wanted them. Every one. Chafing dishes steamed, containing what smelled like beef bourguignonne or coq au vin. Perhaps both. My mouth watered. There were warm rolls and plates of little quiches, a salmon and a cold meat platter, a ham, salads, crab puffs, and heaven knew what in the kitchen still. French pastry? Trifle? Black Forest cake? Fruit flans? Hadn't anyone thought to inform the caterers that the anticipated hundred had diminished to five? Did I care?

"Leslie, do you mind if I fix myself a plate of food?"

Leslie glanced up absently. "Go ahead, everyone. Eat."

Dolores dumped her glass on the mantel and glowered as she passed Yves on the way to the dining room, then Connie followed, leaving his flask and notebook on the table. I came next, but stopped outside the door next to the statue of Poseidon to slip out of my shoe and rub the joint of my big toe. It was then I heard Yves speak.

"You're tired," he said to Leslie, when there was nobody else in the room. His tone wasn't solicitous, but almost blunt. That she was tired was a statement of fact.

"Yes," said Leslie. "It's been a long day."

"Have something to eat."

"I have no appetite."

"You haven't eaten all day. You must eat something." Yves's command was parental in its firmness. A moment later he led her into the hall by the elbow. His mouth twitched when he saw me. Maybe he had the hots for Leslie and was playing his advantage? If he was anything like his father he'd have no scruples about that. I trailed after them into the dining room where Connie and Dolores were silently loading food onto their plates. There was easily enough to feed a hundred. It was ridiculous. Were the caterers malicious or merely stupid? Four stacks of plates a foot high sat at the end of the long table. An entire section was dedicated to cutlery and serviettes. Two wait-ers stood by to assist in spooning out casseroles or pouring wine. Yves picked up two plates, which he presented to me and Leslie. We helped ourselves and ate in silence in the living room.

The party (if it can be called that) broke up shortly after dinner. Grandfather declined my offer of a lift, claiming he had some calls to make. I kissed him on the cheek and watched as he slowly made his way down the walk. Dolores pulled on her mink, perfunctorily bussed the air beside my cheek then strode past Connie and climbed into her Audi. Daddy ambled behind her, pressing his attaché case to his chest. It was still raining. Water dripped from the tree branches and gushed from the drainpipe at the corner of the house. Through the darkness sounded the melancholy clang of a swing chain as it hit the hollow aluminum bars of the jungle gym. I shivered and closed the door.

I wanted to check on the children before I left. It had been an unsettling day. Leslie and Yves were nowhere to be seen so I proceeded upstairs by elevator, a period piece with accordion grille doors that creaked and shook as it ascended. A plaque on the wall stated that the weight capacity was a thousand pounds but I doubted if it had been inspected in the past forty years. It shuddered and stopped with an ominous thunk.

The third-floor landing was lit by a ten-watt night-light plugged into a floor outlet, which shot elongated shadows of table and chair legs up the papered walls. It reminded me of my attic room, although the paper wasn't quite as ugly or tattered. The pattern here was yellow and white stripes. The floor, as in my attic, was covered in brown institutional linoleum. No carpet. Its surface was marred by scribbles of a black laundry pen—hopscotch squares, games of Xs and Os, drawings of stick animals and stick people—I had a fleeting regret that I hadn't been more trouble as a child. Excess weight gain was only a marginally effective irritant. These children were masters of offensive exasperation.

I removed my shoes and holding them in one hand turned the knob of their door and tiptoed in. Except for the faint inkstains on one wall, the room was immaculate. They had probably been too preoccupied to create disorder. Beside each of the four beds was a fuzzy white sheepskin and on each little bedside table sat a small lamp, a story book, and a glass of water. All the drawers of the bureaus were evenly shut, and there wasn't a crayon mark in sight. One of the children stirred in his sleep and coughed. A vaporizer hissed in the corner. It was time to go home.

I didn't trust the elevator and crept down the stairs in my stocking feet. I don't know why. I suppose because the house was so dark and quiet I didn't want to make any more noise than was strictly necessary. The back staircase emerged beside the library at the far end of the atrium, behind the pillars and the statuary. I sat on a bench to put on my shoes when through the darkness I heard a soft, low-pitched female voice humming the Blue Danube Waltz. I sat very still. If one of the maids was still working, she'd have left the lights on.

I peered around the column under the outstretched arm of Hermes and in the center of the marble floor, dancing, were Leslie and Yves. He was still dressed, but she had changed into a long nightgown made from silk, almost gossamer in its delicacy. It floated in her wake as she spun. His large hand rested against the small of her back, then they stopped. He pressed her against a pillar and kissed her. She lifted the shoestring straps from her shoulders, and the negligee billowed to the floor. Yves stepped back and Leslie assumed the pose of the statue of Demeter. In the nonlight, all her fair coloring transformed into alabaster whiteness. Only her lips and the tiny tea-rose nipples that budded on her breasts had any shading. Yves stared like a Pygmalion who had just witnessed his Galatea turn back to stone. Then she extended her long, thin leg and touched his crotch with her foot. He shuddered slightly but didn't move.

What was I doing? I had never thought of myself as a voyeur but the scene was riveting. I looked at Yves objectively and realized that he was quite attractive if you went for the gaunt, intellectual type. The facial structure was well defined, his eyes were deep, and his hair thick and dark, like the boys'. Unlike Jules, who had been only five eight or nine, Yves was quite tall— over six feet, with long legs and narrow hips.

I remembered meeting him for the first time when I was on a brief trip home from England, at a dinner party marking Leslie and Jules's first wedding anniversary. He was still a priest at the time, reorganizing the archives at one of the seminaries and involved in legal work for the diocese. His conversation that evening had been monosyllabic, and I mentally condemned him for arrogance. The popular wisdom among those who knew him was that he'd make cardinal before fifty. We were stunned when, shortly afterward, he left the order. We were even more surprised when the Vatican released him from all his vows. (Dolores was convinced his father had bribed the Pope, but the rest of us knew Jules would never have parted with the money and didn't give a hoot whether Yves remained a priest or not.) The suspicion was that he had a lady on the side but she had never materialized. He had leased offices in a downtown high-rise, practiced litigation, and made money hand over fist, but beyond taking the boys to church on Sunday, we never had the vaguest idea what he did with his spare time. I had thought maybe he was gay.

I was obviously wrong. Leslie knelt before him and unzipped his pants. He threw back his head and gaped soundlessly at the glass roof then lifted her to a standing position and pressed her against a marble column. She wrapped her legs around his hips and buried her face in his neck. Their actions had a ritualistic choreography. I snuck along the corridor and let myself out through the servants' entrance.

So there I was, coatless and barefoot in a puddle, while isolated raindrops from the passing storm plopped forlornly on the roof of Leslie's green Volvo. I dropped my shoes to the asphalt and stepped into them but I wasn't going back into the house for my coat and purse. I would rather have caught pneumonia and died than intrude on the scene being enacted in the atrium. A gust of wind shook loose the overblown blossoms from the crab-apple tree, sending a flurry of petals across the driveway. It had to be the only goddamned tree in the city with leaves. A sign of grace from the body of a saint. Some saint. No wings. Oh, holy shit. Yves and Leslie. How long had that been going on, and why was I surprised? Yves had the house and the money, and Leslie had Yves. Tidy.

God, I was cold. A hard rain had begun pelting the ground once more. I walked over to the car and opened the door to retrieve the umbrella that lay on the floor of the backseat. It popped open when I pressed the spring.

Now what? I was too mad to go home. I didn't want to be alone in my apartment. I wanted to go dancing. I wanted to lounge on a bar stool sipping on a brandy Alexander. I wanted to be thin and beautiful. I wanted to wear a black silk jersey dress cut up to my faint blonde pubic hair and down to the blushing pink aureole of my nipples. I wanted to dab Shalimar in my cleavage and between my thighs. I wanted to paint my lips crimson. I wanted the bartender to give me another drink—one I hadn't ordered—and point to the handsome businessman in a pin-striped suit sitting at the other end of the bar. I wanted him to nod and smile and stand, holding his scotch on the rocks, and walk over to me and put his drink down and take my arm and guide me to the dance floor and press his hand into the small of my back and rub his loins against mine. I wanted him to kiss my neck. I wanted him to take me to a hotel. I wanted him to bang me on the floor, in the bed, in the Jacuzzi, right side up, upside down, sideways. I wanted to wake in the morning, sore and spent and alone. No note, no explanations, no apologies, no telephone numbers. I wanted to be Leslie.

I headed down the street. Grandfather was probably at the Ritz. Since my purse was with my coat he could buy me an Irish coffee and lend me taxi fare. I had to face it—no one wanted to fuck a fat lady. As if to reinforce the negativity of the moment a bus roared past and drenched me with a spray of water from the gutter. My shoes squelched as I walked. I sneezed and my nose started to drip. My kleenex, like my money, was in my purse, so I sniffed. What a pathetic wreck. What a creaking, groaning, heaving monstrosity. The doorman at the Ritz touched his fingers to the visor of his cap and opened the door. I folded my umbrella shut and stepped in. If he hadn't known me he would have barricaded the portals. The lobby was still humming with activity, and glancing to my right I saw that the restaurant was packed. What time was it anyway? I glanced at my watch. Only nine forty-five? Lord. It felt like two. The well-bred patrons of the establishment ignored my saturated bulk as I dripped steadily onto the carpeting.

The telephones were unoccupied. I asked the coat-check girls if Connie'd been there and they replied that he had, but they thought he'd gone to the downstairs bar. I thanked them and ducked into the powder room where a congregation of teenage girls in formals were freshening their makeup. God, I was a mess. I grabbed wads of tissues and tried to blot myself dry. The black wool dress clung damply to my breasts and hips and my hair was plastered against my head. At least mascara wasn't dripping down my cheeks. I wasn't wearing any. I blew my nose and stooped under the hot air blower, rubbing my hair briskly. It was dry in a matter of minutes, one of the advantages of baby fine hair. The only advantage.

Another gaggle of graduates rustled in, primping and preening. Likely not a virgin in the bunch. I borrowed a comb from one and ran it through my hair. Bloody virginity. Best to lose it young at a necking party in a friend's basement with a randy sixteen-year-old or in the backseat of Daddy's car at the lookout or . . . or where? I couldn't think anymore. Needless to say, the opportunity had never arisen.

I returned the comb to the girl, complimented her on her ruffled black minidress, and slipped out of the washroom. There were two people using the phones—a pimply boy in a rented tux and a lady conventioneer with a plastic nameplate.

No Connie. I walked through the lobby and downstairs to the Maritime Bar and Grill. I had always loved the name. It should have been a dive on the waterfront frequented by stevedores where they served greasy fish and chips, but it was an elegant, dimly lit subterranean after-hours haunt of the Montreal business establishment. The hum of discreet conversation was muffled by napery and thick carpets. I caught sight of Grandfather eating a meal several tables across the room and threaded my way over, sitting down before I realized that the gentleman wasn't Connie at all, but a total stranger.

"Oh! Excuse me," I stammered. "I thought you were someone else," and prepared to slide off the banquette.

"Perhaps you thought I was Constantine Fletcher?" he said, wrapping his mouth tightly around Grandfather's name. The voice was accented, but so slightly I couldn't identify his nationality. I studied the man. He placed his cutlery on the plate and dabbed at his mustache with the heavy linen napkin. He looked like Connie, with the same wiry build and thick gray hair. He even affected the same style of dress—prickly tweed suits of a slightly antique cut—and he was certainly old.

"You know Constantine Fletcher?" I asked, curious.

"He is my cousin," the man replied.

"You're Ivan!" I blurted. My adrenaline pumped. The notorious Ivan, father of the murdered Michael and the simple Alex.

"Yes. My name is Ivan Petroff. I'm afraid I'm at a disadvantage."

"I'm sorry. I'm Greer Payton. Connie's granddaughter. I guess that'd make us . . . cousins?"

"That would make us first cousins twice removed." He rose and performed a little bow, then lifted my hand from my lap and kissed it. "But not *too* far removed, I trust."

"You're so like him. But I thought you were in Brazil."

"In this world one is separated more by time than space. Please, join me for dinner."

"Thank you. I've eaten."

"The fish is excellent."

"Well—" I hesitated "—perhaps."

Ivan summoned the waiter and ordered another portion of sole and more wine. He took an enameled cigarette case from his pocket and offered me a smoke. I shook my head. His fingers were yellow with nicotine stains but his teeth were white. I supposed they were false.

"Did you see Grandfather?"

"Oh, yes. Stanzi was here. He went home a half hour ago."

"Stanzi?"

"A childhood diminutive. I suppose I'm the only person still living who knew him as a child."

"I suppose." The waiter came with a glass and poured me some wine. Ivan leaned into the table and resumed eating. "What were you doing in Brazil?" I asked conversationally, unprepared for his answer.

"I went to buy the blue egg, but he beat me to it. I think he must have had an informant in the old lady's employ."

"Blue egg?"

"Yes. A very fine Fabergé egg. That must make about six he has. The man is obsessed."

"He didn't buy an egg. He bought ceramics."

"Yes. Those, too, but he really wanted the egg. The woman's father had it made in 1889. It's very fine. Hasn't he shown it to you?"

I shook my head. He certainly would have, so there was certainly no egg. Certainly not *six* eggs. Jesus. Only museums and Malcolm Forbes had as many as that. Ivan didn't know what he was talking about. Did he? If Connie had six Fabergé eggs, it would certainly explain where his money went, but that was insane. He would have confided that to me.

"The old woman was gracious enough to show me. It is fantastic. There is a rude little cherub inside with a waggling prick. I've never seen anything like it. I tried to convince her to sell it to me but she had promised Stanzi."

Why was he going on? The only egg Connie had was a replica of one owned by his mother. There were no others. Ivan was concealing something. He toyed with his cutlery in silence. The waiter appeared with my order of sole accompanied by a platter of fresh asparagus and filled my wineglass.

"I don't recall meeting you at my son Michael's funeral."

"I was studying in England."

"Ah. What is your field of interest?"

"I suppose *objets de virtu* would cover it. And I know a little about furniture, art, and silver. I work in an auction house." I ate the fish. It was such an elegant little portion it took about five bites. Then I started on the asparagus with a knife and fork. I have never felt entirely comfortable eating with my fingers when I am being observed, and Ivan was observing me. His beady blue eyes peered over the top of his wineglass with radiant intensity. I chewed self-consciously and swallowed with downright difficulty.

"It's nice to see a woman with a healthy appetite."

I don't think he was making a crack. He patted his mustache and poured more wine. I put down my knife and fork and pulled my still-damp dress farther over my knees.

"I'm fat," I said, stating the obvious as though he mightn't have noticed.

"Fat? No. You have the wrong attitude. All my wives have been lusty, strapping girls, like you. You must really look at yourself sometime."

"I have. I don't like what I see."

"But you're beautiful."

"Beautiful?" I snorted. "Surely you jest."

"Look in a mirror. Your flesh is firm and your skin tones are exquisite. Glowing."

"Alcoholic flush."

"Nonsense."

"And I don't make a habit of mirror gazing."

"You must learn to like yourself."

"I like myself well enough. I just can't stand the way I look."

"But your contours are magnificent . . . you're like a primitive earth goddess. Mankind could get lost in your thighs, your breasts could nourish a tribe."

"Uncle Ivan, really!" I felt the blood rise to my cheeks.

"Just Ivan, please. You are a very desirable woman. Rubenesque." He drew the word "desirable" into five syllables and "Rubenesque" into four. I could have sworn he was leering.

"Then why are you the first person to have told me that in thirty-five years?" I snapped. He reached over and caressed my hand. I yanked it away. His touch was hot and dry like parchment.

"North Americans are blind. They can only appreciate what fashion dictates. Heavens! Look at the women in bathing-suit advertisements. Some men might find that attractive, but personally I think it would be like sleeping with a skeleton. There are places where your figure would be considered opulent."

"Yeah. Jupiter."

"Oh. A little nearer than that, I think." He reached over and tucked my hair behind my ear, brushing my cheek with his fingers, then he winked. God. The dirty old man.

"I've got to go. It's late." I didn't want to be at the table with this superannuated pervert but when I removed the serviette from my lap he clapped his hand on my knee and clutched the flesh with his bony talons.

"You haven't finished your asparagus."

"I've lost my appetite."

"They have a wonderful dessert cart."

"I know, but I'm not hungry." I pried his fingers off my knee.

"Come up to my room for a nightcap."

"I think not," I responded, coolly polite. Jesus. How could I borrow taxi fare? I didn't want to be indebted to this person and I'd already accepted a dinner I couldn't insist on paying for. I'd have to walk home. I didn't even have my goddamned bank machine card. Why was it that the only time in my life that someone found me attractive and tried to seduce me it had to be a lust-crazed fossil with hair sprouting from his nose and ears?

"Some other time, perhaps?"

"Perhaps."

"I will see you to your car."

"I'm walking."

"But it's raining."

"I'm prepared." I lifted Leslie's umbrella above the level of the table and waved it around for emphasis.

"Well." He stood, smoothed his mustache then extended his hand. I raised mine and before I knew it he'd clasped it, turned it over and was slavering into my tender palm with his lips. I wrenched my hand loose and wiped it on the fabric of my dress.

"Have a pleasant walk home." He winked again. I clutched the umbrella and slid off the bench.

"Thank you for dinner," I said perfunctorily. He remained standing as I supposed he would until I had departed. I smoothed my dress and headed to the door where three Iranians stood with the maître d'. They nodded to me, then joined Ivan at his table. I was desperate to get home to my little apartment, to my hot shower. The day had been entirely too strange. Too many words and images were swirling through my mind. My feet hurt. I felt sullied.

Fortunately, the rain had stopped.

CHAPTER EIGHT

"Mith Bayton." Ponsonby, suffering the aftermath of yet another extraction, had wadded his inflamed gums with saturated gauze, and the atmosphere around him reeked of oil of cloves. One cheek was distended and he looked like a squirrel with a mouthful of nuts. "You're wate." He sounded like Elmer Fudd and I wanted to laugh but his expression was so anguished (either from pain or the fact that I was indeed very late) that I didn't.

"I'm sorry. My car was towed and I had to pick it up. The paperwork took forever."

"Thomeone ith waiding do thee you." He moaned and pressed his hand against the side of his face. "In your offith." A tear rolled down the side of his nose and lodged in his greasy mustache. He sniffed and wandered out the door to the parking lot. I supposed now that I was there he'd go home—a small consolation for the morning so far. I had parked my car in the reserved space before the Russian consulate, and it had been towed away. I slipped my raincoat off and groaned over the regrettable state of my shoes and legs. Rubber boots would have been more appropriate in the impound yard. The car jockey had sped past me in my own car and I was mud-spattered all around the hem of my skirt, which was three inches longer than my coat.

So who was waiting to see me? A widow with a house full of used furniture to unload because she was moving to a mobile home in Fort Lauderdale? I didn't feel diplomatic today. I threw my coat over a chair, delegated one of my assistants to negotiate with whoever was in my office, and resolved to tackle an inventory of things that weren't moving because bidders wouldn't meet the reserve price. Auction after auction our shills had been compelled to bid against each other in a pointless farce because the sellers had unrealistically inflated the value of their goods. I wouldn't have minded seeing the last of the gilded Statue of Liberty with a clock in its belly or the moth-eaten moose head or the orange piano. Didn't people donate to the Sally Ann any more? I ran my hand over the badly applied and almost impossible to remove plastic paint and wondered what had possessed the owner to vandalize a piano in such a fashion. I peeled off the old lot sticker, stuck on a new one, and entered the number in my notebook. If I had my way, I'd round up all the orphan garbage and hold a garage sale in the parking lot. It would give me intense pleasure to tag the clock at $1.50, the piano at $75.00.

There was a commotion across the room as two stockroom boys attempted to wrestle an armoire against the wall. I turned and smashed my shin into a veteran of eleven auctions—a coffee table four feet in diameter constructed from a single six-inch-thick horizontal slice of a sequoia, stained black and lacquered to a high gloss. I yelped in pain and screamed at the boys who were dragging the heavy piece across an antique Turkish prayer rug some incompetent had been asinine enough to lay on the floor. The small metal castors scored the delicate weave, and I was about to throw my three-ring binder at them when someone behind me cleared his throat and I turned to see a pair of amber-green eyes staring bemusedly at me from across a walnut bed-room set. In one hand he held a tweed cap and in the other an unlit cigarette. He slipped the latter into his handkerchief pocket and extended his palm toward me in greeting. Stupid cow that I was, I just stood and gaped.

Simon? Here? Simon Beauchamp standing in scuzzy old Ponsonby's? Simon whom I had loved unrequitedly for two years of my life? What in the name of God had brought him here and why hadn't I spent the past fifteen years on a starvation diet? Why did I have to be a hundred and fifty pounds overweight, looking forty-five, in a baggy jumper with my hair twisted into a greasy knot, screeching like a fishwife? Lovely. I felt my face flush. It had been years before I'd stopped thinking about him every day, but I never forgot. He was the standard against whom I measured all other men, and here, inexplicably, fifteen years later, he was.

"My dear Greer." I absorbed the remembered endearment as he took my hand and cupped it between his like a precious found object. I was still speechless and wondered if he'd noticed my muddy feet.

"Small world, isn't it? I see we wound up in the same business." He hadn't changed a bit. Still slim and firm and sexy as all hell.

"Are you s-still in New York?" I managed to stammer. God, he was beautiful. Fifteen years had enhanced his physical charms. There was an attractive ruggedness about him. Life was not fair. He should have been bald and overweight. Weren't all objects of extended fantasy invariably revealed to have altered for the worse? He released my hand to adjust his tie in the mirror of a nearby dressing table and his reflection smiled at me. Simon. There. A yard distant.

"Yes. But I'm not with Christie's anymore."

"Oh?" I didn't know he'd ever been with Christie's. "Who are you with?"

"I'm an independent consultant. And I deal a little."

"Oh. I see. How is Portia?" I could hardly bring myself to utter the hated name. The first and only time we'd been introduced was in the receiving line, she, the radiant bride dripping in antique Belgian lace and ropes of pearls and I, the unknown guest. The mystery guest. The fat unattractive mystery guest. Her eyebrows had arched at Simon's familiarity and she had accepted my best wishes without mentioning the fruit knives, but I hadn't been invited to her bridal tea and could only imagine that what I had considered their Georgian splendor had paled beside her other gifts. Perhaps they hadn't been displayed at all. I had drowned myself in Mumms as a succession of petty thoughts and ill wishes cluttered my brain. For a person with such exquisite taste, he had displayed an appalling lapse in his choice of bride. Didn't he realize she was to be the mother of his children? Could her bridal portion possibly be that alluring?

Simon took out his cigarette, looked at it, and put it back in his pocket before answering my question.

"I suppose she's fine. I haven't seen her for two years. I hear she's remarried."

"Oh." Oh, oh. My heartbeat skipped. He had dumped the Honorable Portia. But had he remarried?

"Okay if I smoke?" His accent had flattened and he employed American colloquialisms with unconscious ease. The cigarette was once more retrieved from his pocket and placed between his lips. I shrugged. It wasn't okay if he smoked. The signs were everywhere. I would have denied the privilege to any other mortal, but I wasn't going to stop him. He lit it with a day-glo orange plastic butane lighter. That surprised me. I wouldn't have expected him to use such a tacky utilitarian device. As though he could read my mind, he tossed the thing in the air and explained.

"I'm trying to quit. A gold lighter would display too great a commitment to the evil weed. I carry only one cigarette with me." Then he laughed. "I suppose you've never smoked and think me a poor pathetic creature."

"No."

"No what? No you've never smoked or no I'm not a poor pathetic creature?"

"Both." Lord. I sounded like a moronic twit. Words of more than one syllable eluded me completely. My head was spinning with the fact of his standing before me. Why was he here?

"What brings you to Montreal?" I asked finally. He sat on the dressing-table bench and tapped his cigarette ash onto the threadbare Chinese rug beneath his feet. Granted, it wasn't a great rug—twenty years ago it would have been ticketed for fifteen dollars at a church rummage sale—but he could have asked for an ashtray. I glanced around for something that could be used as one.

"You, actually."

My heart leaped. Me? "I don't understand," I said.

"Well, your name kept popping up in conversations I had with fellow dealers. Last year I was admiring a small Corot at a friend's gallery and when I asked where it came from he told me he'd picked it up for a song at a funny little auction house in Montreal managed by a G. Payton. Then, around Christmas, I was in a shop where I saw the most magnificent Georgian silver tea service and again was informed that it had been acquired at Ponsonby's in Montreal. The owner showed me the catalogue. Such a funny eclectic mix of junk and treasures. When I commented on this, he said the manager, a lady called Payton, was fabulous. My curiosity was piqued. Could this Payton possibly be my dear Greer, I thought? I was about to check, but it was Christmas and events carried me away." He waved his hand and held up his smoldering cigarette butt. I found a loose glass castor dish on the floor and slid it across the table.

"Then just last week, I ran across a set of eight Biedermeier dining-room chairs and once again was told they'd been obtained in a Montreal auction house. When my friend confirmed the place was run by Greer Payton I vowed to jump in the car and check out your operation. So here I am." He smiled and his amber-green eyes sparkled and crinkled up at the edges. Oh holy hell. My fondest dream, my worst nightmare.

"Oh. Well. I see." But I didn't see. A third-rate Corot, a tea service, and a set of chairs were hardly things to cause palpitations—not in a business where a Van Gogh can fetch forty million. Not by a long shot. Yet here he was, Burberry raincoat draped casually over his shoulders, divorced, gorgeous.

"So there are auctions this week?"

"Yes. Thursday through Saturday."

"Anything interesting?"

"Not really. Pretty run-of-the-mill stuff." In truth, the stock that month was dismal. A few semi-interesting carpets, one piece of jade that might have been K'ang-hsi but probably wasn't, a standing bronze Tiffany lamp with an exceedingly dull shade in rust-and-yellow geometrically cut glass, and a 1958 Corvette under a tarp in the parking lot. The showroom was otherwise chock-full of banal furniture.

"That's too bad. You will put me on your mailing list, won't you?"

"As you wish." Was that it? He could have called and spared me his beauty.

"And your grandfather, is he well?"

My grandfather? Had I mentioned Connie, all those years ago? I guess I had. And he remembered. I couldn't look at his face and stared instead at the bloodstone on his left hand. I recalled he had been born in March. One of those blessed years in London I had seen to it that we were served up a small *mille-feuille* cake with one symbolic candle at our favorite hangout. Rain had streamed down the windows and small droplets clung to his hair like jewels. He was astounded that I'd even known and I laughed and said I was psychic, embarrassed to admit that I'd clutched at his passing reference to the date like an archaeologist to the Rosetta stone. I'd spent the weeks leading up to his birthday scouring shops and markets for the perfect gift and settled on a first edition of William Morris's *The Earthly Paradise*, a slender volume with an ornate leather binding conceivably designed by the author himself. But when the moment arrived, I was too shy and never took it from my bag. It remained in a trunk with my lecture notes and books, still in its festive gift wrap, a card still wedged under the satin ribbon.

"My grandfather is fine," I answered. "He's still very active as a dealer."

"Yes. His name crops up regularly. Remarkable, really. He must be over ninety." Simon nodded approval.

"Yes. I imagine you hear his name a darn sight more regularly than you hear mine. Those Biedermeier chairs you mentioned were his consignment cast-offs; things he wouldn't waste his time bothering with."

"Do I detect a tone of self-deprecation?" He smiled and

tsked and draped his arm over my shoulder like in the old days, applying pressure to the bulge of my upper arm. Oh God, I wished I was skinny. I recalled that he had always tried to get me to speak up in class, to overcome my shyness.

"No. But I'm hardly in the same league, am I?"

"My dear Greer ... I'm just going to have to take you in hand to work on that negative self-image. Let's begin over lunch."

"I'd love to but I really can't. We're doing inventory." As if to emphasize the sincerity of my statement, I held up my binder.

"Oh, come now. Don't you take a lunch break?"

"Not today. We're far too busy." And I was a mess. If I was to sit across a table from him for two hours I wanted to wash and set my hair and wear some makeup and perfume.

"Dinner then. I'll pick you up at eight."

"Yes. I'd like that, but don't you have to go back?"

"My time is my own and I want to spend tonight with you. I'll drive back tomorrow. What's your address?" He took out his wallet and removed two business cards. One he handed to me and he pulled the pencil out of my hair knot to write on the back of the other. My greasy hair fell over my face. I wanted to run away. Why wasn't I beautiful? I bent my head and studied the card so he wouldn't see me blush. It was plain cream board with engraved black print that read: Simon Beauchamp, and in the lower right-hand corner was a telephone number with the area code. Nothing more. No address, no occupation. Nothing.

I told him where I lived as I escorted him to the door. A red Lamborghini was beside the tarped Corvette. What a Leslie car. As Simon climbed in and started the engine, as he glanced up at me to wink while the car reversed, I could only think that Leslie ought to have been sitting next to him. They matched. Some people were designed for sleek powerful sports cars and some people were designed for four-door, bench-seat, six-cylinder, automatic-transmission sedans. The sight of him driving off infused me with misery. If he picked me up in that car, could I fit into the seat?

The remainder of my day at work passed swiftly, especially

since I cut out at two o'clock, estimating that six hours was the barest minimum required to make me into an acceptable escort. I cut my own hair with scissors once or twice a year but felt this occasion warranted a professional treatment, so I managed to book an appointment at Leslie's salon for five. That gave me three hours to find a dress. I headed for 16 +, a shop I frequented that catered to, as they put it, queen-size ladies. After trying on twenty items, I settled on a jade-colored wool crepe. It looked like a tent but so did all my other clothes and at least it was a pretty color and wasn't stained down the front with food. (Thin people rarely consider that fat people look like slobs because our food drops onto our chests and not directly onto the napkin.) I chose a large colorful shawl-scarf to tie around my shoulders and decided that the result was pleasantly Gypsyish. If I couldn't look slender, I'd go with interesting. I had a pair of jangly gold Indian earrings at home that would enhance the effect. I turned and admired the ensemble in the store mirror. It was a good mirror, a slimming mirror adapted from the type found in circus fun houses although not so radical as to transform Ollie into Stan. All we patrons knew it was an optical illusion, but we didn't care. In the peach-tinted lighting we looked lovely.

At the beauty salon they gave me a soft curl that fell below my ears and partially masked my chins. The *maquilleuse* redesigned my face, creating hollows where no hollows existed and accenting my eyes with shades complimentary to the dress. I looked okay for a fat person. At home I sponge bathed to preserve their efforts, climbed into the dress, and waited. I had a date. My date was Simon. I had the anticipatory angst of a child waiting for the birthday guests to arrive. It was only seven o'clock. I returned to the bathroom and sprayed Chanel No. 5 behind my ears, on my wrists.

I lined up the completed pieces of my chess set. Seeing them vicariously through Simon's eyes, I noticed that they looked kind of deformed. I carefully placed them in a box and slid them under the worktable, then straightened the sketches. Seven-ten.

The duvet wasn't plumped. I shook it, fluffed the pillows, and kicked my slippers under the bed skirt. Why was I fussing with the bedroom? Simon wouldn't come in the bedroom, would he? I mean, it wasn't really a date, was it? What constituted a date anyway, form or content? Seven-fifteen.

I closed the shower curtain, cleaned the countertop and sink, hung fresh hand towels, and placed a new bar of Pears soap in the dish. The toilet was fine. Was there sufficient toilet paper? I placed another roll on the tank just in case, then switched off the light. Seven twenty-seven.

I'd forgotten the flowers—they were sitting in their wrapping on the hall table. I filled my Bohemian crystal vase with water and dumped the flowers in—blue iris, flaming daylilies, and peach tulips. I sat them on my marble table and wondered if I ought to open a bottle of wine. Would there be time? Did he have reservations somewhere? Of course he did. I'd chill a bottle of white and invite him in for a glass after dinner. I washed two of my good glasses. I used them so rarely they were sticky with grease and dust. Seven forty-five.

Was I sweating? I lifted my arm and sniffed. Not too bad. Music. I didn't want him to think I'd just been twiddling my thumbs waiting. I opened my cabinet and slipped a cello concerto on the CD player. Was it too dour? I ejected it and put *Tapestry* in. No. Too pathetically boomer-nostalgia-like. Oh shit. I was sweating. Stevie Wonder's *Secret Life of Plants*. Good. Fine. I turned down the volume and grabbed a book from the shelf, the latest Irving. That would do. I opened it at random and placed it across the arm of my stuffed chair. There. I was ready. It was five to eight.

I looked out the window just as he pulled up. He was on time. He hadn't stood me up. He climbed out of the car holding flowers. My heart leaped. I stepped back from the glass and tried to compose myself. It was just a date. I couldn't delude myself into believing it was the beginning of an affair to remember. Just dinner. I felt nauseated. I wanted to splash cold water on my face but it would have ruined my makeup. I sat down and rested my head on the table. Why was Simon here? The door-bell rang. Eight-oh-one.

The restaurant was close by and we walked, thus avoiding the problem of bucket seats. There was fresh boiled lobster on the menu. Simon sat next to me on the curved banquette, poured wine, and offered me warm bread.

"Just like old times, isn't it?" He laughed. I laughed and agreed although, just as in old times, I couldn't understand why he bothered with me when he could have been dining with any woman he wanted.

"Simon ... " I turned the stem of my wineglass between thumb and forefinger. "Back in London, when you could have chosen to be friendly with anyone in the group, why did you pick me?"

"I liked you. You were sweet."

"But you didn't know what I was like when you sat down that first day."

"If I hadn't liked you, I'd have moved."

"But I was so ugly."

"No, you weren't, but I'll admit to you now that it was rather obvious you were shy and self-conscious, and I wanted to see what else was there."

"So I was a charity case."

"Nonsense. There you go putting yourself down again. I repeat, if I hadn't liked you I wouldn't have bothered. I thoroughly enjoyed our little talks over coffee. You may find this hard to believe, but being attractive is almost as big a curse as being plain."

"Sure."

"No, really. People see a handsome face and they assume you're either arrogant and unapproachable or totally vacuous so they don't bother making any effort at all. It's frustrating to constantly have to prove your value to the human race beyond being nice to look upon. You were always kind and considerate. Why, remember the time you ordered a birthday cake? I was so touched. Portia didn't remember my birthday that year, or any other year for that matter, but woe betide me if I didn't remember hers. She wasn't satisfied if I didn't give her an expensive piece of jewelry every birthday or Christmas or Valentine's Day. Winston's used to roll out the red carpet when they saw me coming, but did she ever give me so much as a crummy magazine subscription? Not on your life. The sun rose and set on Portia. Forgive me. I'm a touch bitter."

"No. It's all right. I didn't realize you were so unhappy. I just assumed . . . "

"Didn't everyone. The perfect couple. Known each other since we were in prams. Our fathers were in school together." He tore the bread, then thought better of it and threw it onto the plate. "The thing is, we were too bloody young. In fact, youth was all we did have in common apart from our backgrounds, and that's nothing. There's more to a relationship than a shared affection for the Beatles and Crown Derby."

"Were you together long?" I ventured to ask. The wound seemed awfully raw.

"Too long. The divorce was finalized a year ago."

"Children?"

"No, thank God. Or maybe children would have changed her—made her less superficial. She refused to have any, in fact, had two abortions that I know of, not that the babies were necessarily mine. She tended to distribute her favors rather evenhandedly. No one could accuse her of being undemocratic. Anyone would do. My friends. The doorman at our building. Her decorator. But her real weakness was artists. Any artist. She considered herself a patron but I think the artists considered her a groupie. The utter shit that cluttered our walls."

"If it was so dreadful, why did you stay?"

"If I could answer that, I wouldn't have. Maybe for our families, I don't know. Perhaps I thought the situation would improve. We're all capable of profound self-delusion."

We certainly were. The waiter brought my lobster and tied a plastic bib around my neck. Simon had ordered broiled salmon. He pinched the lemon wedge over the pink flesh then leaned back on the banquette and took my hand.

"Look. I'm really sorry. I didn't invite you out to dump all my gripes."

"No. It's fine. I don't mind listening. Sometimes it helps to unload." And I really wanted to hear every horrible little thing about the Honorable Portia. I felt vindicated in my original judgment and was positively reveling in Simon's litany of complaints. She sounded just like Leslie. "What finally provoked the split?" I asked. He released my hand and I began attacking the pre-cracked lobster shell with a little fork.

"It was just too unbelievable."

"Please. You can tell me and you might feel better confiding in someone."

"Apart from a judge and several hundred lawyers?" He flaked the fish apart with his fork but didn't eat any. I thought I was going to be the one with no appetite, but true to form, I somehow managed to eat and, indeed, was growing hungrier with every word he spoke.

"Was it messy?"

"When is it not? How many amicable divorces do you know of?"

I shook my head.

"She got possession of the co-op, which we bought fifteen years ago and has a current market value of three million dollars. We're talking eight large rooms in a corner apartment with views. And they gave her the car and all the jewels I gave her, plus a lump sum settlement, which just about cleaned me out. I'd collected some pretty fine art, and they even gave her half of that."

"I didn't think they did that anymore. She must have had some pretty slick legal advisers."

"She did indeed." He poured us both more wine and ate a few halfhearted bites of salmon. "The worst of it is, I was the wounded party, but since I was the one who actually 'abandoned' her and initiated the action, she came across as the victim and nothing I could say made an iota of difference. Besides, she probably slept with the judge."

"Why did you leave?"

"It's a bit hard to explain. Among her other sterling attributes, she was deathly afraid of being attacked—anywhere, on the street, in her bed, although that happened regularly enough. She carried a twenty-two in her pocket and went to target practice twice a week—wearing a choice assortment of those nice jewels, I might add. One might think she wanted to bait someone to rob her so she could shoot him. I was afraid she'd shoot me when I came home, mistaking me for a homicidal maniac, although our flat had more security systems than the Tower of London. I literally had to spend ten minutes deactivating the alarms before I opened the door. But that wasn't enough.

"One evening I entered to see three corpses in various states of dismemberment littering the foyer. I nearly had a coronary. There was a dripping head perched on the hat rack and an arm, severed at the elbow joint, the hand clutching the closet door handle. One of the corpses still sported a meat cleaver in the cranium and brains spilled out on the parquet. Intestines hung from the chandelier. Greer, the place was an abattoir. A cat was nailed to the wall slit from the throat to the hind legs. A woman sprawled on the floor, eviscerated, her breasts sliced off and strewn to one side. I threw up.

"Just as I was turning to run out and call the police, I noticed that one of the corpses, the one with the meat cleaver in his skull, was wearing my sports jacket, then I realized that he was me. I mean, he looked just like me. I reached down and touched his face. It was made from plastic epoxy.

"They were sculptures. Even the brains on the floor were plastic. I recognized the head on the coat rack as representing my business partner, the only man whom I knew for a fact to have resisted Portia's overtures. The woman on the floor was a lady friend Portia had believed I was involved with. I didn't recognize the cat. We didn't have a cat. The whole tableau was unspeakably disgusting.

"I found Portia in the bedroom, hooting over the closed-circuit video monitor. She had commissioned one of her protégés, a man who specialized in anatomically precise sculptural depictions, to create the carnage in our foyer, thinking it would discourage any lunatic who might actually penetrate the alarms. She was the lunatic. I packed my bags then and there.''

"And yet the property settlement was in her favor? That's amazing.''

"Her lawyers made the successful claim that she was mentally disturbed and I was a cad to leave. They dragged three psychiatrists onto the stand to support the diagnosis. What was I to do? My own testimony wasn't contradictory. She ranted and raved that she loved me and didn't want the divorce at all. At that point I would have given anything to be free of her. I am mildly impoverished, but much relieved.''

"No one should have to go through that.''

"It's over. You know that all those years of hell, I'd think of you now and then and be heartened that there were actually nice, normal, kind, thoughtful women in the world.''

"You must have met lots of nice women. Come on now.''

"I don't know. They might have seemed nice at the outset, but really, they were self-interested or bound up in their work. There never seemed to be any time for thoughtfulness and consideration. That was all sacrificed on the altar of efficient scheduling. There was no just being with a person, one had to be doing something or they felt their time was wasted. You are the only woman with whom I've ever had a friendship.'' Simon put down his fork and ran his fingers through his thick hair. Friendship. Was that why he was here? If he missed our friendship, why had he waited fifteen years to contact me? Had he tried? Were people that difficult to trace? I could have found him if I'd decided to, but I wasn't going to ask. I didn't want to know. He was sitting beside me and nothing else mattered.

He had to drive back to New York for a morning appointment and declined my offer of a nightcap. Taking the keys from my hand, he unlocked my door, like in the movies, then kissed me gently on one cheek, then the other, before brushing his brandy-scented lips against mine like a slow warm breeze. He left with a promise to return the following weekend. I watched the elevator close before going in. My mind raced. How could I possibly sleep? The speakers were buzzing. I'd forgotten to turn the stereo off. From the window I could see Simon climb into his car and speed off into the night. I put *Tapestry* on the CD player and sang along to "So Far Away." I wanted to laugh. Cry. Simon. Simon.

I grabbed my key ring from the bowl on the hall table and walked to the storage cubicles, which were located on each floor in a room near the washing machines. I turned on the light and fiddled with the padlock to my cubby. The trunk sat beside two suitcases and an electric fan. It wasn't locked. I flipped the latches and opened the lid. The tray contained documents, birth certificate, outdated passports, high-school diploma, certificate from the V. & A., some old scarves, and a pair of baby shoes. I picked them up and imagined the babies Simon and I could make. I lifted the tray and sorted through the stuff beneath. I couldn't believe I'd saved so much junk: magazines saved for God knows which articles, loose-leaf binders with my notes, play programs, and curled photographs.

Then I found it. The gift wrapping was tatty at the corners and the bow limp, but it was just where I thought it would be. Laying it aside, I closed the trunk and opened the card I'd written more than fifteen years ago, only to cringe at the soppily sentimental poem inside. I'd signed it, "Affectionately, your dear Greer."

I'd been too shy that day over the birthday cake, but not anymore. He'd be touched and laugh and kiss me. I wouldn't even change the wrapping, only the card, and this time I'd write, "With all my love, your dearest Greer."

CHAPTER NINE

"Where are the boys?" I looked around suspiciously, anticipating an ambush. There were plenty of places for four small bodies to hide since most of the furniture in Leslie's house was untidily stacked in the atrium. Chairs sat on tables and beds, beds on chests of drawers, bureaus in bathtubs, rugs on sofas, desks on rugs. Leslie tapped her foot impatiently and since she was barefoot, the resulting sound was a faint noise such as a seal makes when its flippers slap. She was encased in an emerald-green spandex leotard and footless tights. Her hair, freshly permed, framed her face in a gauzy pre-Raphaelite aura.

"They're out with the new girl."

"A new nanny?" I asked.

"Yes. The agency sent her over. She doesn't speak a word of English. Hauls them around by the scruffs of their necks and curses in Lithuanian. I think she'll work out. Now why can't you have the truck here today?"

"Because it's loading up an estate in Senneville. I told you we couldn't do it until Wednesday."

"What if I hired a truck?"

Oh hell, I thought. Just what I need. Two loads arriving at the same time. There wasn't enough space to sort things out.

"Please, Leslie. Can't you wait two lousy days?"

"I could send it somewhere else."

"I'd be grateful if you would. You're doing me no favor by hiring Ponsonby's. Look at this shit. Didn't I explain that we don't deal in bathroom fixtures?'' I ran my hand over the cool creamy glaze of the antique porcelain double bathroom sink and its chrome fixtures that had taken on the patina of pewter over the decades. ''Why don't you want to keep this stuff anyway? It's beautiful. The stuff they make nowadays is all flimsy fiberglass and costs the moon.''

''It's boring. I'm keeping it in the servants' quarters and the nursery but I want marble bathrooms and Jacuzzis. Did I tell you I'm making a gym in the basement, and a sauna? I think I might even see about a pool. You once mentioned a pool in here, didn't you?'' She pushed her jaw out in an attitude of determination. Poor Yves. ''You know what'd be really stunning? If I was to put a glass floor in the atrium and have the pool underneath. I'd like some natural light. I saw a picture of something like that once. The glass would have to be thick, but it could be like tiles on a grid. The thing I like about thick glass is its green tinge. Remember old Coke bottles?''

''I think the color depends on where the sand comes from or what mineral is added.''

''Whatever. Anyway, I think it would be nice if there were murals around the pool, and palms and things. Maybe rattan garden furniture.''

Christ. Jules had only been dead two weeks. What was the goddamned rush? I let her blather on and took my notepad from my pocket to scribble down the name of a company that specialized in architectural salvage: fireplace mantels, paneling, doors, windows, hardware, and, I supposed, bathtubs and sinks. I pressed it into her hand.

''What's this?'' she asked, glancing at the paper. ''Limited Heritage, Ltd.''

''They'll probably buy your precious porcelain.''

''Will they pay me what it's worth?''

''You'll get a better price from them than you will elsewhere.'' I assumed it would all be going into her private bank account and not to defray the cost of her extensive renovations.

''Will they pick it up today?''

''How should I know? Call them.''

"The decorator is coming later. If possible, I'd rather he didn't see this stuff. It's embarrassing."

"Well, too fucking bad. I can't speak for the salvage people and we only have one truck," I snapped. I hated people who required instant gratification.

"What about Alex? He has a truck."

"Good grief. You can't expect Alex to carry all this. Besides, he's doing a run for Connie."

"Shit."

"I'm sure your decorator won't judge you too harshly if you pay him enough. How does Yves feel about your plans? Are the home improvements coming out of his pocket or the boys'?"

"What? Oh, Yves is paying. It's his house."

"I assume he gave you permission to sell his furniture. I wouldn't like to be a co-defendant in a lawsuit."

"It's fine with Yves. He gave me carte blanche to fix the place up."

"Perhaps he only intended a paint job and slipcovers."

"He said I can do what I want. The house is a dump but it has potential and it's cheaper to renovate than move."

"That's very generous. Are you paying him rent, or what?"

"Rent?" Leslie looked baffled. "Why should I pay him rent when we're getting married?"

Had I blinked and missed something? I knew they were lovers, but the ink was still wet on the death certificate.

"Didn't Mother tell you?"

"I haven't spoken to Mother since the funeral. Isn't there some Catholic prohibition against marrying your stepson?" I asked, bitchily, but she didn't take offense. Maybe she didn't notice. Bitch was her native tongue.

"Yves still has connections at the archdiocese. A dispensation for that sort of technicality is comparatively inexpensive."

"Compared to what?"

"Burying Jules in sanctified ground."

"Oh." I'd forgotten that the world believed Jules was a suicide.

"You don't seem surprised."

"About what? The marriage?"

"Yeah."

"I'm not. I figure you two have been at it for a while."

"And I thought we were so discreet."

"If it's any consolation, I don't think anyone else knows. I guess you'll have a small private ceremony if you don't plan on waiting. Are you pregnant?"

"Good Lord, no. Never again. I've done my bit for the human race."

The doors burst open and the boys tumbled in, muddied from head to toe, with branches stuffed in pockets, waistbands, and neck openings. Camouflage. They fanned out and secreted themselves in, behind, or under various articles of furniture. Moments later, a woman of about forty-five huffed through the door. She was also muddy, although I doubt there was any deliberation on her part. Bits of dead leaves and burrs clung to her wool coat and hair, and a length of twine that was knotted to her wrist trailed along the floor. She marched up to Leslie, glared at her for a full thirty seconds, then announced in heavily accented English:

"I go now. For goot."

May and the tulips were up. Simon flew in for our third date and took me for a calèche ride around old Montreal. We ate hot dogs in the old port and he bought me an emerald-green hand-dyed silk scarf he insisted matched my eyes. We sat on a bench at the end of the pier and threw bits of bun at sea gulls who swooped and fought over the scraps. Simon called them pigeons of the sea and claimed they'd lost the capacity to fish. When the sky streaked orange and purple and the night air chilled, we returned to my apartment and drank a bottle of wine while we watched *Now Voyager* starring Bette Davis and Paul Henried. Daddy had given me the tape the previous Saturday.

I told Simon about the remake game and he proved an enthusiastic player. We had a problem figuring out why a contemporary man would hesitate to divorce, and settled on the wife having a debilitating illness that affected her mental capacities. Then we couldn't figure out why a modern couple would abstain from sex and decided that aspect would have to be updated.

I rather hoped he would attack me then and there, as the furthest we'd ventured to that point was nuzzling and stroking, but he only poured more wine and pondered how the heroine could have been under her mother's domination for so many years unless she was intellectually deficient or paralyzed from the neck down, and in the end concluded that there was no way the plot could be salvaged, so we chucked the idea.

Then I asked him who he would cast as a latter-day Claude Rains and he wasn't sure who I was talking about until I mentioned *Notorious*, *The Invisible Man*, *The Phantom of the Opera*, and, perhaps his best-known role, Louis in *Casablanca*. Simon scratched his head and confessed to being stymied. We necked a bit more then he called a cab to take him to the airport for the last flight out. Early the next morning, a single perfect stalk of speckled orchids was delivered to my door before I left for work with a note that endeared him to me more than any protestation of love could have. It read:

"Re: Claude Rains successor. How about John Hurt?"

I arrived for our weekly tea at five on the nose and hung my briefcase from one of the brass coat hooks by the door. The tearoom was crowded and warm. The regulars were there: the chess players and the old lady with her book, but our usual table was occupied by a trio of well-dressed matron types. I finally spied Connie in the farthest corner, practically touching foreheads with Ivan, so deep were they in conversation. Ivan saw me first and rose to his feet, beckoning me with a broad arm gesture. Why had Connie asked him to our tea? I felt a little put out. Wasn't this our private place? I threaded between the tables, knocking two purses off the backs of chairs, and took my place in the vacant seat against the wall. Connie squeezed my hand and smiled.

"I understand you've already met Ivan?"

"Yes. The night of Jules's funeral."

Ivan reached under the table and squeezed my knee. I kicked him in the ankle. He gave a small yelp and removed his hand.

"Stanzi tells me this is your favorite haunt. What a pity it's going to be demolished."

"What!" I exclaimed. "Since when?" I looked around the room in a panic as though it might suddenly vanish in a puff of plaster dust. My eyes came to rest on the portrait of the girl with the monkey. How could they do this to me? First Ogilvy's, now my tearoom. Didn't anyone have any reverence for the permanency of institutions?

"You know they own the building and rent out the shops downstairs," Connie said.

"Yes. That's why I figured they'd always be here."

"A developer offered them three million dollars for the property. The taxes were prohibitive. They decided the time was right to sell out."

"That's terrible."

"For you, not for them. How is Dolores?"

"Mother?" It took me a moment to switch channels. "Fine, I suppose. Why do you ask? She's preoccupied with the strike at the factory. She hired scab carvers and several beefy types to see that they enter the place safely."

"She slipped a note through my mailbox asking me if I'd attend a garden party at her house in six weeks. I found that most peculiar. Have you any idea what it's all about?"

"I don't know. She hasn't asked me."

"It was only this noon. I have no doubt you too have been honored."

"If I had to guess, I'd say she's having an engagement party for Leslie. Did you know she's engaged to Yves?"

"You don't say?"

"Who are Leslie and Yves?" asked Ivan. He'd poured me a cup of tea and pushed the sandwich plate in my direction. I helped myself to three egg and two ham. Since when did we bother with sandwiches at tea? That had to be his preference. Tea was for pastry.

"Leslie's my twin, and Yves is her late husband's son."

"How baroque." He leered and I turned to Connie.

"A garden party, you say? Six weeks hence is getting into mosquito season. Why is she doing this anyway? It's in the worst possible taste. Jules is barely dead. You'd think Yves would at least show him some respect, not that the old bugger deserved any. I don't understand any of this. Why is it that money seems to be the motivation for, well, for everything?"

"Because money is power and one would have to be a fool to choose to be powerless," said Connie, ever the pragmatist.

"Then I'm a fool."

"But you, my darling, have never been compelled to make the choice. If Leslie doesn't want to be poor, at least by her standards, she has only one option: to marry well. After all, she'll never head a large multinational corporation."

"I'd rather starve than sell myself to the highest bidder."

"There are other choices. A principled person might call them moral choices and pass judgment as you have with Leslie, but if the choice is yours, any number of rationales will tip the scales on the side of personal convenience and gain."

"I don't believe you. I think most people would rather act honorably."

"And how many honorable people can you claim to know?" Ivan smiled patronizingly as he poured what smelled like brandy from a flask into his coffee. I felt so young.

"Connie's honorable."

"Oh, Greer. Don't be naïve. Consistency isn't honor."

"Alex."

Ivan snorted into his coffee when he laughed.

"Alex has the simplicity of a child. He hardly counts for the purposes of our discussion, as children are rarely able to make a choice for personal gain."

"Well—I've been meaning to tell you this—I met a man, actually I've known him since I first went to London, but we lost touch and only lately became reacquainted, and he's both honorable and charming.''

''Honorable *and* charming. Gracious! A rare combination. Wouldn't you say that was a rare combination, Ivan?''

''Yes, I'd say so. In my ninety-odd years I'd say I haven't crossed paths with more than two persons who were both honorable and charming. One was a madam in a New Orleans brothel and the other, as I recall, was an unambitious priest.''

They giggled wickedly. I hated being teased. Ever since I was a small child even the slightest hint of mockery was enough to send me stomping off to my berry-wallpapered attic to sulk, but Connie had never made sport of my sensibilities before and I felt utterly betrayed. I resented Ivan's influence. They were like two naughty little boys, goading each other on. The pastry plate arrived and Connie nudged it toward me. There was a large selection of miniature treats, none of which appealed, but I took a strawberry tart and two cream puffs anyway. There was no chocolate sauce, but then, why should they bother restocking the kitchen when they were going to tear the place down? I was in a filthy mood. Even the thought of Simon couldn't lift my spirits.

''And just who is this paragon, might I ask?'' Connie stopped laughing, wiped a tear from the corner of his good eye with his napkin, and poured more hot water into the teapot.

''His name is Simon Beauchamp and we took the Victoria and Albert course together,'' I answered defiantly, like a sixteen-year-old defending my choice of a prom escort to a possessive father. Connie raised his eyebrows.

''Beauchamp. A British fellow? Worked at Christie's for a few years, then struck out on his own?''

''You know him?'' I asked, astounded.

''Know of him. Have you run into him?'' he asked Ivan.

''Once or twice. I've outbid him at a few sales. He would seem to have a cash-flow problem, no doubt because he places honor before profit. He was in Brazil the same time we were.''

''He was?'' Connie narrowed his eyes. ''What was he after there?''

"You know very well what he was after. The same thing as you and I."

"Simon has as much right as anyone to try to buy ceramics."

"Ceramics? He was after the blue egg," said Ivan.

"Egg?" questioned Connie. Aha. So I was right. He knew nothing about an egg.

"The cupid egg. If you didn't buy it, the old lady was a liar," said Ivan.

"She had an egg?"

"Perhaps Mr. Beauchamp charmed it away from her after all."

"Stop it," I protested. "He's very nice, and one of the few people apart from you who treats me well."

"Well—" Connie hesitated "—he'd better. You deserve to be treated well. But try to be cautious. I'd hate to see you hurt."

"I'm not going to be hurt and I refuse to be cynical."

"How much do you know about him?"

"I know enough to know that I trust him. He's been very candid with me."

"I could make a few discreet inquiries. . . ."

"Don't you dare!" I snarled under my breath. "Don't you understand? Simon is a decent man. He means a great deal to me. I don't want my grandfather skulking around behind his back trying to dig up dirt."

"Very well. As you wish. Would you care for more tea?" he inquired, with a wounded expression on his face.

"Thank you, no."

"Would you care to bring the incomparable Mr. Beauchamp to tea?"

"Where? Here?"

"No. They're closing as of tomorrow."

I glanced around the beloved room with sorrow. No more teas.

"Bring the boy up to my house. If he's all you say he is, a little clutter won't offend him."

"If you like. When?"

"Whenever you say."

"Fine. I'll consult Simon and let you know."

"Good."

As I finished my tea, my grandfather and Ivan talked across me about people and places I didn't know. At a certain point, they lapsed into Russian, excluding me completely, not that it mattered. I was annoyed. He shouldn't have brought Ivan to our place, and I irrationally concluded that if he hadn't, it wouldn't be about to be torn down. If Ivan weren't there, Connie would have shared my happiness about Simon and wouldn't have made nasty comments. I drained my tea and excused myself. Enough was enough.

That night, I dreamed that two boys, perhaps twins, were rowing me out to the middle of a northern lake. The pine woods receded and every so often one of the oars slipped and splashed me with icy water. Reeds from the shallows vanished, giving way to deep still water. We were so distant from the shore even the insects disappeared. The boys stopped rowing and rested the oars along the sides of the boat and the boat rocked as they stood and reached for me as I sat in the stern. I struggled but they grappled with me with their strong arms and tossed me into the water. I couldn't swim and flailed about screaming for help. Their oars dipped in the water and I managed to reach one but was shaken loose. It was then I noticed that the rowers were no longer little boys, but Connie and Ivan, and they were laughing at me. One of them started singing "Que Sera, Sera." I forced myself into consciousness and punched the clock-radio alarm button to silence the unbearably cheery voice of Doris Day.

There were certain rituals in my routine, such as my sporadic pilgrimages to customs to pay duty and excise on carefully packaged bottles of prewar whiskey located by Connie's agents. They appeared from as far afield as Tasmania and Beijing (traced to a British consul posted there during the Boxer rebellion, a man who placed a high value on his cellar—twenty-three bottles of Mortlach malt were discovered in a bricked up sub-basement during demolition). Connie declared that he wouldn't wash his feet in the plonk they distilled today. The old stuff, he said, was aged in sherry casks, but now they dumped in caramel for color. Simply dreadful. He also preferred unblended malts and claimed that forty or fifty years in a bottle mellowed it nicely. His contacts were authorized to purchase any prewar pure malt whiskey they could get their hands on. It was an expensive taste but understandable, for Connie's whiskey was dark and smooth and as like the brands you could buy at the liquor store as silk stockings are like support hose.

It was a still, sticky, low-pressure day, the sort of a day when mosquitoes thrive and birds fall out of the sky. It had to be ninety. May was so damned unpredictable, a result, one presumed, of the greenhouse effect. The carpets in my apartment were moist from the damp, and I didn't want to get dressed. The air conditioner made little difference to my discomfort. The phone rang. It was Connie asking me to pick up a package at customs. Four bottles of Bladnoch (a lowland malt laid down before prohibition and found by one of his agents in a New Hampshire barn when he was on the trail of some Revere silver) had arrived.

The storm was slow in breaking. An impatient hot wind had risen, blowing leaves up so their pale undersides quivered in expectation, but still the rain waited. I parked at the end of the drive under the limpid lilacs and let myself in through the garden door. The basement, usually cool because of its thick walls, was hot and the scent of burning paper filled the air. I consigned the bottles to slotted racks in the wine cellar, a dank little room bounded by two exterior walls, and applied sticky white labels to the painted wood identifying the distillery and year of bottling. Then I locked the door and returned the key to its hook under a filthy pair of oven mitts.

I had a memory flash of the kitchen, shining and dustless. Little billows of flour puffed from Mrs. Ben's apron as she bustled around baking Sacher torte, strudel, cookies, pies.

I forced myself to see it for the dismal ruin it had become. Bartleby, who must have been asleep because I hadn't noticed him on arriving, whined pitifully and crawled across the floor on his belly, panting and whimpering, to scurry under the sink. His untrimmed claws clicked against the tile. I changed a burned-out light bulb and noticed Connie's flask on the old coal-burning stove. (There were two stoves, a "modern" gas range from the 1930s and a vast enamel and cast-iron monster that I supposed had been left in the kitchen for its tremendous ability to warm the cellar even on the coldest days of winter.) As I neared the stove I became aware of its warmth. A faintly acrid scent rose as I lifted a burner and saw inside the curled remains of blackened paper.

Connie had said that Alex was away so I poured some of Bartleby's dry food into the empty bowl and ran the tap until the rusty water turned clear, changed his drinking water, and left it on the floor near the sink. Bartleby yelped when he saw my hand and pressed himself farther into the plumbing. I scratched his ear and went upstairs. Stupid dog.

It was even hotter upstairs. The mad tangle of forest outside had done nothing to prevent the heat from permeating the walls. A low growl of thunder rumbled distantly and the sky darkened. Connie wasn't there, but there were some items spread over the coffee table. I sat on the couch and removed my shoes. My feet had swollen. I was retaining fluids.

The old photo album was open at a portrait of Connie's mother holding a baby, taken in 1916. Connie had scratched the date on the black cardboard in white ink, along with the names, Irina and Stefan. I recognized his handwriting. Stefan was the brother he'd never met. The brother of the ermine. I flipped the pages. There was Connie in uniform, and Connie with Maude on their wedding day. I closed the book and found a letter underneath. It was in a plain white envelope with a Russian postmark, addressed to Grandfather, but Constantine was spelled Konstantin. The envelope bore no return address. The letter was written in Russian and went on for five pages of dense black script. I couldn't even make out the signature.

I put my feet on the table and ate the chocolate bar that was in my pocket. Then I noticed the ring. It had fallen to the floor and glimmered on the dusty rug. I plucked it up and slipped it on to the first joint on my third finger. It was a simple gold band with delicate engraving of vines around its outer circumference.

"What are you doing here?" Connie stood behind me in a light bathrobe, his hair dripping.

"I just delivered your booze."

"Good. And since you're here, I must tell you the news. I've just found out that my youngest brother, Stefan, is alive. I'm going to Russia to see him."

I glanced at the letter on the table and the photo in the album.

"This was lying on the floor." I removed the ring and he took it from my hand.

"This was my mother's wedding band." He slid it onto his left pinky and rubbed it with his right thumb, a faraway look on his face.

"How did all this come about? I thought your entire family had died?"

"In 1918, when Ferdy and Ivan arrived at my family's country house, they found the bodies of my mother, Karel, Sascha, and Nicky, dead of typhoid, but they never found Stefan. They assumed he'd run away and died of exposure in the woods. But according to this letter, sometime before they arrived, our woodsman, Nicholaivitch, had found the boy wandering through the house, half starved. He was only three. The woodsman took Stefan home and raised him. Nicholaivitch informed him of his true parentage when he was grown, and Stefan has been trying to locate surviving members of his family ever since. He recently found a distant cousin, who told him that I was alive and gave him my address."

"Petroff is a common-enough name. Rather surprising he made the connection."

"The man has been looking for over fifty years."

I felt highly suspicious of this fantastic tale. Stefan raised by a woodsman—it came straight out of the Brothers Grimm.

"And you're convinced by one letter? You'd want more pro-

venance than that for any crummy antique, and on the strength
of it, you're going to Russia? You haven't been there since
1914.''

"The ring is his provenance. It wasn't among the valuables in
the house. Stefan says that his adoptive father took it off our
mother's finger to save for him.''

"Then why didn't he take the Fabergé animals, too? It
doesn't make sense that he would take one thing and not the
others.'' I lowered my feet to the floor and stood up.

"The other valuables were tucked in bed with her. She'd died
of typhoid. He was probably scared half to death. I'm surprised
he so much as touched the corpse to take the ring. It isn't likely
he'd have stripped the bed looking for loot.'' He seemed determined to rationalize any inconsistencies, but I was equally
determined to point them out.

"Might you consider, for a moment, that Ivan could have
stolen the ring when he found her corpse? You told me you'd
once believed he'd stolen your mother's Fabergé egg.''

"No, he discovered the egg in Detroit in 1932 and returned it
to me. If he'd stolen it, he would hardly have bothered to return
it so many years later.''

"The entire story is full of holes. I'll bet Ivan stole the egg
and the ring before your uncle turned up. By 1932 he'd probably decided it was more lucrative to be on your good side and
concocted a story about finding the egg when he had it all
along.''

"I didn't know you were so cynical.''

"I learned at the feet of masters.''

He sat on the couch and withdrew a hanky from his pocket to
wipe the perspiration from his brow. My entire body was dripping. What was I getting so worked up about? What the hell did
it matter if Connie went to Russia? Maybe his brother *was* alive.
But why did I have such a bad feeling about it? I sat beside
Connie and he patted my knee conciliatorily.

"Think for a minute. What would it benefit Ivan if I were to
visit Russia? What would it benefit anyone, except me? I've
wanted to go back for years, to relive my youth, but never got

around to it. I was always too busy. Now I have a chance to meet my baby brother, and if he turns out not to be my brother . . . well, I'll have been home. What fault can you find with that?"

"None, I guess." He was right. He didn't get to be ninety-five without knowing how to take care of himself. I was being silly and overprotective. "How long do you plan on being there?"

"A couple of weeks, if I can get a visa. You know, if Stefan *is* alive, it's a miracle."

"Yes," I concurred. "A miracle."

CHAPTER TEN

"May I help you with that? I see we're a little overloaded." Simon relieved Connie of the large oblong silver tea tray and deposited it on the coffee table that I had cleaned and dusted that morning along with everything else in the room. The floor, polished for the first time in years, gleamed in the radiant sunshine that entered unrestricted through the windows. The still, gray dawn had found me yanking tenacious ivy tendrils from the living room screens. Consequently, the room was infused with a normal complement of daylight. I don't know if Connie had considered my violation of his precious vines an unspeakable sacrilege, but he was in a foul humor. Acting the perfect stereotype of the crotchety old sod as he lowered himself into the Victorian parlor chair, he muttered incoherent Russian expletives and shot poor Simon a glare that could have withered a plant at thirty paces.

"*We* were managing nicely, thank you," he snapped as he waved his hand, abdicating Mother's duties in my favor. I sat on the couch next to Simon, viewing him through Connie's eyes and trying to analyze the hostility. If it was true that Simon had beaten him to the punch on a deal in Brazil ... But there was no blue egg. That was nonsense. Ivan was an inveterate shit-disturber.

I speared a lemon and plopped it into Connie's cup. The cloves with which I had studded the pith emitted a faint perfume. I had dug out my grandmother's lovely Crown Derby tea service that Connie said I could take whenever I wanted. It lived in a box at the foot of the closet of my room upstairs, a remnant of my past preserved as though in amber. I still slept there occasionally, when Connie was away and wanted me to receive a delivery, and I kept the place clean, but it hadn't altered by so much as the addition of an ashtray or the changing of a lamp shade. I'd only remembered the tea set that morning when I was cleaning and Connie was making phone calls at the Ritz. He took a plate and examined it as though it had just arrived in a shipment.

"I bought your grandmother this set for our first anniversary. It was old then."

"It's a lovely set," said Simon.

"She never used it. It's been sitting in a box for nearly seventy years," he said with some bitterness. "She was always saving it for some special occasion, but no occasion was ever special enough."

Simon hunched forward, resting his elbows on his knees, and attempted to catch Grandfather's eye, but Connie was assiduously pushing cuticles from the moons of his fingernails with the blunt edge of a penknife. The room was so silent I could clearly hear the buzzing of bees as they collected nectar from the honeysuckle blossoms out in the yard. Why didn't Connie make any effort to be nice? Had he investigated Simon despite my objections? I dismissed my thoughts as paranoid and poured the dark Ceylonese blend, taking pleasure in the transformation of the color to pale orange as it interacted with the lemon.

Grandfather sat, waiting to be served, compulsively shaking one foot as it dangled over the freshly vacuumed carpet. He was in an old-fashioned but well-preserved (mothball-smelling) suit and vest, across which dangled a heavy gold watch chain. His hair and mustache were neatly trimmed, and he looked a bit like Charlie Ruggles (though lacking the sweetness). I could tell he was annoyed, but for the life of me I couldn't figure out why. If it was the vines, or my insistence on cleaning the place, he was overreacting. Maybe it was the mere fact of the visit. He hated visitors, but damn, it had been at his instigation. He'd wanted to meet Simon. It wasn't every day I had a boyfriend. Didn't he want me to have a boyfriend?

I watched Simon as his amber-green eyes took in the details of the room and Connie. What had he been doing in Manaus? I hadn't had the opportunity to question him, nor was I sure I wanted to. Word got around in the business. If there was an interesting estate up for grabs at the summit of K2, dealers would claw up with picks and oxygen masks to grab a share of the loot—such was the nature of the game—but what nagged me was Ivan's claim to have seen the blue egg. The only thing I knew was that Connie didn't have it.

I decided his lousy temper had nothing to do with the visit at all, but rather a fouled deal or waylaid delivery. Three times in the past month, Canadian customs had held items for unpaid duty although they were clearly antique and therefore exempt. He was considering using abandoned crossings and had spent the week poring over old maps. He had discovered four. If it was simply a matter of tampering with the wiring on the barriers or of a little creative carpentry, it would certainly be worth it to avoid the confrontations with customs officers. It didn't help that Alex ran all the deliveries. Alex was officially Libyan (from the distaff side presumably) and traveled on a Libyan passport. This invariably provoked the paranoia of American customs officers who perceived in simple Alex a bomb-concealing ter-rorist. The poor kid was regularly hauled into the office while they ran him through their computers. Fortunately, the worst outcome of these harassments was that he had once failed to provide a certificate proving that Bartleby had been inoculated against rabies, and some sadistic turd had threatened to have the dog destroyed. His replacement on the next shift (a humani-tarian with a firmer grasp of the fundamentals of international diplomacy) permitted them to leave, and Alex ever after avoided that crossing. (He also obtained a rabies tag.)

Grandfather always claimed that acquiring art and antiqui-ties was easy—the difficulty lay in getting them from point A to point B, and to that end he lacked scruples entirely. He was, in fact, a smuggler. Both Italy and France have enacted laws prohibiting the export of works of art considered of national importance. Connie, who had for decades been happily conducting a one-way flow of treasures from those countries to South America, the United States, Hong Kong, and Japan, considered the policy stupid and shortsighted. His attitude was that if French and Italian museums were unwilling or incapable of obtaining and preserving their treasures, they had no moral jurisdiction in the matter of their ultimate disposition. Better a Rembrandt in the climate-controlled vault of a Brazilian industrialist than moldering away in the damp hall of a château because the Louvre couldn't come up with the scratch to buy it.

Connie spirited off national treasures in a variety of ways, from plain old smuggling to forged export certificates or, in many cases, outright bribery of officials. Though I didn't disapprove of Connie's methods, I worried about what might happen if he was ever caught. Couriers could talk.

Simon stood and handed the cup to Connie. He also passed him a small plate, a linen napkin, and offered a platter of sweets that I had chosen that morning at my favorite pastry shop. Connie selected a baba au rhum and spread the crisp white square across his knee. I'd bought the napkins yesterday. All household linens had been whisked off by Dolores when my grandmother died. Connie's style of living was pretty casual and he made do with paper towels. I prepared Simon's tea and he examined the pastry plate. I hadn't the slightest appetite myself. In the past I could have scoffed them all and still hungered for more. Love was the best diet. Days passed in which the thought of food never entered my mind. My dresses were actually loose. Here and there was the intimation of a bone.

"So, Mr. Fletcher, I understand you're still very active in your trade." Simon leaned forward, balancing his cup on his knee. He was dressed informally in a pair of tweed pants, an open-necked shirt, and a bulky brown sweater with reddish flecks that complemented his hair color but turned his amber-green eyes to a shade of light mud. Connie grunted a response, which could have been given any number of negative interpretations, but Simon, undeterred, persisted in his effort to be sociable. "Those are wonderful little pre-Columbian artifacts on your mantel."

"Those aren't pre-Columbian. Greer made them when she was five." (You imbecile, he implied in his tone.) It was an honest mistake, at that distance. Once, a collector, making the same error, had offered to buy them, and Connie had almost taken him up, so I don't know why he was being so supercilious.

"I arrived in Manaus three days after you departed," Simon began again.

"Oh," replied Connie, uninterestedly. I was relieved I didn't have to ask Simon myself, relieved that there was no secrecy.

"You must have been pleased to have beaten the competition."

"I have no competition," Connie sneered as he picked a speck of lint from his sleeve.

"I'd love to see it."

"See what?"

"The blue egg." Simon sipped his tea, his eyes unwavering from Connie's face, which suddenly looked so angry I thought he was going to do Simon an injury. So there *had* been an egg. Why the hell hadn't he mentioned it?

"I'd like to see it, too," I demanded, rather aggressively.

"Then you'll have to go to Singapore," said Connie acerbically. "I sold it."

"That's too bad." I spoke through clenched jaws. "I'd love to have seen it. Why didn't you tell me about it?"

"I forgot."

Bull, I thought. "The way Ivan described it, it must be unique."

"Ivan?"

"Yes. Remember? He said the lady who owned it showed it to him but said she'd promised to sell it to you. I didn't believe him because you hadn't told me about it. Then you denied it to us both. What's the big secret?''

"Perhaps I don't care for every Tom, Dick, and Harry to be privy to my dealings."

"Am I every Tom, Dick, and Harry?"

"Perhaps I should say Tom, Dick, and Ivan. Greer, I was there for the ceramics but when she showed me the egg, I remembered a client who wanted one, so I bought it, as well. It was off my hands twelve hours later. If I didn't tell you, it's because it slipped my mind." He shrugged as though it couldn't have been less important. A real Fabergé egg. I could have held it in my hands. We sat in awkward silence for some minutes. I poured more tea.

"How did you get into the business, Mr. Beauchamp?"

"Oh, I don't know. I was raised with beautiful things so it seemed a logical way to make a living."

"Simon's family home is one of England's great houses," I added.

"Was." Connie uttered the cryptic monosyllable, still preoccupied with lint. "That was an unfortunate sequence of deaths in your family, Mr. Beauchamp."

"Yes." Simon shook his head solemnly. "But, please, call me Simon."

"What deaths? Simon, you didn't mention anything."

"I don't like to talk about it, but my father died, then my two older brothers."

"In order of birth." Grandfather shook his head and tsk-tsked exaggeratedly. "Not only was his family wiped out, but the estate was hit with three sets of death duties in two years. If those deaths had occurred in a mystery novel, the chief detective would have concluded that there was no foul play or that the murderer was unspeakably stupid, provided, of course, that the motive was financial gain. A sensible murderer would kill off his brothers first, then his father. One set of death duties instead of three."

"Yes," said Simon, smiling patiently but returning his cup to its saucer with rather unnecessary force. "If I'd wiped out my family, I flatter myself that I'd have managed it for the maximum gain."

"Yes," agreed Connie. "I imagine you would."

"Simon. I didn't know. Your entire family. How dreadful. And the divorce, too. Why didn't you tell me?"

He brushed his forehead lightly with the fingers of his left hand, an odd little gesture of frustration and despair.

"It was too much. First Portia, then all those deaths, then the taxes. The death duties were impossible. I had to sell."

"The house and contents?" I asked, incredulous. But that couldn't be. Why hadn't he mentioned this? That lovely house. Beauchamps had called it home for over three hundred years.

"And the title," added Connie in a singsong voice. He was enjoying Simon's misfortune.

"You seem to know a great deal about Simon's situation." I didn't like any of this. It was obvious Connie'd been checking up, and as much as I loved him, I resented his interference. For God's sake, I was over thirty. Way over. "I dislike your nasty insinuations. You had no right to dig around in Simon's affairs." There. My heart was thudding and I felt a bit light-headed. I wasn't used to confronting Connie.

"I assure you, I've done no such thing. Nothing could interest me less, but I am blessed, or cursed as the case may be, with an excellent memory. Accidental deaths, it said in the newspaper. They didn't elaborate."

"That's no excuse for being rude to Simon. He's my friend and I brought him here because I actually thought you'd enjoy his company."

"I'm sorry, Greer." He was contrite, but I feared insincerely so. "You're perfectly correct. I have been a less than gracious host, Mr. Beauchamp. I am truly sorry for my disagreeable behavior."

"It's fine. Really. Don't give it a second thought."

"I shan't. I'm disagreeable to most people. It's become something of a habit. You'll find when you reach ninety that patience and the social graces aren't your strong suits, either. One simply hasn't the time."

"Well, I understand. I am seeing your granddaughter and it's only reasonable that you have reservations. To set your mind at ease: Father died of a massive coronary, my eldest brother drowned while sailing . . . "

"A week before he was to have been married. Most unfortunate," interrupted Connie.

"And my other brother smashed his car on the M1," Simon finished, almost defensively.

"And both without issue."

"Harold was gay."

"Well. I expect despite the succession duties you made a tidy profit on the sale."

"Grandfather!"

"But selling the title, now *that* was a peculiar move," said Connie. He took a long slow sip of tea. "I have always wondered why you did that. Aren't there social advantages to being a peer of the realm?"

"Few things in life are as pathetic as an aristocrat with no property. I discovered my peers, if you'll forgive the pun, were not particularly supportive, since the adversity suffered was financial. It was much easier to continue in the States where I'd made my way as plain Simon Beauchamp."

"But you missed a wonderful opportunity. Americans dote on titles. Then again, I suppose a title that has been on the books since the conquest commanded an interesting sum."

"Interesting enough to reestablish my solvency after my divorce." Simon said no more. I busied myself filling teacups and prayed Grandfather would let up.

"I was at the sale," he continued, relentlessly. "It was mildly diverting. Of course, your brothers had sold off the real gems: the Raphael, the van Eyck, and the two Rembrandts, but it was a good show nonetheless. An extraordinarily fine collection of furniture, and the library was a real surprise."

"Yes. Until the man from the Bodleian Library looked the

collection over, I had no idea of the value of that. Our family hasn't produced any scholars in the last few generations, and the cases were only unlocked to be cleaned.''

"What was there?" I asked.

Connie answered without missing a beat. "Four illuminated manuscripts: one Italian, two French, and one Russian from the tenth through the twelfth centuries, a First Folio Shakespeare, believed to have been lost and discovered wedged into a binder supposed to contain land deeds, some rare maps and botanical drawings made on an early expedition to the Caribbean, and a great many incunabula, most predating 1475. Is that right?" Connie had rattled off the list with his hands demurely folded as though in prayer—only the index fingers pointing up.

"Yes," said Simon, obviously impressed. If he had begun by patronizing Connie on account of age, he was now on his guard.

"I noticed you sold the Pecks as 'possibly attributable as early work of J.M. Turner.'"

I was momentarily taken aback that Simon would have permitted them to be sold at all. I didn't want Simon to share Connie's larcenous propensities, which had robbed me of so much sleep over the years.

"I was out of the country when the catalogue was compiled and had them withdrawn from the sale when I found out. I have them still. Feel quite sentimental about them, actually." He squeezed my knee and offered me a pastry. I declined, gloating over Connie's discomfort. He couldn't belittle Simon. Charming and honorable. So there!

"So what is your line now, Mr. Beauchamp?" He emphasized the word "line," turning the question into a piece of double entendre.

"This and that. A jack of all trades, one might say. I still keep my hand in as an independent dealer, like yourself, but the major source of my income is the market. Commodities. Currency. Real estate development."

"Yes. I see." Connie rested his chin on the tips of his upraised index fingers and regarded Simon through half-closed eyes. "But your real expertise is antiquities?"

"Familiarity, perhaps, but not expertise. I'm a talented amateur. My years at Christie's taught me that. It's futile competing with the likes of you. What was left by the time I got to Manaus wasn't worth shipping back to New York."

"Oh?" Grandfather cocked his head and raised an eyebrow. Simon shifted his weight and crossed one leg over the other. What was going on? Simon turned toward me and flashed a reassuring smile before thrashing ahead with the conversation, if one could call it that. More a duel.

"Greer tells me you went to Oxford. When would that have been?"

"A goodly long time ago."

"I'm a Cambridge man."

"Indeed." He sipped his tea and brushed some invisible dust from his knee. Then he withdrew his notebook from an inside coat pocket and scribbled a few lines. Simon, I noticed, was trying to decipher what was being written, but unless he could read Russian upside down it was a futile effort.

"What did you read?"

"History." Grandfather replaced the book in his jacket and began eating the baba au rhum.

"Were you in the war?" Simon asked.

"No." I had already told Simon that he had lost an eye at the Somme, and Connie's prevarication was not only transparent, but a barrier to further conversation. His parchment-like skin was taut across his whitened knuckles. It was time to step in.

"Simon was at the Windsor jewel auction," I said, thinking, naively, that I could get them chatting about the sale of the century. I was wrong.

"So who wasn't?" Grandfather snapped rudely. "Second-rate baubles of a third-rate courtesan. Much ado about nothing. Seven times the estimated value. The buyers were fools."

"Oh, Connie," I moaned. "Weren't you at least touched by the romance of it all?"

"He had the intelligence of Bertie Wooster, and she had the beauty of Olive Oyl. They richly deserved each other, and now every jeweler and pawnshop in the world is going to begin selling knock-off junk and claiming that it was once a fragment of 'the greatest romance in history.' Rot.''

My, but he was in a wretched mood. For someone who could ooze charm with no perceivable effort, Connie was trashing my tea party with glee. He reached over to the table and helped himself to another sweet, this time a raspberry tart. As his appetite was unimpaired I concluded that his health was intact. He was merely acting the bastard.

''May I show Simon the animals?'' I asked. He shrugged, so I stood and unlocked the cabinet with the key from the cloisonné bowl. Simon followed and received each piece from my hands, admiring the intricacy of the carving and jeweled details. Then I took the egg from the upper shelf and handed it to Simon. ''But this is exquisite,'' he exclaimed, genuinely delighted by the elegant toy. ''Translucent daffodil enamel on an engraved field enclosed by gold fretwork of grapevines enameled pale green and set with seed pearls.'' He recited as though for an auction catalogue. ''Five inches. Let's see the base.'' I handed him the nest, composed with three colors of gold and duplicating the interior decoration. ''How marvelous. Is it clockwork?'' I pushed the camouflaged button that activated the mechanism and opened the top. The roof of the house opened and he grinned with pleasure as the pigeon turned and flapped its wings. The mechanism whirred and the melody chimed. ''And you keep it here, in the open? What's the inscription?''

''It reads, 'I love you.' ''

''Is it catalogued? I'm unfamiliar with it. Not Imperial. Certainly not Kelch, but it's early.'' He squinted as he examined the underside of the pedestal. ''Crossed anchors. Signed MII. When was this done?''

''In 1926.''

''What!''

''It's a fake. A recreation.'' Connie sneered.

''You're joking?''

''No. The original was stolen from my family. I had this duplicated decades ago by the very artisan who crafted the original. He fled Russia when it became clear there would be no place in the new order for Fabergé fripperies."

"Remarkable."

"Considering that you claim to have no expertise, you seem to know a fair amount about Fabergé," Connie baited as he removed the egg and stand from Simon's hands and replaced them on the shelf.

"Not really. Mother had a picture frame and a clock, and a few eggs passed through Christie's when I worked there."

I grinned at Connie. No points.

"But who could tell the difference?"

"No one. After I die, it will be sold as a genuine Fabergé egg and become part of his catalogue of known existing work. Since the original is on the books, this will simply be regarded as having been misplaced for a time. There will be nothing I can do to set the record straight. As you say, it is a remarkable copy, if you think an identical design by the same artisan is less than genuine." Grandfather smiled a whimsical little smile, immensely pleased with himself. "And that is why I know that the Windsor jewels—what were they evaluated at? Seven million? And they sold for fifty-two?—can only devalue. Any competent jeweler can fashion a leopard pin, a ruby and diamond plume, or a flamingo. Gullible suckers the world over will be paying through the nose for ersatz pieces of your great romance until Windsor jewels will have the same credence as fragments of the true cross or the thighbone of St. Sebastian." He concluded his speech with a flourish of his hand and swooped in on a *mille-feuille*.

"May I show him the eye?"

"I don't care."

I removed the creamy box and handed it to Simon. Since I'd already filled him in on the history, he studied the artifact in concentrated silence before returning it to its shelf. I locked the cabinet and clinked the key back in the bowl.

"A forger would have to wait decades to reap profits," Simon said after a moment.

"You don't plant trees for yourself, but for your children's children. The real game would be faking provenances. Sneaking phony orders and duplicate bills of sale into jewelers' archives. Obtaining stationery from museums and creating false testimonies of authenticity." Connie was on a roll now. Flakes of pastry fell on his chest as he talked. Simon returned to his seat and stared, enthralled, like a student before a master.

"Manufacturing ships' manifests and slipping them into portfolios at the British Museum. You could invent ships that never existed, much less sank."

"But what about carbon dating?" I asked.

"Piff. Old paper is easy to come by. Blank pages in the back of folios. Diaries. Any able chemist can make a vintage ink."

"But isn't that a tad larcenous?" Simon asked with the caution of a skater nearing thin ice.

"I didn't say *I'd* do it. I merely claim that it's the way to go for an enterprising party." He peered slyly over his teacup at Simon. "But you're in the business. You must know a trick or two."

Simon smiled hesitantly. To confess knowledge of unscrupulous practice that he had almost certainly been an accomplice to at one time or another or to admit ignorance of such doings was to be equally damned, since Grandfather was obviously determined to take exception to either answer. He took the only possible course and chuckled noncommittally.

"But of course you do." Connie's false eye tended, disconcertingly, to stare off to the far corner of the room. It was hard to tell if he was looking at you, or at the fireplace. I noticed that Simon, in his confusion, was alternating between Grandfather and the andirons.

"Well, when I was in the business I came up against a few unscrupulous characters who tried to put things past me," replied Simon, hesitantly, to the ashes in the grate. "And there were practices in the business I didn't hold with."

"Registering a phony bid at auction; selling a Carpaccio that wasn't really a Carpaccio; wink-wink. Didn't Berensen and Duveen do it?"

Simon wasn't looking very happy. As a matter of fact, he seemed angry.

"I am informed," Simon drawled, "by an unimpeachable source, that there is a booming market in falsified export certificates."

I'd seen a few of them stapled with Connie's import manifests: official-looking documents with glossy seals and stamps. Damned fine fakes. I had faith that Connie's tracks were well covered, but the fact that Simon had brought the subject up made me nervous. I put my teacup down to prevent it rattling.

"I understand," he continued, "that excellent forgeries can be obtained from a source operating out of this very city."

"Oh, really?" said Grandfather, seemingly uninterested.

"Yes. Mexican, French, Italian, Greek ... any country you'd care to name that prohibits the export of important art and artifacts. But I don't suppose you know anything about that?"

"No. I can't say that I do. Are you with Interpol, then?"

"No more than you are. I expect you'd sell a Modigliani that you knew for certain was painted by de Hory?"

Oh, God. I knew for certain two de Horys had passed through this very living room. I prayed my face wouldn't flush.

"That would depend on the buyer. I'd sell it to you."

Touché. Grandfather stood and brushed a few crumbs of chocolate from his jacket onto the carpet.

"Now if you'll excuse me, I must make a phone call." Without further ado, he left the room. I heard the outer door close, then glanced at Simon to gauge his reaction to the encounter. He raised his eyes to the ceiling as he flung himself back against the cushions of the couch.

"My, my, my. That was an experience."

"For me, too. I'm sorry. If I'd any idea he was going to behave like that I'd never have brought you. I really thought you'd like each other."

"So you have no idea why he hates me?"

"No. Have you?"

"He seems to think I did away with my family."

"Oh, no. He was just being a pain. He can be."

"He was certainly anxious to leave my presence. You don't have to leave home to make a phone call."

"Oh. That part's true. He doesn't have a phone."

"You're joking?"

"No. He sees them as an invasion of privacy, and he values privacy above all. He make his calls at the Ritz."

"I value privacy, too. How long does it take to get to the Ritz, take a call, and get back?" He moved across the couch until our thighs touched and draped his arm over my shoulders. The teacup I held began to shake. He slipped off his thin Italian loafer and stroked my calf with his foot. The warm scent of moist leather drifted up. He took the cup from my hand, put it on the coffee table, and gently pushed me back until I reclined against the cushions on the arm.

"I expect he'll be some time. What are you doing?"

"Unbuttoning your dress."

He did. Right from the neck to the hem. I clasped one arm over my bosom and the other across my hips in an effort to keep myself decently covered, but he unfolded them and, still holding my hands, leaned over and kissed my chest above the brassiere (an industrial cotton device with ribs). I could feel myself blush all over.

Thus far the extent of our "romance" had been a few kisses and some petting. At least I think it was petting. In fact, his old-fashioned courtesy had surprised me. In our student days, he had been disdainful of conventions, as we all were, yet here he was, holding doors, ordering for me at restaurants, helping me on and off with coats, and he always saw me to my door. Not once was I dumped at the curb. The only thing that concerned me slightly was that he hadn't bedded me. I thought men wanted to go to bed with women. I wanted to go to bed with him.

The problem was, I didn't know how to make him. That sort of talent took practice from the age of three when you sat on Daddy's knee and flirted. It took giggling with other girls at the boys in the schoolyard. It took the awkward first mixed party where eventually one brave girl worked up the nerve to ask a boy to dance, so everyone did (except me). It took the first date, alone with the spotty kid down the block at the early movie, then out for a burger, and the first excruciating kiss on the front porch. It took the first petting session on the basement couch with the Beach Boys' *Pet Sounds* album playing loudly on the stereo and your parents upstairs watching the Stanley Cup play-offs as his hand slid down your underpants and fingered the moisture between your legs, and you unzipped his fly and were awed at the size and hardness of his thing. Leslie had never spared me any details.

It took the first time you actually "did it," at a friend's party when her parents were away for the weekend, when, slightly drunk after making free of the wet bar, you and he slipped into one of the vacant bedrooms and allowed a violent session of necking to go beyond that, and discovered after the first two or three times that you really liked it. It took the first time at the gynecologist's, one whose name you got from a phone book, because you didn't want to go to your mother's or she'd find out you'd been messing around and you'd get hell and be shipped off to boarding school, and standing in front of the pharmacist with your prescription for the pill, then feeling very important and grown up as you hid it in your bookcase wedged in a copy of *Steppenwolf*. It took the first time you moved away from home and set up housekeeping with your current lover, mandala post-ers on the wall and black lights for the nights you lay on the threadbare carpet and smoked joints and maybe didn't much care who you were screwing at any particular moment because, really, what difference did it make anyway, weren't we all just a small part of something much greater? And I suppose it took the first time you really loved, and were prepared to commit yourself to that person forever, and it took the first time you lost faith. It took many things, none of which I had experienced. And I felt at a total loss. Not only had I never played the game, I was ignorant of the rules.

He pulled his sweater over his head and tossed it onto the

floor. A few sparkling dust motes rose in the still air. I attempted to close my dress.

"Don't," he whispered.

"But I've never . . . "

"You're so lovely. So real." He exerted a subtle pressure on my back with his hand until I was sitting up, and he ever so gracefully slipped the dress from my shoulders, then unhooked my massive bra, coercing it from my restraining arms and fingers until my breasts were exposed. He simply stared. I've never been so embarrassed in my entire life.

"You have the most magnificent chest."

"Swinging bags of lard."

"Stop belittling yourself. You're a wonderful, beautiful woman."

"I'm fat," I stated bluntly while hiding my pendulous boobs behind a cushion that wasn't quite large enough. He caressed my upper arm.

"I don't understand the delusion all women seem to harbor that men admire anorexics. Have you any idea what it's like to hold a girl, to make love to a girl whose hipbones are grinding into your flesh? And they all look like adolescent boys: no tits, no curves, no bum. It's so refreshing to meet a woman who looks like a woman. Feels like a woman." Simon drew the pillow away from my body and cupped one of my breasts in his hands, then he bent over and delicately licked the aureole of my nipple. I tensed up, closed my eyes.

"Your flesh tones are fabulous. Like a Rubens or a Renoir." God. He sounded like Ivan. But did he mean it? What did he have to gain by loving me? Only me. He was sucking my nipple. Actually sucking. I held my arms tightly at my side and clenched my fists. I wanted to hold his head but was paralyzed with fear. He released my bosom and I cautiously opened my eyes to see him throw his shirt on the floor beside his sweater. He had hardly any chest hair. I thought all men had chest hair. Then he reached for his fly and I shut my eyes again and clasped my arms around my chest. The next thing I knew, he was rolling my panties over my hips and down my legs. Oh, God, how I wished I was a size seven—even a size twelve—and wearing ivory lace bikini panties, a sexy garter belt, a slip of a bra.

"What's this?" he asked, tentatively stroking at the faint scar tissue on my buttocks and upper thigh.

"A burn," I explained, my eyes still tightly shut, while his fingers continued to explore my skin surface.

He hoisted my legs until I was lying on the couch, and he then straddled my upper thighs as though he were mounting a horse. His soft warm penis brushed my flesh. I turned my face into the couch fabric. This was so humiliating. Why couldn't I respond? Hadn't I dreamed and fantasized about this moment for years? I felt like a piece of drugged meat. I felt like I was on the other side of the room watching this inane proceeding. He pried my legs apart and kneeled between my knees before lowering himself over me. He buried his head between my breasts, and with his hands compressed them against his cheeks. I didn't know what to do with my arms. Then he forced my face out of the couch cushions and kissed me. His tongue traveled along my teeth seeking entrance to my mouth. I loosened my jaw and it flew in, damn near gagging me. What was I supposed to do with my tongue? Reciprocally lunge it into his mouth? I tried and found the exercise quite awkward. He tasted faintly of pink icing. Then without warning there was a tremendous pressure between my legs and a sudden searing pain. He was writhing all over me, wallowing on my flesh and sliding in and out. Was that sex? Where were the skyrockets, the waves crashing against rocks, the pealing bells? Simon moaned, his eyeballs rolling up into his head to reveal the whites of his eyes. Then he was done. He slumped over me, breathing deeply, seemingly half asleep. The three cups of half-drunk tea sat on the coffee table. A fly lighted on a raspberry tart. Grandfather's cigarette butt still smoldered in the ashtray. The sunlight made a square patch on the carpet where Simon had flung my underwear. My hands were still clasped to my sides, but I wasn't a virgin anymore.

He shifted to the edge of the couch and kissed me gently on the lips. "That wasn't very much fun for you, was it? I'm sorry it hurt, but I'm afraid that can't be helped. It'll be better next time."

I felt tears drip hotly down my cheeks.

"It was fine. Really. I was just ... "

"Shh. I know. You're so lovely." He kissed me gently on my cheeks, my forehead, my lips.

"I'm falling in love with you, Greer. Do you think you can stand it?"

I laid my head on his chest, speechless.

CHAPTER ELEVEN

Simon kissed me gently on the lips, then held me for a few moments. The smell of his suede jacket and freshly shampooed hair mingled in the warmth of his neck. One of the stockroom boys gawked as he staggered past carrying a large mirror I recognized as having come from Leslie's house. The last truckload of three was in the process of being unloaded. Mirrors, bad art (the likes of which was usually marked fifty cents in the white-elephant corner of rummage sales), and beds. I'd finally convinced a reluctant and greedy Leslie that no one would bid on stained, sagging, fifty-year-old mattresses and she'd best throw them out.

The statues were another problem. I'd suggested a garage sale, or an ad in the classifieds. There wasn't a large market for nine-foot-tall vandalized plaster statues of Greek gods. It was soon obvious, even to her, that you couldn't give the things away, and I arranged for Alex to cart them to the city dump. Leslie refused to pay him for his trouble, rationalizing that as a relative, he'd be gratified to offer assistance, and the infuriating thing is, he was.

Since the day of the funeral he'd worn her veil knotted around his neck. When I asked him if he'd remove the statues for Leslie his eyes lit up and I had to physically restrain him from racing over to her house that very minute to wait upon her. Since Leslie refused to pay, I slipped an envelope with a hundred and thirty in tens under the sun visor in his truck with a note saying, "Thanks for moving the furniture." He could think what he wanted and it would keep Bartleby in ground round for a few weeks.

An ugly painted screen that I'd never seen, depicting Susannah and the Elders, bobbed past. It must have been in a spare room. (Where had Jules picked up these things?) That, with the *Allegory of Spring*, a Fragonard knockoff with shepherdesses, and a gruesome representation of St. Sebastian looking more porcupine than martyr, made four in all. I was curious to see who'd buy them.

"Eight o'clock then?" I plucked a strand of my hair from the shoulder of Simon's jacket. It was a possessive gesture, like lint picking. Women did it all the time in old movies. Barbara Stanwyck. Vivien Leigh. But I wasn't confident enough to feel the right of ownership. The action was unnatural. I had to will my way through it. I thrilled to the soft feel of the suede. Simon didn't notice that I'd done anything at all.

"Veal with lemon?" I asked, consciously lowering my voice to what I imagined was a sultry intimate huskiness.

"I love—" he simultaneously squeezed my bum and nibbled my earlobe "—pale, tender flesh." Then he left, angling between a scratched desk from Jules's library and the sideboard from the children's dining room.

"Personally, I prefer firm, tanned flesh." Leslie stepped out from behind one of the screens like a magician's assistant and brushed a little dust from her coat. "And just who was that?" she asked, a little too interested.

"I don't appreciate your spying on me."

"I wasn't spying, darling. I only came by to see that my things were being displayed to their best advantage."

"For this trash, there *is* no best advantage."

"Now, now," she admonished, wagging a finger. "Any unattractive third-rate article can be presented in such a way that, astonishingly—" she paused, removed the pencil from behind my ear, and straightened the shoulder strap of my jumper "—some sucker with more money than taste will experience the overwhelming urge to possess it. One sees it all the time. Now who was that man? He had more on his mind than used furniture."

"It's none of your concern, Leslie."

"Hey, hey. I have Yves. I'm not interested in stealing anyone's man, least of all yours, dear," she purred.

Sure, I thought. You with your Siamese-cat eyes.

"Really. I couldn't be happier for you. I was beginning to worry that you'd never get cored. Well, it's quite clear you've accomplished that."

"I suppose it's written all over my face."

"To be less subtle there'd have to be a public ceremony with someone breaking a bottle of champagne over your head and saying: 'God bless this broad and all who sail in her.' "

"You're so crass." I slapped a numbered sticker on the desk and jotted the corresponding entry in my notebook.

"No. I'm delighted, really." She bent sideways to straighten the seam in her nylon. There were cunning leather rosettes at the back of each shoe. Her hair was tied in a neat chignon, and she was wearing one of those artful little hats with a starched veil that circled the head at nose level, accentuating the brilliant crimson lipstick and sharp line of her chin. It was hard to believe I had a chin just like that under the blubber. She looked around the room with proprietary interest. I suppose she had the right. Half the stuff belonged to her.

"They're coming to dig out my basement for the pool. At first they said they weren't free until August but I told them if they finished by the end of the month I'd pay them double their usual rate."

Jules had only been dead for six weeks. I thought you couldn't get contractors to do your bidding for love or money. Perhaps sex and money?

"You're very lavish with Yves's money."

"The boys' money, actually."

"Why? Did Yves balk?"

"No. But I can extract house expenses from the boys' income. Dependent minors. A good deal of their money isn't taxable. Their trust officer explained it all the other day. He's a darling man. Took me to lunch at the Castillion and used his personal credit card."

Trust Leslie to notice that. But then, the trust company might have questioned his use of a corporate card for the room rental, where she, doubtless, permitted him to ravish her after cappuccino.

"And are the boys buying the furnishings as well?"

"No. I'll give Yves the pleasure."

"Something just occurred to me. What happened to Paul LaRivière's furniture and paintings? Didn't Louise inherit the house and contents?"

"Oh please. Don't ask." She rolled her eyes and touched her hand to her forehead in a gesture of exasperation. "Once upon a time the house was quite decently furnished—art nouveau right down to the Tiffany lamps, custom-made rugs designed by artists, and real art. I mean, the man bought Renoir and Matisse in 1903. I've seen photographs. When every other house in the square mile was dowdied up by gloomy Scots in Victorian velvets and mahogany, LaRivière with his arriviste arrogance did up a jewel, and you know what? Jules sold it all in 1937 to finance some investment."

"I thought LaRivière didn't make his fortune until the depression?"

"The big money, sure, but he inherited a load from his father. Jesus. Look at that!" She waved at the prickly St. Sebastian with contempt and disgust. "I don't expect, when this stuff sells, it will finance a trip to the dry cleaners."

"Well, the dry cleaners maybe, but not a block of AT&T."

"Yeah." She adjusted the foxtails around her shoulders and cast a disparaging glance at the chairs and tables and bureaus and screens and desks and carpets and me, then she shrugged. "There's no accounting for taste."

"The house is a disaster. Can I change here?"

Leslie stood at my door with an overnight case. At least I feared it was an overnight case. She waited expectantly on the threshold in a smart dress of dove-gray silk crepe, a long string of pearls with a topaz and diamond clasp, matching topaz earrings, dusky sheer stockings, and gray shoes. Her hair was pinched back into a frizzy puff at the nape of her neck, and a small gray hat with a curled plume of multicolored feathers that fanned behind her left ear perched on her head. She looked elegant, discreet, young, and . . . well, rich.

"No," I snapped. Simon was coming at eight, and it was already a quarter to.

"Have mercy. They're at it with jackhammers. There isn't a square foot of the house that isn't inhabited by an Italian with an overactive libido."

"So what's your problem? Go for it." I tried to close the door on her but she wedged her case in the opening.

"Could you put me up for a night or two?"

"Absolutely, emphatically not. If you must crash, crash at Mother's."

"That's where the boys are crashing. Literally."

I had a vision of the Cats at work among Dolores's china figurines. "She has plenty of room."

"If they're impossible at home they're unbelievable at Mother's. They've already removed the goldfish from her pond, pruned a row of rose bushes to the ground, set fire to the tool shed, and they've only been there twelve hours. I don't need to listen to Dolores lecture me on child rearing."

"She wouldn't lecture you. You're her fair-haired child."

"Oh yeah? You try marrying an old French Canadian and producing four hyperactive sociopaths, and see if you aren't lectured. You might get dumped on because you're fat, but I get everything else. All *you* have to do to shut her up is lose weight. She expects the moon from me. I honestly believe Prince Charles wouldn't have made an acceptable mate. I have to be the perfect hostess. I have to involve myself in good works. God, do you know how dreary it is hanging around Junior Leaguers? I have to join the ladies' volunteer committee for the symphony orchestra. I hate the symphony. It puts me to sleep. Thank heaven we have a loge. It's only three steps from the bar. I've developed quite a rapport with the bartender over the years during the second movements of orchestral works.''

"Then why on earth are you marrying Yves? Won't it all go on the same as before?" I was fascinated. Leslie had made her way into the room and unpinned her hat.

"I love Yves."

"Get real."

"I do. He's very sweet."

"He's a cold fish."

She shrugged.

"If you're so crazy about him, go stay at his place."

"I can't do that. It wouldn't look right."

"Since when was that a concern?"

"Yves is going to run for office."

Jesus. Leslie a political wife? I couldn't see her lasting ten minutes in that scene. "Stay at a hotel. I don't have any room."

She dumped her case on the floor and sat demurely at the table. "There are three conventions in town."

"Come off it. There has to be one lousy room in the city."

"The American College of Orthopedic Surgeons, the Shriners, and some cosmetic company that awards pink Cadillacs to its top salespeople."

"Well, go crash with a friend. I don't have a bed for you."

"I'll sleep in the chair."

"Stay at Connie's. He's in New York. I'll get the key."

"No. He's at the Ritz. I saw him about ten minutes ago. He introduced me to some vile old man he says is his cousin. The pair of them are enough to make your skin crawl."

"Leslie. For heaven's sake." Actually, the thought of Ivan made my skin crawl, too, but with cause. On the surface he was perfectly charming.

"I don't like being around old people, all right? Having to put up with Jules did it for me."

"That was your choice. No one held a gun to your head." I uncorked the wine so it could breathe for an hour. In truth, I couldn't tell if a wine had breathed or was suffocated but I went through the actions anyway.

"Why is Connie so healthy, anyway? People shouldn't live that long. It's disgusting. Wrinkles. Hair sprouting from noses and ears. They always forget to do up their flies and they spill food on their ties. Between them they have enough liver spots to make a small negro."

"And you have enough deliberate malice to make a small bitch."

"Better a small bitch than a large one," she said, staring me straight in the eye.

"Oh, get out." I was cross. She wavered and danced before my eyes like my reflection in the fun-house mirror. My tauntingly thin self. I wanted to throw a rock at her and see her shatter into a million glittering pieces at my feet.

"You have two places set." She flicked one of the wineglasses with her shiny red nail, and the crystal rang.

"Get the hell out, Leslie."

"Remember when you watched me and the gardener in the gazebo?"

"What?"

"You know. When you watched us make the beast with two backs, as someone elegantly put it."

"Leslie . . . "

"Are your voyeuristic tendencies general or am I specifically targeted?"

"What are you talking about?"

"I saw you. A few weeks ago. Behind the pillar. Was the light poor? I apologize if you didn't get a sufficient eyeful."

"Do you think I wanted to watch you cavort with Yves? I was saying good night to the boys and stumbled on your little seduction scene as I was leaving."

"Uh-huh. And it took you seven minutes to recall the way to the door? Were you taking notes for future reference? I'd be happy to give you some pointers. You have some catching up to do."

"Well, for immediate reference, my door is over there." I could feel my face flame. If she saw me then why hadn't she said anything? Maybe she liked an audience.

"I'd love to watch you."

"What?"

"You know . . . watch you screw that man. Tit for tat. I could hide in the cupboard."

"You're disgusting."

"Does he roll around on top of you? How does he manage to squeeze between your thighs? I can only presume he is well hung. I can't imagine you on top. The poor man would asphyxiate."

"Go away." I picked up her suitcase and threw it in the direction of the door. "Just go."

"I'd rather stay." She pulled off her gloves and tossed the fur over the chair back. Then she poured herself a glass of wine from the bottle I'd opened. I'd been angry in my life but I'd never really understood that the expression "seeing red" was an accurate description. Blood seemed to be pulsing into my retinas and my ears hummed. I was just about to drag her into the hallway and ram her into the elevator when Simon appeared at the door holding a bouquet of spring flowers. He smiled at me, then noticed my sister. Leslie held the wineglass up to her flawlessly glossed lips and drank without once allowing her seductive glance to stray from his amber-green eyes.

"These are for you." Simon pecked me on the cheek and handed me the flowers as he entered the room. "And this is . . . ?"

I was so angry with Leslie the last thing I wanted to do was introduce her to the only man (except Ivan) who'd ever shown an interest in me. My knuckles whitened as I clenched the fist I wanted to sink into her fine facial structure. Simon crossed the room, gentleman that he was, and waited for an introduction. Leslie rose and held out her hand, palm horizontal to the floor as though she expected it to be kissed. Well, I wasn't introducing anyone to anyone. I plunked into my oversized chair and waited.

"How do you do? I'm Greer's sister, Leslie. But I suppose she's mentioned me."

"Actually, no. But I'm delighted to make your aquaintance.

I'm Simon Beauchamp." He shook her hand. He didn't kiss it. That was a good sign. A small ripple of surprise crossed her face.

"You mean to say she never mentioned that she had a twin? An identical twin?"

The royal bitch. But I had to hand it to Simon. He didn't flinch, or express surprise, or shock. He simply smiled politely and said, "No."

"Leslie is just leaving," I stated firmly. "She has to head off to her convention." Leslie clenched her fist around the stem of the glass and was about to interject. "She's the top representative in the Montreal area. Well, you can see how beautiful she is, who wouldn't buy makeup from her? She won a pink Cadillac."

"She's joking." Leslie glared at me through a frozen smile as she stood and approached the door and stooped to retrieve her case. "But I am late for a dinner engagement."

"Oh, and about the accommodation problem—have you tried the Mr. and Mrs. Smith Motel on Montée de Liesse?"

She glowered at me. "Thanks for dropping by. Come again." I shut the door. "That was my sister."

"Yes. So I gather."

"She's very pretty, isn't she?" I prodded, scrutinizing his face for a sign of interest.

"I suppose so, if you like the type."

"What man doesn't?"

"This man."

He kneeled before my chair and gave me a deep passionate kiss while his hand slid up my dress and caressed my inner thigh. Oh! That was better. A warm glow spread between my legs. The caress lingered to a conclusion and he stood and smiled down at me.

"Would you care for some wine?" I asked.

"I'll get it."

Leslie's gloves lay on the table next to her glass. Her bright red lipstick stained the rim. There was only one other glass. He filled it, handed it to me, and took Leslie's into the kitchen, where I heard him run water. He emerged a moment later rubbing it with a dish towel, looking pensive and glum. What was wrong? Did he have something unpleasant to tell me? The pace of my heartbeat increased and I was suddenly chilled. The comparison with Leslie had been too extreme. He saw me for all my homeliness and no longer wanted to know me in the biblical sense. I could feel the "I-think-of-you-as-a-really-good-friend" lecture approaching like an oncoming train.

"Is anything the matter?" I asked, dreading his response.

"I'm concerned that your grandfather doesn't like me."

Shit, was that all? I was lighthearted with relief. I wanted to sing. I was giddy. He didn't want to dump me. He really did like me. I sprang to my feet and threw my arms around him.

"Oh, don't mind Connie. He's a bit peculiar. He feels age gives him exemption from civility."

"Is he unpleasant with everyone?"

"He can be perfectly delightful when he chooses. Actually he didn't treat you any worse than he treats my mother." I withheld the fact that Connie hated Dolores.

"I pity your mother." He kissed one of my chins and turned to get the bottle.

"Don't. I cannot imagine anyone less deserving." I drank my wine in one swig. He filled my glass and his own.

"Your grandfather still travels a great deal. It's hard to believe he's as old as he is. He looks about seventy."

"He attributes his healthy longevity to the beneficial effects of alcohol and tobacco. My great-grandmother's brother lived to be a hundred and seven."

He shrugged philosophically. "The body has to give out eventually."

"I suppose so, but Ferdy was shot. No one in my family dies of natural causes."

"No one?" There was a skeptical little twist to his upper lip.

"Not on Connie's side, and not since the turn of the century—unless you consider five—" (or was it really only four, I wondered) "—family members wiped out by typhoid natural causes. I don't."

"You've piqued my curiosity."

"Well . . . Connie's father and one of his six brothers were shot as traitors by the Red Army during the Russian revolution. Another brother was imprisoned. He vanished with a trainload of fifty officers. We assume he was shot, too."

"And the rest of the family died of typhoid fever?"

"Yes. When the Bolsheviks appropriated my great-grandmother's Leningrad residence and partitioned it to house twelve families, her patrician sensibilities were appalled by the prospect of the unwashed hordes stewing borscht in her drawing room. She removed her four younger children to the country house on Lake Ladoga. The picture is on the back of the eye I showed you. My uncle Ferdy, her brother, and Ivan went to rescue them and get them out of Russia, but by the time they arrived, the family were all dead. Typhoid. They couldn't find the youngest. Stefan was only three and it was assumed he must have wandered off to freeze in the woods."

"Assumed?"

I went on more slowly. "A few weeks ago, Connie received a letter from a man claiming to be Stefan with some cockamamy story of having been rescued by the family woodsman."

"Well, that's possible, isn't it?"

"But not probable."

There was a pause. Simon sipped his wine. "It's remarkable that those Fabergé animals weren't lost," he said finally.

"When Ferdy moved Irina's body for burial, he found all the Fabergé animals tucked beside her in the bed, but no egg and no wedding band. Connie suspected that his cousin had discovered the corpse first, and had hidden the egg to keep for himself, but years later Ivan claimed to have found it in Detroit, and he gave it back."

"I thought your grandfather said the egg was a fake."

"It is. He sold the real one."

"Why are you so willing to believe the worst of your grandfather's cousin?"

"Because he's a sleazy opportunist and I don't trust him. He probably sold the egg, and the ring."

"But why? If that was the case, wouldn't he have taken the animals, too?"

"Not if his uncle had interrupted the theft. Call it intuition if you will, but Connie is now planning on going to Russia, and I think it's a wild-goose chase. I don't know what it's all about, but every instinct tells me that Ivan is behind it somewhere."

"What do you think he's up to?"

"I have no idea, but I trust my instincts. Now let's just drop it, shall we? Where was I? Oh yes, our record of unnatural deaths. Connie had twin sons, about fifteen years older than Dolores. They were killed when a bomb hit their airfield in 1943. My cousin Michael was stabbed by persons unknown, and my grandmother froze to death in her own backyard. So far as I know, everyone else is alive."

"Froze to death?"

"That's what Dolores says. Accidentally locked herself out of the house in winter when Connie was out of town on a business trip. She was found in the potting shed. Way before I was born."

"What was she doing in a potting shed when it was that cold?"

I shrugged.

"And how does a centenarian like Ferdy get shot?"

"He gets caught in the act of selling arms to black Rhodesian rebels in the sixties." I drank. He refilled my glass. We needed to open another bottle. To breathe.

"And why was your cousin stabbed?"

"Of that, we are not at all sure. I was in London when it happened. He ran Connie's antique shop but there were private dealings on the side. I suspect drugs. The police thought it was a hire job."

"Colorful family."

"Yeah."

"What about your father's side?"

"Dull as dishwater. No taint of scandal since great-great-grandfather was run out of Ireland during the potato famine."

"Did your grandfather ever deal arms?"

"Fess up. You *are* Interpol," I teased, ruffling his hair. "There's more wine on the kitchen counter."

I sat in my favorite chair and let the room whirl around me while Simon rattled around in a drawer trying to find the cork-screw, which was sitting on the table in the living room. Odd how quickly booze could go to your head if you hadn't eaten. Odd that I hadn't eaten—hadn't thought about food all day. He emerged with the uncorked bottle. Why did he want to know if Connie traded arms? Downright suspicious. Probably wanted to know if it ran in the family, like green eyes and a gift for evasion.

"The corkscrew's there." I pointed and he opened the bottle.

"Don't get me wrong. I'm not judgmental about such trans-actions. If I was in the business, I'd run guns to black South Africans."

"That isn't his style. Strictly art objects."

"How can you be certain?"

"I just am."

"He trusts you?"

"Insofar as he trusts anyone. Now are you going to bore me to death with irrelevant inquiries about my grandfather or are you going to ravish me? I've waited for over a third of a century for someone to sweep me off my feet, metaphorically speaking, because I'm too fat for anyone to accomplish the literal act...."

"Shut up," he commanded.

I did. He took me on the carpet, then broke the sad news to me that he had an unavoidable meeting and departed before nine-thirty with profuse apologies.

I didn't bother dressing and simply pulled on a bathrobe. My appetite miraculously reasserted itself and I ate all the veal, all the rice, all the asparagus, the entire flan, and finished the wine. I put the second movement of Tchaikovsky's second piano concerto on the turntable and felt sorry for myself. I had expected that Simon would spend the night. I walked into my bedroom with a tumbler of Grand Marnier and a Toblerone and sat at my worktable. I clicked the light on. Simon's birthday present sat on my sketches. I'd planned on presenting it to him that night after dinner but fate had dictated otherwise. I sighed. Another time. My drill sat where I'd left it three weeks previous and was coated in a fine film of dust. A small block of carnelian lay waiting for me to transform it into a sea gull. Why a sea gull? Nothing noble about a sea gull. Pigeons of the sea. I gulped some liqueur and switched on the drill. The high-pitched whine soothed me with its familiarity. I touched the bit to the stone. The doorbell rang. Simon. I turned off the drill and raced to the other room.

"Hi." Before I could bar her way, Leslie darted in, her eyes scanning the apartment. It was clear from where she was standing that my bed was made and my bedroom uninhabited. An element of animation was automatically abandoned.

"You're alone."

"Yes." No point wasting energy in elaboration. I collected my drink from the other room and returned the tone arm to the beginning of the second movement.

"I forgot my gloves."

"Sure."

"I need a place to change."

"Try the elevator."

She placed her case on the table and unsnapped the clasps. It popped open. "You seem upset."

"Surprised?"

"At what's his name?" Leslie unpinned her hat and put it on the windowsill.

"Simon. Simon Beauchamp. As if you didn't remember."

"He left early," she said cattily.

"He had an appointment."

"Sure. I have a date and I must prepare. I'll just be a minute, then I'll leave you to your sulk."

What gall. Why did I put up with her? I could have kicked her out. I was bigger. I could have knocked her onto the floor and sat on her. That would have fixed her. I mean, she couldn't have drawn breath and there would have been no marks. It would have been elegant. Poetic. She unbuttoned her jacket and hung it over the back of a chair, then she unzipped her skirt, slid it down to the level of her knees, stepped out, and laid it across the seat. She wore only a peach-colored camisole, matching silk panties, and a garter belt. Typical of her not to draw the curtains. I drank some more. She lowered her firm little buttocks to the seat of the other chair and removed a container of cold cream from the case. This she slathered over her face and neck. The shoes came next, then the stockings slid into shadowy puddles on the floor. Her legs even looked slender without them. She unhooked the garter belt and folded it across her purse. My bathrobe had fallen open, revealing my dumpling of a knee. I pulled it together again. Leslie stood, her stomach perfectly flat, and went into the bathroom.

"There's no mirror in here," she called out.

"You wouldn't have a mirror either if you looked like me." I retorted, beating her to the punch. She emerged brushing her hair vigorously, then proceeded to slide her silky camisole over her head. Her small perfectly formed breasts had a slight upward curve like a pubescent teenager's, and the faint shadowing of ribs shaded her fair skin. When she slid off the panties the delicate jut of pelvic bone contradicted the fact of her maternity. And no stretch marks. How could one carry quadruplets and have no stretch marks? Then again, I was freighted with an excess of adipose tissue and had none either. Come to think of it, Dolores had no stretch marks. Must be genetic.

"You have no pubic hair," I stated when she turned to face me, too drunk to feel surprise. She stood before me, brushing her hair, looking for all the world like a twelve-year-old. "What happened? Waxed off so you can wear bottomless bathing suits?" I chortled, thinking myself witty, and downed more Grand Marnier.

"Muslims can't make love to a woman with pubic hair, and I got bloody tired of shaving. He was so fussy. Every little goddamned hair in every little goddamned crease."

"Of course," I mumbled. Ask a stupid question . . .

"I like it. It's cool and clean and yes, I don't have to wax for

bathing suits. Besides, he still comes to town a few times a year.''
Her hair spun in a cloudlike corona. She looked ethereal.
Virginal.

"You slut.'' I suppose I shouldn't have said it, but I couldn't
restrain myself. ''Sex is so easy for you, isn't it? You'll screw
anything in pants. Isn't it enough that all men worship you?
Must you also sleep with them?''

"What's your problem?'' She lay on the carpet and began
doing leg drops. ''Sex *is* easy. It's like breathing or eating or
sleeping. I like it. If I allowed myself to become a fat old thing
like you I'd have a big problem. No one would want to make
love to me. And get this straight, men don't screw me or ball me
or fuck me or plank me or hump me or slam me. They make
love to me. With all the attendent perks.''

"I guess you mean gifts.''

"Sure, gifts, and consideration. One of my lovers massages
my entire body with scented oil for an hour before we begin
lovemaking.''

"Must be hell on the sheets. So you're not a slut. You're a
courtesan. Semantics.''

She completed fifty leg drops and performed pelvic thrusts,
arms stretched out to either side, palms facing the ceiling. With
every thrust came an involuntary grunt.

"Are you happy?''

"Happy?'' She sat up and crossed her legs. ''Yes. I'm happy.
You look disappointed. But why shouldn't I be happy? I have
everything I want.'' With a tissue she wiped the cream from her
face and neck.

"But don't you care for anything beyond your immediate
personal concerns?''

"No.'' Perfume came next, behind her ears and knees, on
her neck and belly. ''I'm a realist.'' She seemed serious as she
stood to remove the makeup tray from her case.

"A realist? You don't have a nodding acquaintance with
reality.''

"Oh yes I do. You've always written me off as a selfish
airhead.'' She shook out a long-sleeved white blouse of the type

schoolgirls wear and slid it on. "I simply know my limitations and live within them. I can take care of my small corner of the universe. That's all. I can't end pollution. I can't end starvation. I can't end war. Any effort I could make would be a pointless gesture. I suppose I could invest only in ethical stocks. I could buy unbleached paper products and recycle garbage. I could donate dollars to Greenpeace. But what difference would that ultimately make? The powers that be will still manufacture missiles and dump toxic waste and hunt whales to extinction."

Jesus. My sister was making a sort of perverted sense. Not that I agreed with her, but it was a position, and I didn't think she had one. Either that or I was drunker than I thought. I grabbed the neck of the bottle on the floor beside my chair and poured myself another drink. Leslie threaded a dark tie through the collar of the blouse, flipped and threaded it into a fat Windsor knot, then stepped into a pair of navy jersey bloomers, navy knee socks, and scuffed black penny loafers. She sat on the floor again, and with a comb parted her hair down the center and braided the left side.

"Governments," she continued with a world-weary sigh, "wipe out their own people with an efficiency that would shame a Nazi. There are nuclear arsenals that will probably be set off by some gung-ho lunatic who mistakes the red eye from New York to Los Angeles for an intercontinental missile, and meanwhile an increasing proportion of the population is succumbing to a lethal virus that probably first saw the light of day in a petri dish in a Pentagon-funded research facility. So my philosophy is to make the best of it."

"And you feel no guilt?" The bottle was empty but for a few drops. I hauled myself to my feet and grabbed the next nearest bottle on the shelf. Gin. Good enough.

"Only when I allow myself to think. I don't feel superior to anyone. I just feel luckier. And I intend to take full advantage of that luck as long as it holds out."

She finished braiding the right side and snapped an elastic band around the plait. A navy box tunic and blazer bearing the crest of a downtown school completed her toilet.

"Going to a school reunion?" What disgusting sort of human being would want to make it with a twelve-year-old? Oh, well. Better a phony preadolescent than a real one. I remembered Hilter's booty and giggled, imagining Leslie locked in a vault. She carefully folded her other clothes and packed them into the case.

"A costume party, actually. The problem with you is that beyond knowing where you'll get your next snack, you don't know what you want," she said.

Funny, there was no coloration in what she uttered. It was stated with a bored, indifferent shrug, as though she was stating a self-evident truth. I had to protest.

"Where the hell do you get off presuming you know anything about me at all? As it happens, unlike you, I want a better world, and I think it's possible."

Leslie, in her little schoolgirl uniform, slowly shook her head.

"And if you love Yves why are you still sneaking around with other men?" The room spun and my head flopped back.

"Because I want to. If I were you, I'd head for the toilet. You're going to throw up." She snapped the clasps on her overnight bag and left.

I threw up.

CHAPTER TWELVE

Alex backed the truck down the rutted weedy driveway and turned off the ignition. He helped me unload the dry cleaning and groceries from the rear as Bartleby cowered in the farthest corner and tried to bury his head under the grungy sleeping bag. The fragrance of warm roast chicken wafted from the bag, and I remembered I hadn't eaten breakfast yet. Alex, plastic bags of winter suits and coats draped over his arm, pssted and waved me to the corner of the house. Late-morning sun flooded the small patch of terrace outside the kitchen door where thistle and wild mustard vied for space in the narrow strips of soil between the flagstones. I looked through the narrow opening, overhung with honeysuckle in full bloom, to see my grandfather standing stark naked and humming the melody I recognized from the Fabergé egg. He stared at a mosquito as it sucked blood from his forearm, then he pinched it. Alex nudged me and made a face. I whacked his arm and shushed him. Connie sat on a rusted iron garden chair and observed the progress of a bee. A scruffy stray cat stretched beside him on the stoop, mindless of the comings and goings of wasps through the interstices in the latticework to their colony under the porch.

Suddenly, and for no apparent reason, he yelled: "If you buggers think you're so grown-up you can haul the boat down to the water yourselves, I'm not helping. You're going to have to learn to manage without me—after all, I'm off to school next month." He closed his eyes and stretched out his legs and arms to the sun. The soft breeze ruffled his gray hair.

Every nerve in my body jolted. Something was terribly wrong. It was all because of this so-called brother. It had to be. Since the letter he'd probably been nurturing an unhealthy obsession with the past. I told Alex to stay put and pushed the bushes aside. Connie heard the rustle and opened his eyes.

"Annushka," he addressed me imperiously. Who was Annushka? Granny Payton used to call me Marjorie, thinking I was a cousin who'd been dead fifty years, but to correct her had only caused befuddlement, so I went along with Connie even though I wanted to shake him into his senses. It was so unreal— Connie, who'd always been so sharp. Who could I call, what could I do?

"Annushka, I'm thirsty. Have you made the lemonade yet?"

So Annushka was a servant. Why was he talking English? Perhaps because of his father they had spoken English at home. But then he began running on in Russian, gesturing to the trees and laughing. The hair on the back of my neck prickled. He stood and rubbed his buttocks where the seat of the garden chair had left the impression of roses, and accidentally stepped on the cat's tail. The animal screeched and leaped into the honeysuckle bushes beside the drive.

Connie entered the kitchen, slamming the screen door in my face as I trailed behind him. He stood in the center of the huge white kitchen, staring blankly at the copper pots suspended from ceiling hooks, green and dusty with disuse. Only the odd blade of sunlight penetrated the ivy curtains. The irritated buzzing of hundreds of trapped flies electrified the air.

"Stanzi?" I ventured, remembering that Ivan said he'd been called that as a child. I placed the groceries on the counter and began putting them away. Connie sank into a wicker rocker and watched flies collect in the sticky coffee dregs of a mug. Was it from that morning? Yesterday? When had he become ill? He spoke rapidly in Russian and pointed in childlike wonder at three flies that circled the rim like highwire artists, then the next instant he dashed it against the wall. It bounced and shattered on the tile floor. I jumped and at the same moment he sprang up and stepped on a shard of china. Three spots of blood marked his route to the counter where he ripped open the foil of the chicken and tore off a leg. He seemed not to notice his injury.

"Stanzi, sit down," I ordered. To my surprise, he obeyed meekly, almost sheepishly. Alex stood at the screen door watching the proceedings with wonder.

"Alex," I commanded. "Go up to Connie's room and bring down clothes."

"What clothes, Greer?" he asked, wide-eyed.

"Oh, for heaven's sake," I snapped. "Don't you dress yourself? Socks, underpants, a shirt, slacks. Go!" He sprinted up the stairs in a panic. I regretted my nastiness, but I was in a panic, too. Why the hell couldn't Connie have installed a goddamned telephone? He stared expectantly. "And some clean hankies!" I yelled. I served some chicken onto a plate and placed it before Grandfather with a knife and fork. I poured him a glass of milk as he ate and fetched a bottle of vodka from the freezer. When Alex appeared with the clothes, I grabbed a hanky and doused it in alcohol. A sliver of porcelain jutted out from the gash on Connie's foot. He obediently raised it for me to clean, but it needed stitches. Oh, well, we were going to the right place for that. I poured more vodka on the cut, then wound the foot with a clean handkerchief while Connie chewed his food. He dressed himself and followed us to the truck without argument.

"Are you taking me to school now?" he asked. I held his hand as Alex backed out of the driveway. Was this it? I thought. No. Please, God, no. Not this way. Not with a whimper. The truck rounded the corner and the house vanished.

"My son tells me that Stanzi hasn't been well." Ivan toyed with the flagon of water, then poured it into the glass of iced cognac. The white-jacketed waiters in the Maritime Bar were briskly serving up luncheon to well-tailored executives. I could see only two other women in the place, briefcased and girded for a power lunch. Why would anyone want to do business over food? Food was business in itself. The atmosphere of the place was enhanced with the scent of garlic and warm rolls. My salivary glands went into overdrive, probably aided by my relief at Grandfather's spectacular recovery. The episode hadn't been of a psychological nature at all, but neurological, and it had passed. Arriving at work, I'd received a summons from Ivan on a matter of gravity that he wouldn't discuss on the phone. This annoyed me because I'd been at the hospital all night and had only taken Connie home in time to return home myself, shower, and dress for work.

I found Ivan in his usual banquette, dressed to the nines in a new white linen suit (single-breasted, no mothballs), a creamy silk shirt, pale blue tie and matching hanky, excruciatingly tasteful gold accessories (tie clip, watch, a ring), and on the seat beside him a wide-brimmed Panama hat with a black band. He smelled faintly of Royal Lyme, a fragrance barely discernible over the wafting odor of a plate of moules marinières being served at the next table.

It took me a moment to realize he meant Alex. I had trouble associating the two—sweet, naive Alex and sinister, lecherous, conniving Ivan. It had been easier to remember that he was Ivan's son before I met Ivan. I slid onto the bench and helped myself to a warm crusty roll. He handed me the menu. An Italian chef was visiting and the selection was heavy on veal and pasta. I decided to begin with the mussels, move on to fettuccine, with veal piccata for the meat course. Maybe Caesar salad, too. Yes. I returned the menu to the far side of the table and tore the roll in quarters, slathering butter on the tender warm white interior. It tasted wonderful.

"What's wrong with Stanzi?" Ivan asked while drawing serpentine lines in the condensation of his glass. I might have believed the concern in his voice was sincere but for the monocle. Perhaps I'd watched too many films with Father where the wicked Hun screws in his monocle while articulating, "Ve have vays of making you talk." There was something altogether too theatrical about it. No one used monocles anymore, for God's sake, no matter how old they were. His hand crept over to my knee and I impulsively tugged at the thin loop of black satin ribbon connected to the eyeglass, and he yelped as it jerked loose and splashed into his drink. He removed his hand.

"Nothing is wrong with Grandfather. He wasn't feeling well. I took him to the doctor and the doctor said it was a temporary indisposition. He's fine now." Darned if I was going to tell him that Connie had suffered a mini stroke. Chances were it wouldn't happen again, but it was certainly none of Ivan's damned business. The waiter came and we ordered. Ivan dipped the monocle in his water, wiped it clean with a serviette, then screwed it in again.

"That's not what Alex tells me. He says that he found my cousin sitting in the garden talking to his brothers."

"Nonsense. Alex isn't an altogether reliable witness." I tore into another roll.

"Quite the contrary. Alex is incapable of lying."

"He is capable of misunderstanding."

"I think not. I think that Stanzi is perhaps experiencing a little senile dementia."

"All right. I'll tell you the truth. He was drunk as a skunk. He cut his foot and I took him for a few stitches."

"Are you certain that was all?" Ivan's mouth twitched. It was clear he didn't believe me.

"Go see for yourself. He's at home with an ice pack and a monumental hangover." Ivan tapped his fingers on the edge of the table.

"I must be frank with you, too. Stanzi is rather heavily involved in a deal I am negotiating. My clients are nervous people and I must be assured of his absolute reliability and discretion. Can I depend on him?"

The waiter served my salad and I speared a forkful, hoping that if I was chewing he wouldn't press me for an answer. Why did Connie allow himself to become involved with Ivan anyway? His own transactions may have been a trifle shady, but innocent compared with what I imagined Ivan's were. Since I was a teeny little kid all I'd heard was what a slippery operator Ivan was. If I'd been worried that Connie'd pass his declining years in an Italian jail, did I now have to worry he'd be shot? I swallowed and decided to take the offensive.

"Look, Connie's as healthy as you, but I must confess, I don't like the idea of his getting mixed up in your affairs." Ivan shrugged and ate a bite of ravioli in crab sauce.

"If anything happens to him, you'll have me to answer to." I stared him straight in the eye. What nonsensical bluster. My threat must have sounded as hollow to him as it did to me. What could I do to him?

"My deals aren't as nefarious as you might think, and Stanzi's role is minor. He is our financier."

"Financier?"

"Yes." He smiled. "All that is required of him is that he keep his mouth shut and sign the cheques. So to speak."

"What sort of money are we talking about?" I didn't know what Connie did with his money, but I suspected that there was a good deal of it stashed away somewhere. Yesterday's episode hadn't quite been a false alarm, but it might have been a taste of things to come, and if so, he needed protection, from Ivan, from Dolores, from everyone.

"Nothing to worry your pretty little head about."

"Stop patronizing me. Now listen, I don't claim to know anything about Connie's business, but I know that he's careful with his money, and if you jeopardize his security with some questionable deal . . . "

"Are you saying, then, that he is incapable of making judgments?"

"I'm not telling you any such thing."

"Excuse me. Then stop worrying and eat your lunch." He finished his ravioli as I finished my salad. After the waiter had removed the plates, Ivan slid a narrow rectangular box beside my plate.

"What's this?"

"Look and see." He grinned and slipped the monocle into his pocket, looking marginally less sinister without it. I unwrapped the tissue paper and opened the hinged box to discover a diamond and sapphire bracelet, then immediately snapped it shut and pushed it to his side of the table.

"Nice bracelet, but I don't wear that sort of thing."

"Well, you ought to." He pushed it back.

"Well, I don't, " I said, emphasizing the point by dropping it into the ice bucket. He gazed at the box as it bobbed in the ice water. The waiter, who witnessed the exchange, wordlessly fished it out and, after wrapping it in a napkin, laid it on the seat beside Ivan. I chewed my mussels. Ivan chewed his chicken. He didn't open his mouth again until the break before the next course. It only occurred to me as the waiter served me fettuccine and Ivan nothing that I'd ordered two more courses than he had. We were going to be there all afternoon.

"How is the honorable and charming Mr. Beauchamp these days?" he asked with a hint of malice.

"I don't care to discuss my private affairs with you."

"None of our common acquaintances seem to have any idea what he's up to lately."

"This and that."

Just then, Connie limped in with a cane, looking none the worse for his experience. He tipped his hat to me and sat in the chair opposite. The waiter followed with a place setting and a neat malt whiskey. What the hell was he doing out of bed?

"Grandfather, should you be on your feet?"

"I'm fine. Georges, bring me some lunch, please."

The waiter nodded and moved off. Connie really had them trained, not that it mattered what Georges brought. Connie would eat anything. He shook open his napkin and laid it across his knees.

"Greer, I have business matters to settle with my cousin before I leave for Russia, but I wouldn't want to interfere with your lunch, so please don't take offense if we speak Russian."

Still going to Russia? I was about to protest, but remembered the tale I'd spun for Ivan. Connie scarcely looked at me and not from any fear of meeting my eyes, for his statement was as insensitive as it was perfunctory. I was being dismissed.

I folded my serviette and left, my throat aching from suppressed sobs. It was becoming clear that in the company of Ivan,
Connie was a different person—someone to whom I didn't matter
much. I paused under the iron awning, tears pricking my eyes.
The doorman asked if I wanted a taxi. I shook my head and started
toward my car, which I'd parked around the corner.

Why didn't he take care of himself? The doctor had told him
to rest. I'd been planning on taking him some supper after work
and spending the night. Didn't my concern count for anything?
Was Ivan's deal so important? Oh, God. I wanted to talk to
Simon. I wanted to be held. I was tired. I hadn't slept in thirty-
four hours. Fuck work. Ponsonby could accept my absence or
fire me. I didn't care. I was going home to bed.

Simon was attentive, sympathetic, concerned. He insisted on
flying up the next day. After dumping on him for an hour over
the telephone I really felt much better. Just discussing my
concerns put them in perspective, and by the following morning, after a good night's sleep and a hearty breakfast of blue-
berry pancakes, I almost cringed at how melodramatic I must
have sounded. If the doctors weren't particularly concerned
about a recurrence of Connie's disorientation, why should I be?
And as for Ivan, well, they went back a long way and were
entitled to their confidences. I had no reason to feel slighted and
couldn't believe I was dragging Simon up over stress-induced
hysteria and lack of sleep. What was he going to say? It was
already too late to call him. His plane was in midair somewhere
over Syracuse, and hell, I wanted to see him anyway. I'd just
have to make it worth his while.

I raced over to the market and purchased the fixings for an
elegant picnic—cold lobster, chilled wine, small dark sweet
local strawberries, a vegetable mousse, buttery croissants,
sliced rare roast beef, freshly whipped cream, stuffed grape
leaves, and packed it all in a huge wicker hamper from Connie's
pantry. To that I added a corkscrew, white damask napkins,

wineglasses, and plates, but no cutlery. I debated on that for a time but thought it was more lustful to eat with fingers, and oh my, but I wanted a little lust along on my romantic *déjeuner sur l'herbe*. I worried that perhaps I was being too ingenuous, too cute, too boring—like a return fare on the Staten Island ferry under a full moon.

I knew exactly where to take him—private and romantic. The tomb. Or outside the tomb. I'd been earlier in the week and the peony buds were popping, the ground dry to the touch. I had a big soft wool blanket the color of moss. It was seventy-two degrees. Vivaldi or no Vivaldi? I pressed the play button on my portable tape deck, thought what the hell, and tossed it in with the blanket.

The only other question was what to wear. Nothing seemed appropriate until I had a flash of brilliance. I'd wear nothing. Simon loved my body. I was still in my nightgown, so there wouldn't be any red welts from bra and panties. Perfect. I had a half hour before Simon picked me up. Just enough time for a shower. Shave my pits. A touch of sandalwood oil between my breasts and legs. Yes. And a garter on my knee. I had one in a drawer that I'd caught at a wedding once. Blue and lacy. Terrific. Yes. Perfect.

Simon hauled the hamper from the backseat and followed me down the narrow path through the tangle of honeysuckle bushes to the neglected semicircle of mausoleums.

"What is this place?" he asked, stooping to avoid recoiling branches. I paused as the tunnel of new foliage opened into the small expanse of grass. My gardening efforts of the past year had paid off, and the area of cleared scrub was sprouting fresh and green. Here and about, huge pillows of peonies ranging in color from purest white to darkest claret emitted a dense heady scent. I shook the blanket and it billowed to the ground.

"This is the Fletcher burial ground." I was itching to rip off the light raincoat that covered my surprise but had to wait for the right moment. Simon's eyes passed over the semicircle of marble facades.

"Why is only one finished?" He walked over and touched the flowers and vines that had given me so much grief in execution, and now made me almost burst with pride.

"I did the carving."

"You?"

"Uh-huh. It was as overgrown and dirty as the others, and I decided to do something about it."

"You said the Fletcher mausoleum? Why didn't your grandfather keep it up?"

"Oh. I don't know. He doesn't bother much with the past unless he can sell it." I laughed. Simon tried the handle on the metal door and, finding it locked, put his eye against one of the decorative perforations.

"How is he today?"

"Fine. Alex told me he was off at six this morning. His recuperative powers are extraordinary."

"What exactly did the doctor say? Is he in any danger?"

"No. Apparently it's not uncommon at his age."

"Is it the beginning of a decline?"

"I don't know. I hope not. They gave him some medication."

"But his memory is normal? He hasn't had another flashback?"

"Simon, he's fine. Really. I'm sorry I was so worked up on the phone yesterday. I was exhausted and not thinking straight."

"I was worried for you. If it happens again, has he told you or anyone the state of his affairs? His finances? Have you any idea where he keeps his personal papers and belongings? A safety-deposit box? A safe in his house?"

"I assume he's made arrangements. He's fairly prudent."

"When my brothers died, they hadn't taken the time to put their affairs in order and the whole settlement of the estate was a nightmare. Do you know where he stores things? His will?"

"He never said." Funny, but I'd never thought about it. I

was the logical person for him to entrust with the knowledge, but he hadn't done so. Not that I could imagine him dying, but if he did, I supposed a lawyer would materialize with all the necessary information.

"Then you must ask him. Is he still planning on going to Russia?"

"Oh yes. It worries me half to death. Suppose he has an episode over there?"

He shrugged. "When is he going?"

"He hasn't said for sure. It depends on the visa."

"He really is amazing. One would never guess he was ninety-five."

"He has the constitution of one of those Russian peasants you used to read about in *LIFE* magazine who eat goat cheese and live to a hundred and sixty-two."

"Does he claim goat cheese is the secret to longevity?"

"No. Malt whiskey and an active mind. Actually, I think it's good genes. Awful Ivan is the same age and still travels around the world stirring up trouble."

"I think I've seen them together at the Ritz. They look alike?"

"Yes. There's a resemblance."

"What business does one conduct at ninety-five?"

"We're not certain. Family tradition has it that he smuggles armaments, but I gather he might just as easily be a white slaver."

"A man of many parts."

"And well-oiled." I stretched a blade of grass between my thumbs and made a rude noise. He tugged at the handle and the hinge creaked.

"Who's in here?"

"My grandmother and two uncles who were killed in the war."

"Oh yes. You mentioned them. Can you get inside?"

"Sure. Nothing much to see. A bench. Name plaques." I took the key from my purse and tossed it over. He fitted it into the lock.

"Aren't you coming?" He waited on the threshold but I shook my head. Once he was inside, I pitched my coat and shoes under some bushes, twisted a few peonies from their stems, and reclined on the blanket, the blossoms scattered about my body. Simon emerged a moment later and, seeing me, burst out laughing. I could feel the red creeping up my neck when he threw himself beside me and kissed my bosom.

"But this is marvelous. You look like a Seurat."

I exhaled with relief. That was precisely what I had in mind—Seurat, albeit a slightly chubby Seurat. "Shall we be naughty before lunch or after lunch?" I asked in my best seductive, naughty voice.

"Before." He ran his tongue around the rim of my rosy nipple. "And during." It slithered down my belly, pausing momentarily to lick my navel. "And after." He threw aside my artfully placed pink peony and burrowed between my legs. Somewhere overhead, in one of the budding chestnut trees, a squirrel chattered. A pair of starlings took wing. I closed my eyes and stretched my arms back and clutched at the satin binding of the blanket. Oh yes. Marvelous.

We lay on the blanket staring at the clouds and I knew it was the right time. "I have a present for you."

"You shouldn't have. I have nothing for you."

"It's your birthday present."

"But my birthday is in March."

"It's for your twenty-second birthday." I took the book from my purse and laid it on his naked thigh. He examined the wrapping with puzzlement.

"I don't understand."

"The year I bought you the cake . . . well, I bought you this present, too, but I didn't have the nerve to give it to you."

"Greer . . . " He unfolded the paper and stared at the book. It was more exquisite than I remembered—the crimson binding had been hand-tooled in an original design of intertwined lilies, and embossed in gold. The flyleaf was signed by Morris himself. I'd forgotten that. I'd only paid a piddling twenty pounds, although the sum had seemed enormous at the time. Simon turned the pages reverently, then put the book aside and kissed me sweetly, gently on the lips. I knew it wasn't possible to be happier than I was at that moment.

I awoke in a cold sweat but I couldn't remember anything about the dream except that it had terrified me. My room seemed so sterile, so empty. Did I dream because I was upset or was I upset because of my dream? Or both? I hadn't seen Simon in several weeks. He'd phoned with apologies and sent flowers and nightgowns. Three nightgowns in three weeks, a peach one, a white one, and a pale green one, all silk and lace, all expensive, and all too small. And Connie was acting odd, not like when he had the stroke, but secretive and wary—even of me. The last few times I'd been up to the house he'd been there with Ivan and they both scrambled to look innocent when I appeared. I found a gun between the sofa cushions and when I asked Connie about it he claimed that there had been prowlers and he'd obtained it for self-protection. A gun. Connie hadn't carried a gun since 1916. What was going on?

I slipped into a loose cotton dress with short sleeves and sighed over my flabby arms. Too bad, but it was hot. The sale of Leslie's furniture had fetched more than I had estimated, and I decided to deliver the cheque before work so I could see what she'd done to the house. I'd had reports from Dolores about simultaneous work crews getting in each other's way and threatening to quit until Leslie waved bonuses in their faces. The boys had moved home so I deduced the worst was over. Four weeks. It had to be a land speed record for a renovation. I hoped the house wouldn't collapse inward. Then again, maybe I hoped it would.

I parked behind a landscaper's truck that was stacked with evergreen shrubs. Men were busy raking soil. The climbing equipment had been relocated to an area beside the garage, and a slate terrace had materialized off the dining room. I rang the bell and was admitted in short order by two naked and dripping Cats. They gazed up at me expectantly. I had to ignore them for a moment while I took in the renovations. The atrium area, although structurally unaltered, was transformed. The floor was indeed glass, but brilliant turquoise-green, a color echoed in the huge abstract oils that lined the inner walls. There were large palms in boldly colorful ceramic containers, and the floors between the pillars and walls were carpeted in forest green. The marble had been cleaned, and the careful lighting design shed unobtrusive illumination on the plants and paintings. The floor shimmered and danced like the sunlit surface of a lake seen from a diver's perspective.

"What did you bring us?" cried the boys impatiently. Puddles collected at their feet, darkening the thick new carpet. I reached into my plastic shopping bag and pulled out four diving masks with snorkels and eight swimming fins. I knew they could swim like dolphins—they'd attended classes at the YMCA since they were in diapers, and now they had a pool. They grabbed at the paraphernalia but I held it beyond their reach.

"Just a moment. I want a tour."

They looked at one another, came to a telepathic accord, and took my hand. I was led, via a narrow spiral staircase to the right of the door, into the basement, but a better, brighter basement. To my right I opened a door to the sauna, and on a raised platform on my left a Jacuzzi bubbled. The two other Cats appeared, also naked, and attacked me like piranhas, snatching the masks and fins, pulling them on. They slapped away on the slate floor, beckoning me to follow.

The corridor opened into an area that must have taken up half the floor space of the cellar. The pool, rectangular and slate-gray, lay under the atrium floor, which was darker and less dramatic seen from below. There was a dropped ceiling surrounding the pool, and the lighting came from behind the translucent panels. A profusion of plants and the walls, which were painted à la Rousseau in a jungle motif with wild animals peeping out from behind trees, aided the illusion of a rain forest. The rattan furniture was cushioned in brilliant oranges and reds and yellows.

One of the boys flicked a switch that turned off all the lights and giggled. A watery light filtered through the glass ceiling and transformed the room into a nocturnal dream. From the dimness between the trees I heard the swell of birdcalls, monkeys chattering, leaves rustling, panthers roaring. It must have cost a fortune.

The lights flickered back on and the boys yelled and made faces at the gardener, who was acting as lifeguard, then cannonballed into the water with four consecutive splashes. The old man shook his head and returned to the chaise lounge to continue reading his *photo roman*. I watched the children indulge in underwater acrobatics, twisting and surfacing and diving like hairless pink sea otters. They were a marvel. It was some time before I realized that Yves had joined me. His hands were clasped behind his back. As he observed the Cats, an expression of perfect pleasure brightened his face. We exchanged pleasantries and I offered him a lift to work, leaving the cheque from Ponsonby's with the mail in the vestibule.

CHAPTER THIRTEEN

Another Saturday night, only now with a theme—Leslie's wedding. Since my sister had announced that she was marrying Yves, Mother had dedicated her nonworking hours, and there were few enough of them, to the arrangements. Cheated out of the first wedding, by God, she was going to make the most of the second. The dubious moral circumstances of choice of mate and timing (Jules but two months in his grave) didn't deter her enthusiasm in the least. I couldn't have worked up enthusiasm even if I'd liked Leslie, since my mind was on Simon. I estimated that at that moment he was in a cab heading for LaGuardia. Heading for me. I would rather have been waiting at home in a scented bath than before the customary selection of raw vegetables and cottage cheese. Father seemed more dazed than usual. He only touched the food to move it from one side of his plate to the other and back again, making no effort to hide his drinking. The bottle of rye sat openly beside his place mat, and he swallowed it neat from a tumbler. He didn't even speak.

"Seen any good movies lately?" I asked. He shook his head glumly and reached for the liquor. The lip of the bottle collided with the glass, chipping the rim. Mother looked askance but didn't bother commenting, having already demoted Father from Waterford to Duralex.

"Daddy, are you feeling okay?" I was alert for telltale symptoms of liver failure but his pallor was the usual gray-pink hue.

Considering the amount he drank, he ought to have turned mustard yellow.

"I'm fine, honey. A little headache, that's all." He smiled his sweet little smile then returned to the business of pushing his food around. Dolores stood and opened the French doors to the garden. Some cool evening air blew in, but mostly mosquitoes. The house had a forced-air system and I really couldn't understand why she didn't install central air-conditioning. She wouldn't even put screen doors up. The problem was, mosquitoes didn't like Dolores. They wouldn't come within two feet of her before suddenly switching direction and heading for more succulent fare, so she thought we all exaggerated the nuisance. When I was a teenager I'd bought two live trout at the market and dumped them in the pond, figuring they'd eat the mosquito larvae, but instead they spent an exciting two days terrorizing the goldfish before they suffocated for lack of oxygen. Apparently what is sufficient for goldfish is not sufficient for trout.

"Yves insists on a Catholic ceremony and he thinks he can book St. Patrick's for the first Saturday in September. The priest there was a classmate at the seminary."

"I assumed they'd have a civil ceremony."

"No. It's important to them to do it properly."

"I meant that under the circumstances, I didn't think they'd want to make much ado about it."

"They're having a proper ceremony, and I am hosting a reception afterward."

"Oh. She isn't going to wear white, is she?"

"Cream with seed pearls," she said icily.

"But it will be small, won't it? No bevies of attendants, no flower girl scattering petals, no trumpet recessional?"

"Five attendants. And yes, I've made arrangements with my florist. We thought we'd do the flowers in shades of pink and violet—roses, larkspurs, delphiniums, lavender." She spoke slowly, as though daring me to dispute the wisdom or good taste of the plans.

"I didn't know she had five female friends."

Dolores narrowed her eyes. "Leslie tells me you have a boyfriend," she said in the same patronizing tone she might have used if she'd been told I'd been taken for a spin on an alien spacecraft. It was a joke, right?

"Yes. I'm seeing someone." I tried to toss it off as though it was no extraordinary event.

"Is he fat?" she asked.

"Didn't Leslie tell you? She's met him."

"Leslie only informed me you had a boyfriend. Of course, I had trouble believing her since you hadn't mentioned it yourself."

"Why should I?" I wanted to level her with a glare but she was staring out into the garden at a snowy owl that had alighted on a branch of the maple tree.

"Look at that," she pointed, changing the subject.

"I see. It's an owl."

"One doesn't see an owl like that every day."

"No. And I don't get a boyfriend every day, do I?"

"Greer, really. I'm very pleased you have a beau." She returned to the table and sat down. "When will we meet him?"

That took me aback. The idea of introducing Simon to my mother had never occurred to me. I didn't know whether Dolores would fawn all over him or insult his taste in women.

"I don't know. He lives in New York and his schedule doesn't permit much advance planning."

"He will be able to come to the wedding, won't he?"

"I don't know, Mother."

"Well, I'll jot his name down on my list. You can give me his address after dinner."

"I don't have his address." The minute I said it, I regretted opening my mouth. A smug expression crept onto her face, as though she was vindicated in her belief of Simon's nonbeing. "I only have his phone number," I hastened to add.

"I see." She bobbed her head knowingly and ate some cottage cheese. No doubt she thought she did. In her mind there could not possibly be a boyfriend, for if there was she'd have to reevaluate her entire mental scenario of my life and admit that her predictions were incorrect. Dolores didn't like being incorrect. Well, if she wanted to believe Simon was an invention, that was fine by me.

"Has your grandfather told you what he's planning on giving Leslie?" She excavated through the salad bowl for cherry tomatoes and spooned them onto her plate.

"I have no idea." Actually, he had made fleeting reference to the battered collection of copper pots that had hung suspended and untouched from hooks in his basement kitchen for thirty years, but I would have been surprised if his generosity extended that far.

"*Howard the Duck* was absolutely the worst movie I've ever seen," Daddy interjected, pointlessly, wonderfully.

"So they say," I said.

"Don't bother to rent it. It's boring."

"More boring than *Ishtar*?"

He put his elbows on the table and rested his chin on his hands, pressing his fingertips against the rim of his eye sockets in a pose of intense concentration. Mother raised her eyes to the ceiling, then turned to me.

"My designer has come up with a stunning design for a bedroom set and my hand carvers are threatening to quit. Not strike, mind you. Quit. And we only just settled the other dispute. The head carver claims the decoration is too complicated to be done on a mass scale and the designer refuses to simplify his concept. He says that if I make him he'll take his design to an American firm, but to hire additional carvers would make the price of the completed set prohibitive."

"Hire nonunion," I suggested helpfully, while taking several croissants from a bag in my purse. "You did when the upholsterers walked out." Her employees were always threatening to strike or quit. I'd never heard of a company with so much labor unrest. "Have you ever thought of keeping a mediator on retainer?"

"Yes, it's more boring than *Ishtar*," said Daddy after careful deliberation. "It's the most god-awful piece of drivel ever committed to celluloid. They should burn every print—every negative—every still."

"And kill the witnesses," I offered with mock gravity.

"I suggested it to the head carver."

I started at the momentary image of massacred Payton employees before I rejoined the drift of her conversation.

"She has a name, Mother. Huberta. Remember? She's only been carving for you for twenty years, for Christ's sake."

"Huberta." She exhaled the name like a curse. "Huberta says if I do that, everyone in the plant will go on sympathy strike. My God. Whatever happened to worker loyalty? You'd think they'd be grateful to have jobs at all. I'd like to fire the lot of them."

"Oh, Mother. You're always threatening to do that."

"Well, this time, maybe I will."

"It would take too long to train the new people. You'd lose too much money." That always closed the subject.

"I could sell the works."

"And do what? Furniture is your life," I said sarcastically. "You're too old to start something new."

"I'm only fifty-seven. A young fifty-seven."

"You can't sell the factory." Daddy shook his head slowly. "You don't own it."

The effect of his few words on Mother was immediate. She shut up. It wasn't often she was reminded of that annoying technicality. She pursed her lips and wrung her napkin before returning to a neutral topic.

"Do you think Father might give her the egg?" she asked. The egg? Whatever put that notion into her head? Yes, Leslie coveted the object—always had (she didn't know it was fake), but Connie didn't like her.

"No. It's mine. He gave it to me when I was five."

"Don't be ridiculous. Nobody would give a Fabergé egg to a child."

"Well, he did. Ask him if you don't believe me." I stuffed a roll into my mouth and smiled provocatively as I chewed.

"Are you dieting?"

"No."

"You ought to. The wedding's in two months. You want to look nice, don't you?"

"I do look nice." I defended myself indignantly. "Just because I don't weigh a hundred pounds doesn't mean I'm not attractive. I'll have you know plenty of people find me attractive."

"Like this so-called boyfriend?"

"Yes," I rasped, an octave below my usual voice. "Simon finds me most attractive."

She cast me a withering but eloquent glance that said, "You poor self-deluding slob. You know and I know there is no boyfriend, you look like hell, and I pity you."

"As maid of honor, I would think you'd want to look your best."

"Maid of honor? Forget it. I want nothing to do with any of this."

"Don't be silly," she said dismissively. "Of course you do."

"I do not." My fist was poised to pound the table when Father interrupted.

"I saw *Lawrence of Arabia* again. It was good."

"Yes," I agreed, briskly. "It's one of my all-time favorites. As a matter of fact, I think it's one of the finest films ever made. By the way, what time is it?" I'd forgotten my watch, and Simon's flight landed at eight. I'd bought a lacy black negligee. The thought of Simon made me smile.

"It's seven-thirty." Dolores squinted to read the tiny face of her watch, too vain to wear glasses. "Why? Do you have to be somewhere?" She popped a radish flower in her mouth, the last remaining morsel on her plate, and winced slightly at the taste as she bit down. Dolores was of the school that the hostess had to have food on her plate as long as her guests were still eating.

"I'm meeting Simon."

"Simon?" She raised one eyebrow. The pretend boyfriend, I could tell she was thinking. Why did I bother with the charade? Why didn't I confess to her that the man Leslie met was simply a client or something? I smiled as enigmatically as I could and let her think whatever she wanted.

"I must leave," I insisted, sliding my chair back from the table and depositing my napkin beside my plate. "My boyfriend will be waiting." Mother believed that I only wanted to get away from her, which was also true. Father stood and offered a consoling fatherly smile. I kissed him on the cheek and left him to the evening's video fare.

I was standing in a terry bathrobe contemplating my sexy negligee when the doorbell rang. He'd have to come in and wait while I dressed. I touched my breast, still damp from my hurried shower, as I walked to the door. Tonight he would sleep in my bed for the first time. Tonight and tomorrow night. That would make it seem real. If it hadn't been for the phone calls I'd have thought I'd imagined the whole affair. It had been so long.

"It's me," he called as I rattled the chain. I ushered him in, allowing my robe to fall open and expose more cleavage than I considered strictly decent, but Simon had accomplished the miraculous. I no longer hated my body.

"Come in. I have to finish dressing." God, he looked gorgeous. He was wearing a creamy silk suit and open-necked shirt that revealed a narrow V of pale freckled chest. No gold chain with Italian pepper. No flashy rings. No heavy bracelet. Just a thin watch cased in stainless steel. And he was wearing sandals. His feet had to be the most lovely clean pink feet I'd ever seen. He handed me a large cone of paper containing stalks of daylilies, crimson and yellow and orange, then curled into the chair with the thoughtless grace of a cat.

I realized that for some time that's what he'd been reminding me of: a sleek, contented cat. It was the only time that I'd attributed feline characteristics to a man. In the kitchen, I clipped the stems of the flowers with vegetable scissors, arranged them in my Bohemian vase, then carried them to my small round white marble table beside the window.

Simon drummed his fingers on his knees. His head had fallen back and his eyes were closed. What was he thinking? I wanted him to be thinking of me. It had been three interminable weeks since he'd been up, since that lovely day at the tomb. We'd talked on the phone regularly, but he'd been preoccupied with business. I wanted him to be a hundred percent here, with me, now. I wanted him to seduce me, but he looked as though he were falling asleep in the chair.

How exactly did one go about a seduction? I guessed I'd seduced him the last time but he hadn't seemed quite so exhausted. I tried to envision scenes from movies but it was always the men doing the seducing. The female role entailed passive resistance, and since Simon wasn't in the least active, there was nothing to resist. I thought he'd jump me the moment he walked in. Men were strange.

"Can I get you a drink?" I asked, leaning seductively (or so I hoped) with one leg bent along the arm of the chair lightly touching Simon's elbow. He turned his face to mine and smiled.

"Love one. Gin and tonic if you have it."

I had. While I was preparing his drink in the kitchen, I knocked back a third of a glass hoping the effects might give me a bit of courage. How would Greer Garson have gone about attracting Walter Pidgeon? She was too dignified and subtle. Carole Lombard would have done it with a wisecrack, and Katherine Hepburn would have played the aloof bitch, but she had such damned fine cheekbones Spencer Tracy would have tackled her anyway. It was no good. I took another swig of gin and stirred Simon's ice with a chopstick left lying on the counter after last night's binge on Chinese food. I had a perfectly delicious man in my living room and I hadn't the vaguest idea how to get him into bed. What was wrong with me? What was wrong with him?

I gave him his drink. What would Leslie do? Stroke his hair with her flawlessly laquered fingertips, working down the temple to the crimson rim of his ear. Too much driving without his hat. I'd warned him he should wear sunscreen. He took my hand in his, guided it onto my thigh, and held it there. It felt cool and dry against my skin but limp as a dead thing.

"You don't like clutter, do you?" he asked, as though noticing my apartment for the first time.

"No. I decided on white because after a day at work I tire of the chaos of things. Like a parent putting the kids to bed at seven-thirty."

"Pardon?"

"You know. Sick of the noise. Every water stain on a dinner table or inkstain on a desk materializes for me some ghostly being until the showroom is as crowded with personalities as on auction night. I have to turn it off and the easiest way I know is either to avoid belongings that summon up images or stuff them in drawers. My sister has five-year-old quadruplets and she has admitted to slipping Gravol into their juice at dinner so they'll conk out early. I don't approve but I think I can understand."

"Oh. Do multiple births run in your family?" he asked, twirling his ice.

"Oh yes. Uncles, great uncles ... "

"And you're a twin and there are these quadruplets. It's hard to believe Leslie has four children." He stood and walked to the window.

I experienced a frisson. Leslie's name tumbled off Simon's lips too easily. Had he been thinking about her? He put his drink down on the sill. The sky was striated orange and blue and mauve and indigo, all delineated by burning streaks of gold. It was an extraordinary sunset. No. He'd only met her the once and hadn't shown the slightest interest. I was being paranoid. I brazenly clasped my arms around his waist and kissed his neck, my heart pounding so fiercely I was sure he could hear. He turned, kissed me on the forehead, picked up his drink, and continued his circuit of the room, opening a door to my wall console and giving a cursory inspection to my record collection. I tried to dismiss my feeling of rejection as imagined. He was acting like a stranger.

"What's your place like?"

"Not much busier than this. In the property settlement Portia kept all the household furnishings." He glanced in the bedroom. "What's this?" He stepped over to my worktable and picked up one of the heliotrope cormorants I was sculpting. On his previous visits I'd hidden them away, but he was so complimentary about the tomb, I hadn't bothered. My carving was as much me as my fat. He might as well see it all.

"It's a chess set I'm carving for my grandfather. This is the queen's knight. The king's men will be a little fussier. More definition for the feathers. The queen will have a higher polish."

"It's very good. You're really talented. Have you ever considered chucking the auction business and sculpting as a career? Bigger stuff you could really get your teeth into?"

"No. It wouldn't pay the rent. I have done larger stuff, though, like that." I pointed to my marble statue and he walked over and stroked it with the palm of his hand.

"Yes. Like this."

"I did it years ago."

"Have you any more?"

"Not as large."

"Show me."

"You don't really want to see them."

"If I didn't want to, I wouldn't have asked. Stop parading your damned insecurity. I know what you can do better than anyone. Now show me."

Chastened, I folded back my cupboard door and carried, one by one, my work from the shoe rack to the worktable. There were only five—my remaining work was in a box in the storage closet, but I wasn't hauling it out. Simon examined and fondled every one, shapeless forms, but to me, a cat, a horse, two women, and an abstraction of Connie. The marble varied in tone from yellow to black and white to pink.

"This is quite different from what you're doing now."

"I guess so."

"Why don't we box these up? I know a gallery owner who could show these."

"There aren't enough," I protested.

"There are for a group show."

"I don't know. I'd have to think about it."

He shrugged. I replaced the sculptures in the closet as he finished his drink. "What about the opposing men?" He picked up one of my rooks to give it a more minute examination.

"Haven't begun them yet, but I've had some lovely carnelian sitting in a box for ages. I think it'd make an attractive contrast."

"Yes. Are you making the board, too?"

"I don't know. I doubt it. Pretty boring. Anyway, Connie has a games table with a leather surface. I don't like the feel of stone against stone. It's not soothing."

He returned the carving to the table and flipped through the loose pile of sketches. I'd never shown them to anyone and regretted bringing him into my room. He was showing more interest in the chess set than in me. Seeing my work objectively through his eyes, I didn't think it was all that good. What was he going on about? I couldn't be a real artist. My anatomical grasp was faulty and my rendering weak. Even the completed pieces, lined along a small shelf behind the table, seemed like a menagerie of mutants. Birds after the bomb. Maybe he thought I intended them to be that way. Expressionistic birds. I suddenly lost heart for the planned seduction scene, and folded my thick terry robe tighter across my chest.

"What's this?" Simon scooped up the negligee, which suddenly looked as huge as a tent.

"A nightie."

"Did you buy it with me in mind?"

"No. I've had it for ages."

He fingered the manufacturer's washing instructions, which I had forgotten to remove, and grinned.

"Well, I'd better get dressed," I murmured, appalled, embarrassed, dying.

"Not so fast. Isn't there a little something you'd like to do first?" He placed the drink on my worktable and before I could think had untied my sash and whipped my robe off. I stood naked and exposed, not knowing what to do. Didn't I want this? I thought of the condoms sitting in the drawer of my bedside table that I had nearly died buying. The slender girl at the pharmacy cash had barely suppressed a snicker when she rang up the sale. But things were moving too fast—Simon had unzipped his trousers and was pushing me toward the bed.

"Bend over," he hissed in my ear.

"What? I . . . "

I found myself kneeling beside the low mattress with my face pressed into the duvet and Simon's hands gripping my hips while he plunged into me. I clutched at the duvet and bit my lower lip. It didn't hurt but I wasn't enjoying myself. Did Leslie do this sort of thing with men? Did she like it? Had Dolores done it with Daddy? Had Connie done it with Maude? I imagined women through history, hunched over, grimacing. I thought this posture was exclusive to the lower species. Did gorillas do it this way? It was certainly degrading. Simon panted and began to moan. His thrusts came harder and faster, then he collapsed on my back. I wanted to shake him off like a parasite, but I wasn't supposed to feel this way. I was supposed to feel tender and close. He rolled over and ejaculate dripped down my leg.

"Ah, Greer, Greer, Greer," he whispered breathlessly. I stood, holding the duvet to my chest for modesty. He yanked up his pants, tucked in his shirt, and zipped up.

"Greer, you're upset. Didn't you like that?"

"Not particularly. But if you did . . . "

He looked stricken and pulled me into his arms, stroking my hair and patting my back. "No. No. I'm sorry. That was insensitive of me, I could have been more delicate. Sometimes I'm just a selfish bastard." He rocked me for several minutes without speaking.

"It's okay."

"No, it's not. You didn't like it, and on top of that, I have to tell you that I can't stay."

"I don't understand. You said you could stay over until Monday." I pulled away and turned so he wouldn't see my tears. I'd stocked the larder. I had tickets for the Kirov and a baseball game. Shit.

"My dear Greer. I'm so sorry."

"But it's been over three weeks. I've missed you."

"I missed you, too, but it couldn't be helped. I have to rake together some financing for a client. It's the Caribbean development I told you about."

"I don't remember your mentioning it."

"Then you've forgotten." He stroked my cheek and dried my tears with a clean hanky.

"I see."

"I shouldn't be here now, you wicked seductress, but I couldn't keep away a moment longer."

"Will I see you next weekend?"

"I don't know. If the deal ties up."

"Maybe I could fly down."

"That would be lovely, but there'd be no point. I'm never home." He squeezed my bum and kissed me, then he left. Just left. Like that. I lifted his half-finished gin and tonic from my charcoal sketches. It had left a wet ring, smearing the details on the wing of a pigeon. Why had he been that way? Why had he been so rough? So abrupt? I felt a little used. Slam, bam, thank you ma'am. But maybe that was the way it was between men and women. I mean, I couldn't expect us to be Cinderella and Prince Charming all the time. And he had been contrite. He wouldn't have come if he didn't like me. A man like Simon could have anyone. Anyone. And he had chosen me.

I stepped over my black negligee and put on my old terry bathrobe. Under the table was a cardboard box. Inside, wrapped in newspaper, lay my treasures. I sat on the floor and withdrew them, one by one: chunks of jade, peridot, topaz, jasper, agate, turquoise. Grandfather had taught me that an artist saw something in the stone—in the banding, the swirls in the mineral. What it was meant to be was there, waiting. It had been waiting since the beginning of time, and was waiting still, struggling for release.

I faced the window and held a large amethyst up to the last ruddy streak of sun, turning it until the hexagonal prisms caught the light. Raised to my eye, the room, tinted purple, danced kaleidoscopically around me. Ancient Greeks believed that amethyst could protect one from drunkenness. What could I do with it? Nothing. Too pretty. Nature had finished it already. And what about the lapis? What did it look like? Gold

flecks winked in the blue stone. It was a quality piece, but it
didn't look like a damned thing, with the exception, perhaps,
of earrings or beads. Perhaps a cigarette box.

Sculptor, ha! Nothing looked like anything. Just rocks. No
magic. A pile of useless rocks. I wanted to throw them all
through the plate glass window into the blood-streaked sky. I
wanted to hear the crash, to see the glitter of a million shards, to
feel the dank warm air of the summer's night permeate the cool,
filtered sterility of the room.

When I woke in the morning, I automatically reached beside
me to see if he was there. It was raining, the first real rain in
weeks, and the dark gray outside my window had moved
indoors. I didn't bother turning on the light. The digital clock
read six-eleven, and my white walls, gray in the gloom, seemed
to contract. My negligee still lay crumpled in a heap on the floor
where Simon had tossed it.

He was in New York, four hundred miles and one hour away.
I bit the edge of the sheet. Hot cocoa. I wanted hot cocoa.
Connie's German cook used to bring it to me in bed those
mornings after I'd spent the night at his place. I had a full
refrigerator but was overcome with inertia. I just wanted to be
coddled.

I curled up under the duvet and listened to children's pro-
gramming, then a show for seniors peppered with music from
the swing era, but I wasn't in the mood for "In the Mood." I
hauled myself out of bed, heated some cocoa, and moped by the
window. Steam hovered like a dense ground fog over the surface
of my cup. The daylilies had released their bright orange pollen
all over the surface of the table. I stuck my finger in the vase. No
water. Typical. I burned my tongue on the scalding milk and
cursed. My feet were cold. I was lonely. Before Simon had
returned to my life I'd been self-reliant and had never understood how people could mind being alone. Now my old ways no
longer fit. I felt like an intruder in my own home. I expected to
hear a key scrape in the lock. A woman would enter and throw
her suitcase on the hall floor, sort throught the mail on the hall

table—someone who had such a full and busy life that she couldn't bother doing the place up—someone who traveled—someone who spent her nights with a lover. Why couldn't Simon have stayed? The gray and dismal rain was falling everywhere.

CHAPTER FOURTEEN

The sky cleared shortly after eight and I decided to attribute my mood to hormones. There was no objective reason to feel so rotten—Simon had come when he could just as easily have canceled. I changed into blue-striped overalls and packed a bag to do some work on the tomb. When I'd been up there I'd noticed that the leaves on the lintel needed spines and the facade wanted a wash before I could consider it complete and show it to Connie. My hand was on the door handle when the telephone rang. I thought to myself, "It's Dolores. I know it's Dolores." I have second sight when it comes to Mother and the phone, but unfortunately I don't trust it, and, hoping it was Simon, I tossed my bag on the floor and picked up the receiver.

Of course, it was Dolores, who summoned me to her house. This was not convenient, and I said as much, but my refusal was dismissed. I asked her to just say what she had to say over the phone and save us both time and effort, but she insisted that my corporal presence was required for an hour. Since she had a ten o'clock appointment (with a representative of a mill in Pakistan that had recently introduced a new line of upholstery fabrics rivaling anything of British, Italian, or French manufacture at half the price), she told me to be there by nine. Then she hung up. I hung the buzzing receiver in the cradle and determined to stay not a minute past an hour.

When I arrived at the house I was greeted with a cheery wave from Alex as he squatted on the grass, dusting a rose bush with

209

powder. Bartleby huddled under a nearby spirea, confettied by a thousand minute white petals. "What are you doing?" I called to Alex.

"Killing aphids," he answered. The dew was still wet on the grass as I walked across the lawn. He pointed to a sticky green encrustation on the stem, which on closer examination turned out to be a seething mass of microscopic green bugs. I shuddered.

"There aren't enough ladybugs this year. Usually the ladybugs eat them."

I squeezed his shoulder and headed for the gazebo where Dolores stood impatiently tapping her foot on the slate tiles. A pot of coffee and two cups sat on the round glass table. Occupying four of the six iron chairs were books of fabric samples splayed open to show a spectrum of color and prints.

I dumped my bag on a glazed chintz of apple blossoms and hummingbirds, sat, and helped myself to a cup of black coffee. There was no cream or sugar, no croissants, no brioches, no Danishes or cinnamon rolls. I reached into my bag and removed the box of assorted doughnuts I had prudently thought to purchase on my way over. Dolores moved my bag to the ground as though it was oozing slime on her precious sample, made an incoherent but disapproving noise, and sat on the opposite chair. She looked serious. What was going on?

"Where's Daddy?" I wanted a buffer. With him around the conversation could at least be maneuvered to the innocuous subject of movies.

"Upstairs watching television. Where else? Must you eat those things now? And what are you wearing? You look like Tweedle-Dum."

I opened the box and selected a honey-dipped twist to precede my coffee. Chewing at her, I brushed flecks of glaze from my overalls onto the slate. The gazebo had been freshly painted, perhaps in preparation for the engagement party, and the smell was overwhelming. The clematis was just coming into flower, and bright green leaves poked through the white trellis. If the flowers were doing well, so were the mosquitoes. I swatted one on my neck.

"Thank you, Mother. You're looking lovely yourself." Actually it was a source of constant awe that she was always so well put together. Was there a well-groomed gene that Leslie inherited and I didn't? My hair was tied back in a spiky ponytail and Mother's was her usual perfectly sculpted roll. Her linen dress was clean and pressed, her shoes were unscuffed, the red in her scarf coordinated with her unchipped nail polish, and she wore makeup. Sunday morning, nine o'clock, when sensible people were either still asleep or else lolling about reading the *New York Times* and eating croissants. She stared me in the eye and said:

"I was speaking with Alex earlier and he told me that Father wasn't himself lately."

"Connie's fine," I snapped. Lord. Why couldn't Alex shut up? I could see it all. Dolores conversationally asking how Connie was and Alex meandering on about his little lapse. Sailboats on Lake Ladoga and dead brothers. "If you must know, he suffered a minor neurological incident. A tiny stroke. It's quite common at his age. The doctor said he was just fine and it probably wouldn't happen again."

"What happened?" she probed, too interested by half.

"Nothing. The incident just stimulated a memory pocket. Like intense déjà vu. He's perfectly well now."

"What if it happens again? He really can't be considered competent to manage his affairs. Perhaps he ought to have a guardian."

"Like you, perchance?" The sun passed above the maple tree at the corner of the property, and its light hit the gazebo broadside. Glittering shafts fell through the trellis and mottled us in brilliance. I sure as heck wasn't going to be the one to tell her he was making a pilgrimage to Leningrad to meet a miraculously resurrected brother.

"I am his closest living relative."

"'A little more than kin, and less than kind,'" I quoted in a mutter.

"What?"

"And a more solicitous, loving, concerned daughter one

would be hard pressed to find." I ripped into a filled doughnut
and jelly dropped onto the overall bib. "Anyway, I hate to
disappoint you, but there's no point in pressing for a compe-
tency hearing. He's as competent as he ever was. Is that what
you wanted? Is that why you forced me to come over? I could
have told you this over the phone."

"That wasn't all. The dressmaker dropped these books and
samples over this morning. . . ."

"It's Sunday!" I protested, irate on behalf of the poor
woman who'd been making clothes for Dolores since 1953.
"Other people like to take it easy on Sunday." From beyond the
fish pond I could hear the gentle snip of Alex's clippers.

"Nonsense. It only took a half hour and she's grateful for the
work. Anyway, decisions must be made if she's to have the
dresses ready on time."

"Too bad you didn't arrange to have it sooner. You could
have used the flowers from the funeral."

She ignored me and stood to close the fabric books and stack
them together on one chair. Under one she found a glossy Italian
bridal magazine and held it on her lap as she sat down again.

"I think it's all in the worst possible taste. I understand he
bought a dispensation to marry his stepmother," I continued.

"A dispensation wasn't necessary. In the eyes of the church
it's doubtful whether Leslie and Jules were ever married."

"What are you talking about?"

"A Hindu ceremony in Nepal hardly counts," she retorted
testily.

"Tell it to the Nepalese. Wait a minute, now. Am I to conclude, then, that the boys are, now how can I put this delicately,
bastards?"

"Greer, really!"

"Did Leslie and Yves have dispensation to sleep together
while Jules lay dying?" I poured a cup of coffee and took
another doughnut. Cinnamon. Sugar clung to my lips and chin
as I munched. I licked it off with my tongue. Mother contem-
plated me with ill-concealed revulsion.

"Jules was dying forever. For years. Leslie's young. She has certain physical needs."

"I give up. Okay. But don't you think it's just the teensiest bit in bad taste to have a big wedding?" I goaded.

"It's not going to be a big wedding. Only a hundred or so. The reception will be at the Ritz. A sit-down dinner, I think. Perhaps a string quartet."

"What fun," I said flatly. "After dinner we can work off our calories with a brisk minuet."

"Greer, I don't recall asking for your opinion, and I don't appreciate your sarcasm."

"Excuse me." I glanced at my watch. I'd been there a half hour. I read once that one could never truly grow up until one had murdered one's parents. Metaphorically. I thought I'd done so, but apparently not. "And use a napkin—there's jam dripping down your . . . chest."

"May I be excused?" I shifted weight in the chair. The metal arms dug uncomfortably into my hips.

"You are to be the maid of honor."

"No, I'm not. I thought I made it clear last night that I wanted nothing to do with this affair. I don't want to be an attendant. I don't want to be a guest. Hell, I don't even want to be her sister."

Mother took the thick magazine from her lap and opened it to a page marked with one of those ubiquitous self-adhesive yellow notes. She held it up to my face. It was a bridesmaid's dress in pink tulle. The bodice was low and frilled, the sleeves puffy, and the skirt so full it must have been draped on six crinolines. For the coup de grace there was a huge full-brimmed hat with ribbons and bows. Scarlett O'Hara would have given a blow job to a Yankee for such a dress.

"You have two months to lose weight. Since the wedding's in September the fabric's going to be dark mauve. Yours will be indigo. I think the maid of honor should be set apart."

"If I starved until the rehearsal dinner, I'd still look like an antebellum blimp."

"You could make a start by throwing out the remaining doughnuts."

"I do not choose to diet. I like eating. I like food. As a matter of fact, I love food. I adore food. I especially adore doughnuts." To gall her, I grabbed another one, chocolate, and ingested it so quickly she was rendered momentarily speechless.

"You, you, you just eat because you don't ... " Her face darkened with frustration and anger and she had difficulty pushing the words out. As she tried I popped a munchkin with coconut sprinkles.

"Don't what, Mother? Screw? Is that what you're trying to say? That pent-up sexual desire is perverting itself into a morbid obsession with food?" I grinned and ate a sugar doughnut.

"Don't be obscene. I was going to say you eat because you don't have much of a life."

"So you don't buy the boyfriend story?"

"You never do anything, or go anywhere. A girl your age shouldn't depend on her grandfather for a social life."

"I don't, but I prefer his company to that of others who shall go nameless. Besides, what do you know of my life? I don't confide in you."

"I can guess."

"Well, you'd be guessing wrong." I sucked the icing sugar off my fingers. "And I refuse to attend the wedding. It's stupid. I feel sorry for Yves. He's too innocent. He should have stayed a priest."

"Did you know he's adopting the boys?" she queried.

"No. I didn't. I haven't spoken to Leslie for weeks." Not since she used my apartment as a way station to tart herself up for a roll in the hay with a generous sheikh, I thought.

"I couldn't figure out how to include them in the ceremony, but Yves suggested they stand up in front with the best man. They'll look so adorable in their little sailor suits."

"If it was my wedding, I'd have them manacled until my plane landed in Jamaica."

"Until you find a man willing to overlook your obvious weakness, the matter of your wedding is academic, so we'll put it aside, shall we? You'll have to diet if you're going to fit into this dress.''

"Forget it. I shall not, will not, wear that dress.''

"You are the bride's only sister.''

"So bloody what?''

"If you aren't in the wedding party, people will talk.''

"Let them. I don't care.''

"You're just bitter.''

"I'm not bitter. I'm disgusted. She gets everything her own bloody way and all because she's pretty. Jesus. If she were judged by personality . . . Sometimes I think the highest priority in her life is the circumference of her upper thighs. She goes down on anyone with a well-lined pocket. Christ. And she's marrying Yves for money, no matter what you think. If I rationalized her behavior as much as you do, I'd have a mental hernia.''

"You don't understand a mother's love. I've always known about Leslie's peccadilloes. They weren't important. It's always been Yves.''

"What rot. And Leslie has enough peccadilloes to have her saying Hail Marys until she's ninety-three. What I don't understand is how a mother could so obviously favor one child over another. More than once you've said to my face that Leslie was your favorite, and you've proven it by word and deed since we were in diapers.''

"That's not true,'' she protested unconvincingly.

"Did you ever love Daddy?'' I asked accusingly.

"Of course I loved him. But I wasn't in love with him, the way Leslie's in love.''

Love, in love, what was the difference? I'd never been able to tell. Was ''to love'' active and ''in love'' passive? I wasn't surprised that she'd never been in love with Daddy. I couldn't see her in love with anyone. The only men she ever saw were connected with the furniture business, and I couldn't imagine Dolores romping in the sawdust with a lathe operator, or in a sleazy motel room with one of her sales representatives. I didn't believe for a minute that she'd ever loved Daddy at all. Poor Daddy. No wonder he drank.

"That's why I'm so pleased that Leslie is marrying Yves," she was saying.

"Come off it. She doesn't love Yves. It's the money."

"They're in love. They've been in love since they first met."

"Yeah. Sure. She's the reason he quit the priesthood."

"Yes," she replied placidly, turning the pages of the *Pronuptia* magazine. She stopped at another marked page and stroked the image of a bride in appliquéd silk. Patterns embroidered in seed pearls swirled over the billowing skirt. An enigmatic smile crossed her face.

"Jules knew."

"Knew what?" What little there was of my patience was wearing perilously thin.

"Knew that they were lovers."

"You mean he knew that she was cuckolding him with his own son?"

"Of course he knew," she said smugly. "Jules couldn't have children."

"He had Yves," I contradicted.

"Before he had mumps."

"So the Cats *are* Yves's. I wondered." ("They are blood of his blood and flesh of his flesh all right," were Leslie's words, but the puzzle pieces hadn't quite clicked into place, primarily because I hadn't known there was a puzzle. Now things were beginning to make sense.) Dolores continued.

"Jules certainly knew. That's why he divided his estate the way he did . . . to insure that the family remained together."

"Okay. I can see that. He knew Leslie was so mercenary she'd do anything for money. I don't see where love comes into it. I give it three weeks before she's off on one of her little solo jaunts to God knows where in a string bikini. Did she tell you all this?"

"Yes. We had a little heart-to-heart the night she told me they were to be married. I imagine she'll want more children."

"After the Cats?" I gasped incredulously. "You know what one of their psychologists called them? The zero-population-growth poster babies."

"It would be nice if she had a daughter," she said dreamily. I slapped the table to rouse her from her reverie.

"Or two," I added, acidly.

"Leslie is lucky to have Yves. Most men are perfect bastards. Jules was awful."

"You're not making any sense. Jules was considerate enough to not throw Leslie out on her ear."

"He couldn't have. The boys are his grandchildren."

"And most men aren't bastards," I argued. "Daddy's sweet."

"He is a disgusting sodden wreck. If it hadn't been for me, the business would have gone bankrupt."

"He could have sold it, and besides, you adore running the place. You'd be lost without it."

"That's not true. I wanted to be at home with my children."

"Bull." I snorted involuntarily.

"Perhaps do charity work. Garden."

"Come off it."

"But I wanted to build something for my children. It's too bad I didn't have a boy to leave it to. I expect Leslie's boys will take over some day."

"Gee, thanks."

"Perhaps if you ever have a child ... " The sentence went unfinished.

"Perhaps the boys will grow up to be bastards, as you put it. They're off to a splendid start." I'd never suspected she had such a negative opinion of men. I thought of Simon and my heart skipped a beat. Simon wasn't a bastard. "And Connie isn't a bastard."

"Connie is the biggest bastard of them all," she said icily.

"If it hadn't been for Connie I probably would have killed myself when I was twelve."

"Don't be melodramatic. You would have done nothing of the sort."

"How would you know? He was kind to me when everyone else, except Daddy, made my life hell."

"He killed my mother."

"Oh, good God! That's the stupidest thing I've ever heard."

"She didn't want to move to Canada. Her life was in England. Her sons were buried there."

"He moved because life was intolerable in England after the war. All the taxes and rationing."

"I was there, remember? There was nothing intolerable about it. Our friends were there. All my relations. The Blitz was intolerable, but we didn't leave. He didn't even evacuate us to the country after our house was bombed—just moved us into an awful flat above the shop. We lived there for two years."

"Admit it, life is better here. I've lived in England, and I couldn't imagine trying to raise a family in London. It's so crowded and expensive."

"You're a North American. You can't understand. Mother faded away after we moved here. She was uprooted."

"Connie tried. He moved your brothers' remains here."

She looked at me with some surprise. "No, he didn't. She begged him to but he refused. He said it was a foolish waste of money. I can still hear him shouting, 'Dead's dead. I refuse to squander my money hauling moldering bones across the Atlantic Ocean.' "

"But I've seen the tomb. They're all there," I insisted.

"The tomb? Oh, yes. I'd forgotten. No one's buried there. How did you discover that?"

"The cemetery office." Now I was confused.

"I recall he bought the tomb then decided it would be too expensive to repair."

"But he *did* repair it. There are even brass name plaques."

"He changed his mind." She shrugged. "My brothers' remains were cremated and buried in a conventional plot. And he didn't bring their ashes over until after Mother's death."

After? Of course, Connie had never told me anything about it at all. I'd assumed he moved the bodies when they moved. I suppose if I'd checked the purchase date . . .

"She hated Canada. She hated the cold. She had no friends. She spent all her time, from May until October, on her knees in the garden. I remember, it was beautiful. There were roses, and lavender, and larkspur. She'd even dug out a small pond and there were bright pink water lilies. She loved flowers. The summer after she died, Father tore up the yard and had trees planted. Trees. Stubbly little pine trees. They grew so quickly that it was a forest by the time I left home. What a petty, pathetic act."

"That's not true."

"Yes, it is. I was there. I watched him yank out each bush and shake the dirt off the roots."

"Well, he must have had his reasons."

"Yes, I'm sure he did," she said coldly. "The thing is, I still dream of her lying frozen out there in the potting shed." She shuddered and shook her head. What was I doing then? Carving an empty tomb? Connie wasn't going to be buried there, but down the mountain. I didn't understand. Maybe Dolores was lying. But why would she?

"I've got to go." I shook all the doughnut crumbs from my overalls and stood to leave. She snapped out of her reverie.

"What size are you? For the patterns and fabric."

"I haven't the vaguest idea."

"Greer!"

I had to get out of there. I had to investigate the tomb.

"No way," I snapped.

"The dressmaker is coming here for the first fitting Tuesday at four. Be here." She slapped the magazine down on the table as she spoke. I nearly knocked a table over in my haste to escape.

"Be here," she repeated as I fled through the garden, sending Bartleby into a tizzy of panic as I brushed past his bush. Alex's goodbyes were lost in the slamming of my car door. Damn. I'd left the window shut and the car was a furnace. Never mind. I started the motor and sped away.

I drove my car as close to the tomb as possible, and walked quickly the rest of the way. I don't know why I expected it to appear different from last week. After all, if Connie didn't own the mausoleum, he hadn't owned it last week, either, or the week before, or last summer when I began working on the marble. But it was the same. The leaves of the chestnut trees

were bigger and a deeper green, the grass was lusher, the squirrels more active. One of the wild dogs—part Alsatian, part
Samoyed—had heard the car motor and waited in the bluebell-
covered semicircle of lawn for his customary treat. I reached
into my purse and tossed him my last doughnut. He caught it
with a low growl and ran off into the bushes. I unlocked the
door and went inside. As my eyes became accustomed to the
gloomy interior, my tools, scattered across the bench, took
definition.

I impulsively seized a chisel and started prying at the facing
of one of the compartments, the one with the plaque marked
Peter Fletcher 1922-1943. What was I looking for? The stone
was firmly attached to the wall, and I could make no headway. I
lit a match and examined the edge. There was no mortar. I had
been whacking at the marble. What was I doing? A person
couldn't go around vandalizing graves. But if he'd moved the
bodies like Dolores said, then they weren't technically graves,
were they?

I ran the chisel along the edge in an effort to find out what was
holding the stone in place. If there were no bodies, why weren't
the niches open? All three were sealed tight, the name plaques
still affixed. None of this made any sense—but then, it
explained the lack of upkeep that had always puzzled me. What
if he had sold it? What if there were strangers buried there? No.
There couldn't be. The names would have been changed. The
place would be kept up. None of this made any sense, but before
I desecrated the tomb, I had to confirm if Dolores knew what
she was talking about. I retrieved my car keys from the bench
where I'd tossed them and drove down to the records office.

The secretary at the office put her sandwich on top of the
cabinet and kneeled beside an open file drawer marked F. She
removed a three-by-five card.

"Cedar Knoll. Shall I mark it on a map?"

"Please," I replied. The odor of tuna fish filled my nose, and
I was tempted to reach over and steal a bite. "Do your records
say when the plot was purchased?"

"Just a moment." She consulted the card. "That was 1950."

"Thank you." I accepted the Xeroxed diagram of the mountain, and studied the path, defined with pink felt marker, that led from the office to Cedar Knoll, a distance of a mere two hundred yards. The secretary resumed eating her sandwich, and I regretted the absence of vending machines. I should have let the damn dog starve. "Excuse me, but could you check and see if there's another plot for Fletcher?"

She finished her mouthful and looked at me as though thinking why hadn't I asked when she was up before, and slid the F drawer out again. "Constantine?"

"Yes."

She shook her head. "That's it."

"Is that ownership or who's buried there?"

"Either, both. It doesn't matter. We're cross-referenced."

"Are there any other Fletchers?"

"Sure. It's a big cemetery." She walked down the file headings with her fingers, reading off names. "Andrew, Celia, David, Edward, Edwin, Edgar, Frances ... "

"Wait. Could you check the card for David, please?"

"Sure. Why not." She pulled the card. "Sunset Circle. I've never come across that. Let me check the map." She stood before the large diagram on the wall with a puzzled expression until I pointed out the area.

"Son of a gun."

"What happened to the other woman who worked here, last year?" It had taken her no time at all to locate Sunset Circle. She must have found the wrong card when I asked.

"Her? Oh, she retired."

"Does it say who owns the tomb?"

"Tomb? Just a sec. Here it is. Constantine Fletcher. I wonder why it wasn't under F? These records are a mess."

"Thanks. You can go back to your lunch now." I left her scratching her head and walked the few hundred yards to a dignified black granite gravestone into which the familiar names were carved.

Maude Fletcher 1900-1950
Beloved wife of Constantine
and dear mother of
Peter 1922-1943
and
David 1922-1943
"Whom the gods love die young."

A ring of mature cedars surrounded the plot. Someone had planted white impatiens at the base of the stone, and the grass was neatly trimmed. Perpetual care. From here I could see Connie's house, high on the opposite hill or, to be exact, I could see the roof and chimneys. A slender pall of smoke drifted straight up from one, and I imagined Connie was busy burning papers again. Since his neurological episode, as he called it, the activity of paper burning took up more and more of his time. I had walked in on him once as he threw a stack of his phony export certificates on the fire, and he chuckled, saying he was destroying evidence before his trip. In a basket at his side were bundles of letters, legal documents, and a large tin of lighter fluid. This he picked up to squirt liberally over the already crackling papers, and flames exploded out and up, blackening the painted overmantel and nearly singeing his gray hair.

I had been standing so still that three squirrels, perhaps thinking I was a new tree, were sniffing around my feet. I shooed them off, then feeling guilty, rummaged in my purse for a package of dry roasted peanuts. I tore at the plastic and scattered the nuts on the grass before driving to my tomb.

I stood in the long green grass, gazing at the rusty cliff, the half-buried facades of the abandoned mausoleums, the ostentatious whiteness of mine. Silence rang in my ears. Why hadn't Connie removed the plaques? They were made of heavy brass, oval with a design of coiled rope around the circumference. The names and dates were engraved inside. I had always admired them. Why, if he decided to buy another plot, had he left them? I stood and touched Grandmother's. Maude Fletcher 1900-1950.

What had she been like? I couldn't imagine Connie married

to anyone. I couldn't imagine him in a clean house. I only knew her from the photo in Dolores's dressing room—that of a woman past her first youth, her permed hair falling in soft waves around a smiling face. On either side stood an adolescent son in school uniform and on her lap, wearing a smocked dress, white shoes, ankle socks, and more ringlets than Shirley Temple, sat Dolores. Connie rarely spoke of her, something I simply never questioned because I figured it was too painful. Did he feel guilty for not loving her enough? That would explain why he'd ripped out her garden. It reminded him of her, of his failure. Every rose.

Why had he bothered sealing the niches? The plaques were three quarters of an inch thick, tinged green with age. I decided to remove them so some vandal with a discerning eye couldn't steal them to polish and use for paperweights. I retrieved my chisel from the floor, wedged it between the plaque and the marble, then levered it downward. Instead of cracking off, it shifted sideways, like a door handle. I pulled the chisel out and grabbed the brass to twist with my hand, hoping that the repeated action would cause metal fatigue on the screw with which it was apparently attached, but it moved smoothly, first ninety degrees to the right where it stopped, then ninety degrees to the left, when it clicked, and the entire rectangle of marble, twenty-four inches square, swung away from the wall like the door of a safe. I stepped back, half expecting to see bones, but inside the cavity were boxes—stacks and stacks of metal boxes varying in size from a few inches to a foot square. I tried the other plaques, and they, too, opened doors to compartments, likewise filled with boxes.

I sat on the bench and looked at the three open doors, at all the little parcels hidden away in this secret place that no one ever visited. No one but me, I thought, because a clerk at the office had made a mistake and directed me to the wrong plot. There was a rustling of leaves outside, probably squirrels or dogs, but I leaped to close the door and light the lantern. That, with the faint light that filtered through the perforated metal door, was sufficient for my task. Although I felt like a grave

robber, I had to find out what was in the boxes. I never doubted
for an instant that Connie had placed them there. It was just like
him to design sneaky little hidey-holes for his goodies. But he
was a little nuts to trust that no one would stumble upon them.
Why hadn't he noticed that the key was missing from his blue
cloisonné bowl? Was it simply dumb luck on my part that he
hadn't hidden anything on the days I'd had it in my possession?
What would his reaction be if he knew I was on to his secret? I
glanced over my shoulder, expecting him to walk in, and shivered. The tomb was as chill and dank and grim as what it was. A
grave.

I walked over to the niches and picked up a largish parcel,
metal like the others, unsealed, about a foot square, and lifted
the top. Inside was an object wrapped in blue felt. I unwrapped
the fabric to find yet another box, oval shaped, of white leather,
mellowed by age to ivory, stamped in gold with the double-
headed Romanov eagle that signified the firm of Fabergé. I sat
down on the cold stone floor, removed my jacket, and laid it
before me. Upon this, I placed the box and pried open the gilt
clasp. Nestled in the molded interior was an Easter egg, the
likes of which I had only seen in museums or Christie's auctions. It was carved from a sold piece of lapis lazuli, and decorated with rococo scrollwork in yellow gold, set with diamonds
and sapphires. The clasp was a star sapphire surrounded by
diamonds. I carefully drew the two halves apart. Inside sat a
gold spaniel with cabochon ruby eyes in a bezel setting, and the
dog also opened, revealing a gold ring set with a ruby, so tiny
only a small child could have worn it on his smallest finger. The
gold band around the egg's circumference was inscribed with
Cyrillic lettering, so I couldn't understand it, but the date was
1905. I found a pencil and paper in my purse and copied the
writing, then replaced the egg in its wrappings.

What on earth was he thinking? The current value of such an
egg was probably around three million U.S. dollars, and any
derelict with a talent for lock picking might have found it at any
time in the past thirty years or whenever the hell he'd put it
there. I put the box on a space I'd wiped on the bench and

removed another from the cubicle. This one contained an irregularly shaped object wrapped in a length of chamois, then a length of brown cloth. It was a silver tankard with scenes from what I recognized as the tales of Baron Munchausen in bas-relief around its girth. The hinged top was ornamented with a laughing wolf. Hallmarks on the underside again indicated the Fabergé workshops.

How many boxes were there? I decided to examine the contents methodically before I left, and wondered if Connie knew what order they were in, and would notice that they'd been tampered with. I wanted a drink. I wanted a hamburger. And fries. On my pad of paper, I sketched the configuration of the boxes in each compartment and taped the sketch above each door. Then I began the inventory.

David's repository on the left contained mostly jewelry. The first box held a magnificent diamond choker, probably from the middle of the last century, judging by the ornate setting. The necklace contained eleven large stones of approximately six carats each and innumerable smaller stones. I couldn't begin to estimate the value. Narrow spears of sunlight pierced the perforations in the door, and the gems sparkled like so much shattered glass. How could he have been so damn sure no one would find his cache? What did he have against safety-deposit boxes? There were seven more necklaces, one emerald and diamond, two ruby, two sapphire with diamonds, one topaz and diamond, and one unusual one of pearl and amethyst. There were also three tiaras—all diamond; eleven pearl necklaces, one of perfectly matched one-centimeter black pearls; and so many unset stones that I didn't bother to count them: sapphires, rubies, emeralds, diamonds of every hue, a topaz the size of a goose egg, ten identical square-cut aquamarines of about thirty carats each, pearls—all neatly compartmentalized in boxes, the interiors of which were indented like egg cartons and lined in natural suede to protect them against scratching. Oddly enough, none of the pearls appeared to have been drilled. They ranged from one centimeter in diameter to a luminous pink beauty the size of a clenched fist.

In the center compartment I found six more Fabergé eggs.
One was rose quartz, about three inches high, with a trellis
pattern of gold and seed pearls, containing an enamel portrait of
a baby also framed in seed pearls. Another, executed of rock
crystal, engraved with vines on a pedestal of green enamel grape
leaves and garnet grapes, was only two inches high and didn't
open. One was enameled gold and incubated a gold pheasant
seated on a nest with four enameled eggs. These opened, revealing four minute mustard-colored carnelian chicks with cabochon ruby eyes. The whole thing was only three inches tall. I
marveled at the skill of the sculptor, for each chick, although no
larger than a large pea, was anatomically exact down to the
feathers.

The two remaining eggs I found were as large as the first. One
was set on its side, as opposed to the others, which were all on
their ends, and was enameled translucent blue on a guilloche
field. It was in the art nouveau style, mounted on a stylized gold
twist of leaves and twigs that spiraled up to opaque white jade
calla lilies with gold stamens. The casket opened to expose a
winged cupid in pale pink enamel, his wings set with rose
diamonds, reclining on a bed of straw made from four colors of
gold. A spring, worked by a button concealed near a leaf,
operated a clockwork mechanism, which when pressed made
Cupid's penis wave up and down while a strange little melody
chimed from within. That old fucker. He hadn't sold it.

The next egg was enamel, too, translucent rose, the hinged
center encircled by pearls. It was austere compared with the
others. The only ornamentation was the faint design of the
guilloche field, and the egg was segmented into ten equal parts,
each outlined in pearls. Inside was a detailed model of a house,
using three colors of gold to achieve definition. It looked
vaguely familiar to me, but then, one Victorian house with
dormers and a veranda was suggestive of any other Victorian
house with dormers and a veranda. It was stabilized on a pewter
base cast in a pattern of waves, and when one was pushed, the
roof of the house opened, but whatever had been inside was
now lost. There was a pathetic grating of gears and the poing of

a mainspring where there should have been music. There was no inscription. I closed it, placing it in its wrappings.

The last egg was a shock. How had Simon described it? Translucent daffodil enamel on an engraved field enclosed by gold fretwork of grapevines enameled pale green and set with seed pearls. I opened the top and activated the hidden switch. The pigeon flapped its wings, the clockwork whirred, and the familiar melody chimed. It had to be the original egg, the one Connie had had copied in 1927. What was it doing here? I wrapped it up and placed it in its case.

The third compartment held a bizarre diversity of things. The first box held a silver and quartz reliquary in the shape of a cross immersed in flames, containing, if the archaic French could be trusted, a bone fragment from the thigh of Joan of Arc. There was a ten-inch-high T'ang figure, not of a horse or camel, but of a cat. I'd never seen a T'ang cat, and if Connie had shown it to me, I would have guessed it was phony, but there was nothing phony in this hoard. There was a blue-and-white ceramic globular jar—Chinese, fifteenth century, and extremely rare. The only reason I knew this was that I'd come across one like it in a twelve-year-old catalogue, and even then the selling price had been more than $170,000 U.S. One box contained a pair of German presentation wheel-lock dueling pistols, engraved, silver-mounted—probably seventeenth century. There was an Italian faience plate from the fourteenth century, the painting in vivid blues and greens depicting Noah's ark. One flat plastic box held coins, mostly gold, some silver, from many countries, representing many ages.

I was about to replace the packages when my hand brushed against a swatch of black velvet that had been glued to the upper surface of the vault about three feet in, to hang down over what appeared to be a brick wall. The bricks were smooth and metal. I lifted the lantern from the bench and held it so its light illuminated a stack of gold ingots. I wiggled one loose from the top of the stack. It was about seven inches long, four wide, and two thick. I turned it to examine all sides, and oddly enough, all six surfaces were unstamped. In photographs there were always numbers on the ends of the bars and, somewhere, a stamp identifying the country of origin and the purity of the gold. I pulled out two more bars, and these too were smooth.

I counted seventy-one ingots, but lacked the energy to examine each one. They were damned heavy. I read somewhere that a standard ingot weighed thirty-five pounds, but thirty-five pounds of concentrated dead weight certainly felt like more. I slid the bars on top of the others and replaced the velvet, then sat on the bench. If the average price of gold was four hundred dollars an ounce, American, I calculated Connie's stash was worth approximately sixteen million dollars.

Holy Jesus. About then I could've used Connie's flask of whiskey. Not being a gemologist, I had no idea of the value of the jewels, but I knew the eggs were worth several millions, and the ceramics, hundreds of thousands of dollars. I tried to duplicate the patterns of the boxes so my discovery would pass unnoticed if Grandfather came up. Then I sealed the doors. I rubbed some dirt from the floor over the scratches made by my chisel and packed all my tools in a knapsack. He'd know immediately I'd been up there, for who else would have done the carving, but he needn't know I'd been inside. Why hadn't Connie confided in me—shared the thrill of acquisition? I'd never seen any of these things. Didn't he trust me to keep his secret? Or did he believe I'd think he was crazy? To do him justice, at that moment I did think he was a trifle loony. There were safer hiding places than in a tomb on the mountain. A Swiss bank, for instance. With his connections, he could have converted the entire lot to cash and made remarkably lucrative investments. The interest rates of the late 1970s alone might have trebled his worth. Was he a miser? Did he ever come up and sit on the bench, opening boxes as I had, holding each object in his dry, wrinkled hands, glorying in their cold, unaltering perfection?

I glanced around the tomb once more to be sure I'd left no evidence and locked the door. Well, I thought as I leaned against the facade in the heat of noon, at least I now knew what he did with his money.

CHAPTER FIFTEEN

The third Saturday in July was a predictably muggy water-retentive sweat-drenched day. A typical day for a Dolores party to fall on. Mosquitoes would be out in squadrons. Simon had kicked off his sheet in the night, and his slender tanned body was beaded in perspiration. The blithering air-conditioning was on the blink. He stirred and burrowed his face in my breasts. His skin was hot.

"Are you certain you can't come today?" I asked, combing his curls with my fingers, fighting the urge to push him away as our sticky warmth merged, overwhelmed.

"The meeting will take most of the day. It's just not possible." He had the good grace to take ten minutes diddling me, bringing me to orgasm, before he rid himself of his morning erection. I opened what windows could be opened, showered, and made breakfast: prosciutto and melon, croissants, St. Andre cheese, strawberries, freshly squeezed orange juice, tea. Simon preferred tea to coffee. I had meant the occasion to be festive—the first time Simon had spent the entire weekend—showing him off to everybody at the engagement party, rubbing Dolores's nose in him. Now he had this meeting in Quebec City. My hand rested on the neck of the champagne bottle as I debated whether to open it. Simon padded into the kitchen in bare feet and nibbled on a croissant. I closed the refrigerator and carried the tray to the table in the living room.

"Nice flowers."

"Alex brought them over from Mother's garden."

"I've never seen daylilies and roses in combination." He touched the petals of a speckled tiger lily. The arrangement covered the spectrum of yellow, orange, and red, and I thought the mix worked, not that I had much choice, only having the one vase. I poured his orange juice and lifted the top of the teapot to bang the bags with a spoon.

"You seem put out."

"I'm just disappointed."

"You needn't take it out on the tea. I'll be back later tonight."

"I thought we'd have the entire weekend. You've been so busy lately, I've hardly seen you." I looked out over the sweltering rooftops. A shimmer of vapor animated the very air.

"I'm sorry, but this deal is extremely complex."

I poured the tea and helped myself to three spoons of sugar and some cream.

"Have some melon."

"I ate one in the kitchen," I said.

"Oh. Croissant?"

I took two, and a slice of cheese.

"What are you doing this morning?"

"I don't know. I thought I'd check on Connie."

"How's he been?"

"Okay, I guess."

In fact, it had been a very strange few weeks. After I'd discovered his cache I realized that I had to show him my work on the tomb because it was purely dumb luck he hadn't gone up in the year I'd been carving. But that didn't explain the cupid egg. Who had put it there? Who else was in on the secret? Why hadn't they mentioned to Connie that someone had been carving flowers all over the marble? I explained how I'd found the place from cemetery records and fixed it up as a surprise. It was a surprise, all right. Connie's face blanched, but he recovered quickly and expressed guarded pleasure. By the time we reached the mausoleum he had worked himself into a fair facsimile of delight with my effort. I didn't mention the cache, nor did he, but I noticed that he tried the door to see that it was still locked.

The following week I snuck up and did a quick inventory, and sure enough, several gold bars were missing. The financing for Ivan's deal, no doubt. That same week, Connie discharged a gun, killing a raccoon he'd thought was a prowler and inciting the neighbors to register a complaint with the police. He hid the weapon and feigned innocence, having had Alex dispose of the incriminating furry corpse.

I was also summoned to the house to witness his will. That made me queasy. Malenfant, Jules's lawyer, sat on the couch with the necessary documents while Alex and I waited. Connie explained that I was the principal legatee, and he had provided for Alex in the form of an annuity. We signed, and that was that, although I had no idea what was what and I didn't want to ask. Connie's apparent immortality was something I accepted on faith.

"He's been invited to the party but I don't know if he'll go." I slathered cheese on the croissant and bit off the end. The cheese was too ripe and tasted like unwashed gym sock. I ate it anyway.

"I take it he doesn't like your sister."

"Not much."

"So he won't give her the fake egg for a wedding present?" He drank his tea clear and ate a slice of prosciutto and melon. Had I mentioned that Leslie wanted the egg—had wanted the egg since she was three? Odd that he'd remembered.

"Not bloody likely, since it's mine."

"Oh."

"The original belonged to my great-grandmother. I doubt if he'll give her anything."

We finished our breakfast in silence. Simon stood and unzipped a leather case he'd left in the corner of the room. He removed a tripod, extended its legs, and attached a camera. For a moment I was afraid he wanted to take my picture, me in a bathrobe with my hair snagged back in a barrette.

"I'll clear off the table," he said, unexpectedly, and stacked the empty plates one on top of the other to convey to the kitchen. "Bring your sculptures out."

"What?"

"Get those carvings. I'm going to photograph them to show to my friend. The one with the gallery."

"Simon . . . "

"Go." He took the dishes to the kitchen and dumped them with a clatter into the sink. I retreated to the bedroom and lifted one of the marbles off the closet floor. Were they good enough? I touched the suggestion of a paw. Well, here was my chance to find out.

Simon had wiped the table clean and moved it against a blank wall. He removed the sculpture from my hands and placed it in the center of the table, then fixed the flash to reflect off the ceiling. I brought the others out as he snapped. For each work, he took three exposures at varied angles. My self-portrait in stone was too heavy to lift, so he photographed it in situ.

"Are there any more?" he asked, and I admitted that several more were boxed in the storage room. He made me get those, and committed them to film as well. I'd almost forgotten my white marble phase, a series of stylized children contorting themselves in play. Then there was my effort with granite, where I was more interested in the color and texture of the material than the subject matter. As I recalled, there was no subject matter, just amorphous shaping. Simon conscientiously recorded them all.

"That's it?" he asked.

"That's it."

He packed up his equipment, helped me put away the sculptures, then departed for his day-long meeting in Quebec. After sulking for a bit, I dressed and stopped off at the grocery store. It, at least, was air-conditioned, and I spent half an hour browsing in the frozen foods section, examining Stouffer's dinners as though they were objets d'art, before gathering up Connie's bananas, nectarines, bran flakes, seven-grain bread, butter, milk, and barbecued chicken. When I arrived at the house I found Alex and Bartleby asleep on the kitchen floor and stepped over them to put the food away. Bartleby growled in his sleep. As I was compressing the bag to stuff into the garbage, Alex woke.

"How'd you get in?" he asked, rubbing his eyes. I was alarmed to see that he had a shotgun at his side.

"The door, Alex, and what the hell are you doing with that?" I pointed at the gun. He could have blown off my head. Jesus.

"Oh. Connie gave it to me. There've been men ... "

"Alex, there have been raccoons."

"No, Greer. Really. I saw someone."

"It was probaby the meter man." What was Connie thinking of, giving the boy a gun?

"Meter men don't come at two in the morning, Greer," he corrected patiently.

"Oh, never mind, but please, put the gun away. You could hurt someone."

He regarded the weapon as though the thought hadn't occurred to him. It probably hadn't. Bartleby scrambled to his feet and crawled under the sink.

"Are you going to the party?"

"No. Wasn't invited," he said resignedly. Alex did Mother's gardening free, would have licked Leslie's car clean if she'd asked, and they didn't even include him in family events.

"Would you like to come with me?"

"I should stay here and watch the house." He scratched and wiped his nose on his grubby cuff.

"You should have received an invitation, you know. There was probably a mix-up."

"No," he said simply. "Mrs. Payton said I wasn't to come Saturday 'cause of the party, but to come Sunday and help clean up." He shrugged meekly and went about feeding his dog. "I don't fit, you know. I don't know what to say to people, and Bartleby doesn't like parties anyway."

I left him and went upstairs, where Connie was rattling the handle to the flue. The metal damper clanked open, and several desiccated birds dropped into the grate, then a gun. He glanced

up, plucked it from the soot, and wiped it clean with a handkerchief.

"Good morning, Greer. I didn't expect you today."

"I brought your groceries." I didn't know much about guns
but the revolver looked old, something Al Capone might have
wielded—big, heavy, dark, and gleaming. I didn't make any
comment.

"Thank you."

"Are you going to the party?"

"I haven't decided."

"Leslie expects the egg."

"Let her expect. Should I give her my eye?"

"Which one?" I laughed. Despite the fact that he was polish-
ing a gun, he seemed to be back in his usual good humor. I was
relieved.

"I thought the good one. She could place it on a little stand
and shock her guests." He removed the last traces of soot and
wedged the gun between the couch cushions. To give the
Fabergé eye to Leslie was an inspired idea. It was altogether too
weird for words. He said he'd tried to wear it for a while, after
all, his mother had gone to the trouble of having it made.
According to legend, a craftsman had copied it from a real eye,
obtained from a St. Petersburg hospital and preserved in for-
maldehyde. But the sentiment was misplaced. It was unsani-
tary. There had been repeated infections, and he was eventually
fitted for a properly designed glass eye. The old one rested in its
creamy calfskin box, an oddity, and although indisputably
Fabergé, virtually worthless. At best it might fetch a few thousand bucks for its novelty value.

"I think that's a terrific idea."

"Good. I'll wrap it up."

"Has she ever seen it?"

"No."

"Has Dolores?"

"I think not."

"That's wonderful. Did you know the bastards didn't invite
Alex?"

"Did you expect them to?" He wiggled the gun out again and walked over to the curio cabinet, where he found a bullet in a teacup commemorating the silver jubilee of George V. He flicked open the cylinder, dropped the shell into the empty chamber, and snapped it all together again with such fluency of movement I was in awe. Perhaps guns were like bicycles—once learned, never forgotten.

"Don't you have a hair appointment?" he asked.

"What? Yes." I looked at my watch. It was twelve-thirty. Connie flipped the safety and laid the gun on the mantel.

"I'll see you at the party."

"Shall I drive you?" I asked.

"Not necessary. I have things to do." He smiled.

Dolores had outdone herself. There was a bar set up on the terrace outside the dining room. Little café tables and little gilded rental chairs littered the lawn. The crowd was filling out, and Leslie and Yves greeted all as they funneled through the house and into the garden via the dining room. I didn't know anyone, since the guest list was composed almost exclusively of their friends. I noticed several priests among their number, including the archbishop of Montreal. Malenfant was there with his wife, who looked as though she'd rather have been elsewhere. I recognized faces from the society page but names eluded me, and there were men in altogether too somber suits who had to be Yves's associates. Dolores flustered about, pestering the caterers.

I saw Ivan sitting in the gazebo smoking a cigar. What the hell, I thought, and in my flapping cotton-polyester blend vertical-striped dress (it resembled mattress ticking) I trotted across the yard to join him. He stood and bowed. I sat and removed the silly picture hat the salesgirl had convinced me I needed to cap the ensemble.

"You have no drink."

"I came in through the hedge and missed the bar, but I see they're passing a tray." The breeze had died so the heat at five seemed more intense than at noon. It was only marginally cooler in the gazebo than in the direct sunlight. A few of the women had had the foresight to carry paper fans and were waving them in the wilting warmth.

"How did you wangle an invite?" I asked, wiping the sweat off my upper lip with a flimsy paper napkin. Ivan shrugged and tried to kiss my hand. I pulled it away.

"An invitation found its way to my suite. Since I am a relative . . . "

"But they didn't invite your son."

"Alex? Well . . . you understand he is a social liability. Shall I get you a drink? They're serving Bellinis, a sickening concoction of peach nectar, peach liqueur, and sparkling wine."

"Sounds good to me."

"That's unusual perfume."

"Citronella. Have you seen Connie?"

"Stanzi hasn't arrived."

A maid brought us drinks, followed shortly by another bearing a tray of shrimp speared on sticks with melon balls. Three wasps hovered over the food. I took a couple of sticks and tried to ignore the pests.

"I was speaking with a friend who tells me that Stanzi did buy the blue egg."

"Yes. I know. He said he sold it to a man in Singapore."

"I don't think so," I answered. "I think he kept it."

He drew a shrimp off the toothpick with his perfect white false teeth.

"I know of three other eggs he has acquired over the years and suspect two others. I only hope he has them in a safe place. Has he? Have you seen them?"

"How can I have seen what doesn't exist?"

"They exist," he stated firmly. Dolores barged over and asked us if we'd move—the musicians were going to set up in the gazebo. We resettled ourselves at a table, regrettably near the fish pond, as the sort of jazz, sort of easy-listening quartet struck up their rendition of "Diamonds on the Soles of Her Shoes." Fortunately, they hadn't bothered with amplifiers. I moved my legs to escape Uncle Ivan's foot, which was rubbing my calf. Suddenly and with unexpected force, he grabbed my hand and shouted:

"Where are they?"

Everyone in the garden turned in our direction. He regained his composure but still clasped my fingers. I was surprised at his strength.

"Where are they?" he repeated.

"What are you talking about?"

"The eggs. Where has he hidden them?"

"I don't know anything about any eggs. The only egg Connie has is a replica of one his mother owned." My mind was spinning.

"You aren't a very good liar, but I won't press you. It's clear that your loyalty is with Stanzi, and you wouldn't tell me anyway. I don't hold that against you. Just one question. Does Stanzi know you've seen them?"

Oh, he was smooth. I nearly answered him.

"Look, Ivan. I don't know anything. What is it about you people and your stupid eggs?" I shouted, then realizing, lowered my voice to a loud whisper. "You're behaving like a little boy who wants to get his mitts on someone else's toys. Is that why you're luring him to Russia—so you can find whatever it is you think he has?"

"Luring him to Russia? What are you talking about?"

"I suppose it's just a coincidence that he got his hands on something you wanted, then you turned up here, *and* his brother contacts him after seventy years in the grave, all within a few weeks? What about the wedding ring, Ivan? You stole it from your aunt's corpse, didn't you? And the egg?"

"I did no such thing. I found ... "

"Oh, yes, we all know the story. You found the egg at an auction in Detroit in 1932 and gave it to Connie and all was forgiven."

"Then you know he has the genuine egg as well as the replica."

"He sold the authentic one."

"If you believe he would sell his mother's egg, then you are a stupid girl, and that is unthinkable. Connie may have a replica, but he also has the original of the yellow pigeon egg. And he has the blue egg, and at least four more that I know of."

"Eggs, eggs, eggs. This conversation is ridiculous. What difference does it make anyway, if he has six eggs? If he does, they're his and have zip to do with you," I hissed and stood. As the sun was lowering, so were the mosquitoes mustering. I snatched my drink and walked away.

Connie had arrived and was standing in a circle of people that included Dolores, Leslie, the director of the museum, and a gnome of a woman I couldn't place. Connie gestured me over and placed his arm around my shoulders. He smelled of citronella, too. I detected a whiff of 6-12 coming from Leslie. Veterans all. Grandfather was looking very dapper in a blazer, white flannels, and a boater. The quartet had launched into a barely unrecognizable string of Cole Porter melodies. Connie handed the square box he was holding to Leslie, whose eyes lit up greedily as she attacked the wrapping. His indifferent utilization of graph paper for the purpose passed unnoticed as it dropped to the grass. She undid the gold-plated clasp, opened the box, and yelped—quite literally, yelped. Connie had positioned the eye to stare directly out of its swaddling satin, and the effect was startling if you hadn't known what to expect. Leslie raised her eyes to Connie with horror and distaste.

"It's my eye," he said unhelpfully and walked away. Dolores looked aghast.

"What sort of present is that?" she asked, pointing at the thing as though it was real. The museum director, who was made of sterner stuff, plucked the eye from its hollow and examined the sphere.

"Curious," was all he said, unwilling to commit an error of expertise.

"It was made by Fabergé." I pointed out the double-headed eagle minutely present in the lower left-hand side of the picture of the house. "When Grandfather lost his eye, his mother had it made. Look at the little veins."

"Ugh," expressed Mother.

"Is it valuable?" asked Leslie. The museum director shrugged. The little gnome woman took it next and stared at the eye side for about thirty seconds.

"I should imagine it's unique," she offered. "But you can't really do anything with it, can you?"

"You could balance it on an egg cup and display it in a curio case, house side out, of course." The director took it from the gnome and returned it to Leslie, who grimaced.

"If a value could be placed on it, and I donated it to the museum, I'd be eligible for a tax deduction, wouldn't I?"

The director squirmed like a worm on a hook. What would the museum want with a thing like that?

"In theory," he replied, diplomatically.

"What about that show you're putting on, the fakes show?" Leslie persisted.

"Apparently this isn't a fake."

"It's a fake eye."

"That isn't the point of the show. It would have to be a fake Fabergé to qualify."

"Oh, yeah."

I thought of Connie's egg.

"What show is this?" I asked, my interest piqued.

Connie had wandered back with a tumbler of Scotch and was smiling happily. "Yes, do tell."

The director looked a little embarrassed. His past three shows had been dismal failures, and he was sensitive to comment or criticism. I didn't blame him. I'd seen the shows and they were terrible. No one went. Money was lost. The minister of cultural affairs was unhappy and threatened to cut their allocation.

"It's a show of great fakes and forgeries," he mumbled.

Connie perked up. "I know where you could borrow a slew of fake Turners."

"Pecks?" asked the director, wearily.

"Yes. How did you guess?"

"We've been offered eighty-seven Pecks so far. The man

never slept. We could do a Beamish Peck retrospective. If only he'd imitated someone other than Turner," he moaned.

"Who else is included?" I asked. "De Hory?"

"Of course. Eight. A Modigliani, the Vermeer, a couple of lesser-known Cezannes ... "

"Van Meegeren?"

"Naturally."

"How about Dolovo?" asked Connie, a wicked twinkle in his eye.

"Who?" asked the director. The gnome woman, who I had finally placed as the social columnist for the local paper, wandered off for a refill and never returned.

"Igor Dolovo. Surely you know of him?"

"No. I don't believe I do."

Leslie and Dolores made their excuses and departed to mingle with more interesting guests. I noticed Leslie hand the eye to Yves.

"Dolovo was an extremely gifted and prolific craftsman who, with the blessing of the revolutionary government, painted icons in the style of the era of Peter the Great. He flourished in Moscow between 1925 and 1950, all the while selling to foreign tourists and splitting the take with local officials. They kept him supplied with the necessary materials: gold leaf, gesso, pigments, and old wood paneling from churches. It was illegal to export genuine treasures and religious art was prohibited anyway, but customs officials in Moscow were on the take from Dolovo and, I expect, from the tourists. Their supposed authenticity was confirmed by experts less expert than Dolovo, and when the value of antique art objects shot through the roof, many were sold to museums at obscenely inflated prices. It wasn't until recently, when a Russian expert was asked by a museum in Arizona to give an evaluation for insurance purposes, that the old scam was detected. The man, it turned out, had apprenticed under Dolovo. But you must know all this. There was a piece in *Connoisseur* magazine a few years back."

The director nodded but didn't say anything. He was a political appointee and didn't know much about art.

"Come now. Your museum does, after all, own three."

The director glared at Connie, quickly glanced around to see if anyone else had heard the allegation, stammered a few incoherent syllables, then walked away.

"Could be a fun show," said Connie with a mischievous grin.

"I'll make book that every loan will be anonymous."

"I dare say. Do you think Leslie appreciated her gift?"

I trudged upstairs to Daddy's sanctuary to find him in his usual place watching *E.T.* on the video. Two of the Cats were squished on either side of him in the recliner, and the other two sprawled on the shag carpeting. They were all sucking Fudgsicles, even Daddy. One of the boys put his finger to his lips when he saw me and shushed softly. E.T. was drunk and staggering through the house. I pulled up a chair and joined them. The caterers brought a platter of food when the film was over, then Daddy popped one of the Indiana Jones series into the slot. The Cats were enthralled. I'd never seen them sit still for so many hours. They'd yanked cushions off the couch, and in spite of themselves were growing heavy-lidded. I wondered who was responsible for returning them home. I ventured back to the party. An orange moon hung low in the west, candles flickered, and guests attempted to dance to the quartet's medley from *South Pacific*. One of the priests (a tenor manqué) belted out "Some Enchanted Evening" at the top of his lungs, Ivan was taking a turn with the gnome lady, and Connie was having an animated discussion with Yves. I couldn't see my sister.

"Mother, where's Leslie?" I confronted Dolores as she swept by, carrying a lazy butler filled with ashes and butts.

"I don't know. Around somewhere."

"The boys are exhausted. Who's taking them home?"

"Leslie, I presume," she said and bustled off. Fat lot she cared. As long as the boys weren't creating chaos, it really didn't matter to anyone what they were up to. I searched awhile longer but couldn't find my sister anywhere so I informed Yves I'd take the boys home myself and see them safely into bed. The singing priest was starting in on "Bloody Mary," and Ivan groped my bum as I walked to the house.

The kitchen was lit. I drove my car around to the rear entrance, parked behind Leslie's Volvo, and herded the children to the back door. Madame helped me with their baths because I couldn't bear to send them to bed sticky—not that they cared. Children seem to regard traces of ice cream, lemonade, Fudgsicles, and jam tarts as a natural augmentation to skin surface. I scrubbed their arms, faces, and legs and committed each one to Madame's toweling. They protested it was too hot for pajamas and we didn't insist. They collapsed on their sheets. The new central air-conditioning wasn't terribly effective on the third floor, and we plugged in a couple of oscillating fans. Madame bade me *bonsoir* and returned to the kitchen and her television. I kissed the boys, turned off the overhead, and headed downstairs.

I wondered if Simon was back from Quebec yet. The brown linoleum of the upper staircase gave way to a boldly patterned broadloom on the second floor. Moonlight, pure and silvery, made it unnecessary for me to switch on the lights. I had to admit, the house was looking nice, although it still gave the impression of an institution, albeit an expensive institution. The upper hallway was a mezzanine overlooking the atrium. Paintings adorned the walls between the bedroom doors, and fuchsias hung suspended midway between the ceiling and the marble balustrade. I took advantage of one of the small benches and sat to pry my shoes from my poor swollen feet.

Where was a phone? Did Yves have a study? I'd phone Simon and ask him to open the champagne and draw the bath. Too bad Leslie was expected home. I could have invited him here for a skinny-dip in the jungle pool. Oh well. I massaged my metatarsals and imagined what it would be like to have Simon rub every square inch of my body with scented oil. Where did one buy the oil? One of those sleazy stores with vibrators and studded leather jockstraps in the window?

I opened my eyes and noticed that the light had changed. Most of the illumination came from below, and shimmering reflections danced off the walls. I peered through the balusters to see that the swimming-pool lights had been turned on and were shining up through the glass floor. Automatic timer? I hadn't heard anyone come in. Maybe one of the staff was taking a midnight dip. My feet wouldn't fit back in my shoes, and I resigned myself to driving home barefoot.

There was a phone in the front hall. I circled to the wide-branching staircase and had just reached the landing when Leslie danced out from behind a pillar and into the center of the atrium. She was dripping wet and stark naked and as she spun, beads of water sprayed from her hair. Oh God. I'd been through that picture before and was about to sneak upstairs and take the back staircase when I heard his voice.

I froze and stared over the railing. He, too, was naked, dripping, carrying water in one of the boys' plastic buckets, which he splashed over my twirling sister. She shrieked in mock fury and flew at him. He threw the bucket aside with a clatter and caught her thin wrists in his hands, laughing. They wrestled briefly until he had her pinned and thrashing on the glistening green floor. She pulled his hair, and he struck her across the face. I flinched with the force of it but she had her teeth in his shoulder. As his hands went to her breasts she clutched his back and they kissed, if it could be called that for its violence. Then they had sex, every which way, screaming and moaning and giggling as I watched. Simon and Leslie. He finally threw her over his shoulder and carried her down the darkened hallway. The light from the pool shivered as they jumped in, and sounds of chattering monkeys rose through the open basement door.

Too stunned even to cry, I walked in a daze to my car, drove home, and drank the champagne by myself—then a bottle of gin. At one point I thought I heard the doorbell. Maybe I answered it. Maybe Simon let himself in with the key I'd stupidly given him. Maybe I even yelled at him—I don't remember—but when I woke the following morning, his bag was gone.

★

I hunched over my worktable with an ice pack tied to my head, smashing random scraps of red carnelian with my little hammer and chisel, wishing they were Simon's face. Goddamn goddamn goddamn was my hushed mantra as tiny fragments of red stone littered my bird sketches. It reminded me of dried blood. Simon's dried blood. Smash. They hadn't seen me. Simon didn't know I knew. What did Leslie want? Certainly not to risk her union with Yves. Yves had money. Simon didn't. Red dust fell from the paper to my thighs. How could I have deluded myself that he was attracted to me? He probably just wanted to get to Connie. The blue egg. Connie's cache. Well, no one would. Not Simon, not Ivan, not Dolores, not Leslie. I shuddered, thinking how I'd taken the man right to the tomb, but he hadn't demonstrated more than a casual interest, and I'm certain he had no idea a fortune had been sitting on the other side of a rusty iron door. If he believed I knew, he also had to know I wouldn't lead him straight to it. I may be naive, but I'm not stupid. Smash. The doorbell rang. I folded the paper into a cone and funneled the dust and fragments into my wastepaper basket. My drawing stared up at me. Ravens. Ravens on the wing, ravens perched, ravens nesting. An unkindness of ravens. A little more than kin, and less than kind. Bitch. I tossed aside the sketch and repressed the urge to pelt a chunk of lapis the size of a fist through the plate glass window into the clustering thunderheads. Instead, I answered the door.

"Greer." Connie stood in the hall holding a large brown paper parcel that looked as though it might be a painting. "Where were you?"

"What do you mean? I was here with a hangover. Where was I supposed to be?" I left him at the door and sank into my chair clutching at my throbbing head.

"The auction at the tearoom."

"I forgot."

"I got the painting for you." He propped the package against a wall and cut the twine with a penknife. The heavy paper fell away, leaving the beady-eyed little girl in furs with a monkey, staring at me. I felt like vomiting.

"You wanted it, didn't you?" He went into the kitchen and reappeared a moment later, emptying his flask into a glass.

"Yes. Thank you. Excuse my ingratitude. I'm feeling kind of shitty."

"So it would appear. Want to talk?"

"Simon is fucking Leslie."

"Oh. I see." He took a long draw on the whiskey and placed both flask and glass on the table. The first raindrops began falling against the plate glass window.

"Aren't you going to make a snide comment about the charming and honorable Mr. Beauchamp?" I said defensively, but he only sat on the arm of the chair and hugged me.

CHAPTER SIXTEEN

I had never seen such a storm. If there was any truth in the maxim "happy is the bride the sun shines on," then Leslie was destined for misery. I inched up the road, visibility being practically zero, and parked in front of Dolores's house. Thunder growled in the distance, and gale-force winds worked the deluge into a perfect frenzy of wet. I'd just come from the hairdresser and there was no way my do would remain intact between the curb and the door. Oh well. Who'd notice me anyway? I pulled the handle and the wind wrenched the door from my hand. The hinges tore and it slammed against the front fender. With considerable difficulty, I was able to ram it back into place, although it wouldn't latch. I had some rope in the trunk, but didn't dare open it since I estimated the damage had already exceeded $1,500. I secured the door from the inside with my trench coat belt and hung on to the door for dear life as I climbed out the passenger side. By the time I rang Dolores's bell, I was a wreck.

"Greer!"

"Don't start, Mother. The signs are not auspicious and I'm half inclined to go home to bed."

She closed the door and helped me off with my coat, which an unfamiliar maid carried away, dripping, down the length of the hall. I stepped out of my sodden shoes and kicked them against the wall. Water streamed down my body and pooled at my feet. From the kitchen I could hear a radio blaring a weather watch.

"Leslie's hairdresser is here. Perhaps he could do something with you."

"Ether would be a good start. I'll just go downstairs first and throw my clothes in the drier. Okay?"

"Fine. By the way, have you seen my father?"

"Yes."

"Is he coming today?"

"No."

"Why not?" she squeaked. Appearances, appearances.

"Because he's in Leningrad."

"Leningrad? But you said you'd seen him."

"I did. Yesterday. I drove him to the airport." His visa request finally approved, he'd moved quickly. One might have thought his two suitcases had been packed in expectation. As well as clothes, he'd taken the Fabergé animals to show to his brother. He gave me the address of an associate with whom he'd be staying, then we checked his luggage and shared a meal before his flight was called. An alarm didn't sound as he stepped through the metal detector, so I supposed he'd returned his gun to the fireplace flue. I waved as the moving sidewalk carried him away to the boarding lounge and hung around for another forty-five minutes until the plane was air-borne.

"Couldn't he have waited one more day?"

"I guess not. Look, I'm freezing. Do you mind . . . " I held the soaking skirt of my dress to emphasize my discomfort.

"Go . . . go." She turned toward the stairs, muttering under her breath. Two attractive women I'd never met floated down, visions in cloudlike mauve tulle. I sensed a headache coming on.

It felt like the night of my high-school graduation. I lay on the guest room bed and stared glumly at the purple atrocity. It was the same shade as grape juice. Leslie's hairdresser had attacked my hair with a curling iron, and the result was a cross between Shirley Temple and the bride of Frankenstein. I was almost grateful for the picture hat. I'd wrapped a sheet around myself and was listening to a radio phone-in show with citizens describing the havoc wrought by the storm. One lady was in hysterics, recounting how a neighbor's tree had just leveled her brand-new, fifty-thousand-dollar solarium. Then Leslie walked in and shut the door behind her.

She was quite the most beautiful bride I'd ever seen. Her hair was tied back in a severe knot from which a length of veil was attached with a small coronet of seed pearls. Her dress was creamy satin, appliquéd overall with a scattering of tiny pearls, long sleeved, the neck cut straight across the shoulder blades, and fitted to accentuate her tiny waist. She sat beside me on the bed and switched off the radio.

"They're taking pictures soon. You'd better get dressed."

"You look nice," I said grudgingly.

"Thank you." She examined her nails. Denuded of their usual reds or pinks, a sheen of pearl was their only polish.

"Is that all?"

"What?"

"Did you come in here to tell me to get dressed?"

As though remembering what she was wearing, she stood and smoothed the front of her gown.

"No. I wanted to ask you if you'd heard from Simon."

"You've got a hell of a nerve!" I snapped.

"I know you found out about us, but I haven't heard from him since July. You've been seeing him, haven't you? Is he all right?"

"I assume so. He's called. I've hung up."

"He doesn't call me."

"Aw. The jilted bride."

"I was worried. I could never reach him at his home."

"No surprise. He's rarely there. Now would you please go?"

"Look, if Simon's back with you, I'm glad, really. I just must know if he's OK. It's been six weeks. He hasn't answered the messages I left on his machine. I hate loose ends. I like to remain friends with people I've been fond of."

"Fond of? Well, I suppose if they like you, they won't blackmail you."

"Oh, please!" She was about to run her hand through her hair but stopped before she did any damage. Her concern appeared genuine. The wind was still buffeting the window, and the sky, if anything, was darker than before. It hurt to think about Simon. I studied Leslie's flawless face. He hadn't seen her—hadn't called her—yet he'd called me. Could it be he really cared? You can't fake affection, can you? He was always so kind. Maybe there was a chance for us after all. I had to know, even if it meant begging Leslie for information.

"I haven't spoken to him since the night I found out you two were lovers. I was hurt and angry. I hung up on him when he called. Eventually, he stopped calling."

"Oh." She sighed and picked at the lacquer on her left thumb and peeled a section. If I didn't ask her then, the opportunity might never again present itself, nor would I have the nerve.

"I have to ask you something. Did Simon ever talk about me, when you were together? Please. I must know the truth. What does Simon think of me?"

She deliberated for a moment, staring at her satin shoes, then answered without artifice or apparent motive. "He likes you. He has a great respect for your intelligence and ability—says you're wasted in a dump like Ponsonby's. He wouldn't allow me to say anything against you. One day when I made a passing comment about your weight, he snapped at me and said I might have looks, but you had heart." She said her piece without once making eye contact. For the first time in our lives, I found myself respecting her.

"Then why did he cheat on me?" I couldn't help myself. The tears just flowed, soundlessly, unbidden.

"Because I went after him. I'm sorry. I really am. It was just another episode for me, and you love him. You must understand, I adore men. I love the way they smell and their firm little asses, their prickly beard stubble and their strong hairy legs. I love their forcefulness and their deep voices. I love the electric charge that surges through me when I'm lusting after someone, and I love screwing, but the bottom line is, it just isn't important. It's

like listening to a favorite piece of music or having a nice long
bath. Simon didn't love me any more than I loved him, but I have
yet to meet the man who would pass up available twat. Trust me.
It was meaningless fun. That's all. Just fun.''

"He likes me?''

"I guess so. It's the first time I've been dumped, and I can
tell you, the experience is not pleasant.''

He liked me. He hadn't let Leslie make snide remarks. He
thought I had talent and tried to encourage me in my work.
There was something more than greed going on. I experienced
a novel gratitude toward my sister, for it must have cost her to
make that admission. I tore a tissue from the box and wiped my
eyes, smearing mascara. "I don't know where Simon is. He's
probably off in South America or something. I suppose he had
his fill of us.'' I blew my nose.

"I suppose.'' Just discussing her concern, and having me
reassure her that there was no special import to Simon's vanish-
ing act, had relieved her. She adjusted her veil in the mirror and
pinched her cheeks. "You'd better dress. I'll help you with the
buttons. They're a bitch. You can freshen your makeup later.''

The only way we could enter the limos without getting
drenched was to have them back into the big double garage that
was connected to the house. There was a bridal canopy at the
church end, if it hadn't blown away. The bridesmaids had just
pulled out, and the second limo that was to carry me and
Dolores was backing up, when Alex staggered into the garage,
Bartleby limp in his arms. Dolores recoiled in horror as Alex
approached me.

"Greer. Help me,'' he sobbed. "Bartleby's dying.''

I helped him lower the dog to the ground, and an examination of the dripping, matted fur revealed a wound in his chest.
Blood was still flowing, but his eyes were already glassy.

"Greer, don't touch that animal. You'll soil the dress.''

"Oh, shut up.''

Dolores waited for a few moments, clearly unable to believe

that I considered an injured dog more important than my own sister's wedding. Finally realizing that I wasn't coming with her, she stepped into the car, which drove away. I tore my hat off, grabbed an old tartan car blanket from a nearby shelf, and wrapped it around Bartleby. His tongue lolled out the side of his mouth, and I feared I detected blood mixed with his drool. I lifted him in my arms and we hurried through the storm to Alex's truck.

The receptionist at the animal hospital immediately led us to an examining room where I laid Bartleby on a stainless steel table. The vet came a moment later and unfolded the blanket, but I knew, and he knew, even before he placed the stethoscope on the dog's rib cage, that we were too late. Alex stood weeping in the corner, his arms wrapped tightly across his chest.

"What happened?" He removed the stethoscope from his ears, addressing the question to me. I shrugged and turned to Alex.

"Alex," I asked, as gently as I could. "How did Bartleby get hurt?"

"How is he? Is he going to be okay?" The tears poured down his face and he began to rock.

"Alex, Bartleby's gone."

He flung himself at the dog and buried his face in his wet fur. The vet disengaged him from the dead animal and directed him into my arms. I patted his back and repeated meaningless consolations in his ear as the vet cleaned Bartleby's wound with gauze. All I could see for a few minutes was his back. Why was he taking so long over a dead dog? My question was answered when he turned, holding a pair of forceps. They held a bullet.

"The dog appears to have been shot."

"Shot? Alex ... how did Bartleby get shot? Alex?" He shook and clung to my soaking purple gown. What a sight we must have looked. "I'm sorry. I don't think we're going to get an answer. He's in shock."

"I'll have to report this."

"Report?"

"To the police. All gunshot incidents have to be reported."

He rifled through a drawer until he found a form and asked me who owned the dog, etc. I looked at the clock and figured Leslie would be marching down the aisle about then.

"Alex. Please!" I pried him away from me and tried to penetrate his grief. He made an effort to control himself, placed a hand on Bartleby's head (which seemed to have a calming effect), and sniffed back some tears.

"Alex ... how did Bartleby get shot?"

"I don't know."

"Weren't you there when it happened?"

"No."

"Where did it happen?"

"I don't know. He came home bleeding and collapsed."

The vet sighed and wrote on the form. "I see this occasionally. Some bozo takes a potshot at a defenseless creature for kicks. Probably from a car." He shook his head in disgust. "Would you like us to take care of things?" He indicated Bartleby with his pen.

"Alex. What do you want to do with Bartleby?"

"I'm taking him home."

I had a fleeting vision of the dog, stuffed, like Trigger.

"I'll bury him somewhere," he added, to my relief.

"Not legal in the city," said the vet.

"Then I'll take him to the country."

"Fine." The doctor folded the blanket over the dog, then dropped the slug into a small plastic pouch, which he stapled onto the form. Alex closed Bartleby's eyes and cradled him in his arms.

Alex wanted to be alone, so he let me off at my apartment. I dropped the purple dress into the kitchen sink and climbed into a hot bath. The storm had abated, but I didn't for a moment consider attending the reception. Once in my bathrobe, I poured myself a stiff drink and sat staring at the telephone for about fifteen minutes before I punched in the familiar numbers. The line clicked and after one ring Simon's answering

machine engaged. The sound of his voice filled me with such longing.

"Greetings. You have reached 555-7569. I'm not home at the moment, but if you leave your name and number at the sound of the beep, I'll get back to you as soon as I can."

"Simon. It's Greer. I'm sorry I've behaved like such an idiot. Please call. I can't begin to tell you how much I've missed you."

I placed the receiver gently in the cradle and wondered how long it would be before he phoned. He might be away for months. I took a long draw on the cognac.

So I'd wait months.

CHAPTER SEVENTEEN

I fell asleep in the chair and was awakened the next morning by the telephone. Simon. I shook the fog from my brain and picked up the receiver. The voice on the other end was distant, echoing, and heavily accented.

"Mees Greer Pay-ton? I haff regret to inform dat your granfa-zer haff ac-cident. His misfor-tunate to die."

The voice continued in its alien stutter, telling me where I might claim the body, and which authorities to contact if I chose to go there. I automatically took down the details but my mind was numb. Connie dead? How was it possible? I had been with him less than forty-eight hours ago. Accident? He wasn't careless. He was the least careless person I knew.

He had been struck by a bus on the Nevsky Prospect and had succumbed to massive internal injuries—another member of my family to die of unnatural causes. The Leningrad hospital had contacted me because I was marked as next of kin in his passport. Struck by a bus? Could he have had another stroke? I wondered if that sort of thing would be detectable in a postmortem. Would they have bothered doing a postmortem on a ninety-five-year-old they believed fell in front of a bus? I hung up the phone and stared at the portrait of the little girl from the tearoom. More likely he was pushed.

I performed my morning ablutions in a daze. Connie was dead, but there was no reality in the words. I tried to picture it, to imagine him falling, but another figure always grafted itself into my vision. Ivan. I pictured Connie and Ivan walking along the street, talking, laughing. I could see the bus approaching and drawing into the curb. I could sense the thrust of Ivan's hand against Connie's back. But why? And how could he have hated him for so long and have his hatred crystallize into such a vicious act just when their time on earth was drawing to an end? Maybe that was something I'd never learn. I dialed the Ritz and had the desk connect me with Ivan's room. There was no answer.

The bells chimed from the church across the street and I remembered it was Sunday. The Soviet consulate would be closed. I'd have to wait to apply for a visa. I wished Simon would return my call. After pacing the floor for an hour I decided to drive up to Connie's.

The big house, shrouded in the blowsy ostentatious growth of late August, was still, and the damp hollow ring of abandonment pervaded the atmosphere. Blackened curls of burned paper rocked in the fire grate as puffs of air found their way down the partially open flue. I twisted the damper handle and the gun fell into the ashes. I placed it on the mantel beside my little dog. A few boxes lay strewn around. I flipped open the lid of one. Nestled in the shredded wood was a small oval platter— the swan service he'd purchased in Manaus. I thought he'd sold it. Maybe he had. Maybe it was waiting for delivery but I had no instructions. There was nothing more.

Crumpled pages of newspaper littered the empty rooms, newspapers from all over the world that had wrapped objects, with print in Chinese, Arabic, Portuguese, Indian. I kicked through a mound of them on the filthy white floor of the upstairs bathroom, remembering when the hexagonal tiles had gleamed, the great claw-footed tub had frothed with scented bubble bath, and huge fluffy white towels were draped over the shining chrome rack, specially fitted into the heating system so the towels were always hot and dry. Connie's shaving cup sat on the glass shelf under the mirror, but his razor was gone. A saucer brimful of cigar ashes was balanced on the rim of the large pedestal sink. The screen was gone from the window and

fingers of ivy had poked into the room and pinched the soap
rack with their grasping tendrils. One shoot had wound its way
half across the shower ring. I slammed the window down and
snapped the latch.

In his scantily appointed bedroom the covers on the double
four-poster were casually thrown back as though he'd just
risen. The pillow was indented from his head. The door of the
cupboard stood open and three ties dangled pathetically from a
rack. Some shirts hung askew on hangers, and one jacket lay
crumpled in a heap on the floor on top of his shoes. They lay
immaculate in a row, trees holding their shapes, gleaming
bright with polish. Why hadn't he taken shoes? Weight consideration? I bent over and picked up one of his brogues. Oxblood.
The shoe was remarkably tiny and fine. Connie had abnormally
small feet for a man. All his shoes had been custom made since
he was a young man by the same firm of shoemakers in Italy.
They kept a cast of his foot, and anytime he needed shoes, he
merely specified type and color. He was like a woman about his
shoes. Some pairs he'd had for decades. Who cleaned them?
Alex? Had Michael cleaned them before him? Or did he take
them to a local shoemaker for cleaning? Did people do that? I'd
never thought about it before and ran my finger around the
seam where the leather upper was stitched to the leather sole.
There wasn't a trace of dirt in the narrow groove. A thin sheen
of clear wax had been buffed over the sole. I could smell the
fresh polish. I put the shoe with its mate and hung up the
tumbled jacket, but it wasn't until I began straightening the
shirts that I realized my hands were shaking. I threw myself on
the bed, buried my face in his pillow, and wept.

The hall of Dolores's house was cluttered with wrapped wedding presents that guests had brought to the reception. The
door was answered by the cook, who told me that my mother
was at the factory. Labor talks on Sunday? I called there, but
was told that she was locked in negotiations with the upholsterers' representative and a mediator and couldn't be disturbed.

(The inexpensive new fabric was hell to work with—it split and shredded under the slightest stress and they wanted Dolores to go back to the old stuff. Dolores, who had burned her bridges with the previous supplier, argued that they were simply sloppy and with careful treatment, the new fabric would be perfectly adequate. Deadlock.) I hung up the phone on her neurotic babbling secretary and trudged upstairs to talk to Daddy.

The drapes were pulled and the only light in the attic came from the television. Snatches of dialogue overdubbed with a soft orchestral melody emanated from the stereo speakers in competition with a droning air conditioner. Daddy sat in his black leather recliner holding a plastic tumbler with sailboats painted on it. A bottle of vodka stood in a bucket of ice on the floor next to a bag of taco chips. He turned his head and smiled his sweet smile as he focused his eyes.

"Daddy, Connie's dead."

"Greer, honey. Come. Sit down. *An Affair to Remember.*" He waved me over, then dropped his hand limply on his lap. I sat on the floor beside him. I could understand why the term "pickled" was used for drunks, for an alcoholic essence seeped through the very pores of his skin. He switched the glass to his other hand and patted my shoulder. On the forty-eight-inch screen, Deborah Kerr was talking with Cary Grant's grandmother—Gladys Cooper or Kathleen Nesbitt. I could never get those two straight. I laid my head on Daddy's knee. He idly stroked my hair.

"Connie's dead," I repeated, assuming he couldn't have heard the first time I'd spoken. I stifled a sob and sniffed quietly, wiping my eyes with a crumpled napkin that lay on the carpet. Cary Grant walked in, and he and Deborah Kerr listened as Gladys Cooper or Kathleen Nesbitt played the piano. Deborah Kerr sang and Cary Grant gazed adoringly. I burst into tears.

"Greer, Greer. It's only a movie." Daddy rubbed my neck comfortingly. Although I'd seen the movie about sixteen times and could recite the dialogue, I never cried until the final reel when Cary comes to her apartment on Christmas Day with Gladys Cooper's or Kathleen Nesbitt's shawl and realizes that

Deborah is crippled. I bawl every time. I bawl thinking about it. But today I was bawling for Connie. I blew my nose and tried to compose myself.

"Daddy, Grandfather was killed in Russia."

"Gee. I'm sorry, honey." It finally penetrated his brain and he looked away from the television screen to make eye contact. "He was very old," he said by way of consolation. "And I'm sure he'd rather have gone quickly, don't you?"

"He was pushed in front of a bus," I blubbered, but I don't think he heard. His attention had been drawn back to the movie. What a pathetic life. Was this what he wanted? Of course it was. Why would he be there otherwise? No one was tying him to the chair. For all his indifference, he owned Payton Furniture, could do with it what he wished, could go where he wanted, see whom he wanted, but what he wanted to do was to watch movies and drink himself into a stupor. He poured more vodka and patted my head.

"I'll tell your mother. She'll want to arrange the funeral."

"That's not necessary. I'm going over."

"Oh. Perhaps it's for the best. Your mother didn't like him very much. Do you think it should be remade?" he asked, thoughtlessly trivializing my sorrow by dismissing it for the sake of the game. Goddamn him anyway. Why couldn't he have been a normal father instead of a booze-drenched excuse for humanity? He could have been there when Dolores wasn't. He could have protected me from her, but no. He'd forsaken the world as effectively as a cloistered monk. At that moment, I didn't like him very much.

The door opened and Alice slouched in carrying a plate of sandwiches and four videotapes. She frowned unpleasantly at me, as though I had no right to be there, and deposited her armload within Daddy's reach. Then she padded around the room, perfunctorily straightening up, collecting dirty plates, glasses, plucking Kleenex balls from the floor, scooping soiled clothes from the backs of chairs.

"This version was a remake, you know. The earlier film

starred Charles Boyer and Irene Dunne. I'd love to see it but haven't been able to get my hands on a print."

Alice stood to the side of Daddy's chair and picked the TV listings off the floor, flipping to that day. "That it?" she asked, pointing to the items circled in red.

"Yes, thank you," replied Daddy politely. "I've seen everything else." He patted her gnarled reddened hand, then took it in his, raised it to his lips, and kissed it. I must have looked stunned, for Alice glared at me defiantly and stomped out of the room with the laundry, dishes, and wastepaper basket. Jesus. I was no snob, but had Daddy descended to having an affair with the help? What was wrong with everybody?

"Can you think of any terribly attractive stars in their thirties? Maybe the male lead could be in his forties."

My head was whirling. Male leads? I couldn't think straight. I needed to sleep. Didn't Daddy care? Or was he so fermented that he couldn't understand? Connie was dead. Kerr and Grant leaned over the ship's rail in deep conversation.

"What about Meryl Streep? Everyone casts Meryl Streep."

"Sure. She's a good actress." I gave up. Why had I come? There was no consolation here.

"Now, the man. Who do you think?"

"Mel Gibson?" I suggested, halfheartedly.

"No. I don't think he's right."

"Robert Redford?"

"A bit long in the tooth." He sat bolt upright and bit into a segment of sandwich. I blew my nose and tried to figure out how to leave. The boat was entering New York harbor. Cary and Deborah agreed to meet at the top of the Empire State Building in six months unless there was a darned good reason why not. For God's sake, Robert Redford wasn't that old.

"Daddy, I've gotta go."

"No. Stay. What about Harrison Ford?"

"He's not drop-dead gorgeous."

"Well, who is?"

Who is? Right. I don't think he was aware when I left.

★

I passed the next few days waiting for visa approval, engaged in mind-numbing inventories at Ponsonby's and endless fried-chicken binges. Simon hadn't called, although I'd left three more messages on his machine. He had to be away on an extended trip—at least that's what I told myself. Dolores called, ostensibly to confirm that I was taking care of things, but actually fishing to see if I knew anything about Connie's will. I told her Malenfant had it, and that apart from an annuity for Alex, he'd left everything to me. After she hung up, I remembered the envelope Connie had handed me at the airport, only to be opened, I was cautioned, should he not return. It was still in my handbag.

I slit the flap and withdrew the paper. It read:

My beloved Greer,
    In the event I do not return from my trip, you must
know of my special collection. Over my lifetime, I have
accumulated some extraordinarily beautiful things,
objects I could not bear to part with. I give these to you.
They are hidden in the mausoleum you worked on, in the
cubicles. You will find the key in the bowl on top of the
curio cabinet. The cubicles themselves are not locked,
and the name plaques turn like handles. Be prudent.
Don't let Dolores know or she'll never give you any
peace.

                                        With all my love,
                                        Connie

Heavens! All the times I'd snitched the key, often replacing it days later, and he'd never noticed its absence. I thought I'd been the only one who'd used it—that it had been gathering dust in the bowl for decades. Lucky timing, and now it was mine, for what it was worth. I supposed that depended on how many gold bars Ivan had conned for his dubious scheme. I chuckled at his crack about Dolores then promptly burst into tears.

★

The consulate expedited my papers and I was in Leningrad by week's end. A "guide" was assigned to me, and I was annoyed until I realized how useful she'd be as an interpreter. The officials were kind and helped me deal with the yards of red tape so Connie could be buried there. He would have liked that.

The doctor who had attended Connie before he died informed me that he had never regained consciousness. They gave me his personal belongings, including the two suitcases, his passport, watch, money, and the wedding band, which I slipped on my little finger. I asked a nurse if she could tell me when the accident had occurred, and according to the file, an ambulance had been dispatched to the scene about three hours after his plane had landed. What had he been doing for three hours? Why hadn't he gone straight to the place he had planned to stay?

A taxi took us to the address Connie had given me. His associate hadn't heard about his death and was shocked at the news. He had been concerned when Connie hadn't shown up as scheduled, but ultimately assumed a change of plans. He served us tea, and my guide translated a series of sanitized stories about his dealings in the antiquities trade.

That night I went through the contents of the luggage, finding only clothes and the old photograph album. No Fabergé animals. What could he have done with them in three hours? Had he met with his so-called brother? Might he have given the animals to a virtual stranger for safekeeping? Perhaps he had been robbed. Was it possible for a thief to have pushed him and stolen the animals? But any thief worthy of the name would have taken his other valuables, especially the foreign currency.

But Ivan wouldn't have. He just wanted Connie out of the way, I was certain of it.

The following day, after I authorized the arrangements for Connie's burial, my guide and I visited the Leningrad records office. A clerk assisted us by spending hours on the phone with all the medical registrars in the Soviet Union, but the only

Stefan Nicholaivitch was thirty-five years old. When contacted, he told us that his father's name was Mikhail, and his grandfather's Vladimir.

I didn't know the address of Connie's childhood home, and even if I did, street names change, buildings are demolished. I showed my guide a photograph of the house, but she wasn't able to do more than suggest a certain district. I walked for days in hopes of recognizing it, but failed. Even to attempt to locate the country house seemed futile. Ladoga is a huge lake, and I didn't even know the name of the nearest town.

I buried Connie and returned home.

CHAPTER EIGHTEEN

W hen I arrived home, I phoned the Ritz to ask if Mr. Petroff had returned from his trip. They confirmed that he had, and did I wish to be connected with his room? I hung up. My first bit of evidence—he hadn't been here when Connie died, so he could have been there—but I needed proof. I called back and arranged to meet him for dinner. When I arrived, he was already sitting at his usual table. He stood when he saw me.

"Greer . . . "

"I have some bad news," I said, seating myself at the opposite curve of the banquette.

"I know about Stanzi." He sidled over until our thighs touched and I was overpowed by the scent of his sandalwood cologne. I suffered his clutching my hand in his under the guise of condolence. "Your mother was kind enough to inform me."

Blast Dolores. If he hadn't known, I might have been able to tell if he was surprised by the news or not. He caressed my neck with his bony beringed fingers and I clenched my jaw as he massaged my shoulders, whispered gently in Russian—so like Connie. The sound swept past my ears like a moist, warm breeze.

"I'm so sorry. I wish you'd told me before you left. I could have accompanied you. Helped you. It must have been an ordeal."

I tried not to think of Connie's body in the morgue—so small and frail—and to concentrate instead on the bastard who put

him there, but I couldn't prevent the tears. Perhaps it worked to
my benefit, making me seem vulnerable. He took advantage of
the situation and embraced me. I was glad the bar was dark.

It was 5:00 a.m. Leningrad time when I got to my apartment.
I tried Simon's number again—left another message. Slept.

Late the following day, I went up to the house to tell Alex
about Connie (if he didn't already know), and to explain the
annuity Connie had purchased. His truck wasn't in the driveway. Bartleby's bowl, half-filled with putrid hamburger, sat
untouched on the kitchen floor. Boxes of china still cluttered
the hall and the gun was where I'd left it, on the mantel. In fact,
there was no sign that Alex had been there since the day
Bartleby had died. I dropped the gun in my purse with the
intention of dumping it off a bridge. Where was Alex? I didn't
know whether to be worried or not. I was tempted to contact
missing persons, but maybe he was off somewhere in deep
mourning. Who was I to interfere?

As I stood in the hall, half expecting Connie to appear at the
head of the stairs in his carpet slippers and bathrobe, I realized
that the house was now mine. If I had an ounce of gray matter,
I'd sell the dump, or patch it up and then sell it. Even in a slack
market, it was worth upwards of two million dollars. Location,
location, location. But, I thought, it is the only home I've ever
known.

September passed. Still no word from Simon, and early in
October, his phone was disconnected. He had never given me
his address. I didn't know what to think. To add to my concerns, Alex was still missing. I finally called the police, and was
told that adult males who vanish generally do not care to be
found, and for the most part aren't. After I explained Alex's
intellectual deficiency, they were a little more receptive but
advised me that he'd probably turn up of his own accord when
he was good and ready.

I considered visiting the tomb, but I couldn't seem to force
myself to go there. The last thing I wanted to visit was the

sepulcher I had spent a year beautifying to be worthy of Connie's remains. The loot had been undisturbed there for years now and it was safe enough without me running up and checking on it. Safer, in fact, because if I were Ivan, I'd have me shadowed.

By mid-month, I finally convinced a contractor to look over the house. I stupidly hadn't renewed my apartment lease, which expired in two and a half months, believing (oh, babe in the woods) that any work I wanted done could be completed in that time. He called me at seven and said he could meet me in half an hour. After waiting six weeks, I felt honored, and grabbed the morning newspaper as I raced out the door. Leslie's entire renovation had been done in the time I'd waited for a lousy estimate. I hadn't fully appreciated her accomplishment at the time. By the time I arrived, Mr. Raymond had already conducted a preliminary examination of the exterior. He tipped an imaginary hat and flicked his cigarette into the grass.

"Checked under the ivy. The stone's sound. The exterior window frames are rotted. Need replacing. The roof's okay but the woodwork on the eaves needs a thorough scraping and repainting. Some may need replacing. There's a big crack in the foundation on the north side of the house. If you weren't at the top of the hill you'd have had major flooding in the basement." He lit another cigarette. A pale plume of smoke shot out his nose as he flipped the page on his clipboard and ran a yellowed finger along his penned notes. "That'll need work. Otherwise you're okay structurally. The front porch needs replacing, the door could use refinishing, and the stones on the walk could be relaid. Frost heave. Ditto for the driveway. If you really want to enhance the value of the house I'd suggest redoing the works with interlocking brick. You said you wanted a garage?" I nodded. The ground descended to the backyard and I thought a garage would snuggle nicely against the rear of the house at basement level. We could knock an entrance in where the pantry was located. I hated a cold car.

"Let's go in." He grabbed a flashlight and toolbox from his

truck and followed me into the house. I led him to the basement and he immediately gravitated to the furnace room.

"Someone put some copper piping in a long time ago—maybe forty years, but that's to the bathrooms. The heating system has lead, and they're shot. Could go anytime." To emphasize his point, he poked a corroded pipe with the business end of a screwdriver. Black, metallic-smelling water dripped onto the floor and down the drain. He aimed his flashlight at the corner for a cursory and dismissive glance at the fuse box. "The wiring's 110. You'll want to change to 220. There probably aren't enough outlets. The furnace is a real dinosaur. You could improve your energy efficiency if you changed it. And your water heater . . . " Apparently it was beneath contempt. He clicked his tongue and scribbled something on the side of the page. A number. It had an ominous five digits. "I hope you got a deal on the house." I trailed after him as he ignored the kitchen and headed up the stairs. He dug a hole in the dining room wall with a chisel, and a chunk of plaster thudded onto the floor. A ruler was inserted between the laths.

"You said you wanted central air-conditioning. The system you got here is hot water. Now somehow we gotta get air ducts up the walls and there isn't a lot of space. I recommend switching over to a forced-air system, since we'd need to replace all the pipes anyway. Then you could also install humidification. The plaster under the paper is powder. We'll need to tear it out and replace it with drywall and while we're in there we can insulate the exterior walls. You lose a lot of heat."

"What about the moldings?" I asked, glancing at the splendid architectural detail. He waved his hand dismissively.

"No sweat. What we can't save can be duplicated." He flicked the cigarette butt into the fireplace and tapped his pen against his teeth. "If you were smart, you'd change all the windows to something double- or triple-glazed. They make some very nice stuff now. R factor of eight. I'll get a catalogue to you. Ah—the floors." He kneeled on the floor and played with his flashlight and chisel under a radiator. "Half inch. No problem. Sand, stain, and refinish. They'll need some repair if we remove the rads." He opened the damper and aimed the flash-light up the chimney. I was glad I'd removed the gun.

"The firebrick could use repointing." He closed the damper and headed upstairs. He didn't like what he saw.

"I recommend that you update the bathrooms."

I shook my head vigorously.

"But they're so old-fashioned," he complained. "They won't help the resale value."

"I'm not planning on selling and I like them just fine."

"Okay. You're the boss. Now the kitchen. Nobody wants a kitchen in the basement. Move it upstairs to the study behind the dining room and I can make you a lovely recreation room where the kitchen is."

"No," I said.

"French door leading out onto the garden. You're lucky that the rear of the house is at ground level. It would be very bright."

"No. I like the kitchen the way it is."

"It's very inconvenient. Won't help the resale value."

"Forget the bloody resale value," I snapped. He glanced up from his doodling, regarding me in an altered light. No push-over, this fat lady. He lit another cigarette and offered me one. I declined and leaned back on the shabby chair, crossing my ankles. The meter was ticking in my head. This was going to cost a fortune and we hadn't gone into painting and decorating yet. I sighed and reached into my purse for a snack, coming up with a Granny Smith apple. It sat greenly in my lap, exhibiting little appeal. Diets sucked. The thirty pounds I'd lost in the month since Connie's death had done little to improve my appearance, and my constant hunger made me cranky, but I was determined to be a thinner me when I saw Simon again. If I saw Simon again. I bit into the apple as though it was fate itself. I wanted to keep the house. It had been waiting all those years for me to find the beauty in it, to salvage it from dereliction. I wanted to make it truly mine, put my imprint on it. The house represented hope and continuity. Here I was, pushing forty, and what had I to show for my life? A family who didn't like me much, whom I didn't like much, no social life, no friends, no job since I'd quit Ponsonby's, a grandfather who'd got himself pushed in front of an oncoming bus, the one and only love of my life (albeit a rat) who was making himself annoyingly scarce, and Ali Baba's treasure hoard.

"So should we go ahead? I have another job lined up if you don't want us." The contractor threw his butt into the grate and tapped his foot. I would have to hire an architect or a designer, I didn't want to make a hash of it.

"I'm thinking. Give me a minute." I went downstairs and sat on the living room couch. The empty curio cabinet was shadowed in the gloom of the day. I'd entrusted my rose quartz monkey and the fake egg to a safety-deposit box until renovations were complete. Only my clay man and dog remained on the mantel looking small and dusty. Thirty long years. I fingered the letter in my pocket that had arrived that morning. It was from the art gallery owner in New York. Simon's friend. In it he apologized for taking such a long time, but said that he loved my work and would be pleased to represent me. How long a time? When had Simon spoken to him? Perhaps he knew where Simon was. A cold rain pelted the window and I buttoned my sweater up to the neck. What a dismal month. I needed a drink. I needed sustenance. Mr. Raymond came into the room and sat in the slipper chair, tapping his pencil against his pad, waiting.

"Perhaps you're right about the kitchen. I don't relish trotting up and down the stairs every time I want a cup of tea."

He lit up. "I can make you such a nice kitchen. Bright, clean, modern. I can even put heating coils under the tiles so that if you wander down on a cold winter night in your bare feet, the floor will be warm." He winked and turned to a blank page where he added fifteen lines of writing and figures as we talked. "I did a nice job for a lady on Sunnyside. Wonderful kitchen. My daughter is a designer, you know. She specializes in kitchens and bathrooms. Are you sure you don't want me to do the bathrooms?"

"No," I blasted. It was fortunate I wasn't doing this on a budget, and that there were people out there with more money than brains who would pay through the nose for anything I chose to sell from the cache. "All right. No need to get steamed." He chuckled at his own bad joke. "You have any color preference?"

"White," I muttered. "I don't know. Black and white. I like a classic kitchen." What drivel. I didn't know what I liked.

"Gotcha. Well, I'll have to get some additional figures. The exterior work'll be a subcontract unless you want to shop around and hire a landscaper yourself. My estimate on the rest'll set you back about—" he sucked on the tip of his pencil and cleared his throat "—ah, approximately two hundred and thirty-five thousand." He flipped the pages so they all lay flat on the clipboard and handed it across to me. "That's the itemized list. So let me know by the end of the week and we can start in two weeks." He stood up and tucked his cigarettes into the waistband of his jeans.

"What about a pool?" I thought of Leslie's house and knew mine could be equally spectacular. I had a view. Why shouldn't I have a pool, too? Wasn't swimming the best exercise? Whenever I wanted to eat, I could throw myself in the water. The contractor's eyes widened. He'd struck the mother lode.

"A pool?" he asked. "Indoor or outdoor?"

"I saw a photograph in a magazine once of a pool in a greenhouse. We could dig a pool out back and have the glassed extension adjoining the room in the basement. Yes?"

"I suppose it's possible. It would be expensive to excavate. That's solid rock down there. Cement or resin?"

"Cement, definitely."

"The greenhouse would have to be double-glazed in this climate."

"I'd like it to be salinated instead of chlorinated."

"Huh?"

"Ask someone who knows, but I think the filtering works need to be noncorrosive. And I'd like solar heating. We could put it on the roof of the house."

"This is a very expensive proposition." He spoke slowly as though cautioning me to fess up if I were unable to pay for it all. Hell. I was Ms. Croesus. I stared him down.

"You get what you pay for, Mr. Raymond," I said in my coolest, most self-assured voice. He gazed at his sheaf of papers then looked at me, a mischievous gleam in his eye.

"Then how would you feel about, say, a sauna, maybe a hot tub, you know, for entertaining, and an exercise room?"

I considered his suggestion for only a moment.

"Everything, Mr. Raymond. I want everything."

After he left I stretched out on the couch to read the newspaper. First the comics, then Landers, who was fielding a slew of letters from people protesting that raising a dog was more ful- filling than raising children. Wars, famines, football. I was about to discard the life-style section, when a *faits divers* caught my eye. It must have been a slow day for the *Gazette* to have lifted the item, as it lacked the prurient content that would attract the attention of most readers. It read:

> New York (AP) Today a spokesman for Christie's con- firmed rumors that seven Fabergé eggs will be up for auc- tion in January. All the eggs are reported to be from a single anonymous seller. At a recent sale, one Fabergé Easter egg commanded a selling price of over $3 million (U.S.). Bidding is expected to be heated.

Seven eggs? There were seven eggs in Connie's cache. *My* cache. I sat bolt upright. I had been so convinced they were safe where they were, I hadn't even checked. Maybe it was a coinci- dence. Maybe some other person had seven eggs. I tore the item out, stuffed it into my purse, and thought it had better damn well be a coincidence. I reached into the cloisonné bowl and the key was there. So far so good. There was only the one key. I dropped it into my pocket.

It was still raining when I parked my car. I pushed through the thick hedges, now brilliant yellow, and found the open patch overgrown with purple aster, and milkweed. The door of the mausoleum stood ajar and whined as I pressed my hand against the cold iron. The interior was damper than the day.

Weeks of rain had permeated the marble, the very earth. I couldn't recall so wet an October. A faint sickly odor of rotting meat was coming from somewhere nearby, and I glanced around to see if there was an animal carcass about. As my eyes adjusted to the dim light I could see that the mausoleum was empty but one of the three covers had been tampered with. The brass disk on my grandmother's cubicle was twisted, and the door hung open several inches. I pulled it fully open and stared at the empty interior. So Ivan had cleared it out. How had he discovered it? Could Connie have confided in him before he was killed? I twisted Peter's plaque and yanked. Empty. Not so much as a scrap of paper.

I touched the third disk—David's. It, like the others, was icy to the touch. Despite the chill, I could feel sweat dripping down my spine, my sides, between my breasts. I twisted and tugged. The simple mechanism that undid the latch had jammed. Something impeded the metal bar from moving downward. I rattled the handle, pushed, pulled, until it finally gave, and I saw the impediment. A foot in a soft leather shoe. A pair of feet. Then, overwhelmed by the sweet smell of decaying flesh, I ran out gasping. I sat for a time trying to figure out a course of action. I should call the police. That was going to require endless explanations. I'd already reported Alex as missing. How could I possibly explain how I found his corpse? Who would want to kill such a harmless soul? The same fiend who shot Bartleby? Poor Alex. I cried for a few minutes.

Wait a minute. I was overlooking the obvious. The same person who had stolen the cache had to have murdered Alex, but would Ivan murder his own son? The thought appalled me. Who else was in contention?

Simon. That would explain why he'd vanished off the face of the earth. He'd last called me a few days before the wedding, and when I'd tried to reach him a few days later, he was gone. That bastard. I leaned against the cold, wet marble and let the rain fall on my face. I had to move Alex. He had to be buried properly. I held my breath, hurried back in, grabbed the corpse by the ankles, and heaved it out. Rigor had passed, and the body was as floppy as a rag doll. It slid to the stone floor in a crumpled heap.

But it wasn't Alex. I ran out the door and vomited. The shock was so great it seemed like an hour before I could force myself to go back in. His fine handkerchief-linen shirt was black with dried blood, and when I turned the body over, there was a corresponding stain on his back. A bullet. I gently straightened the body out. My precious Simon. I found myself remembering his kindness when I'd been a hopeless seventeen. Flies buzzed around his face, and maggots seethed where there should have been eyes. I raced outside and threw up again, then lay on the ground shivering, a shrill ringing in my ears, spots swimming in the blackness surrounding me.

I no longer wanted to call the police. I had as valid a motive for killing him as anyone, and it could have been done before I went to Leningrad. Who else? Back to Ivan. It had to have been Ivan. I held my breath again and with a hanky from my purse carefully wiped the smooth marble and the brass disks for any fingerprints, cautiously stepping around the seething corpse. Maybe Ivan had forced the secret out of Connie in the three hours between the time his plane landed and his death. I imagined him, stripped of his secret, dazed, shoved under a bus.

I pushed my dripping hair from my face and groaned. I didn't want anyone to stumble on this corpse. If I didn't move him, how long would it be before he was found? It had already been months. Years, probably, and by then he'd be bones. How long did it take a corpse to decompose? Why didn't I know anything practical? Simon had vanished and the chance of anyone connecting some unidentified bones with his disappearance would be unlikely. My car was nondescript. No one would implicate me. There was no evidence. I'd leave and never return. Someday I'd read in the paper of bones being discovered in the cemetery. Then again, maybe not. Maybe the wild dogs would carry them off and bury them here and there. There were always bones in cemeteries. Nothing unusual in that.

I entered the tomb one last time to remove Simon's wallet and keys, then checked his pockets for any further identifying material. I left his watch, for I couldn't bear to touch his rotting flesh.

Then I returned to Connie's house wanting nothing less than to be unconscious. I opened a bottle of Scotch and carried it up to my room where I collapsed in one of the club chairs, and drank until the sky was black and I passed out.

CHAPTER NINETEEN

"How is the house coming?" Ivan flagged a waiter and ordered a refill of his brandy and soda. He reminded me so much of Connie it made my heart ache and my teeth grind—this man, who had murdered both my grandfather and my lover. He would pay. He would pay dearly, as soon as I had irrefutable proof.

"Won't you have a cocktail?"

"No, thanks." I sipped my Perrier with lime and concentrated on keeping my hand from reaching into the basket of buns. They baked their own bread at the restaurant and had some of the best beef in the city. I studied the menu and found grilled filet of sole and plain green salad. No butter. No potatoes. No rice. No wine. No pastry cart. No cake and ice cream. I'd read that the greatest pitfalls for dieters were the exemptions they allowed themselves to pig out on on special occasions. Some birthday this was going to be. "The work's coming along. They finally finished tearing it apart, and started on the new windows yesterday. I think they went through twenty dumpsters."

"Then you must have found his safe?" Ivan asked, staring longer than was necessary into my eyes. I hated being stared at, especially by him. I wanted to whack him over the head with a clenched fist, but smiled instead. Being nice to Ivan was doing terrible things to my gastric secretions.

"Connie had no safe."

"He had to have hidden the blue egg somewhere, and all his other goodies."

"I told you he sold the blue egg, and there *are* no other "goodies." God, he was conniving. Talk about covering bases. If I knew about the cache, then he was telling me he didn't. If I knew that it had been looted, he was telling me he wasn't the looter. All these messages without telling me anything. I'd just keep on denying the existence of a treasure, because if he knew I knew, my plan wouldn't work.

"Wasn't Stanzi given to squirreling things away in odd places?"

"Not that I know of," I said with the most ingenuous expression I could manage. "Connie bought things, he sold things, but he didn't hide things."

"He left you well provided for?"

"You've asked that about twelve times. He was extremely generous. I shall never want for anything," I lied. I wanted a lot. "Did he leave you anything besides the house?"

"Just a fake egg, a quartz monkey, and some porcelain that he bought in Manaus last spring." I tried to read his eyes. "I was rather surprised," I said, baiting him. "I expected that there'd be a few things he couldn't bear to sell, but ... " I threw my hands up and shrugged. "I suppose he wasn't a hoarder."

"And nothing in his personal belongings from Russia?"

"No. You know, that puzzles me. He took his brothers' Fabergé animals with him, but they weren't with his things, and I could find no trace of his so-called brother. I suppose he could have left them somewhere for safekeeping, but I'll never find them. It's too bad. He was wearing this." I wiggled my pinky with Irina's gold wedding band.

"Oh," he said with a trace of suspicion. "By the way, have you seen Alex?"

"No. I've been worried. He hasn't turned up since the day of Leslie's wedding. At least, not that I've seen. Have you?"

"No." He relaxed. Relaxed? "I shouldn't worry, though. Alex manages."

"I told the police he was missing."

Did I perceive a jolt of alarm in his posture? Maybe a man in his position simply didn't care for the mention of any law-enforcement institution. He feigned polite interest and reached into his jacket pocket to place a small box on the tablecloth beside my drink. It was wrapped in pink tissue paper with a pink rose tied up in a pink satin bow. Very feminine. Very pink. I'm not a pink person. The image he harbored of me was so far off the mark, it made my duplicity easy.

"You shouldn't have," I protested in an unconvincing feminine squeak. I didn't do it very well, not having had any practice.

"I couldn't neglect your birthday. Our dinners together are such a pleasure. You have given me cause to hope that perhaps ... " The sentence trailed off and I let it. I picked up the gift and plucked at the ribbon. The wrapping came away easily. I recognized the peacock blue Tiffany's box and braced myself for what it might contain. I wasn't up to a proposal tonight—not on an empty stomach, anyway.

I removed the lid and lifted the cotton wool to find a pair of black pearl earrings with a matching pendant. That reptile. Scum of the earth. Sewer gas. He had taken three of the unset pearls from the cache and put them into a contemporary design, but he would catch no flicker of recognition in my eyes. Who did he think he was dealing with, anyway? As I'd told Connie, I had learned at the feet of masters.

"How lovely," I crooned, and they really were. Set in platinum with details of pavé diamond leaves, the pearls were a good centimeter in diameter. Not a bad gift, if they hadn't legally belonged to me in the first place. I reached into my purse and presented him with my box, which I'd wrapped in tin foil. It had been a sudden inspiration.

"But it's not my birthday," he said with faint surprise. I could imagine he didn't get many gifts.

"I don't know when your birthday is," I replied sweetly. He peeled off the foil and opened the hinged leather container.

"A watch. How splendid."

"It was Connie's," I explained. "I'm sure he would have wanted you to have it." After all, you have everything else, I thought. "I'm afraid the crystal is cracked. It must have happened when he fell under the bus. Give it back to me and I'll have it replaced." Ivan's mouth was frozen in a smile as I took back the watch. I returned it to my purse without another word. Greer:15, Ivan:love.

The December 1 auction was scheduled to capitalize on the spirit of generosity and open pocketbooks that precedes Christmas. New York had girded for the onslaught of festive consumerism with decorations in every store window, every plaza. Even the blinking signal lights receding down Fifth Avenue contributed to the glitter of the season. I slipped on a patch of ice and grabbed at a lamp standard to prevent a fall. Noontime crowds surged past with shopping bags, briefcases. I trod gingerly around the frozen puddle and pushed through the revolving doors.

In my short, curly, black wig and tortoiseshell glasses, I was confident that Ivan wouldn't recognize me. I checked my coat and took a seat to the center left of the podium, fifteen rows back. The room was filling up and a young woman relieved people of their cigarettes, pipes, and cigars as they entered. I thought, with a pang, of Simon. He'd been here many times, and I could picture his apologetic grin as he handed his smoke to the girl, flung his coat over his shoulder, and sauntered down the aisle to a seat near the front.

The atmosphere was expectant, as it is before the curtain rises on a successful play—only a producer couldn't hope to make in a decade the profits that would be garnered today. How completely the antithesis of Ponsonby's. This was real. I glanced around me and recognized many faces from the pages of *Vanity Fair*, *Vogue*, and *Fortune*, but no Ivan. At the preview I'd checked off items from Connie's cache against their entries in the catalogue, and if memory served me, most were accounted for, with the exception of the jewels. Perhaps he had a more

lucrative system of disposal for them. I hoped he wasn't breaking them up for resetting.

The chief auctioneer pounded his gavel and the din subsided
to a hush broken by the odd cough. Certain items were on
display at the perimeter of the room. Prominent among them,
to the right of the podium, sat the Fabergé eggs. Perched
against a backdrop of matrix-gray velvet and illuminated by
concentrated halogen spots, they dazzled. There was no other
word for it. They dazzled with provenence, romance, and pure
aesthetic power. I had only seen them in the gloom of the
mausoleum by a kerosene lantern. In full light, they were
extraordinary. They shimmered and sparkled. The colored
enamels glowed as though lit from an internal source. I could
almost understand why Connie had kept them a secret, but oh,
how I wish he'd shared them with me.

The bidding commenced on a small Pieter de Hooch, a
typical Dutch domestic scene somewhat blackened by varnish,
and stopped at $925,000. I couldn't tell who'd bought it, but sat
tight as I methodically scanned the rows for a glimpse of Ivan.
He had to be there. It would be too great a coincidence if he had
just happened on the pearls he'd given me for my birthday.
Then again, one big black pearl was the same as any other. I
supposed it was possible that Connie had slipped under a bus
after secreting the animals, and it was also possible that Simon
was followed or accompanied to the tomb by a confederate who
then killed him and stole the treasure, but it was improbable. I
laid my bets on Ivan. I wanted him for a villain, and anyone,
anyone, who was selling what was being sold would be there to
watch, especially if the motive for selling was unadulterated
greed.

I paid scant attention to the bidding, as I had no intention of
buying anything, and examined faces until I was alerted by the
twelfth item, the Fabergé tankard with Baron Munchausen in
bas-relief. The bidding was light and it went for six thousand
dollars.

The auctioneer's assistant then held up a tray with seven
items on it. I strained to get a better view and whipped to the

correct page on the catalogue just as the descriptions were
intoned through the P.A. system. How had I missed them? In
my single-mindedness over the more valuable items from the
tomb, Connie's menagerie of small carved animals had completely slipped my mind. That almost clinched it. Who other
than Ivan could have both the animals *and* the eggs? I rapidly
calculated how much cash I could raise. I wanted them back.
No one else had a right to touch them, but could I risk Ivan
seeing me? I hunched down in my chair and waited. The bidding was started at two thousand dollars and rose in increments
of a hundred. It quickly passed four thousand, then slowed
down. I raised my hand at forty-five hundred and clinched the
sale at six. I had Stefan's ermine. Next was Karel's lapis
rabbit—seventy-one hundred. Sascha's nephrite chameleon
was a steal at fifty-nine. Perhaps people were anxious to get on
with the main event, but then interest perked with Peter and
Mischa's bear cubs, sold as a pair. They set me back fourteen
thousand dollars. What were these things anyway? Stocking
stuffers for the filthy rich? Well, they wouldn't get these. The
sardonyx fox, Nicky's, was enhanced by the previous bid, and I
had to go as high as seventy-five hundred. This was killing. The
fact I was bidding on all the animals was upping the cost consid-
erably. The auctioneer glanced my way after every bid waiting
for a signal. Finally Connie's onyx raven was held up. I surrepti-
tiously checked the room for Ivan but couldn't see him. The
bidding soared to six thousand and I entered the contest when it
reached seven-three. It was mine at eight. I relaxed in my seat
and filled out the slips the patient porter held while waiting for
me to complete my marathon session. I filled in a pseudonym
until I could figure out a better way to preserve my anonymity.

A curator from the Met who was sitting two rows ahead of me
acquired the St. Joan reliquary and the Chinese globular jar,
which went for an astounding $550,000. The Noah's ark plate
was snapped up by a Canadian collector (who'd once bought an
eighteenth-century English harlequin at Ponsonby's) for
$21,500. I marked each price next to the catalogue entry, just to
keep track. This was a lot of loot. Perhaps Ivan didn't have

Connie's connections in the field of fine art objects, for Connie would certainly never have exposed his profits to a system that demanded commission and capital-gains taxation.

From the corner of my eye I saw the rear door open. There he was, bundled in a black overcoat with an otter collar and a hat. The young woman removed the smoking cigarette from between his lips, and an usher directed him to a vacant seat at the very end of the front row. Thank God he hadn't been there to see me bid on the animals.

The next item up was my swan service. Because of its rarity, the bidding was carried to half a million. Very gratifying, and a bit of a relief as it took the sting out of having to fork over forty-five thousand for the menagerie. It went to a Canadian collector who also picked up the T'ang cat for ten thousand. Ivan nodded with satisfaction, the cretin. It was worth far more than that. They proceeded to non-tomb objects, and I kept my head low lest Ivan should turn around. They were obviously keeping the best for last to build expectation, and as each item passed, the buzz increased. Ivan removed his hat and smoothed back his thin gray hair. Dear Lord, how I hated him.

After four hours and only one break, people were becoming giddy and bid-happy. A perfectly ordinary Meissen bowl went for seventy thousand dollars, and a seventeenth-century earthenware posset pot for twelve. Ivan mopped his brow with a large white hanky and took a pull from his flask. It was warm and close. The doors were opened to let in some air. A camera crew from one of the networks installed themselves in the center aisle and switched on a powerful light. A loud murmur swept through the room. The auctioneer signaled the porter, who handed him the small lapis Easter egg. His voice crystalized through the speakers.

"Lot number 195. An important decorative item from the workshop of Carl Fabergé. An Easter egg, made in 1905 for the Czarevitch Alexis, authenticated, hallmarked, lapis lazuli with scrollwork ornamentation in yellow gold set with precious stones. The surprise—" he theatrically pried the two halves apart to show the gold spaniel "—is a gold spaniel which also opens, and contains a child's ruby ring. The bidding will open at one million dollars and rise by five thousand."

Phew. That was hefty. The bidding didn't begin for at least thirty seconds. It took that long for the whispers to die down, but once begun, the competition was fierce. Imperial eggs had a cachet that others lacked, and I wasn't at all surprised when it went for three million. The wee two-inch egg of rock crystal reached a million five before the bidding stopped, and it wasn't even Imperial, and didn't open or anything. The rose quartz egg, three inches high and likewise a solid piece, realized a million seven. The three-inch enameled egg with the pheasant and chicks, which I had found so remarkable, obviously appealed to someone very much, for he was willing to pay three million four. The room roared and the auctioneer gaveled to bring order, then summoned the porter to present the Cupid egg.

"This extremely important Fabergé Easter egg was commissioned by a South American landowner for his mistress in 1889. One of the earlier Easter eggs, it has a unique erotic automaton operated by a clockwork mechanism. The bidding will open at a million dollars."

Four million. It went for four million; a new plateau. The person beside me whispered that it was probably Malcolm Forbes. The egg of translucent rose enamel with the broken clockwork and lost automaton lowered the bidding, and it went for a mere two and three quarter million. Then it came up. Irina's egg.

"Another extremely important Fabergé Easter egg, commissioned by an expatriate Englishman for his aristocratic Russian wife in 1895, to commemorate the birth of their heir. It features a rare combination of automaton pigeon and a melodic chiming mechanism. The bidding will open at one million dollars."

The porter opened it and activated the clockwork and chimes. There was a collective gasp. Ivan stole a glance around the room and grinned gleefully as the bidding carried the price to $4,300,000.

It was as well they had reserved the eggs for the last. Anything following would have been anticlimactic. I waited until

Ivan was ushered into the administrative area before I presented myself to conclude my purchase.

"The elderly gentleman who just passed through . . . " The young man who knew me as the seller of the Meissen accompanied me to an upstairs room. "Isn't he Ivan Petroff?"

"I believe so."

"Have you any idea why he's selling off his collection of Fabergé?"

He shrugged. "Taxes? Who knows?"

My heart raced. So there was no mistake. It was Ivan. The slime. I glanced down the corridor, but he was nowhere in sight. I arranged that my name remain anonymous, that Ivan be kept in ignorance of who bought the animals. My young man understood perfectly, being accustomed to the publicity-shy.

I flew home the following day, locked the animals in my safety-deposit box, and drove up to the house. Painters were at work on the windows and eaves. As I parked the car, Mr. Raymond emerged from the driveway and met me on the curb.

"Miss Payton. Do you know a young man named Alex?"

"Yes. He's my cousin. Is he here?" It had been more than three months since Alex had driven off to bury his dog. The police had had no leads, and he was too old to have his face on milk cartons. I was beginning to fear he was dead in a ditch.

"He came looking for you yesterday and locked himself in one of the bathrooms. We tried to reach you."

"I was out of town."

"Is he sick?" He used a smoldering butt to light a new cigarette and threw it on the grass. Why was he asking if Alex was sick?

"No. At least I hope not. He's a bit simple." I went into the house and stepped over tarps and wires and pipes. Upstairs, one of the workmen pointed to a closed door and shrugged. I knocked and tested the handle.

"Alex," I called. "It's me. Greer. Open up." There was a scrambling noise, then the door opened and he pulled me in, locking the door after. I sat on the toilet lid. Alex sat on the edge of the tub. His hair was cropped close to his scalp and he was wearing what looked like hospital pajamas under a cheap plastic raincoat. His face was puffy and he didn't look at all well.

"Alex! Where have you been?"

"In a hospital."

"What happened? Why didn't you call me?"

"They didn't let me. I wanted to. I didn't like it there. They gave me pills that made me sick."

"Were you sick? Did you have an accident?"

"No. My father put me there. He said that if I didn't go to the hospital, they'd hang me."

Ivan?

"Hang you, Alex? Why would anyone hang you?" I moistened some toilet paper and wiped his face. He couldn't have bathed in days, nor eaten.

"My father said that when you kill someone, they put you in prison and hang you unless you're insane, so he put me in the hospital." He looked terrified. I held his hands in mine and tried to calm him.

"Alex, you didn't kill anyone, did you?"

"Yes," he admitted softly. "I think so."

My mind was spinning. Alex, a murderer? It didn't add up. There had to be a simple explanation. "Do you want to tell me about it?" I asked, soothingly.

"You won't send me back to the hospital, will you?"

"No, I won't."

"Promise?"

"Cross my heart and hope to die." As I moved my index finger across my chest he seemed to relax. I was touched by his trust.

"Do you remember the day Bartleby was shot?"

I nodded.

"Before Connie left, he told me to get two gold bars from the tomb, to give to my father."

"You knew about the tomb?" I was incredulous. "It was you who put the packages in?"

"Yes."

"But didn't you notice the carving and tell Connie?"

"No. I thought it was something he'd arranged. We drove up. Remember, it was the day of that big storm."

"Who's we?" I asked.

"Me and Bartleby. When I got there, there was this strange man poking around, trying to force the door with a crowbar. I told him it was private property and to go away. He pulled a little gun and told me to go away. The wind was real bad, blowing the trees around and all, and Bartleby must've got scared all alone in the truck 'cause he came running out from the bushes and the man shot him. Bartleby yelped and fell down. I had Connie's gun, so I shot him."

"Just like that?" I croaked through my constricted vocal cords. Was he saying that my Simon had been shot *not* because he had somehow figured out the secret of the tomb and was attempting to steal the treasure, but because he shot the damned dog? I could imagine it . . . the storm, Alex coming out of nowhere, then the stupid animal, who in that context must have looked like the bloody hound of the Baskervilles. Anyone would have panicked.

"I had to, Greer," he whined. "Don't you see?" Tears were streaming down his face. I took him in my arms and rubbed his back. Of course I saw. That was my problem. There was nothing else Alex could have done. Absurdist drama demanded a logical conclusion.

"Yes. I see. Did you put him in the niche?"

"Yes. After I took the boxes out."

"What did you do with the boxes?"

"My father took them. He said they weren't safe there anymore."

"So you told your father?"

"Yes. I had to explain why I didn't have his gold. I didn't want to go back. He came up to the tomb with me."

"When was this?" Things were clicking into place like the numbers of a combination lock. Here was my ultimate proof. My justification. Alex spoke.

"After he came back from Russia."

Bingo!

"He made me move all the boxes and the rest of the gold into the truck, then he told me to put the man into the cubbyhole. He said I couldn't tell anyone, and that if anyone found out, I would be hung."

That bastard. He didn't have to stick him in an asylum. The body wouldn't have been found in a hundred years, hidden in the vault. He just wanted to keep Alex away from me.

"Then he took you to the hospital?"

"Yes."

"Where was this hospital?"

"Ontario, I think."

"How did you get out?"

"One night an orderly left the door to the ward unlocked. I just walked out. No one noticed."

I blessed his dumb luck. God watched over drunks, children, and Alex.

"Then I hitchhiked here. You won't let them hang me, will you, Greer?"

"Nobody gets hanged in Canada anymore. Besides, what you did wasn't murder. More like self-defense, and no one can connect you with the death anyway. Let me think." Of all the motives I could have imagined for someone killing Simon, shooting Bartleby had not sprung to mind. Poor Simon. Poor Alex. Poor me. I didn't know who to pity anymore. Now I had to prevent Alex from telling Ivan that I knew anything or I'd get no revenge.

"You put the gun back in the flue, didn't you?"

"Yes. How did you know?"

"I found it. Don't worry. It's at the bottom of the St. Lawrence. Do you have your passport?"

"It's in the pantry."

I pulled him to his feet and we headed for the basement. Work hadn't begun there yet, although I noticed a few of the whiskey bottles were missing. Alex reached into a lower cupboard and withdrew a tatty manila envelope. It contained his passport, birth certificate, and immigration documents.

"Alex," I said. "You're going to visit your mother. Don't contact your father or he'll put you back in the hospital."

"Okay."

"Promise!"

"Cross my heart and hope to die."

CHAPTER TWENTY

Fifty pounds and counting. My doctor informed me that the plateau was over, that I'd squeezed out the retained water and my body was now consuming my fat. The image made me want to run out and eat a large porterhouse steak drenched in béarnaise sauce. He recommended I see a therapist to whom I could talk so I could discover the root of my compulsion, but I knew the reason well enough. It had been hostility. Now it was giving me resolve. I taped a photograph of Leslie on my refrigerator as incentive, my poor refrigerator, which contained only skim milk, cottage cheese, light yogurt, vegetables, and fruit. I installed two full-length mirrors, one in the bedroom and one in the living room. I forced myself to look at myself naked. I did sit-ups. Leg drops. Deep knee bends. Jumping jacks. I joined an aerobics class at the Y and bought a Jane Fonda workout tape for the VCR. I bought a scale that enunciated my weight in an uninterested synthesized monotone.

Revenge—the great motivator.

Leslie was doing Christmas dinner. I decided it was time I saw my family again—seasonal reconciliation and all that. Actually, after months of avoiding them, I was curious to see what effect they'd have on me. I stamped my feet on the doormat and rang the bell. A few stray snowflakes drifted aimlessly in the still air, and "Joy to the World" rang up the mountain from the Sun Life carillon.

Leslie greeted me at the door in a sweeping, romantic, cranberry velvet gown with a matching snood. I wasn't surprised when a moment later the Cats attacked me wearing little white hose, velvet knickers (green, red, blue and purple), and floppy silk bows tied under round-collared white shirts upon which someone had thoughtfully embroidered their names in black thread. The nice wool crêpe dress in medium gray, which had pleased me so much at home, made me feel like a dowdy little domestic sparrow trapped with birds of paradise. The brilliantly patterned shawl I'd flung over my shoulders paled. Only my birthday pearls from Ivan held their own here. It was the first time I'd worn them and I was conscious of their weight dangling from my lobes.

Then Yves appeared in his usual nondescript gray suit and I felt a bit better. I could imagine twenty or so of them lined up neatly in the cupboard in Jules's old dressing room, each with the requisite two pairs of pants. The drawers would be filled with perfectly pressed white shirts and subdued silk ties—not too wide, not too thin. Socks, black. Shoes, black. He couldn't quite shake a priestly dress code.

"It's been months. We all assumed you were hibernating." Leslie kissed the air to either side of my face. "And maybe you have been at that. You've dropped a load. Look at you. How much?"

"Not enough." I hated the way she assessed me and was sorry I'd agreed to come. Why did I assume anything would have changed? She still drove me crazy. The Cats tore at the large bags I carried. Leslie had laid an Oriental carpet over the glass floor and removed all the tropical plants, replacing them with evergreen garlands and an eighteen-foot-tall Christmas tree. The balance and proportion of the decorations betrayed the deft hand of a professional. How to take the fun out of Christmas. Beneath the tree sat the gifts, ostentatiously displayed in open boxes—four small two-wheelers, Lego kits, an illustrated, leather-bound set of children's classics in ten volumes, Playmobile sets, a telescope (I could only imagine to what use the Cats would put that), a toy printing press. I assumed the mink coat and gold necklace were Leslie's and wondered if Yves had got anything.

Poor Yves. I'd found him a seventeenth-century edition of St. Augustine's *Civitatae Dei*, which I hoped wouldn't wind up as paper airplanes. I bore him no grudge, in fact, was beginning to like him. At least from him I knew what to expect. I emptied my bags of gifts on the floor next to the ones still in wrapping—presumably for the parents and myself.

"Merry Christmas, Greer." Yves relieved me of my overcoat and kissed me on both cheeks. His lips were cold.

The Cats found the presents marked for them (dropping the pretense that they couldn't read) and ripped off the Santa Claus paper, exposing stained cardboard boxes. Leslie looked at me sideways and picked a pale blonde hair off her sleeve. Yves kneeled beside the boys and helped them remove the industrial tape that kept the flaps down. They threw the wood shredding every which way in their efforts to find the presents until Pascal freed a red caboose. Honoré extricated two passenger cars and a sleeper, Anatole found the coal car and two freights, and Émile the engine and a flatbed. Yves rummaged in the bottom for the rails and the transformer, seemingly as thrilled as the children. Boys with their toys, I thought. That would keep them busy for hours . . . weeks.

"But, Greer," Yves exclaimed. "I haven't seen a model train set like this since I was a boy. Wherever did you find it?"

"Connie gave it to me when I was about their age, but it's much older than that. See that they take care."

"I will."

"Do we say something to Greer, children?" Leslie tapped her foot and motioned the Cats over. They leaped on me with wet, velvety kisses. I missed the "gringe bidous" of old. What was going on with them? They were acting normal. I asked Leslie if they had a new psychiatrist.

"No." She laughed. "It's Yves. He instituted a policy of divide and conquer. You know they entered grade one in September?"

"No."

"Well, they did, but instead of sticking them in the same school, he enrolled them in four different ones. I mean, really different. Pascal is at Selwyn House, you know, blazers, ties, hockey, rah rah. He adores it. There are all these little boys who don't resemble him in the least. That's been the predominant reaction of all four. I do believe they thought all six-year-old boys were just like them." She caught my dubious frown.

"I don't mean appearance. They've seen other boys, but haven't played with any. My mistake, I suppose. I couldn't stand the idea of more little boys whooping it up here, and couldn't imagine inflicting them on anyone else. Besides, they were sufficient unto themselves. They all think alike." She gazed fondly at the seething mass of colored velvet that was trying to fit segments of rail together. It was the first time I'd ever seen any sign of affection from her toward the Cats.

"Anatole is at Marie de France. They're really French French. Terribly strict. Hours of homework. All stress on the academic. Honoré is at St. George's, where the emphasis is on allowing the child to develop at his own pace. If he wants to sit in a corner and examine toe jam, so be it. Actually, he's developed a close friendship with a Jewish kid and made us buy a menorah for Hanukkah. We light the fourth candle tonight and he mutters a Hebrew prayer. You can imagine how thrilled Yves is about that. Émile is at Westmount Park School. Half its enrolment is from Little Burgundy and some of the kids are really poor. At lunch, any child who can't eat all his food is instructed to put the leftovers in the center of the table for the children who haven't any. Émile has the cook make him three extra lunches so he can give them away. Often he doesn't eat his own. The quality of the education is inferior to the other schools, but he's so bright that a few years won't do him any harm. I've got to hand it to Yves. I was reluctant to split them up, but it seems to have done the trick."

The door crashed open as Daddy and Dolores blew in. It was turning into a real storm, the first of the year.

"It's snowing," Dolores said, unnecessarily. "It'll be a white

Christmas after all. That's one thing I love about Canada. Christmases here are so much more Christmassy." They doffed their coats and hung them in the hall closet. Dolores sized me up and kissed me without commenting on my weight loss. You'd think after not laying eyes on me for four months, and after nagging me for thirty-six years, she would have seized the opportunity. "How is the house coming?" was all she said. "I drove past the other day and there were three trucks."

"It's fine. I have no interior walls but exquisite heating pipes."

"Father must have left you a pretty penny for you to be able to do this renovation," she said through her teeth. Oh, this was killing her. Me with money, or so she thought. Since quitting Ponsonby's, I'd been living off the small sum of money Connie left. The auction money was financing the work in progress, and if my plans didn't come off, I'd have to sell the house to pay the contractors.

"I'm comfortably off," I answered vaguely.

"You'd think he would have remembered Leslie and the boys."

"Please don't start, Mother." I hugged Daddy and gave him a big kiss. He reeked of rum. Too much punch.

"Greer," he whispered conspiratorially. "I've got *It's a Wonderful Life* in my pocket."

"You could have called." Dolores twisted her pearls around her finger. She was wearing a bright cherry-red wool dress with one of those Christmas corsages with miniature glass balls and sparkly gold holly pinned to her left shoulder. Every year it went into a box with the tree ornaments to be retrieved and used the next. It was becoming a little tatty and the white satin bow had turned gray. Her hair, hennaed to an alarming shade of orange, clashed with her dress.

"Mother, let's just drop it, okay?"

"I haven't seen you for months."

"You couldn't have missed me too much. You never called."

"There was the strike at the factory...."

"Oh yeah. Right. And you were too preoccupied to pick up

the phone. Don't be such a hypocrite, Mother. You were delighted that you didn't have to bother about me. It rankled, didn't it, that Connie excluded you from his legacy, but I don't know why you expected otherwise, the way you treated him.'' Jesus. I was ranting. Dolores stared, her mouth pressed in a tight red line, then walked the length of the atrium, to the table where Leslie was ladling eggnog into cups. So much for good-will.

Daddy had given the Cats their presents, Polaroid cameras, and was helping them load the film. They immediately began snapping pictures of each other without waiting for the flash to recharge, and were cross when most of the exposures were dark. Yves tried to explain, but the novelty had worn off and they dumped the cameras under the tree. Daddy shrugged and returned to my side.

''Do you want to watch it now?'' he asked, but I wasn't quite ready for Capra's feel-good opus. Besides, I'd seen it the previous night on the late show. George Bailey could wait.

''After lunch, Daddy. Okay?'' I squeezed his arm when his shoulders sagged. Poor man. He took pleasure in such tiny things, one forgot how easy he was to disappoint.

''Daddy, do you know what I have for you under the tree?''

He brightened. I trotted over, scooped up the package I'd deposited there (scooped, mind you—the gruesome calisthenics were paying off), and presented it to Daddy. He sat on one of the benches on the perimeter of the room and unwrapped the green-and-red striped paper. Tears welled up in his eyes. He stroked the videotapes as though they could feel.

''Look,'' I said. ''Here's *Holiday Inn* and *A Christmas Carol*, the good one with Alastair Sim, and *The Holly and the Ivy*, and *One Magic Christmas*, and *Santa Claus—The Movie*, and *Desk Set*, and yes, I even got *It's a Wonderful Life*. All our favorite Christmas films. We can have a movie marathon.''

He held the seven cassette boxes to his chest and smiled his sloppy smile. ''They're colorized.''

''What?''

''Colorized. Some of the originals were black and white.''

"Oh, I'm sorry."

"No. It's wonderful. I love color. Thank you, sweetheart." He planted an inaccurate kiss on my ear, then added, "I missed you."

Guilt, guilt, guilt. Leslie approached with two cups of eggnog.

"Those are lovely pearls," she observed. Typical that she made no comment on my nice new dress or my hairdo, but then, she wouldn't have been caught dead in my dress or hairstyle. "Did you buy them for yourself?"

Daddy stood, his eggnog in his left hand, the tapes crooked in his right arm, and wandered away.

"They were a gift." I waved my hand as if to suggest that they were of little consequence.

"From whom?"

"A passing Saudi chubby chaser." I winked, took my egg-nog, and wandered off to play trains. The remainder of the day was a jumble of turkey, videos, and booze, but mostly booze.

CHAPTER TWENTY-ONE

Spruce have shallow root systems, and after tractors had ripped the trees from the yard, a cratered and ravaged expanse of frozen, rocky soil stretched for about two hundred feet to the edge of the cliff and a low stone wall I had forgotten about. It commanded a view over rooftops of newer houses that lined the road winding down to the valley. The granite monuments in Côte des Neiges cemetery ordered the opposing landscape with their bleak presence. Snow lay thickly on the ground everywhere but my backyard, where a steam shovel had scraped it clear. Soon they would excavate for the pool and greenhouse foundations.

A stiff wind rippled the plastic sheeting that covered a hollow window, and the room was freezing in spite of portable heaters hooked up by the contractors. Unprimed drywall was finally up, concealing the cotton-candy insulation, heating, plumbing, and central vacuum pipes, so I assumed things were progressing.

Across the hall, the dining room and study had been flipped, and a kitchen was now taking shape at the rear of the house. I told myself I ought to feel satisfaction, but I didn't. The only thing I had accomplished was the exorcism of ghosts—fond, dear ghosts, utterly and irrevocably banished by the banging and sawing and drilling. Nowhere could I sense Connie, hear him chuckle over some deal, picture him impatiently crowbarring open a crate to show me his latest acquisition. His presence had been carted off in the dumpster with the old walls, windows, cast-iron radiators, wood stove, and I had to accept and live with what I'd done.

By the time I returned from Europe, the bulk of the work would be finished. There were three house auctions on my itinerary, and I planned to buy rugs, furnishings, and paintings. Since quitting Ponsonby's, the idea of a home filled with things had ceased to dismay—as long as the things were exceptional, would stupify Dolores and Leslie, and I wasn't paying for them.

I glanced at the ring on my finger, a pink tear-shaped diamond of eleven carats circled by smaller white stones set in platinum. An intensely feminine article, it looked incongruous on my hand. I wasn't particularly feminine, and why Ivan hadn't figured that out had to be attributed to a stubborn illusion on his part. That kind of jewel suited Leslie, not me. But however he perceived me, he wanted to marry me and that was just fine. After months of appearing to warm to his advances, I had finally accepted his proposal, his only regret being my insistence on saving myself for our wedding night. The expectation, fueled by whatever appetite-whetting morsels I doled out, was driving him crazy. He was ninety-six years old. Once he had me, how long could he possibly last?

I collected my purse from the mantel, which remained attached to the gutted wall, and saw that my clay figures still sat there, partially buried under small chunks of plaster and lathe. I brushed them off, blew at the dust, and examined the chunky little man. One could still discern tiny finger indentations on the torso and legs. The man was smiling. So was the dog. They did look a bit pre-Columbian—not half bad for a first attempt at sculpture. Then I remembered that I'd never responded to the letter from the gallery owner. Well, there was no time now, and I didn't know what to say anyway. I felt an overwhelming surge of melancholy as I stowed the figures in my purse and took a final look around the room. There was no turning back. I would avenge Connie the only way I could.

★

I insisted on a will. Amazing. That age, six marriages, and he'd never made one, the suspicious old son of a bitch. I informed him that according to Quebec law, if he died intestate a third of the estate would go to me and two thirds to Alex. If Alex ever turned up. Did he really think Alex was competent to manage the bulk of his money? "No," he agreed, reluctantly. Nevertheless, he was taken aback when I appeared at the door of his suite with Malenfant and his secretary.

"Greer," he squealed, shoeless and rubbing his eyes, having been awakened from his nap. "What is this all about?"

"You agreed to a will. I brought a lawyer so we could get it done before we catch the plane. That's all right, isn't it?"

He looked really uncomfortable standing there in his socks. I gave him a big wet kiss, which shifted his thinking to his gonads, and guided him to a chair. Malenfant sat on the bed and opened his briefcase. The secretary set up a portable typewriter at the desk.

"Now, Mr. Petroff, what constitutes your estate, and what disposition do you care to make?"

Ivan squirmed. I suspected, apart from being secretive about his net worth, that he was one of those people who figure they'll croak the moment they sign a will. Granted, that was more or less my plan.

"For instance, real estate. Do you own property?"

"No," he replied. "No real estate."

"Stocks?"

"No." He shook his head.

"Bonds, T-bills?"

"Some."

"Good. Anything else?"

"Bank accounts," he almost whispered, "in Switzerland and the Bahamas. Do I have to tell you what's in them?"

The old miser. As though I didn't know bloody well what was in them. Malenfant shook his head.

"No. Institutions and account numbers will suffice. Are they all in the name of Ivan Petroff?"

Now that hadn't occurred to me. Malenfant was smooth. No

wonder Jules had retained him. He didn't even look up when he asked that, nor did the tone of his voice alter. Ivan cleared his throat and studied my expression as he answered.

"No. For reasons I don't care to divulge, some of my holdings are in the name of Sergei Nemirovitch."

Aha, I thought. Now we're getting somewhere, but still, it was like pulling teeth.

"Is that it?"

Ivan compulsively knit and unknit his fingers. He hesitated for a good minute before answering.

"There's a safety-deposit box."

"In what name?"

"My own."

"Do you want to itemize the contents or simply designate someone to inherit the contents?"

"Leave everything to Greer," he said impatiently.

"What about Alex?" I reminded him.

"Who is Alex?" asked Malenfant.

"My son," replied Ivan, with a tone of regret. "But he's a simpleton."

"Then I suggest a trust, or better still, an annuity."

"Fine, fine," he agreed, eager to be done with the entire business. A provision was made and the sum settled upon—five hundred thousand dollars, the assumption being that Alex would always be an addenda to someone else's life, probably mine. That done, the secretary typed in the specifics of Ivan's holdings, and I was named sole beneficiary. A chambermaid was dragged in from the hall to act as the second witness, since I was happily ineligible. Ivan signed the two copies. It was done. They packed up their paraphernalia and left. As a reward for his compliance, I permitted Ivan to touch my bare breast while I closed my eyes and pretended he was Simon.

We were married in Paris on a cold, wet March day. Our suite overlooked the Place de la Concorde where a vortex of traffic circled Cleopatra's Needle, and I stared at the hypnotic play of light on the glistening street as I drank my champagne. Ivan presided over the remnants of the meal and scrutinized my every move.

"More, please." I held out my glass. He cocked his head slightly, then did as I asked. I was feeling unpleasantly like an acquisition, wearing the pink peignoir he had insisted on purchasing for me that afternoon. It was humiliating to see the expressions on the faces of the saleswomen as they sized us up. What a pair we were. I flushed, thinking about it, and gulped down the champagne. The peignoir was ridiculous—all flouncy with a marabou trim. I filled the glass myself and finished the bottle.

"Order another, will you, dearest?" I asked sweetly through an increasing alcoholic buzz.

"You've had three already, Greer."

I detested his red-and-yellow striped pajamas. He hadn't had much wine, no doubt to reserve his energies for the night to come, but I needed a lot more, for the same reason.

"Champagne relaxes me. It makes me feel sensual." I removed the outer robe to reveal a transparent nightie. He picked up the phone for room service.

After the fourth bottle of bubbly, my recollection of the evening becomes hazy, but I remember performing my own version of the dance of the seven veils with Ivan's freshly laundered pocket handkerchiefs, and making him chase me around the suite many times before letting him carry me to bed. At least I think he carried me, staggering under the weight. Maybe he dragged me. I don't know, but I found the whole thing absurdly funny, especially when he shed his silly pajamas. In the history of sex, can there have been a more unlikely coupling?

When I woke the next morning, I was distressed to find that not only was he not dead (I was certain the excitement would do him in), but he didn't even have a bloody hangover, whereas I couldn't keep down my café au lait and brioche. No wonder he'd lived so long—he had the constitution of an ox. I leaned over the toilet bowl and retched while Ivan read *Le Monde* and stuffed his face. How long would I have to bear his attentions? I couldn't drink four bottles of champagne every time he wanted to exercise his conjugal rights, and I wasn't so dedicated an actress that I could convince him I was in on the fun. With my luck he'd live to be a hundred and twenty. What had I been thinking? I sat on the cold tiles and rested my throbbing head on the toilet seat.

Suddenly, the bathroom door was flung open and Ivan staggered in, his eyes bulging and his face purple. He pointed to his throat and gesticulated frantically for me to do something. He was choking. He was actually choking. Adrenaline kicked into my bloodstream and my nausea passed. I'd taken the St. John's Ambulance course and knew the Heimlich maneuver. Fat people frequently die from choking, so it's a handy procedure to know, and so simple you can perform it on yourself using the back of a chair.

"Can you talk?" I asked, calmly, soothingly. If the victim can talk, then he can breathe. I hauled myself off the floor knowing full well he could neither talk nor breathe. That much was obvious. His gestures grew wilder—more desperate.

"Let's see if we can get that lump of food out. Now stop panicking and open your mouth," I ordered.

He did, as obediently as a child, and I peered in. That killed a bit of time.

"Nope. Can't see anything. Let's try patting your back." I slapped him between the shoulder blades, a pointless activity, the obstruction wedged as deeply as it was. How long did it take to suffocate, anyway? Three minutes came into my head. Ivan clutched at the edge of the sink and fell to his knees. His whole body heaved and he raised his head to beseech me. I nearly weakened at that point, he was so old, so pathetic. All I had to do was clasp my hands together under his rib cage, thrust upward, and the obstruction would pop out, but as I moved to do it a vision of Connie crushed under the wheels of a bus came to me. It was so vivid that for a moment I was there with him, feeling his horror, disbelief, betrayal. I stared coldly at the face, so like Connie's, and stepped away.

"How could you?" I rasped. "Connie trusted you, though

only God knows why. What was it, Ivan? Hate? Greed? Yes. That would be it, wouldn't it? Greed. I know all about the tomb. Alex told me.'' Ivan lunged at my legs as the realization struck him that I wasn't going to save him—had no intention of saving him. He clawed at the insubstantial marabou feathers. "You walked along the Nevsky Prospect, you laughed with him, you reminisced, then you shoved him into the traffic. You didn't think you were going to get away with that, did you Ivan? I loved Connie. And guess what? Now it's all mine—every ill-gotten, blood-coated penny you ever managed to put aside.'' He grabbed my ankle but I shook him loose and stepped into the bathtub where he couldn't reach me. His face was turning blue. "Are you afraid, Ivan? Of what? Hell? Oblivion?'' His features contorted and he made a last berserk attempt to reach down his throat, then collapsed on the floor and with a final convulsive shudder was still.

What astonished me was how little I felt. No relief, no ela-tion. Emotion was suspended as I regarded Ivan's body. So he was dead. What now? I twisted the ring from my finger and left it on the rim of the sink.

I decided it would be prudent to wait twenty minutes before I called the front desk, to be absolutely certain he was beyond resuscitation, and switched on the heat lamp so his body tem-perature wouldn't drop too quickly. Then I returned to the breakfast table where I ate two croissants and drank a toast to Connie with a glass of orange juice.

The confining elastic bandages were extraordinarily uncom-fortable, and my entire body, from jowls to ankles, felt like a huge bruise, which was, in fact, precisely what it was—a giant hematoma. The surgeon had refused to touch me until I'd lost a hundred pounds, so the month following Ivan's cremation (I flushed him down the john, illegal but immensely satisfying), I starved myself while traveling through Europe buying lovely things for my home. Whenever I felt the urge to eat, I bought another table or painting or carpet.

The greatest risk in liposuction is blood clots, so they had me on massive doses of anticoagulants. I had no idea the procedure would be so painful. I'd thought they just vacuumed out the fat globules and sent you home in a day or two. Not so. All I wanted to do was lie on my bed and die, but nurses kept rolling me over and rubbing my poor violated flesh. The sadistic bitches. The first couple of days I counted minutes between morphine shots.

Baths were the worst. I was lowered into nasty pulsating jets of water and commanded to move or my muscles would stiffen, as if I cared. Everything throbbed. Fluids were pumped into me through one tube and drained out through another. I couldn't even focus on the mountains that brooded malevolently outside the walls of the clinic. What consciousness I had was a daze of Demerol and agony. I wanted to crawl out of the pain.

Then, just as I was feeling vaguely human, they told me further surgery was required because I had too much skin. It hung on me like oversize clothes, and two plastic surgeons went at me, cut, tucked, stitched, and removed enough skin to graft on half the burn victims in Switzerland.

I was there for six weeks of physiotherapy, group therapy, diet and behavior modification therapy, and exercise classes. When I checked out, they presented me with a booklet defining their maintenance regimen, and I clocked in at one hundred and fifteen pounds. I hadn't weighed a hundred and fifteen pounds since I was nine. I headed straight for a dress store where I learned I was size eight. I bought eight outfits to celebrate the fact.

I had my face done up and my hair styled, and treated myself to dinner at one of Lausanne's finest restaurants. Two men offered to buy me cocktails in the bar, and a third joined me for the meal—a distributor of fine chocolates in from Chicago. Halfway through the grilled sole, I was horrified to see Leslie at a table across the room until I realized that I was staring at my own reflection in a mirrored wall.

I sent no letters or postcards. No one knew of my marriage to Ivan, or of his death. I merely sent money to my contractor and furnishings to my interior decorator.

By July, the renovations were complete, on me and my house. I booked passage home.

CHAPTER TWENTY-TWO

Perhaps I am naive, but it never for a moment crossed my mind that I would be so consistently mistaken for Leslie. My first week back, I took Alex to the clothing store frequented by the men in our family, to banish once and for all his grungy jeans. I'd only ever been there before to buy Daddy presents and was surprised when the sales staff began fawning all over me. At one point there were three, yanking cords and crew-necks from the shelves, and it wasn't until one of them called me Mrs. Dansereau that I figured out this wasn't their customary attitude. But I let it go, rather enjoying their obsequiousness. When I pulled out my American Express card, there was an impromptu conference, two of them vanished, and the third made a point of checking my creditworthiness. The nerve. My card was platinum.

My first dinner at Dolores's, she called me Leslie six times. After taking credit for my transformation, she invited me to a symphony luncheon (I declined) and suggested that I join the Junior League. It was as though Greer had ceased to exist and she had twice as much Leslie to deal with.

Daddy must have thought that I *was* Leslie because he wouldn't talk to me at all. I tried to play the game, asking him how he'd cast a remake of *Arsenic and Old Lace*, and he just mumbled into his vodka.

"How about Maureen Stapleton and Angela Lansbury for the old broads?" I asked.

He sighed.

"And Danny de Vito for the Peter Lorre role? You could use Steve Martin for the Cary Grant part. But who would you have for the Raymond Massey character?"

No response.

"Daddy, it's me, Greer." I poked his arm and he looked at me with an expression of woe similar to Bartleby's. "Come on. Someone tall and menacing. How about what's-his-name? He played the heavy in *Moon Over Parador*. Oh, you know . . . Raul Julia. He'd be good, wouldn't he? And how about Robin Williams for the nephew who thinks he's Teddy Roosevelt digging the Panama Canal in the cellar? Wouldn't that be funny?"

Nothing. Dolores shook her head and pointed to the vodka. Regretfully, I gave up.

The next time I was taken for Leslie, I had just concluded a meeting with one of Connie's agents, now mine, who had apprised me of a houseful of antiques in Nova Scotia that could be snapped up for a song. We parted under the metal awning of the Ritz lobby and I was about to ask the doorman to hail me a cab when a Middle Eastern gentleman grabbed my arm and ushered me through the lobby and into the elevator.

At first I thought he was the house dick and was working myself into a state of righteous indignation when he literally swept me into his arms and kissed the breath out of me. Fortunately we were alone in the lift. What was this, I wondered? Upper-class rape? Then he whispered "Leslie" in my ear.

Aha, I thought. The Islamic lover. This was an interesting development. I admit to having had ample opportunity to inform him of his error, but as I had nothing planned for the afternoon, I opted to suspend whatever ethics I still possessed and kissed him back.

We stopped on the sixth floor where he guided me along the corridor and into a suite of rooms overlooking Sherbrooke Street. I excused myself and slipped into the bathroom where I found a razor and shaved off my pubic hair. I kept on a garter belt and stockings, which concealed my scars, and had a delightful afternoon. As Leslie. I don't think Greer would have enjoyed herself. Greer would have expected conversation, and the man didn't speak a single word other than "Leslie" the entire three hours.

Between sessions of active lovemaking, he stared at my very white skin, occasionally advancing a tentative finger to my nipple or cheekbone or eyebrow. I was concerned that he'd question the minute scars from my cosmetic surgery, but he didn't. At four o'clock, room service delivered a cart laden with tea, sandwiches, and cakes. I thought Moslems didn't drink tea, but he had two cups. We ate naked and in silence. It was very sedate and most peculiar. We made love once more, he presented me with some exquisite ruby earrings, then dressed and left the room. I waited for several minutes before doing the same.

The following day I was wakened by my sister pounding my door knocker.

"What's the problem?" I asked, rubbing my eyes as I tied up my bathrobe. She stomped in waving a newspaper in my face. I took it from her hand, thinking the headline might enlighten me, but it didn't.

"How dare you!" she screamed. I winced. Such volume is difficult to take at seven in the morning.

"How dare I what? Look, I'm half asleep. You'll have to be a bit more specific in your accusations." She followed me to the kitchen and noisily scraped a chair across my nice black slate before sitting. I put a kettle of water on the Aga cooker. From the basement came the sounds of the vacuum. Since returning from his mother's in Libya, Alex had been subdued, and I thought of buying him another dog. I poured boiling water into a teapot, threw in two bags, and left it to steep. Leslie drummed her fingers impatiently on the tabletop. She looked like hell. Hadn't she slept last night? She ran her hands over her unbrushed hair and glared at me.

"I didn't believe it when Mother said you looked exactly like me."

"Is that what's bugging you? We *are* identical twins, you know. It was inevitable that if I lost weight, we'd look alike." I took two cups and a creamer from the cupboard.

"You could have dyed your hair."

"Why should I? It's my hair. If it bothers you, dye yours."

"You're wearing it exactly like mine. Your makeup is like mine. Your clothes are like mine." She pounded the table. I filled the jug with milk and put it, the sugar, and cups on the table.

"Well, isn't imitation the sincerest form of flattery?" I said flippantly. Actually, I hadn't been trying to look like Leslie, I just did. The type of clothes that looked best on her naturally looked best on me, too. She picked up one of my pretty Susie Cooper teacups and pelted it onto my hard stone floor. I yelped involuntarily. They were extremely pretty teacups and I'd been lucky to find a complete set.

"Leslie," I lectured. "You really must behave. You may be annoyed with me, but don't take it out on my poor teacups."

"Behave! You have the nerve to tell me to behave? You, who pretended to be me and slept with Faoud?"

"Faoud? Is that his name?" I swept the fragments of china into a dustpan and took another cup from the cupboard. I supposed she was bound to find out what I'd done.

"He phoned and asked me if I liked the earrings. I didn't even know he was in town. Then he said he'd like to meet again before he leaves."

"Did you enlighten him?" I don't think I'd ever seen her so angry.

"Of course not."

"Oh, but you should." I smiled as I poured the tea. "Maybe he'd like to have us both at the same time. Stereo."

She clutched the edge of the table until the tips of her fingers turned white.

"I mean, the man's not averse to a little kink," I lied. More conventional sex than that which I'd experienced with Faoud was unimaginable. "He tied me to the bed and tickled me with an ostrich feather."

"I don't believe you." She spoke deliberately but dumped three heaping teaspoons of sugar in her cup. Leslie, the perpetual dieter, usually took her tea straight.

"Then someone came in and watched him ravish me. I think it was his assistant. Then he watched as his assistant took a turn." I embellished the tale as her eyes widened. "I think he'd be thrilled if two of us turned up. Identical blonde pale bodies. He'd be in heaven."

"I don't share my lovers."

"Why not? They share you."

"Faoud has never done *that* with me."

"I beg to differ. He did yesterday."

"He must have known it wasn't me," she protested.

"Then why did he call you and ask to see you again?"

"Why are you doing this to me?"

"Doing what? Sleeping with one of your boyfriends? I don't know. I couldn't help myself. He dragged me into the elevator and was all over me, and well, it was nice. I just love screwing. I adore men. I love their hairy chests and their rippling pecs. I love their basso profundo voices. I'm sorry if you're upset. If it's any consolation, it didn't mean a thing. You can have the earrings, if it'll make you feel better, even though I did earn them."

She was positively horrorstruck, confronted, as it were, by her clone in behavior as well as appearance. At that moment, I was Leslie. Was that what I wanted—to be Leslie? I capped my performance by laughing in her face and she knocked the remaining china on the floor, then stormed out of the house. I gazed regretfully at the designs on the tiny shards that littered my floor and pondered whether the destruction of my tea set was worth the pleasure of giving Leslie a taste of her own medicine.

All at once I felt like crying, taking a bath, and attacking wet clay. Instead, I cleaned up the mess, packed the earrings in a padded envelope marked with the room number of Leslie's sheik, and had Alex run it down to the Ritz.

Months passed. I made a trip to Mexico to smuggle out some Mayan silver, which I sold to Connie's cocaine broker in Maine.

Some Renaissance panels that appeared in Paraguay I sold in Tokyo. In St. Vincent I collected some seventeeth-century Spanish jewelry from a treasure hunter who'd found an undisturbed wreck, and spent a month in Lisbon tracing its impeccable provenance. Big profit. No pleasure.

Winter came. For my father's sake, I endured another Christmas with my family, although I don't know why I bothered, since he was so gone with drink he didn't even bother watching movies. I flew to Ireland on Boxing Day to attend four estate auctions on behalf of some nouveau New Yorkers who wanted authentic Georgian furnishings and two hundred and forty-three feet of attractive leather book spines. It was of no interest to them what the spines were glued to. By February I needed a break, and treated myself to a month-long vacation in Antigua, where I swam and read a book a day, repelling the advances of every lust-crazed middle-aged businessman with a wife who didn't understand him.

And I thought about Simon.

The police, represented by a plainclothes detective with a bushy mustache, rang my bell, wanting to see the owner of the house. Alex, after years of dealing with customs inspectors, wasn't about to question his authority and showed him down to the pool where I was doing laps to keep my muscles toned. (An academic awareness of the maintenance requirements of a home or a size-eight body are light-years distant from the realities—I seemed to spend most of my time exercising, paying bills, and shopping.)

A heavy snow blew in drifts around the greenhouse, contrasting dramatically with the potted hibiscus and stands of bamboo around the sides of the pool. Alex brought down my afternoon tea and placed it on the unpolished stone slab beside my chaise longue. I continued swimming.

"What can I do for you?" I asked the detective. I was glad my quivering legs were under water and wondered if his call had anything to do with the itty-bitty Donatello bronze I'd snuck out of Italy a few weeks past. But that would be Interpol, not the municipal police. Had Connie been this paranoid? The officer crouched by the edge of the pool and flipped open a pad.

"I'm sorry to have to bother you, but the files at the Mount Royal cemetery list a Constantine Fletcher at this address as the owner of a certain mausoleum."

My heart went arrhythmic and I sidestroked to the other end of the pool. It had been more than a year and a half. I'd almost stopped thinking about Simon's poor corpse. Had it been discovered? I ducked under water, hoping it would cool my flaming complexion, surfacing at the man's feet.

"Constantine Fletcher was my grandfather," I said as I trod water, my eyes level with his polished black shoes. "But he died a year ago last August."

"What do you know about the mausoleum?" His eyes were glued to my cleavage. I shrugged and affected a blank look. The damn clerk at the office must have tidied up the files.

"My grandmother and two uncles are buried there, but not in a mausoleum. What's this all about?"

"A moment." He wrote something in his pad. "There was some decorative work done on the facade quite recently. Do you know who might have done that?"

"I don't know about a mausoleum at all. There must be some bureaucratic error. Why would my grandfather have had two plots?" Had I left incriminating fingerprints that could identify me as the perpetrator of floral carvings? If they learned I was lying about that, they might suspect me of anything. Maybe if I seduced him he'd ... he'd what? Stop the inquiry? What was I thinking? This was no time to do a Leslie. He didn't suspect anything. I had to relax.

"It's just a routine investigation, but we have to follow up all leads. A jogger's dog raced out of the bushes with a bone in his mouth, and the jogger, who happened to be a doctor, recognized the bone as a human femur. He didn't think too much about it, but when the dog led him to the mausoleum and he discovered a badly decomposed body on the floor, he notified us."

How had the dog gotten in, I wondered? I'd closed the door. Someone had probably opened it and received the shock of his life.

"How dreadful, but I'm afraid I can't help you." I glanced at the door, hoping Alex was out of hearing. The last thing I needed was him bouncing in to make a confession.

"Do you recognize this?" he asked.

I rested my arms on the side of the pool and took the thin stainless-steel watch from his hand. Either it had been wound or had a quartz movement, for the sweep hand was still moving. I had a sudden black vision of John Cameron Swayze speaking into his mike, informing the viewing audience that: "This watch was placed on the wrist of a moldering corpse and left to suffer through a sweltering summer and two brutally cold winters, and look—it's still ticking!" My head spun. Would an innocent person display any curiosity? Probably. "Have you any idea as to the identity of the . . . ah . . . ? Was there any . . . ah . . . foul play?"

"Definitely foul play." He took the watch and put it in a Ziploc sandwich bag. "He was shot. The coroner estimates the body's been there for well over a year, but he doesn't fit the description of any reported missing person."

"Oh." Who, I thought, would miss Simon enough to report his absence? Not Leslie. She was too wrapped up in her new incarnation as a pillar of society. Business associates would have shrugged off his disappearance as unremarkable. His ex-wife never saw him anyway and her settlement had been a lump sum. His family was dead. Maybe his landlord—but that was in New York, and how effective was computer cross-checking? What had happened to his car? Stolen, probably, and since he hadn't been around to report the theft . . .

"We estimate he was thirty-five to forty years of age, Caucasian, six feet, reddish hair, in good health."

Why was he telling me this? Why would he expect me to know any more about it than anyone he could stop on the street? Would he speak to anyone else in the family? I hoped not. Leslie could easily deduce that the corpse was Simon and the whole wretched mess would be stirred up. If he believed I knew nothing, he wouldn't bother following pointless leads. The most he might do would be to contact Dolores, but she didn't know anything. She'd probably suggest, helpfully, that Connie had killed Simon. The cop seemed to be waiting for me to react.

"I don't think . . . " I put on a frowning, concentrating face. "Reddish hair?" I shook my head and pushed off, kicking backward across the pool. He flipped his pad shut.

"You've been very cooperative. I'm sorry to have bothered you. An abandoned tomb is a convenient place to dispose of a body. If the door had been fastened it mightn't have been discovered for years."

Damn. I should have locked it.

"No ID?" I asked.

"Just the watch. Probably a settling of accounts. No loss to society."

Yeah. No loss to society. Only to me. I smiled. The cop smiled back, then saw himself out. So that was that. I floated on the surface and speculated as to why my relief wasn't greater— my satisfaction complete. Where had I to go from here? I dove to the bottom of the pool and came up gasping. The afternoon darkened and the dying wind relaxed its grip on the falling snow. It lighted softly on the glass roof, blotting out the sky. The winter night enclosed me, and the corresponding silence was absolute.

The process of disencumbrance was oddly cathartic, considering what I had gone through to get my hands on Ivan's estate in the first place. I endowed African orphanages, established scholarships for the poor, donated to medical research and UNICEF. My largesse only just stopped short of riding down St. Catherine Street in an open car tossing loose bills to the masses on the sidewalk. I gave it all away—all the blood money, then I sold my house, furnished, to a Hong Kong businessman and invested the profits for my own use.

My trunks were packed and passage was booked for myself

and Alex on the *QEII* out of New York. From Southampton we were to proceed to London for a week, then we would fly to Rome, rent a car, and drive to Florence. I planned to buy a villa in the Tuscany hills where Alex could garden and keep dogs and I would learn whether I was an artist or not. The New York dealer had sold five of my pieces and had provided me with letters of introduction to several Florentine sculptors.

My hotel window overlooked Central Park, where a green haze of budding leaves appeared to hover in the mild spring air. My decision to leave Montreal must have been correct, for no one objected. Dolores, ever the pragmatist, had me officially resign my position on the board of Payton Furniture Ltd. Daddy drank vodka in his La-Z-Boy, not once shifting his eyes from the TV screen. He seemed as unaware of my presence as he would be of my absence. Leslie and Yves had invited me for a farewell dinner and dutifully promised to visit if they ever came to Italy. Leslie's relief at my leaving was palpable. Only the Cats expressed regret, probably because they wouldn't be getting nearly as many presents from now on. They had kissed me, then vanished with their new Nintendo cassette—Super Mario Brother 14, or some such number.

The tickets and passports lay on the bureau. I zipped them into an inner compartment of my purse, noticing as I did so my hands. My sister's hands. In the bathroom I removed the crimson lacquer from my fingernails and filed them short. That was better. Then I scrubbed my face and brushed my hair until I felt I achieved a look that didn't resemble Leslie. I changed into a plain, slightly baggy, moss-colored dress, cinched it at the waist with a yellow scarf, and slid into leather sandals.

Alex knocked on the connecting door and I let him in.

"Greer. I was going to get something to eat. Wanna come?"

In the past year he'd gained a bit of weight and with his new wardrobe he had become fairly presentable.

"Alex, my boy, this is a holiday. No muscle will be moved before its time. Behold, one of the great amenities of a five-star hotel—room service. What would you like?"

"I dunno. A hamburger?"

"Hamburger, hell. A filet mignon."

"French fries?"

"It goes without saying."

"Onion rings?"

"Why not?"

"A chocolate sundae? A milkshake?"

"Anything, Alex. Anything." I dialed room service and gave Alex's order.

"Will there be anything else?" asked the voice on the phone.

"Ah... well... yes. Sure. Just a sec." I sat down and rested my feet on the coffee table. "A large pot of English Breakfast tea with cream, not milk, please, and, ah, four éclairs. The whipped cream filled, not the custard. Thanks." I hung up the receiver, wiggled my toes, and smiled at Alex. Life was good.